MOON'S ARTIFICE

MOON'S ARTIFICE

TOM LLOYD

GOLLANCZ

LONDON

First published in Great Britain in 2013 by
Gollancz
An imprint of the Orion Publishing Group
Orion House, 5 Upper St Martin's Lane, London WC2H 9EA
An Hachette UK Company

A CIP catalogue record for this book is available
from the British Library.

ISBN 978 0 575 13116 3 (Cased)
ISBN 978 0 575 13117 0 (Trade Paperback)

1 3 5 7 9 10 8 6 4 2

Printed in Great Britain by CPI Group (UK) Ltd, Croydon, CR0 4YY

The Orion Publishing Group's policy is to use papers
that are natural, renewable and recyclable products and made
from wood grown in sustainable forests. The logging and
manufacturing processes are expected to conform to the
environmental regulations of the country of origin.

www.tomlloyd.co.uk
www.orionbooks.co.uk
www.gollancz.co.uk

For Ailsa Rebecca Lloyd-Williams

CHAPTER 1

The prohibition on gunpowder weapons for lower castes has been in force for centuries and is obeyed across the Empire of a Hundred Houses. No such ban on lenses or telescopes exists, yet with our Gods residing in bright constellations in the nearer sky, common sense remains the first obstacle to progress.

From *A History* by Ayel Sorote

For one glorious moment he was flying. Starlight shone wetly on the black slates below – the air around him was still, but charged like a God's breath before the thunder. On the edges of his vision were faint yellow strands of light that spilled around doors and half-shuttered windows. He stared down as though trying to count the cobbles below the slate-tiled roof. Night's serene hands cradled him and for that moment he felt the cares of the world slough away as sudden, beautiful clarity washed over him.

Bastard fucking fox.

Irato fell. With shocking speed the awning jumped up to meet him and black lights burst before his eyes. Head and chest smashed into the tiles with a crack that seemed to rip right through his skull. His mind filled with the white noise of pain that momentarily tore him from the world as the air was punched from his lungs.

The divine stars burned a trail through the night as he was yanked around by the force of impact. Then the ground struck him with the heavier thump of meat on the butcher's block. The delicate tinkle of glass vials chimed around the cobbled street. Irato felt pieces patter as gently as summer rain on his close-cropped hair. A sense of warmth flowed over the black emptiness where his body had once been.

Numbness fleetingly consumed him, sucked him down into the belly of the earth before pain burst hot and jagged to wake him. Unable

1

to command his limbs, Irato lay helpless and stunned – too dazed to recognise the sensations flowering in his damaged body. His arm lay crookedly beneath his chin, tilting it up to look over the blurry grey cobbles of the street. A pale, indistinct shape wavered directly in front of his eyes. His heart thumped two loud beats before the sight suddenly resolved into sharp focus. It was a shard of glass two inches long and shaped like a stiletto, pirouetting delicately in the groove between cobbles, barely a hand span from his eye.

Irato felt a lurch in his gut as he watched the shard slow and topple, spent of its energy – a message from the Gods now done and delivered. Combat-trained senses kicked in, observing with cold detachment while the man they belonged to stared with drunken incomprehension at the glass.

His moment of respite was short-lived. From the damp cobbles rose a new terror, like a cobra roused to anger. A wisp of greenish-white vapour curled before his eyes, then another and another. A quiver of spectral snakes regarded him with lethal intent and the detached voice of observation inside faltered, diverted by this new, unanticipated happening.

As though in automatic response, his lungs shrieked for air and it took all Irato's strength of will to refuse. His eyes began to water and a single tear slid onto his nose, down to skirt his nostril and pat onto the ground below. A wet presence on his eyebrow followed, sharp pain and the touch of blood that took the place of tears in his right eye. Irato was forced to stare at the vapours with one eye, begging for them to dissipate, but they refused. The snakes watched him patiently, knowing their time would come soon – that they would not be denied their prey.

He tried to move but couldn't fathom the tangle of his numb limbs. His chest began to burn, that particular hot sting of cracked ribs, and below that a more distant, discordant pain. He became aware that one hand was pinned and useless beneath his stomach, while the arm under his chin was wrapped in a bright-burning pain.

No choice.

The realisation seemed to clear Irato's thoughts. His body refused to obey, to drag him from the cruel vapours waiting to pounce. His vision started to blur and shiver as the ache for air increased, but instinct was fought to a stalemate by fear. It took the man inside to overrule both, to cast the bones and accept the fate they determined.

There's a chance. I still have time.

He made one last effort to roll himself over, but neither arms nor legs could shift his limp frame and reluctantly he took a long, shuddering breath. The air burned hot and cold in his lungs as the vapour snakes struck, filling him with ecstatic horror as a cacophony of hurts resonated through his body. At last his limbs started to obey. Irato flopped onto his back, face screwed up at the light of the Gods above – the Order of Knight's piercing glare momentarily pinning him to the cobbles like a doomed moth.

Irato winced and stared at the constellation above, far brighter than the lesser stars of the further night sky. There were four in a diamond shape around a fifth; Shield, Knight's ever-steady protector. He paused to blink away the dark ethereal shapes that danced before his eyes and realised coils of cloud covered three constellations in the Order of Knight. What remained were Shield, the twin pistols of Lord Knight and the scales of Lawbringer.

A cold-hearted divination, that one, he thought drunkenly, *Lady Pity hides her eyes and the bastards in her Order come out to play. Not the omen I'd like right now.*

He struggled to his feet, trying to cradle a damaged arm with one that hurt only marginally less. He stood low, hunched over and knees bent while he tried to outlast a bout of dizziness. He was a heavily-built man, of average height but appearing larger because of his broad limbs and a startling speed of movement. Right now he felt feeble and insubstantial, all that speed turned to sluggish inertia.

The clink of glass fragments sounded inordinately loud in the deserted night-time street as they cascaded off his body. Irato blinked around at the buildings surrounding him; by the decorations he could tell he was not yet out of House Dragon's district of the Imperial City. The last drips of the night's rain fell from gutter heads shaped like that nation's ubiquitous emblem. If he had made it to the Harbour Warrant they would be curved crests of waves instead – symbols of the Vesis and Darch merchant house who held the Imperial warrant for that district, rather than the noble House Dragon, but he had fallen short of his goal.

He shuffled forward a few steps to test his balance, feebly brushing the last of the broken glass from his body and glad his leather armour had at least protected him from that. A fragment of memory came back to him; his coat snagging and tearing open, the glass vials spilling

3

out like bloodless guts. He hissed in pain and tried to make sense of
his memories.

*Did something hit me? Was it the fox-spirits? Did Shield himself reach
down from the heavens?*

Irato took another few steps until he was in the shadows of the
building ahead, out of Shield's starlight. He had never seen a God
descend from the heavens – they rarely noticed the actions of one man
and interfered even more rarely – but the fox-spirits had flooded the
rooftops with silent signals and daemon-song that even now echoed
through Irato's mind. If Shield had been looking down at the Imperial
City, the Ascendant God would have surely heard their fury and hatred.

The ambush was most likely a ploy – they were unlikely to kill him
themselves, Irato knew. But they were sly little bastards, these foxes;
they'd happily attract the attention of something he couldn't handle
quite so easily. Some demon of the night, God or Astaren warrior-mage
could have heard the clamour resonating out through an unhearing
city and come to investigate.

I have to get off the street, he realised. Whether or not something had
been called by the foxes, he didn't want to find out. And of course,
given what he'd just inhaled, time was running out anyway.

Scouting desperately around, Irato at last spied a glimmer of hope in
the form of lines of light around the shuttered window of a teahouse.
It was late in the night and anyone there was surely smoking opium
or balese. Irato didn't give a damn which it proved to be – both would
numb the pain of his injuries and he had more than a few streets to
travel in a short time. If he passed out, or more than an hour elapsed,
it would be all over.

That's not going to happen, Irato told himself. *There's a cure, I still
have time.*

He remembered his mentor's voice describing just what would take
place, accompanied as always by the scents of aniseed and honey that
had been ever-present in the man's study. The old doctor had been
an exacting master, but scrupulously fair to each of his protégés. Irato
found himself drifting into the warmth of fond memories before he
caught himself.

Knowing how much it would hurt, Irato shook his head as hard as
he could to clear his thoughts.

Wake up, you bastard. You let yourself drift off again, it's all over.

He headed for the teahouse, reaching behind his back with his right hand to try and free one of his hatchets. A band of pain clamped around his stiffening wrist; not broken, he guessed, but it wouldn't be much use and he gave up the effort to unhook it. His heart drummed a fearful tattoo in his chest as he reached the window. He was an easy target to anything that found him out there. Even a common thief was a danger now. Normally, Irato wouldn't break a sweat if attacked, the Blessings imbued by his mentor's spells had seen to that, but this wasn't a normal evening.

A dull pain was building in his head, his thoughts clouded by dizziness from his fall. It felt like his skull was cracked and the numbing chill of night was slowly seeping into his head. Any sort of blow or stumble could see him collapse and once down he knew he wouldn't be getting up. Even if something did, it wouldn't be him any more; of that, his mentor had been chillingly clear.

With skin darker than most natives of the Imperial City, jet-black hair and hooded eyes, few guessed his heritage correctly and Irato had lied about it so often even he found the truth rang false when spoken. A chill ran through him as he imagined that truth being lost to him.

He reached the window and listened a while, trying to peer through the cracks but able to see nothing of the inside. Wincing, Irato drew a knife with painful care and listened again, hoping to catch any small sound that might tell him if the room was empty or its occupants were still conscious. A tiny noise came from somewhere on the other side, perhaps a floorboard as someone shifted their weight slightly. Irato began to ease backwards and raise his knife.

He never even saw the shutter move. Light exploded across his eyes as it struck his head and smashed him backwards. The ground disappeared from behind him and the light faded to nothing as he fell. Blackness enveloped him and went on for ever.

Investigator Narin leaned cautiously out of the window, stave at the ready. There was a big man wearing black crumpled on the ground outside, a long-knife visible at his side.

'Who is it?' Lady Kine whispered from behind him.

Narin raised a cautioning hand and she fell silent while he checked left and right down the street. It was empty, but the starlight illuminated a glittering trail of glass fragments and some fallen slates further down the road. He returned his attention to the supine man. He appeared unconscious and Narin didn't doubt it was true. He'd kicked the shutter open as hard as he could and, from the cut to the man's forehead, had caught him square on.

Narin peered closer. There were several scrapes on his forehead, one of which had bled down to his chin. He turned and motioned to Kine that she should stay silent. The dark-skinned woman nodded, lips pursed and hands pressed protectively to her belly. The green kohl around her eyes had smeared and he'd knocked one of the white combs in her hair loose so a trail of dark hair hung down to her shoulder. The ache in his heart intensified; a bitter-sweet mix of joy, fear and longing, but a cool breath of wind from the street returned Narin's thoughts to the man he'd injured.

He wore black leather armour underneath a ragged grey cloak. More glass remained on the man's chest; there were lines scored in his armour and tears in the cloak, while his left arm lay at an awkward angle. Narin grimaced. In his fear, he'd lashed out – thinking someone was spying on them – but this man could just as easily have been looking for help.

He picked his way over the window sill, stave still ready to deflect any attack, and looked toward the fallen tiles. He couldn't hear anyone coming to investigate yet, but it was crucial Kine was not seen with him.

A small sound came from inside the teahouse. He turned and saw Kine beckoning frantically so he hopped back through the window and returned to her.

'What's happening?' Kine whispered in a pleading voice. As she spoke she tugged the ivory cinch of her cord belt tight. Having also realised the danger, Kine had wasted no time in pulling on her long coat, ready to leave. Sinuous wyverns were embroidered in blue down the left-hand side, the sign of her House.

'I'm not sure.' He glanced back towards the unconscious man. 'I think he's a thief, or a goshe maybe.'

'Goshe? You think he's an assassin?'

Narin took hold of her arms and brought the small woman close to his face. 'Don't worry; no one's going to hurt you.'

'What if *he* knows?' she insisted, eyes wide with terror. Against her dark skin the whites of her eyes were even more startling, her fear even more pronounced. 'What if he's sent someone to kill us?'

6

'Then they've lost the element of surprise,' Narin said calmly, 'and have backed off. Otherwise they'd be in the room by now. I think he was just crossing the streets by rooftop and fell – he's nothing to do with us. All that talk about the goshe being assassins is only rumour; the Lawbringers have found no evidence of anything like that. And anyway, your husband wouldn't be hiring an assassin – that would mean trusting low-caste outsiders when he's got loyal men in his own household.'

Kine opened her mouth to argue, but couldn't seem to find the words so he ran a reverential finger down the side of her ebony cheek, catching the errant trail of hair in his fingers and tucking it behind her ear.

'You need to go,' Narin urged, kissing her full on the lips and walking her towards the door. 'Go out the south door, cut down the alley and onto Wyvern's Walk. I'll head out into the street and attract the attention of anyone watching.'

'You're going to make yourself a target?'

He forced a smile for her and gestured at his pale grey jacket and trousers. The badge on his breast was the only adornment, but it spoke volumes to every citizen of the Empire; an upright spear before a yellow sun casting two rays down to the ground. The sun was the Emperor's own symbol; coupled with a spear it showed him to be an Investigator of the Lawbringers, the body which technically ruled the streets of the Imperial City.

'There's a man injured in the street – injured by my actions. I have to see to him, but I'm an Investigator of the Imperial House so I'm hiding in plain sight.'

He opened the door for her and hugged her tight. 'Please, Kine, go now. I'll write to you soon.' He hesitated and kissed her again, one hand reverentially brushing her belly. 'I … I don't have the words for … but I love you. I'm sorry it's happened this way and …'

The words dried in his throat and he found himself just gaping at Kine, breathing the sweet faint scent of her perfume and feeling her tremble under his hands.

'I know,' she said in a small voice, 'it's a shock. I've put us both in danger with my carelessness.'

He wrapped his arms around her, this time his smile entirely genuine. 'We were both careless,' he breathed, lips brushing hers, 'and still I couldn't be happier.'

'What if he finds out? He will find out, he must! I cannot get rid of it; I'd rather die myself than kill our baby.' There was a sudden fire in her eyes that made Narin hold her even tighter.

'That won't happen,' he said firmly, 'I need time to think of a plan, but I'd never ask that. I couldn't ...' He shook his head. 'We must have a few weeks before he finds out you're pregnant, no? So we have a while.' He released her reluctantly. 'Now go. I will see you soon, my love, I promise.'

Kine nodded, biting back the tears that threatened and kissing his hand once before she fled. He shut the door behind her and extinguished the lamps before heading back to the window. The man was still unconscious, so Narin stepped over the sill and closed the shutters behind him. He crouched to check the man for a pulse, suddenly afraid he had killed him with the solid wooden shutter.

'Thank Pity,' he breathed when at last he felt one, slow but regular.

Narin glanced up at the stars. He wasn't much for religion, but right now he was more than willing to bow his head, two fingers touched to his forehead, towards the occluded constellation of the Ascendant Goddess, Lady Pity. He cast around at the other stars to get his bearings. Taking a step out from under the eaves of the teahouse to look east, where the nearer Ascendants in the Order of Empress would be visible, it was Lord Thief, not Healer, that he could make out.

Narin looked down at the goshe, trying to think. He had an obligation to help the man no matter what the circumstances, of that he was very aware. His father had been a merchant's clerk and a timid man, but he'd revered the Lawbringers and Narin had grown up with the oaths hanging on the wall of their home. Long before his parents had died and he'd become a novice to the Palace of Law, Narin had been able to recite them by heart.

'Thief, eh? Maybe that's a better Ascendant to be looking down on this goshe anyway,' he muttered.

'In that, you are correct,' called a deep voice from a way down the street.

Narin yelped and whirled around. His hands moved automatically, bringing his stave up to the guard position before he even saw the threat. The Investigator hesitated as no attack came. All he could see was a bearded man ten yards off, but one who'd appeared silently and now stood in the middle of the street watching him.

'Who are you?' Narin demanded, moving away from the injured man to give himself space if an attack came. The tip of the stave he kept in line with the stranger's face, but it was the dark corners of the street he was more concerned with.

'I have many names,' the stranger said, not moving. 'I think you'll be able to guess one at least.'

Narin stopped and gave the man his full attention. He was big, extremely big in fact – a few inches taller than Narin but vastly broader. His face was tanned and weathered; darker than a local's, with a long neat beard of black curls that suggested southern origin, House Redearth or somewhere within its hegemony of lesser House-states. The man had long hair drawn back like a nobleman's and the cut of his white clothes suggested warrior caste, but he wore no sword or pistol – nor was there a badge of House visible on his clothes. Instead, there was only a black spiral embroidered on the left-hand side of his coat, studded with glinting crystals, the pattern continuing seamlessly down an ornate silver vambrace on his arm.

Narin blinked and looked again at the vambrace. Suddenly the stave felt like lead in his hands. Unable to help himself he glanced up at the constellation directly above.

'Do not worry, the stars still shine without me,' the Ascendant God standing before him said in a level tone. 'You have more pressing concerns right now.'

'I ... ah ... Lord Shield?'

The God inclined his head. 'Investigator.'

'But ... why ... ?' Narin stopped and turned back to the unconscious man with dread slithering down his spine. 'Ah, who is ... ? Oh Empress, have mercy!'

'Investigator,' Shield said sternly, 'don't be so foolish. My Brother-under-Knight would be most displeased in his servant.'

Narin turned cautiously around. The street remained dark and empty. 'Is ... ah, is Lord Lawbringer here too?'

'No, nor any other. That is a man at your feet, just a man.' Shield took a step forward, head slightly tilted to one side as though listening to a voice on the wind. 'You have inconvenienced me, Investigator.'

'What? Ah, I mean, I'm sorry, Lord Shield.' Narin gaped for a moment, then checked himself and dropped to one knee. 'I did not realise.'

'Clearly.'

Head bowed, Narin waited. The cool night air prickled on his exposed neck and he started to feel terribly vulnerable. Just as he was about to ask what he'd done, Shield made up the ground between them in the blink of an eye. Gasping, Narin fell back, barely keeping a grip on his stave as he scrambled to recover himself.

'That man was a thief, I believe,' Shield said distantly, eyes fixed on the black-clad goshe.

Another blurring movement brought him to the man's side and he knelt, touching one finger to the man's injured temple and a second over a closed eye. The God bowed his head in concentration and Narin saw pale light glow from his half-shut eyes. It lasted just a few moments then Shield withdrew his hand and straightened, giving Narin an appraising look.

'A thief of what, however, I do not know,' Shield continued eventually. 'I had hoped the rat would return to its lair to lick its wounds, but then you got in the way, Investigator.'

'You threw him from the roof?' Narin asked in astonishment. It had to be a miracle the man was even alive after such a fall – that he would be able to walk home even less likely.

Shield tilted his head to look at the damaged roof. 'He is hardier than he appears,' the God said by way of reply. 'Unfortunately, only in body.'

'But he's alive; you can still question him when he wakes!'

Lord Shield gave him a look that froze him to the spot. 'Your intervention has precluded that.'

'You can't heal his injuries?'

The God turned to the goshe. He reached out again and brushed his fingers over the man's head injury, then tapped twice against his chest. 'Some. Not everything can be undone.'

He stood and gazed down at Narin, who had recovered himself and knelt again. Shield's stare was unblinking. Narin flinched under the intense scrutiny, though there was no anger in that look. If the God felt any emotion, he betrayed nothing.

'This is a problem for you, Investigator,' Shield added gravely.

Narin's guts went cold. 'My … my apologies, Lord Shield, I thought he was spying on me.'

'Why would he spy on you?'

'I, ah, I do not know.'

A massive hand reached down and took hold of Narin's tunic. Shield lifted him to his feet with no appreciable effort, his expression grave. 'I choose to forget you lied to me there. Try again.'

Narin gaped – his mind blank until a tiny light flickered in the recesses of Shield's eyes and startled him into life again. 'I'm sorry, Lord – I meant only to protect another.'

'I can keep a secret, unless you think to protect them from me?'

'No! No, of course not. I was meeting someone; she ah, she gave me some news.'

Shield bared his teeth in what Narin hoped was a grin. 'Husband found out?'

The Investigator's heart gave a lurch. For the hundredth time he wanted to rap his knuckles against his forehead.

What sort of a fool falls in love with a noblewoman? A married noble-woman? A married noblewoman of House Wyvern, second only to its cousin House Dragon in its obsession with honour?

'Close enough. How did you … ?' he asked weakly.

'I still remember mortal life.'

Narin lowered his eyes. Lord Shield, carried dying into the heavens by his lord, the Ascendant God Knight, to serve him there as he had in life.

'Of course, I'm sorry. Ah, why have I inconvenienced you, Lord Shield? Surely he will wake still?'

'He will wake.'

'Can't you interrogate him then? He won't be able to lie to you either.'

Again the distant light flashed, white-green in the blackness of the Ascendant God's pupils, and Narin felt it like tiny claws brushing his mind. He winced at the sensation and Shield released him. Narin sagged with relief and staggered back a step before catching his balance.

'It would be of no use,' Shield said slowly. 'Tell me, Investigator, your oaths – you have a duty to any you harm or place in danger, no?'

Narin's mouth fell open as the memory of his father's stitched wall-hanging appeared in his memory. The words were etched into his heart; the first he'd learned to read, long before Narin could fully understand what they stood for.

'I – yes.'

'Then you bear a duty to this man and a debt to me for your interference.' Shield gestured to the goshe on the ground. 'You will make amends.'

'How?' Narin asked in a hoarse whisper.

'You will investigate,' Shield said simply. 'This man carries secrets with him, secrets he cannot now tell. You will find them out or you will die in the attempt, do you understand me?'

Narin found himself unable to speak. Only a tiny wheeze escaped his throat. The moments ticked by, the crisp salty air caressed his cheek and still he did not reply. With an effort he managed to nod, realising his hands were shaking as he did so.

'Good. Once you know this man's secrets, you will answer me this – who is the moon?'

Narin blinked. 'Who … ?'

The words died in his throat as Shield vanished from sight. Narin reeled as though struck around the head, black stars bursting before his eyes. The night seemed to have twisted and snapped like a hungry creature, enveloping the Ascendant God and leaving no sign he had even been there before.

A voice echoed down the empty street. He didn't hear the words, but it stirred him into action all the same. An Investigator of the Imperial House he might be, but Narin still didn't want to have to answer any questions about why he was out here all alone with an injured goshe.

'Who is the moon? What in Lady Pity's name does that mean?' Narin muttered in disbelief. 'What have I got myself into?'

He looked around at the dark, still streets. The faint scent of wood smoke mingled with the ever-present salty tang of the sea. The breeze was light, brushing unhurried across his cheek. He stared at the empty cobbled ground where Lord Shield had stood and tried to work out what had happened. Foreboding was a cold weight in his gut, despite the mild night air.

The city seemed to stop around him, silent and harmonious while he alone struggled. For a man used to solitude, Narin suddenly felt more alone than ever before. The weight of all he'd learned tonight pressed down as though the light of the stars themselves had him snared in a web. Narin bowed his head and closed his eyes briefly. Kine's smiling face came easily into his mind; her dark skin fading into the shadows, her beauty like a fire's warmth against his skin.

He opened his eyes and looked down at the unconscious man. The goshe was dark-haired and tanned of skin, with scars on his face and faint stubble on his cheeks. What House he belonged to, Narin couldn't tell. The Imperial City included districts ruled by each of the ten Great

Houses – once just extended noble families, now synonymous with the nations they ruled. Public thoroughfares under the rule of the Lawbringers cut through each district, but beyond those the Emperor's law was always in competition with the Great House who claimed sovereignty there.

'You're obviously not House Dragon or any House under it,' Narin said to the goshe, 'but looking at you I can't fit your heritage to any House I know.'

The Imperial City had spent five hundred years under the steward-ship of House Dragon, a hegemony that ruled its own nation and those of the lesser Houses under it. Thickset, black-skinned Dragons were a common sight on these streets, as were their lesser cousins, House Wyvern, to which Kine belonged. The other states within Dragon's domain maintained less of a presence in the Imperial City, but Narin had seen enough of each to at least know a Darkcloud citizen from a Smoke. Beyond that, there were so many shades and tints of skin and eyes in the city that most were as impossible to discern as the dark Dragons or near-albino Leviathans were obvious.

'So what do I do now?' he asked the man at his feet. Narin shook his head in disbelief and almost smiled. 'I've no idea – what would Lawbringer Rhe do? What would Enchei do?'

That last thought seemed to trigger something inside him and he stirred into action. 'Enchei'd just deal with it as though nothing strange had happened,' he said with a sigh as he knelt and hauled the goshe into a seating position.

'Come to think of it, this is all the old man's fault anyway.' He ducked his head under the goshe's arm and manoeuvred him until he was draped over his back.

'All Enchei's fault,' Narin repeated as he tried to stand. 'Stars in heaven you're heavy!' he gasped, wavering and almost dropping back down to the ground.

The goshe was a dead weight on his shoulders, all hard muscle and bone. Crab-like, Narin hauled the man over to the window sill and grabbed hold of it to drag himself up. For a moment his knees wavered before he at last straightened them with a gasp.

'Damn you, Enchei,' he continued through gritted teeth. 'If I'd never met you I'd not be in love with another man's wife. Not be dragging this Gods-cursed lump home for reasons that'll probably get me killed – if my friend doesn't find out about me and his wife first.'

13

The layout of the city unfolded in his mind, a broken wheel of streets and districts that followed the curve of the Crescent River around the Imperial Island. Narin's home was on the near-side of the island, between the Tier Bridge and the vast Imperial Palace, but he would have to cross a lot of ground to get there.

'The Harbour Warrant,' Narin said to the weight on his shoulder, 'That's just a few streets away. I'll take you there and find a patrol to help me. Lord Shield, if you're looking down, steer me clear of House Dragon's soldiers or I'll never get him out.'

He started off across the street, staggering to the nearest alley to be swallowed up by the shadows there. Something pattered down onto his feet as he went. He looked down and saw the sparkle of glass fragments glint in the starlight.

'Who is the moon?' he repeated under his breath. 'What sort of a question is that?'

Under the glare of Shield's starlight he didn't dare voice his thoughts entirely out loud. The God might still be watching him, might even be listening to anything he said.

The High Gods and their Ascendants had not figured largely in Narin's life. There were traditions and rituals he knew as well as most in the Empire of a Hundred Houses, but the Lawbringers were the religion his father had taught him; the ideals they stood for and the order they had brought.

'When has the moon been anyone?' he wondered as he turned a corner and shifted the goshe to a more comfortable position. 'The moon's a lump in the sky where no God lives, and a Great House far to the west. Moon's water is a drink I could do with a few of right now, but it's no man or woman I ever heard of.'

The night seemed to grow colder, his breath casting clouds of vapour before him as the effort of carrying the man increased with every step.

'I'm dead then,' Narin muttered miserably. 'Dead and buried one way or the other.'

Scowling, he shook his head and plodded on, trying to focus on his anger rather than the strain on his back.

'I'll be dead,' he continued to the uncaring night, 'and Enchei won't have a friend in the world again. That might shut the bastard up for a while at least. Should've thought of it sooner really.'

CHAPTER 2

In his dreams Narin walks home through the streets of the Cas Tere Warrant alongside a man he hardly knows. A tattooist of the Imperial House called Enchei Jen, he is a grey-haired man once of House Falcon, foremost of House Eagle's subordinate nations. Narin has been surprised how quickly he has warmed to the man since they first met, just a few weeks before. Enchei's ready smile and mocking humour reminds Narin of the bullies he endured during his years in the novice dormitories, but somehow he senses no malice in the man – only a quiet strength and peace Narin instinctively envies.

His arms ache from the effort of two hours' hurling a leather ball with all his strength, only to see it batted back or deftly deflected away. They have played dachan once before so Narin is not surprised he has lost to a man two decades his elder. His thigh also hurts; a straight blow from the fist-sized ball that hadn't seemed intentional until Enchei had cheered the strike.

It is late in the evening, but the air is still sticky and warm. The summer afternoon heat is too fierce to play in so they played in the hours before sunset, then ate at a strange back-street eatery serving racks of griddled prawns. Narin carries his dachan stick in hands stained yellow by his food and they talk of inconsequential things, ambling along as men do after a good meal.

Crossing the Fett Canal into the Tale Warrant, they pause to admire the lanterns strung along the bridges and shopfronts even at that late hour – white, red and purple. The purple lanterns hang outside teahouses where men and women alike sit on the wooden decks and smoke cigars or pipes of balese, while inside the opium users have likely crawled onto a pallet to sleep and dream.

Tale is quiet this late. The occasional burst of noise comes from a tavern or gaming den, but nothing that Narin feels he should investigate. Moths and tiny flying lizards dance in the bright starlight of the Gods on a cloudless night. The entire Order of Shaman is displayed in all its glory, the stars of each distinct constellation seeming to cast a purer light than the aged moon.

They turn a corner and stumble to a halt. There is a body on the floor before them. It takes Narin a moment to fully comprehend the sight after a convivial evening, fatigue and wine both dulling his thoughts. Then the black pool of blood and brutal gash in the dead man's neck snap into focus – as do the long braids of hair and white embossed holster that marks him as a warrior caste of House Wyvern.

At last he looks up and sees more dead men, two in labourer's clothes and three more of the warrior caste. He is astonished by the sight; the idea that trained warriors could be cut down by so few lower castes surprises him as much as the sight of slaughter.

The starlight shines down on a strange tableau in the middle of the street. Propped up against a stone water-trough is a nobleman, trousers cut away and lying in tatters around his ankles. Bent over him is a scarred man with a bloodied knife, while around him five others are frozen by the sudden appearance of Narin and Enchei.

Then the spell is broken and they surge forward together. Narin feels a cold knot of fear in the pit of his stomach, realising his Investigator uniform will serve as no defence here. He hurls his dachan stick over-arm at the nearest, causing the man to throw his arms up to protect his face. It gives Narin just a moment's respite, but long enough for him to pull his stave from behind his back.

A darkened blur flashes across his view. His placid companion has not needed to think, has experienced no moment of uncertainty and fear – he has simply acted. He watches Enchei in the staccato movement of dreams, leaping towards the dead House soldier and rolling across the fallen man. Narin doesn't even see him pull the pistol from its sheath. One moment Enchei is diving, the next he is crouching with one arm extended.

The crack of gunpowder breaks the quiet – the dirty yellow muzzle-flash casts a sudden light over their attackers, illuminating bloodied knives and cleavers. A man falls, one side of his face torn open by the shot, and the rest hesitate, realising they have left the prohibited weapons alone after killing their owners. One looks down for the body of the nearest soldier and Narin lashes out, hammering his stave into the man's shoulder.

Enchei drives forward, dachan stick in hand. With the same casual flick that had the beating of Narin earlier, he shatters a man's jaw. In the next movement he kicks forward to catch another in the midriff. As Narin readies for a second strike, Enchei spins and deflects a wildly-swinging cleaver. The weapon flies away and the butt of Enchei's stick is driven into the owner's throat.

16

Another lunges and Narin dodges, turning the movement into a shattering blow. Before the man he kicked can recover Enchei has made up the ground between them, striking down at the man's head. Narin sees blood fly like a soul escaping and the man is dead before he hits the ground.

The man Narin hit staggers towards Enchei, weapon abandoned and clutching his shoulder. Enchei senses the movement and strikes as he turns, a near-perfect horizontal sword-stroke that the assassin never sees coming. Soon he joins his comrade lying supine and pawing feebly at a shattered throat. Enchei glances around and sees only the dying. He abandons his stick and runs to the humbled nobleman, assessing his wound then tearing away a piece of his shirt to staunch the blood.

'Thank the Gods you came, Investigator,' Enchei says in a strangely level tone – not even needing to pause for breath. 'You've saved the life of a Wyvern lord.'

'No,' Narin finds himself saying feebly, still stunned by the deaths happening around him. 'No, it wasn't me.'

'Of course it was,' Enchei says, turning to look at Narin. Over many such dreams his eyes have become black and empty in Narin's memory. 'You saved this man's life. Who else could it have been?'

'Emari! Emari?'

Kesh put her head around the door and surveyed the empty hall beyond. A long wooden table occupied the centre, over which hung a wide wrought-iron chandelier. The bright morning light streamed in through the open shutters off to her right, showing Kesh the chandelier had fresh candles in at least, though the floor remained unswept. The young woman paused to listen, head tilted to one side, but there were no sounds of sweeping from elsewhere in the boarding house either.

'Honestly, that girl,' Kesh said with a small smile. 'Give her one job she finds boring and suddenly she's as flighty as a butterfly. Lord Monk give me patience!'

Her eyes twitched to the left as she spoke, instinctively looking towards the grey sweep of the temple's concave roof as she invoked its Ascendant God.

A muscular woman of twenty with a sailor's tan and long plaited hair, Kesh stepped inside the doorway, brandishing her rug beater.

'Emari?' Kesh shouted again, 'I'm not so tired I can't swing this a few more times!'

There was no response from the house beyond. Kesh gave a tut of annoyance and returned to the warm sunshine outside, as aware as Emari that her threat was empty until their mother, Teike, returned. Though the woman loved her adopted daughter no less than Kesh, she had fewer qualms about smacking Emari's nut-brown behind if she slacked in her duties.

There was no one else in the house; each of their five lodgers was out at work and Kesh was unmarried, having been promised to a young man who'd drowned alongside her father several years back.

The slow, sonorous clang of the wreck buoy beyond the harbour wall carried up to her on the breeze. From where Kesh had laid out the rugs, she could see its red-painted flanks bobbing on the tide. Further out, past the limits of the Harbour Warrant's authority, floated the threatening shape of a House Eagle warship.

Kesh frowned at the sleek warship before returning to her work. It had been there for a week now, not interfering with trade yet, but a silent threat that the harbour folk recognised well enough. With a shake of the head she attacked the rugs again, hammering away with the beater until her arm was near-shaking with fatigue, then moving on to the next after a gulp of lukewarm yellow tea.

A smile appeared on Kesh's lips as she took a second swallow. The spring sun was warm on her shoulders, the breeze coming in off the sea clean and salty. On such a day she could only enjoy the exercise as she put the strength of her thick arms to work. The courtyard faced south, catching the morning sun and affording her a fine view of the harbour's three main wharves. The nearer two were long, wooden affairs for the fishing fleet and trading cutters that plied the Horn Coast – while the furthest was the old stone deep-water dock for ships ranging all across the Inner Sea and beyond.

Kesh crossed the courtyard and hopped up a few makeshift steps until she could look over the perimeter wall. Their house was on an outcrop that loomed above the road leading to the nearer docks; a district of taverns and cramped markets that had been Kesh's whole life until her father died. From there she could see the glazed blue tiles of the fishermen's market and glimpse piles of yellow cockles gathered from the sandflats off the coast.

'A good crop,' Kesh muttered, looking around the various stalls for her mother. 'Let's hope Mother thinks so and brings a bag home.'

She sat on the top of the wall, brushing her fingers over the yellow petals of a flowering gull's foot as she listened to the clatter and voices of the harbour. When she had gone away to sea to cover the last seasons of her father's bond to the Vesis and Darch merchant house, which controlled the harbour and much of the shipping that used it, this view had been what Kesh had missed. The breeze over the wildflowers, the cries of gulls and the bustle of busy lives – not the unearthly sight of the Imperial Palace or the ice-white roofs of Coldcliffs to the east. As arresting as those enormous, ancient structures were, they never changed. The harbour was man-made and ugly to some, but it lived and breathed in a way the places of the old ones didn't.

She returned to her work and finished the last few rugs before hauling the pile up onto her shoulder and returning inside. There was still no sound of activity from her little sister so Kesh dumped the rugs over her father's chair at the head of the table and headed through to the corridor beyond.

'Emari,' she called ahead, 'Mother won't be long coming back.'

'Kesh, come look,' came Emari's reply at last. 'Come look at this!'

She followed her sister's voice through to the stairs that ran up the centre of the house. Emari was sitting on the windowsill on the second floor, her favourite place to watch the busy streets of the Harbour Warrant and marvel at the Imperial Palace on its distant island hilltop. The street curved around the outcrop of their house so from that window Emari could see a hundred yards down the warrant's public thoroughfare with the Palace rising behind. Today however, Emari was looking up towards the roof.

'What have you found, little one?' Kesh asked, slipping an arm around her sister's skinny shoulders. Emari was a bundle of scrawny arms and legs; still of that awkward age where her body didn't quite seem to fit together yet.

Emari turned to face her, big black eyes wide and questioning. 'There's a rope on the house.'

'A rope?' Kesh laughed. 'What do you mean?'

She leaned out across the little girl. As she looked up, a seagull on the roof just above them cried loudly, making Kesh jump in surprise. Emari below her dissolved into giggles, prompting Kesh to laugh and tickle her sister into submission before again looking out. It seemed Emari was right; there was a cable attached to the apex of their roof which ran taut across the street to the tavern there.

'So there is,' Kesh mused, 'painted grey too – to blend in with the sky maybe?'

'Why's it there?'

'I don't know,' she said with a shake of the head.

Kesh ushered her sister off the window sill and stood where Emari had been. After a few seasons on a merchant ship she had no fears about clambering around an open window and levered herself almost entirely out to inspect the cable more closely. Reaching up she could just about grab it and an experimental tug told her the cable was securely fastened to the main beam of the roof, tied with a knot that wasn't meant to be undone easily.

'Maybe this is what Master Greycloud heard a few days back,' she called down to Emari. 'Remember he complained about a cat or some-thing making a noise on the roof? That's his room right there.'

Emari nodded, hands clasped together in delight. 'It was someone tying the rope on! But who? Oh! It could be Master Shadow; I told you he was an Astaren!'

Kesh tutted at her sister. 'Don't be so silly, and don't say such things where the guests might hear you, Master Shadow in particular. He's not the sort to take kindly to idle gossip about him. As for this, I think it's a thief's road – an escape route over the rooftops.'

'Really?' Emari squealed. 'What sort of thief?'

'I don't know!' Kesh clambered down again. 'How would I know that? All I'm saying is everyone knows thieves use the rooftops to keep off the streets when the fog comes, but this road's too wide for anyone to jump. You can get all the way to Dragon District from the tavern, but you can't cross this road easily because we're on the public thoroughfare – it has to be wide enough for nobles of different houses to pass without starting an argument.'

'The thieves run across it?'

'No, but I used a cable like that a thousand times on board the *Piper's Lament*. You hang under it by your hands and feet, and crawl like a monkey underneath. Even at night I'd be across in no time and ready to cut the cable if anyone tried to follow.'

'Or a goshe!' Emari gasped. 'A goshe could run across and anyone following would fall!'

'Not at night,' Kesh said dismissively. 'You'd need eyesight like a cat to see it on the run and balance better than the best-trained goshe could have.'

'Do you think Master Shadow is a goshe, Kesh?'

She ruffled Emari's tangled dark curls. 'How should I know, little one? But it's not polite to ask; some people don't like the goshe and might take offence. He carries himself like a fighter – I bet you he's good too – but he's not warrior caste, that's for certain. Most likely he trains at a Shure, yes.'

'He is goshe! I'm sure I've seen him dressed like one, all in black. Do we like the goshe, Kesh?'

'Of course! Whatever folk whisper about them, they cured your fever when you first came to live here, remember?'

'So why don't others like them?'

'Money and tradition mostly,' Kesh said with a sigh. 'Some members bequeath their money to the Shure they trained at rather than their relatives and high-castes don't much like low-castes being taught to fight at all. '

'So Master Shadow might take it as an insult if I asked him?'

Kesh shrugged. 'All I'm saying is think before you speak, understand me? Don't ask such things of folk you don't know. If it turns out they're warrior caste, you might get a slap for the insult.'

'Or Master Shadow might turn out to be an assassin and kill us in the night to protect his secrets,' Emari said gravely.

'No! Pity's light! Have you been listening to old man Pethein again?' Kesh demanded, wagging a finger in Emari's face. 'I've told you not to loiter in the tavern once they've got stuck in for the evening. Next time I think you have been, I'll slap the brown off your legs, hear me?'

'Yes, Kesh,' Emari replied in a quiet voice. 'Sorry, Kesh.'

She grabbed the little girl and hugged her. 'I know you are, but you've got to be more careful round these parts. Sailors come from all over and get troublesome when they're out drinking. You keep clear after dark, you hear me?'

'I will,' Emari promised.

The girl fell silent for a while, her lips pursed as she thought. Kesh saw she wanted to ask something, but the little girl was trying to be mindful of what she'd just been told about thinking before she spoke. It was enough to make the older sister laugh, but she fought the urge. Emari tended to blurt out every thought that crossed her mind; it would be good for her to start controlling that before she got much older.

'Kesh?' Emari eventually said in a small voice.

'Yes, little one?'

'Is there going to be a war?'

'Between the Houses?'

Emari nodded.

'Well, I don't rightly know,' Kesh said, kneeling on the landing to look Emari in the eye.

When they'd taken Emari in, her father a shipmate of Kesh's father, Kesh had promised herself she'd never lie to her new sister. Something about hearing their neighbours tell Emari her father had sailed off with the Gods had jarred with Kesh. The Empire was not a happy place to live in sometimes, and Emari needed to know what it was really like without fearing it.

'The Houses like to fight,' she said by way of explanation, 'it's what noble folk do a lot of the time. If you're high-caste you're not allowed to work or learn a trade – House soldiers are warriors trained from birth to do that job alone. Now it might be that Eagle and Dragon end up fighting, but the Harbour Warrant isn't controlled by either and they have to respect the Emperor's domains – otherwise the other Houses would step in against them.'

'Master Steelfin said House Eagle could attack the harbour all the same, block us off so we can't fish or trade.'

'Pah, Master Steelfin's a stupid old man,' Kesh said quietly, 'and he knows little more about the Empire than I do. If they do blockade us, it won't be for long. The warriors have their own code for fighting; they're only allowed to kill other warriors. The Gods say it's a sin to kill someone of a low caste – as you'd remember if you came to temple a little more often.'

'Doesn't stop them all, mind,' called a voice from the bottom of the stairs.

Kesh turned to see her mother, Teike, leaning against the banister post and looking up at them, a wicker basket full of food slung over her shoulder.

'But don't you worry about the Eagles, my girl. It'd embarrass House Dragon if the city began to starve and Dragons don't like losing face.'

Teike slipped her scarf off her head and brushed her hair back away from her face. Once order was restored again she nodded towards the common room, one eyebrow raised. 'If you don't hop to your sweeping however, you might have me to fear!'

Emari gave a squawk and jumped up, clattering down the stairs and barely stopping for a kiss on her forehead on the way. Teike smiled after her and beckoned Kesh down also.

'Help me with the shopping?'

Kesh pulled the load from her mother's shoulder. 'Emari's seen a rope attached to the roof, it looks like a thief's run.'

Teike made a dismissive face. 'Tell her to look out for Master Shadow, not thieves. The man promised to give me the next week's board by yesterday and has yet to show his face.'

'He must have left very early this morning,' Kesh said, 'or he didn't get in last night. I was up with the dawn and heard no one before you.'

Her mother scowled. 'I knew he was going to be trouble, that one. Too full of himself was Master Tokene Shadow, all but propositioned me his first night here. I've seen his type before; in debt or in trouble, and either way he'll cost me money.'

'Don't worry,' Kesh said as she headed for the kitchen, 'his sea-chest is still in his room; he'd have to be dead not to come back for that. It's not like he'd just forget it.'

'Well, boy, I'm inclined to agree.'

Narin narrowed his eyes at the older man. Enchei sat back and looked down at the long-knife in his hands. It was a street fighter's weapon, not a soldier's, yet it couldn't have looked more natural in the man's callused hands. Enchei tucked a stray trail of grey hair behind his scarred left ear and returned the weapon to the pile at his feet.

In front of him was the half-naked body of the goshe, still unconscious. The man was bound to a makeshift bed, ankles tied to the frame Narin had dragged out of his bedroom and a sheet wrapped across his chest to pin his bandaged arms. He had no idea if it would hold the man, but he was terrified the goshe would wake and disappear when his back was turned, leaving him to explain that to an angry God.

'You think the tattoos are fake?'

Enchei glanced up, a sly smile on his face. 'I meant you really *are* buggered.'

Narin sank down in a chair, too deflated for any sort of joking. They were in his assigned quarters in the Imperial District; a two-room affair on the first floor of an Imperial housing compound. Sunlight streamed in through the open windows, the brightness of spring after a long, damp winter. Enchei took a deep breath of the fresh afternoon air that raced through the quarters. He touched a palm to the injured man's chest.

'He's hot,' Enchei commented, 'even in this draught.'

'Fever?'

'Mebbe.'

Narin jumped up again and crossed the room to stand over Enchei. 'But what about the tattoos?'

'Ah yes, the tattoos. Seems your Investigator instincts are gettin' better.'

'They're fakes? Truly?'

Enchei squinted up at the younger man, silhouetted against the bright window frame. 'Aye, they're fakes.'

'But how? Magic?'

Narin walked back to the table, unable to stay in one spot for long. By contrast Enchei slowly lifted himself up out of his chair and reached for his pipe to fill it.

'Magic?' he said eventually, 'mebbe.'

He jammed the pipe in one corner of his mouth and shrugged off his long leather coat. The old man wore it most of the year round; it put Narin in mind of a fussy little boy the way he always kept the coat to hand, even on warm days.

Enchei had re-stitched the lining with dozens of patches; some sort of protective charms, Narin guessed. Feeling like a child himself, he'd once sneaked a feel of the coat. Each closed pocket seemed to contain some sort of coarse powder or soil rather than padding.

Enchei draped his coat over an armchair and went to the iron stove in the far corner to fetch an ember for his pipe. Once it was lit he returned to the goshe, again picking up the long-knife in a way that looked as if it was more out of habit than for any real reason.

His skin was stained with ink from his trade; blues and reds swirling around his tanned, greyish fingers. After years working as a sanctioned tattooist – in an Empire where every man, woman and child were marked with their caste and House – it was a mark of honour, one that showed his experience.

Like many looking for a fresh start in life, Enchei had joined the House of the Sun rather than been born into it. Every noble House had authority over its subjects; to leave your nation of birth and join another would have been unthinkable before the power and domain of the Imperial House became more than nominal – before the Emperor's authority had been changed from temporal to spiritual. Even now the act was not to be taken lightly. It meant placing oneself at the whims and greed of officials, but Enchei had a skill that was always in demand and little interest in advancement.

'However they faked it,' Narin continued at last, 'that detail alone is enough of a scandal. The temples have been looking for an excuse for years to go after the goshe order, half the entire Empire's warrior caste too. Treating all their members as equals is enough provocation, but changing the caste tattoos too …' Narin shook his head. 'They'll see it as great a threat to the Empire as any merchant house manufacturing guns. Stars above, there are Shure training houses in every city you could name – the goshe order is probably bigger than any one merchant house!'

'Quite a step from here to there,' Enchei pointed out, 'so I don't reckon that's your first concern. More likely it's professional killers learning their skills from the goshe and you've pursued assassins before.'

'Wish it was as simple as that.'

'Aye, Lord Shield spoke to you. That's interesting right enough. Bet you he didn't bring up the tattoos though.'

'I think Shield threw him from a damn roof!' Narin hissed, trying not to shout in his alarm. 'What in the name of Pity's tears have I got caught up in?'

Enchei puffed on his pipe, frowning. 'Something, that's for sure. Remember those spirit traps I set in the summer?'

'Spirit traps? You mean those bloody bone charms I helped you hide? I remember coming a hair's breadth from falling off a bloody roof and you laughing about it. You told me they were protective wards.'

Enchei grinned briefly. 'Aye, I did, didn't I? Well they're there ta keep me safe, sure enough.' His hand went to the fetish at his neck, an animal bone of some sort. 'Anyways, they trap spirits; knot 'em up good for a few hours they will, but they'll also catch echoes.'

'Echoes? Echoes of what?' Narin demanded, startled that the spirit traps had been anything more than heathen superstition.

Enchei claimed to hail from the north-east, some obscure region of House Falcon's sovereign land no one had ever been to. Narin knew such remote parts were of little interest to the ruling lords, so old superstitions and shaman magic quietly survived in the shadows.

25

Compared to the Gods-fearing folk of the Imperial City, Enchei looked eccentric and anachronistic with his pagan trappings, but Narin had always assumed it was just a facade.

'Calls, screams, warnings; depends, really. What's important is this – one o' my spirit traps caught the echo of something big and noisy. My guess is that was your little encounter.'

'Big and noisy? Like a man falling off a roof?'

Enchei waved dismissively. 'Don't be daft, nothing like that. It was nothing you'd hear yourself, but if this one's not just some simple goshe, it'd have startled the shit out of him. Mebbe enough to make him lose his footing and fall – certainly enough to attract the attention of any nasty that happened to be in the area.'

'Like a God?' Narin asked, already knowing the answer.

The old man nodded. 'Shield was in ascendancy last night, no? If he was looking down at the city, he'd have heard it, along with any spirit or demon in the vicinity. My spirit-traps can only tell me there were screams in the night, not what they said. Lord Shield would've heard it all clear as day.'

'Shield asked me a question – "who is the moon?" – he expects me to investigate this goshe and find the answer.'

'So he don't know what's going on most likely, just caught a fragment of the screams and hopes you can provide him with a few pieces of the puzzle. Not good that a God's involved, but it could be worse.'

'Worse?' Narin exclaimed. 'How, exactly?'

The older man shrugged. 'There ain't a God at the heart of it. Shield's late to the game and just taking an interest because he's a God and can stick his nose wherever he damn-well wants. If this was his game though, or another God's, you'd be more buggered than you know. As it is you've got a divine charge and mebbe even an ally if it all goes to shit. Not the finest hand a man ever got dealt, but not certain death either.'

Narin scowled as he recognised the truth in Enchei's words and bent over the goshe. The man's face was a little darker than Narin's own, his stubble and hair almost black while his features were small and surprisingly neat, considering his fighter's build. The man was heavily muscled, marked with more than a dozen scars in addition to a mass of bruises from the previous night. Narin had dragged a bonesetter he knew out of bed to tend him. The man had been furious at being woken so early in the morning only to discover no obviously broken

26

bones – the result of Shield's intervention, Narin guessed. All the same the bonesetter had wrapped the goshe's left arm, ribs and right wrist and stitched the cut on his forehead.

On the goshe's right shoulder were symbols tattooed in black, something required of every citizen of the Empire, but these ones had troubled Narin. He hadn't been able to explain to Enchei exactly why that had been, but the two were close friends and Enchei had been happy to indulge a hunch.

'House Shadow,' Narin read, 'military service, craftsman caste. No goshe mark, but I don't think they all do that anyway.'

'He look Shadow ta you?' Enchei asked.

'I don't know. You don't exactly get many of them round here.'

The old man shook his head at his friend's ignorance. 'Well fortunately for you, one of us has left this bloody city and seen something o' the Empire. Travelled a ways through Kettekast and can't say I'd have guessed he was a Shadow.'

Kettekast was the sovereign land of House Moon – one of the Empire's ten noble Great Houses that ruled the known world. Within that domain lay House Shadow's own lands, a subordinate nation but Narin couldn't remember exactly where it lay. Most maps of the Empire he'd seen only marked the domains of the ten Great Houses and tiny Imperial warrants granted to merchant houses. Everything was secondary to the Great House hegemonies and for outsiders the details mattered little.

'It's hardly proof the tattoos are fakes,' Narin said.

'No, what makes the tattoo a fake is that I say so. It's a good one, would fool more'n a few tattooists I reckon, but it's not old enough to be the one he got as a child.'

'I don't buy the military service either,' Narin added, 'doesn't seem to fit him.'

'No? Big man with scars in the military – not beyond the realms of possibility?'

Narin shook his head. 'The goshe use physical training to purify the mind, the Shure teaching martial arts anyway. It's all about enlightenment through perfecting skills, even at free hospitals the basic idea remains the same. They're also Shure, just teaching medicine instead.' He pointed at the thick slabs of muscle on the goshe's arms and chest. 'A man this size, taught to seek perfection in the martial arts? Doesn't strike me as someone not to be noticed and promoted. He's a few years older than me so must have served a full term, and if he was an idiot it's unlikely he'd be caught up in something Lord Shield would take interest in, certainly not on a solo mission.'

Enchei nodded. 'And there're no scars on his back, so a bad attitude wasn't holding him back.'

'Do you … do you think he could be an Astaren?' Narin asked quietly.

In spite of everything, saying the word sparked a flicker of excitement inside him. The Imperial City was a sheltered world to grow up in and the House of the Sun's elite Astaren warrior-mages had been obliterated centuries ago along with its warrior caste. Like the rest of the city, everything Narin knew of the Astaren came through rumour and myth. A secret kept even from the lords and generals of their own Houses, the Astaren were warrior-mages who formed the secret core of each army, performed the impossible and answered only to the Gods.

Enchei puffed out his cheeks and frowned at the goshe. His curled greying eyebrows twitched as he thought, absent-mindedly twisting the bone fetish around his neck through his fingers.

'Doubt it. They'd probably have tracked you down by now if you had one of their own,' he said eventually. 'Let's hope he ain't, eh? Near enough the games of Gods in terms of us getting out alive.'

Narin let out a deep sigh and nodded his agreement. Normal folk getting caught up in the machinations of the Astaren rarely fared well and it was one additional complication he didn't need.

'Quite a night you had, then,' Enchei commented. To the older man's astonishment, his idle comment seemed to deflate Narin completely. The Investigator's head dropped and he dropped back into a chair and slumped.

'Stars above, what's come over you?' the old man exclaimed. 'Don't tell me you argued with that girl of yours? That's where you found him, right? Out seeing Kine?'

Narin shook his head miserably. 'If only we *had* argued,' he admitted.

The Investigator fell silent, unwilling to say more. Enchei was his closest friend and the only other who knew of Narin's relationship with Kine, but somehow he feared to speak the words in the light of day. The idea of children had been a small fantasy they had each mentioned on occasion over the last year; wilfully dreaming of a life they'd never have. While it remained just between him and Kine, it wasn't quite real yet – but telling another would make it so.

'Well, spit it out, boy. It's because of me the two of you met; reckon I feel some sort of responsibility.'

Enchei stood and headed around the makeshift bed Narin had set up. He put a hand on Narin's shoulder and bent down until the Investigator met his arresting, cobalt-blue gaze.

'Better we hadn't met I think,' Narin sighed.

Enchei made a disgusted sound and stepped back. 'You say that again and I'll smack you round the head. I ain't saying it's the best way of falling in love, her being married to a Wyvern nobleman and all, but we all get dealt a shitty hand sometimes. I could've picked life to go a better way too.'

'You don't understand,' Narin insisted, 'Enchei, she's pregnant.'

The older man stopped mid-reply. 'Pregnant? Ah. That could prove inconvenient.' He scratched his jaw and held up a finger like a schoolmaster waiting for his pupil's attention. 'Now I know I'm old and forgetful, but when you saved that nobleman's life like the hero you are, hadn't they just cut his balls off?'

Narin groaned and pressed his fingers against his temple. 'What was I thinking? As soon as she starts to show, he'll know she's taken a lover and have her killed!' His voice became panicked at the very thought of it, his heartbeat jumping rapidly though he couldn't even find the strength to rise.

'Don't be so foolish,' Enchei said in a sharp tone, 'it's not so drastic as that.'

'What? The man's been castrated! He knows he's not going to be the father, how long before he works out it's me?'

'Hah, Lord Cail Vanden Wyvern? For a man of the noble caste, he's a spineless bureaucrat and not the cleverest either. I'd be surprised if he got that far in nine months – which is, by the way, how long you've got to find a solution.'

'He'll know long before then!' Narin protested, only for Enchei to dismissively wave his words away.

'That there's a child coming, sure, but the man's not going to announce to the whole of House Wyvern he's been cuckolded, is he? Remind me why he thinks you're the greatest Investigator of all time?'

'Ah, because you saved him from assassins and made me take all the credit?'

Enchei wagged a finger in Narin's face. 'Try again.'

'What? What are you talking about?'

'Poor Kine, the child's likely to be simple,' Enchei sighed, shaking his head theatrically. 'Saving his life was one thing, but covering up the fact his balls got cut off for not paying a gambling debt? That's what made you the shining sun of the whole Imperial House, in Vanden's eyes.'

Narin was so bemused he didn't even bother objecting to Enchei's irreverent turn of phrase comparing him to the Emperor. The old man had joined the House of the Sun gladly enough, but had only ever managed a sort of gruff affection for their young Emperor descended from Gods.

'So I helped ...' Suddenly it all fell into place and Narin gasped. 'Oh for Pity's sake, I must need more sleep. Of course – it's the only heir he'll ever have! He'll not endanger that, no matter how angry he is with Kine. It's not as though he can prove the child isn't his, someone'll ask why. He'd most likely take his own life than live with the shame of the truth getting out. Wyvern skin varies quite a lot – might be he can accept the child as his own even if I am the father. Kine's darker than he is. So what do I do?'

Enchei looked down at the unconscious goshe beside them. 'You've got more pressing problems, hey? There's a God waiting for answers from you and when this one wakes up, my guess is you'll not have time to worry about Kine for a week or so.'

He headed back over to the stove, beside which he'd deposited a hessian bag. From the bag he pulled a clay wine bottle and several wrapped packets which were each set out in an orderly line. 'Go find the lovely Sheti, ask her if she wants to eat with us after she's finished her duties. There was squid and dappled crab at the market today – what I'm planning requires a more appreciative audience than you.'

Narin didn't move from his seat, watching the man with astonishment. 'You hear all my problems and all you care about is cooking to impress a widow?'

'The best solutions are always found over a meal,' Enchei said with a flourish of a kitchen knife. 'Have I taught you nothing these last two years? If you think it's just the sum of my wisdom on the dachan court you should be picking up, you're more simple than any of us are willing to admit.'

'And what about him?' Narin demanded, pointing at the goshe. 'What do you propose I tell Sheti about him?'

Enchei shrugged and fished from his bag a knobbly vegetable Narin didn't recognise. 'Tell her the truth, or some approximation of it. That woman's seen life in all its colours and was no fool to start with – plus, she does chores for this whole compound,' he said, gesturing to the square of housing Narin's rooms were within.

'That means not only is she around during your shift hours to keep an eye on him, she also hears gossip from all over the city.' He smiled and looked up with a comically wistful expression. 'Us lonely old men love to gossip with a pretty face – and anyways, it's not as if she's the only one you'll have to tell.'

'What do you mean?'

Enchei laughed. 'Investigator Narin Deshar, your life is not your own. You might be the rising star of the Lawbringers, but there's one star risen higher than yours that you still bow to.'

'Rhe?' Narin said with a sinking feeling. 'Stars of Heaven, why?'

'Aha! The one and only Lawbringer Rhe,' Enchei exclaimed, arms raised in theatrical adulation. 'Scourge of the criminal classes, slayer of generals and insufferable bore. Lawbringer Rhe indeed; the man under whose tutelage you'll ascend to the rank of Lawbringer, assuming you don't get yourself brutally murdered first. The man whose sharp eyes will soon enough notice his protégé's distracted state and time spent on a side matter – then do what comes naturally to such a sanctimonious, arrogant shit: investigate.'

As the evening light turned the vast white walls of the Imperial Palace golden, Sheti realised she had been lost in the sight and shook herself back to her senses. She set her sewing aside and blinked out through the window at the skyline beyond, breathing in the scents of jasmine and honeysuckle that drifted up from the garden below. Far in the distance, around the towers and sharply peaked roofs of the Palace, long-winged birds turned lazily through the thermals. The day's warmth remained and when she leaned out over the window to look down at her small corner of the garden, she could hear the contented hum of bees as they attended to the flowers.

It was an indulgence, she knew, to have her part of the communal garden taken up by flowers, but her needs were modest now that family life was behind her. The tall plants and bushes provided a snug, secluded spot in the sun where she could work, partitioned from the rest of the grounds by a prickly hedge the chickens and geese steered clear of. She turned her head right and looked down the length of the communal garden. It was empty of people, but a pair of geese waddled between neat plots of beans and tomatoes, their bamboo frames shaded by lemon trees.

'My boys are improving,' she said with a smile. 'I'll make peasants of them yet!'

Though she had two grown sons of her own, Sheti had spent almost a decade working in this one Imperial compound for unmarried men. She had moved there soon after her husband's death and regarded many of the residents with maternal fondness. The Imperial staff who lived there had mostly grown up as orphans within the colleges of their professions. After a childhood in college dormitories and being worked hard from an early age, most were shy of anyone beyond their own small world and so unused to the presence of women they frequently never married.

Even Investigators like Narin, who saw the harsher side of the city, were often as wary as little boys around her. Sheti knew it was only at the urging of his worldly friend, Enchei, that Narin had first invited her to eat with them, more than a year ago now. The invitation was now a regular one and she had found the pair enjoyable company in a way her stern and weary daughters-in-law were not. Spurred on by the occasional invitation to these convivial evenings, others in the compound had tentatively followed suit. Now a growing sense of family was developing; Sheti playing matriarch to two score men mostly young enough to be her own sons.

Sheti straightened and shook her hair out. Pulling it deftly back she slipped a scarf – black, denoting peasant caste – over her head and tied it underneath her hair in the style of a married woman. She paused and blew a kiss towards a small painting of a young man that hung above the fire. It was a typical sailor's portrait; simple and quickly-made, but accurate enough to stir her memory.

The portraits were traditional wedding gifts for the brides of sailors, as so many men were lost to the sea-fogs and rocks of the Inner Sea. She had almost refused it when Oshene had presented the portrait to her, feeling immediately guilty at the idea, but for once he had been insistent. The pain of his loss was dimmed and distant nowadays, but forever present. It remained one of the reasons why she had chosen to work in the compound rather than live with one of her sons.

Only in the quiet moments did she remember him properly, felt him at her side as the bed creaked gently at night or a breeze brushed the sheets. For that ghostly memory she was glad to put up with long hours of work at the compound, cleaning and mending for careless young men, and the twinkling smiles from that aging fool, Enchei.

'No, he's no fool that one, my love,' she said with a wag of one finger towards Oshene's portrait as though her late husband had spoken through it. 'However much he plays one, that old boy has us all well worked out.'

She closed the shutters and slipped the latch, gathering up her shawl as she headed towards the door though her journey was as short as could be.

'No, far from a fool is our Enchei,' she continued under her breath as she went out into the compound's courtyard, 'even if he does like teasing me to the point of getting a smack.'

And there's the crack in his armour, she added privately. *The man might like to argue about the sun and stars given half a chance; but it's always with a smile and never a raised voice. That smacks of a man who misses his wife, to my mind. Oshene and I squabbled the same way often enough.*

Curtseying with a smile to one of her younger neighbours as he hurried out, tugging his Investigator's robes straight as he went, Sheti crossed the packed-dirt courtyard and made for the stairway on the other side. She could hear Enchei long before she reached the door, clattering a pan on Narin's stove while singing in his strange native tongue.

Despite the racket, somehow the tattooist still managed to know she was coming and as Sheti jerked open the door, Enchei stood there with his arms wide in greeting. In his hands were a large knife and a rusty-red crab with long dangling legs.

'Mistress Sheti!' Enchei declared with apparent delight, 'your timing is impeccable as always.'

'Indeed? And for what this time?' she said with a raised eyebrow at what he held. 'That crab doesn't look cooked yet to me.'

She curtseyed briefly to both men despite their friendship, each being of a higher caste. The formality was a reminder to all of them, a polite boundary to their familiarity. Enchei offered a half-bow in return, one that had less to do with caste than theatre, and swept out of her way to deposit the crab on the table. The creature's claws flopped over the edge, almost pleading for its life as Enchei prepared it for the pot.

33

'That it isn't, but Narin was just contemplating stripping his guest naked and naturally I thought of you.'

Sheti gave a start as Narin rose from the other side of the room. Still in his Investigator's robes, Narin wore a strangely fearful expression, but any question at that dissipated when she noticed a bandaged man tied to a bed in the corner.

'What is going on here, Master Narin?' Sheti demanded, bewildered by the sight.

'Official Lawbringer business,' the younger man said stiffly. 'I'm not at liberty to tell you everything, Mistress Sheti, but this man will be staying here for a few days.'

'Official business?' she echoed. Sheti blinked and looked from one man to the other. Narin was a handsome young man, well past the age he should be married, but a liar he was not. That, coupled with Enchei's apparent delight, told her all she needed to know there. 'Narin, we're friends, are we not?'

He hesitated, frozen like a rabbit for a moment before nodding. 'I think so.'

'Excellent, so do I,' she said, advancing a step towards him and nudging the door closed with a flick of her heel. 'Now please don't insult your friend and give me an explanation I'm going to believe.'

He deflated almost instantly. 'Very well, I'm sorry. I'm … I don't rightly know what's going on, though.'

'Give me something,' she advised.

'I knocked him out last night, while out seeing a friend. He took me by surprise and I reacted without thinking. He'd fallen from a rooftop and was injured – I think he was being chased by Lord Shield at the time and he's ordered me to find out who this man is and what he was up to.'

'Lord Shield?' she gasped. 'You spoke to a God last night? This is your idea of a more plausible explanation?'

'I swear it's the truth! I wish I was making it up, but I think I'm in real trouble if I don't find out what he was doing out on that rooftop.'

Sheti didn't speak for a while. She approached the bed and looked down at the man. He was asleep or unconscious and half-naked already, a sheet only partially covering his broad chest. The man was older than Narin, but still in the prime of life given his build. The ghost of a black beard lay on his tanned cheeks, while a pile of weapons sat atop some stained black clothes on the other side of the bed.

'Who is he?' she breathed, edging closer.

'I've no idea. That's what I have to find out.'

'Is he dangerous?'

Narin hesitated. 'He's a goshe – dressed and armed like an assassin. We have to assume he's dangerous, but mostly I didn't want him moving before he woke and I had to leave him alone for half the day.'

'You honestly spoke to Lord Shield?' she said, confusion taking over again. 'What game is he playing with you – how can you manage anything he cannot?'

'It seems Lord Shield doesn't want to be too actively involved,' Enchei supplied from behind her. Sheti glanced back to see the man reverse his knife and drive it down through the shell of the crab with a practised movement. 'He must want Narin to stir up trouble first, see what rises to the top.'

'And then?'

Enchei shrugged and turned his attention back to the crab, neatly cracking it open.

'What are you going to do, Narin?'

The younger man scowled and gestured to the pile on the other side of the bed. 'Firstly, go through his belongings. See if there's anything that might help me.'

She shook her head. 'First you fetch water and a cloth.' Sheti sighed and knelt down beside the injured man. 'I don't know much about Gods, but I do know about injured men. He needs to be washed; you don't leave a man stinking in his own sweat and blood like that.'

As Narin went to fetch a bowl, Sheti started to untie the cord around the unconscious man's ankles. 'As for after, how about you just leave a note on your door for him? When he wakes he can come find me.'

'I can't risk him running away!' Narin protested. 'He's probably a fugitive, remember? The word of a God's good enough for me—'

'Then take him to the Palace of Law!' Sheti interrupted angrily. 'That's where you take criminals isn't it?'

'It's complicated.'

'Enough to make you act like a fool?' She rose and faced Narin. 'You've told me often enough how much of a stickler Lawbringer Rhe is – what would he say about all this? Would he approve of you confining a man without record or trial? You *are* still trying to impress him, aren't you? Prove to him you're worthy of promotion?'

Narin raised his hands to stop her. 'I know, I know, but please listen. I have no evidence, no crime under Imperial law, no clue what is going on other than a God giving me orders I don't understand. I'm going to speak to Rhe tomorrow – tell him everything and ask his advice. You know what he's like; Rhe is the most scrupulous and uncompromising Lawbringer in living memory.'

'So you'll take his opinion but not mine?'

'He's a Lawbringer,' Narin protested, 'my superior and as much an expert in the Emperor's law as anyone I can trust. I don't mean it as a slight on you.'

'Enchei – are you just going to stand there silently and not offer any sort of opinion? Normally we can hardly hear ourselves think for your thoughts on every subject under the stars.'

The older man looked up. 'You want me to help persuade him? Sorry, I've never been one for rules and regulations. Anyways, our friend there looks like he's seen his fair share of trouble. Doubt he'd be so happy if he woke up at the Palace of Law.'

'So you're happy to tie him up and keep him hidden? Let him disappear from the world no matter what he wants or who might be looking for him? Have you no morals?'

Enchei grinned. 'Sold 'em off years ago. Got a good price too.'

'Now is the time for jokes?'

He stopped and put down his knife, the smile vanishing from his face. 'Jokes? Who says I was joking? You strip and wash him; I'll even help you if you want. You look at the marks on his body and I'll tell you what most likely caused 'em. That man's lived a violent life and if he's goshe he's probably good at it. Men like that live by different rules and Imperial laws of confinement don't figure much in them. I doubt he'll be overly upset by being cared for and hidden for a week, whatever the constraints.'

He walked around her with a grim look on his face and knelt at the goshe's side. 'But sure, we could try it your way and worry about Lord Shield later. Gods are notoriously easy to stop when you've pissed them off.'

Sheti didn't reply. After a moment she joined the two men in stripping off the remainder of the stranger's clothes and sponging the sweat and dried blood off his body. It didn't take them long, half the job already having been done, and swiftly she saw Enchei was right. The tattoos on the man's shoulder proclaimed military service, but she doubted all of his injuries had come from that. A life of crime afterwards seemed likely. Gang fights or assassinations she had no way of telling, but this was a lifetime of injuries unless he had been a remarkably inept soldier.

'Now his belongings,' Narin declared once they were finished, retrieving the pile from the other side of the bed. Enchei left them to it, returning to his cooking while they picked over each item in turn and looked for clues.

It didn't take long, everything being plain and unremarkable, but at last they found something tucked into an inside pocket of the man's tunic – a rough piece of paper with small, neat writing on it. Narin spent a while peering at it then handed it over to Sheti. 'A list of street names?'

She didn't reply immediately. There were numbers on the paper as well, accompanying some but not all of the words, while each string of numbers and words ended in one written just a shade more definitely than the rest.

'I know some of these streets   Tessail leads off Grand Adahn over in House Dragon's district. I don't see where all the numbers fit in though.'

'Door numbers?'

She shook her head. 'Tessail's a poor street; I doubt any of the houses will be numbered there. The next words are Cettas Han though, that's a few streets away from Tessail – they're not connected.'

'If you're following a route, you need to count streets to know when you're turning,' Enchei called. 'Otherwise how do you tell where you're going? Half the streets won't have posted names so you can't go directly from one to the next.'

'Does that fit?' Narin wondered aloud. He took the paper back and ran his finger along the words, muttering each one under his breath. 'Ah, I can't tell, I don't know these districts well enough to remember.'

Sheti pushed the goshe's weapons under the narrow bed and stood. 'There you go then, there's your evidence. Tell Rhe your story and show him the paper. Between the two of you, you should be able to follow these directions. There are what, four destinations by the looks of it? Find something to tie them and you might know what you're involved in. Don't find something, maybe you stop assuming this man is a dangerous criminal. There are enough disappearances in the Empire without you adding to their numbers.'

Narin looked down again at the paper and nodded briefly. 'Got to start somewhere, I suppose.'

'And come and eat your greens, young man,' Enchei added with a laugh. 'Your mystery will still be there once we've eaten.'

CHAPTER 3

With the ascension of mortals to the heavens, some hoped the old Gods would simply fade into history or be destroyed. One must now wonder whether the God-Emperor and God-Empress instead felt kinship for beings they would now share eternity with – or more worryingly, they are not strong enough to defeat those we now call demons.

From *A History* by Ayel Sorote

Cotto padded noiselessly along the peak of the roof until he reached the great clay-brick chimney at its centre. He glanced back and nodded to Shir, watching the small man hop the gap between houses and follow Cotto's path. The breeze was faint on his skin and a layer of clouds hid all but a glimmer of the moonlight. Despite the dark he could see the lines of the city clearly, each roof and tile outlined in pale starry white. On the streets below was a veil of mist, creeping tendrils enveloping the city's houses like an octopus's embrace.

'No sign?' Shir whispered, crouching beside Cotto to present a smaller outline against the sky.

'Sign of what?' Cotto growled back. 'This is a fool's errand. What in the seven hells are we likely to find out here?'

He remained standing, one hand hooked on the hanging jaw of a terracotta dragon's head that protruded from one corner of the massive chimney. His skin was so dark that the whites of Cotto's eyes seemed to shine by contrast.

'Our lost brother!' Shir insisted. 'Some clue about what happened to him.'

Cotto scowled. 'Just shut up,' he muttered, watching Shir's jaw clamp shut. He felt a pang of contempt at that, at how obedient the man was. 'Whatever happened to our brother, he'll be long gone – dead or alive.'

Little more than dogs, they are, he thought to himself. *Starsight's wasted on them; they'll always be less than a normal man. I can hardly see why the Elders bother giving them any of the Blessings – 'cept it means fewer true men like me to give the orders.*

He moved around the chimney to look north from where they were, toward the palazzos of the Dragons where lesser men ruled; his countrymen, who'd likely not even acknowledge his presence except to summon their guards. Blade-like towers reached up into the sky, set with long curves of glass that faintly glowed green or blue. Ancient magic, a jealously guarded secret that illuminated the towers and arches of House Dragon's district, but mere toys compared to the Blessings Cotto now possessed.

'Keep moving,' he muttered, giving the docile Shir a nudge with his boot. 'We search these streets and return to report.'

They set off at a faster pace, Cotto leading the way along the rooftops of the district's lower-caste areas. As they went, the city seemed to close in on them; mist rising up from the Crescent and the sea to fill the streets with a pale, insubstantial blanket even their Starsight could hardly penetrate. They kept to the rooftops, working their way into the corners between buildings and ornate chimneys for their lost brother or a clue to his disappearance.

It was slow going – even with the Cat's Paw Blessings the Elders had imbued into their muscles to let them walk silently – but they moved steadily down the lines of houses as the night drew on. They paused at a crossroad, peering down at the dirt-packed ground below with wary, unblinking eyes.

All was still, the mist undisturbed by man or beast, God or demon. Over the crossroad stood a grand structure, a four-pillared archway canopied by a shallow roof of red tiles. A black dragon statue stood at the very peak of the roof, facing north-east down the larger of the streets leading away from the crossroad – claws raised and silently roaring a challenge to the cliff-top palazzos of House Eagle.

Cotto was about to leap onto the tiled roof when he heard a faint sound from his companion, a hiss of warning. He froze and heard a click of the tongue come from Shir, then a second. Turning his head slowly, Cotto scanned the street to the right as the signal had told him to. At first he saw nothing, then he noticed a slight disturbance in the white spread of mist on the street below. He shifted his body slightly and felt the reassuring press of a long-knife in its sheath as he watched the mist drift like a lonely spectre.

Something moved in the street, something smaller than a human. Against the mist it was hard to tell what, but Shir had been right to warn him. There was no sound coming from that direction, no pad of feet or panting that might indicate a stray dog. Cotto eased himself back against the peak of the roof and slowly slipped a hand behind his back, reaching for the small crossbow stowed there. With practised fingers he unshipped the weapon and brought it in front of him, ratcheted the string back and locked it into place without taking his eyes off the curls of mist below. It wasn't a powerful weapon, but if that was a fox in the street, it would be enough to kill it and send any demon inhabiting its body fleeing.

He eased a bolt into the trace and paused, weapon ready to aim. Through the mist he saw a small shape, slinking down the side of a building in parallel with them. Not a rat, though demons could use them too, but smaller than a dog for certain. He raised the bow and looked for a shot, drawing in shallow breaths while Shir waited silently behind.

Nothing happened. The fox, or whatever it was, seemed to melt into the night. The layer of mist went undisturbed on the ground; the street frozen like a sheet of ice. After two dozen breaths, Cotto lowered the bow and turned to Shir.

'Did you see it?' he whispered.

The small man with greyish skin opened his mouth to speak, but no words came out.

Cotto frowned and waited a heartbeat longer before his senses screamed in panic. Light burst all around him and a clap of thunder seemed to burst in his head as a fox screamed just behind Shir. The smaller man jerked and juddered, looking pleadingly at Cotto for help, but he was already scrambling out of the way. Cotto fired the crossbow and the bolt cut a trail of white through the night sky as a narrow vulpine head appeared over the crest of the roof. He hurled the spent bow at it, but the fox dodged with unnatural speed and shrieked again.

This time he felt it, the demon touch they had all been warned about. It drove into his ears like a stiletto. Searing pain and a cacophony of sound filled his head, causing Cotto to lurch on the shallow slope of the roof. Somehow he found his hand around his long-knife and he tore it from the sheath, slashing wildly towards the fox but catching nothing. At the back of his mind, against the mess of noise crashing on his ears, came a second sound, the long deep note of a tolling bell.

Cotto gasped with relief and fought for balance, swinging his knife wildly as he sought purchase underfoot. The clatter of the demon touch dimmed, eclipsed by that sonorous peal rising from inside him – another Blessing, this one buried deep within his mind to combat the chattering voices of demons. The fox vanished from sight but Cotto kept moving, desperately seeking an escape route. Shir was still slumped against the roof, his jaw working as though still trying to warn Cotto, but his limbs were frozen in place.

Venom, Cotto realised, *he's gone.*

He ran to the edge of the roof, intent on jumping to the grand arch. Before he could leap, something struck him in the side and spun him around. Cotto was thrown from his feet, sliding and scrambling down the shallow roof. Knife abandoned, he flailed for purchase and after a moment of panic found the ornate cornice at the edge of the roof. The muscles of his wrist screamed as his weight pressed down on it, but he managed to fight the pain and hold himself long enough to twist and plant a foot.

He looked up and saw a nightmare staring back. Four angular limbs held it steady at the peak of the roof while a mass of eyes fluttered and twitched madly on its misshapen head. Cotto flapped at his knife sheaths for a moment before tugging a slim blade free. As he hurled it the demon darted to one side and then it was on him. The forelegs slammed into his body and Cotto felt its claws bite flesh. Only his raised forearm prevented the demon from burying grey fangs into his face and still he cried out as the force of the bite crushed his arm.

Cotto struck back with a closed fist, the steel knuckles of his gloves crashing into the side of the demon's head, but it was like punching stone. The demon jerked sideways and hurled him back up towards the peak of the roof, pouncing after him like a striking spider and biting down again. This time it tore through the leather spaulder and down into his shoulder. Cotto had drawn a knife by then and hacked at one of the limbs pinning him. The blade scraped down the limb, tearing through velvet-black skin before catching and digging into bone or chitin.

The demon ignored the injury and used a free limb to drive Cotto onto his blade-arm, pinning the weapon while it tore at his armour. This time it found a vulnerable point under his arm and ripped at the

41

flesh. Cotto howled, then screamed as the demon slammed a clawed limb into the wound and snapped the ribs below. Pain flooded his body. Cotto felt the strength drain from his limbs as the demon hooked multi-jointed limbs around his shoulders and pinned his arms back, turning him face-up to stare at the uncaring clouds above.

The fox appeared again, a malevolent arrowhead against the darkened sky. Its pale pelt faded to black around narrow eyes in which Cotto could see jerky, twisting bluish light. The air around it flickered and shuddered, lambent and ghostly. Pinpricks of white light burst before his eyes, jagged shapes that hinted at a huge hunched wolf looming over him. The fox advanced and screamed again, needle-sharp teeth showing as the sound ripped into Cotto's mind and he howled with it. The phantom wolf lunged at the same time and he felt its teeth scrape down his belly, his muscles shrieking as the crackling maw bit down. Again the peal of the bell rose up unbidden from the depths of his memory, but this time the fox was undeterred.

A second cry burst Cotto's eardrums. He couldn't tear his eyes away from the fox as it came close enough to sink those slender teeth into his face. Pale light thrashed like a storm all around it as the white wolf continued its assault, tearing underneath his leather armour. He tried to free his arms, but the misshaped demon was far stronger, its grip unbreakable. Inhuman voices screamed through his head and the tolling bell became increasingly distant. The bursts of light in its eyes intensified and Cotto felt a searing pain in his own as he tried to hide from the light, but he couldn't move. The fox's eyes blazed bright and—

Without warning the demon was thrown to one side, almost spun around by the force of a crossbow bolt tearing into its gut. It screeched and turned to flee, the wolf collapsing into eddies that folded back into the fox. Over the far side of the roof appeared a black, expressionless face. For a moment Cotto felt a fresh pang of fear, seeing only unnatural, inhuman lines of brow and jaw. Then he realised it was a mask as the figure slammed a slim axe into the fox's neck. There was great spurt of blood and the fox's head tumbled while the wolf-spirit seemed to explode and evaporate into nothingness.

The monster holding Cotto released its grip and scrambled to attack. Before it could, another black-masked goshe appeared and hooked one of its legs, dragging the demon off-balance before chopping into its shoulder joint with a second axe. The demon threw itself around, driving up with lightning speed to claw at its attacker, but somehow the goshe was faster. It deflected the limb and whirled around with the grace of a dancer – slashing at the demon's bulbous body as it went, before hooking another limb and dragging it close once more.

The demon lurched unsteadily towards it, but this time the goshe drove in to meet it and smashed a lightning-wreathed fist into the snagged limb like a hammer. A cracking sound cut through the night and the demon yowled, but then the first goshe was on it and hacking down at its head. Both struck in quick succession and the creature spasmed and fell limp.

Cotto managed a croak, a gasp for air as everything fell still around him. The second goshe looked down and slid up its mask, revealing a woman's face. In the white light of his Starsight, Cotto saw pale skin and light eyes, a wisp of hair creeping down her cheek towards a thin scar that seemed strangely bright in the augmented light.

'Kodeh,' she said briskly to her comrade, pointing at the larger of the demons with her axe. 'Take that one and head back before anything comes to investigate.'

'And the fox?' Kodeh asked, accent and black skin marking him as a fellow Dragon – a native of this district in some fashion, just as Cotto was.

'Leave it, it's just a vessel. The demon-spirit's gone, but the other is one of their soldiers. The Elders will want to study it.'

'As you command.' The big man spared a glance down at Cotto. 'What about him?'

She looked down and Cotto drunkenly tried to pull himself upright with his good arm. 'They have his scent now.'

'Syn ... Synter,' Cotto gasped. 'I can walk.'

Her face was blank. 'I doubt that,' she said. 'Kodeh, I'll meet you at the safehouse. First I need to warn Father Jehq.'

'Of what?'

The woman's face tightened with anger. 'This was an ambush; they knew we'd be looking for signs of Irato. That fox was digging into Cotto's mind, we've no idea how much they know. We need to cover our tracks and protect the artefact.'

'What ... about me?' Cotto panted, fear taking him as Kodeh tossed the dead monstrosity over his shoulder and trotted back across the rooftops.

Synter ignored him and went to see to Shir. She crouched down over the man for a few moments then drew a knife from her belt and cut his throat, tossing the body with ease down the sloped roof until it fell to the ground.

'Synter!' Cotto pleaded as she stood over him. 'Don't!'

There was no pity in her pale eyes as she returned to him, nor remorse. Focused on the task at hand, the female goshe didn't even seem to hear him.

'Let's hope they got nothing from you,' she muttered to herself, 'we're too close now.'

She reached into a pocket and withdrew a small bag, hefting it in her hand as she gave Cotto an appraising look. 'Time to clear up behind us. Wouldn't want to leave anything for the Astaren to find now, would we?'

The blackened blade flashed once more in his star-lit eyes and then all was dark.

CHAPTER 4

Blood stains his hands and streaks the grey of his trousers. His knees are damp, sodden by the dark, sticky mess of death surrounding the unconscious Wyvern nobleman. The stink of human waste hangs thick on the air, the voided bowels of those who have died, but there is no time to be disgusted. Enchei tears a surcoat from the body of one fallen guard, uses a knife to cut away the bloodied front. This he wads up and, pulling Narin's blood-slicked hand away from the nobleman's crotch, he presses the fresh bandage against the wound.

'He's still alive?' Narin hears himself ask as the first compress peels jerkily away from his palm and flops to the ground.

'He'll live,' Enchei confirms, 'but this needs proper bandaging.'

'Can we carry him? It's not far to Dragon District.'

Enchei is silent for a while. There's a smear of blood on his forehead – not his own, he's just wiped away the sweat of his exertions with bloodied hands.

'No, I have a better idea,' he says at last.

'Better than taking him to safety?'

The tattooist nods. 'I know a woman, not far from here. A midwife, she'll have clean bandages.'

'You'd trust her over a Great House's finest doctors?'

Enchei shrugs. 'I'll do it myself.'

'Yourself?' Narin looks around at the bodies of their attackers. He is reminded of how quickly Enchei killed them, the quick efficiency with which he made corpses of six killers. 'How are we even alive?'

'Told you I was a soldier,' Enchei says gruffly. 'Was a damn good one, 'cept the bit about taking orders from fools.'

'And you learned to wrap wounds too?'

'In war men get hurt quite a lot.'

Enchei looks the nobleman up and down and for the first time Narin does so properly. The man they've saved is not typical of his countrymen;

45

he's short and rotund with a thick neck and lighter skin than most Wyverns. Without warning the tattooist grabs Narin's hand and uses it to take the place of his own. That done he begins to strip off the nobleman's once-grand jacket to reveal the plain linen shirt beneath.

'Why?'

'Why? All those weapons lying around. Bound to be an accident o' some sort.'

'Why dress it yourself? Why take his jacket off?'

The tattooist's eyes seem to shine now, each tiny vein of his iris edged in light. 'Make him less obvious.'

In his dream Narin hears the words echo distantly as Enchei begins to fade into the dark shadows behind – all except his eyes, which remain bright and terrifying.

'Why?'

'He's been castrated,' he hears Enchei say as his view begins to recede and he finds himself in front of the narrow, whitewashed house belonging to Enchei's midwife friend. 'You realise how that's seen where he's from? He'll be disgraced, for this and running up debts. Those were enforcers I'm sure, out to punish a man who couldn't pay, given what they've done.'

'You want to hide it,' Narin says as the door opens and a wizened face peers and ushers them in, the darkness enveloping them all.

'Might as well try, give the man a chance. Without that he's done – most likely he'll kill himself through shame and his family'll forget he was ever one of 'em. I ain't saying this'll work; you need to find his steward or manservant, hope they're loyal and competent enough to keep the secret.

'He'll be the best friend you ever have,' Enchei says from somewhere in the dark. 'Forever thankful – and in this life that's worth as much as gold.'

Narin woke with the dawn. Grainy, feeble light slipped through the angled slats of the window shutters along with a damp breath of wind. He scowled and rolled over to face the open doorway that led into the main room. A moment of panic gripped him, but then he heard the soft exhalation and relaxed again. The goshe was still there; he hadn't woken and fled in the night.

He eased himself up off the floor where he'd spent the night, barely sleeping, while his unconscious guest remained in the bed next door. A sharp ache behind his eyes blossomed as soon as he moved; his limbs were sluggish and heavy with fatigue. Unsteady for a moment until he found his balance, Narin straightened and stretched his arms up to brush the whitewashed ceiling, slowly tilting to each side to work the stiffness from his back. He grimaced at the twinge in his right shoulder when his arm was fully extended and rolled it in slow circles to work the discomfort out. A nagging injury from the dachan court, his shoulder hadn't enjoyed a night on the wooden floor.

Narin crossed to a small washstand and scrubbed away the greasy feeling on his face, blinking at the reflection in his small mirror as though not recognising himself. Once his brain had caught up, Narin wiped a cloth over his chest and armpits. The damp chill raised goosebumps over his skin until he turned away again, swinging his arms to shake off the last vestiges of sleep.

Opening the window shutters, Narin stared out across a city rendered ethereal and alien by the blanket of mist. The familiar lines of buildings and streets were broken up by a tattered curtain of white, the waters of the Crescent almost entirely obscured. The Imperial District was an island three miles across − nestled in the protective embrace of the mainland that extended around four-fifths of its shore − with the Crescent that band of water separating the two.

His eyes were inexorably drawn to the huge structure that dominated his view, one that even fog could rarely hide. The great arcs of the Tier Bridge rose high in the sky; as white as ice and, to Narin's eye, just as cold. The ornate grey towers of the temples on both banks looked tiny in comparison to the bridge's oppressive bulk, curving slightly left as it stretched to the far bank in House Dragon's district.

The bridge had no straight lines; each tier was suspended from a twisting spray of white arches that rose from each corner and crossed diagonally to the opposite corner. Anchored to the cold forest of arching supports on each bank, ramshackle houses ran along the shore behind a bustling network of market stalls.

Against the haze of morning Narin could make out little of the white flags bearing the Emperor's sun at the nearer end, but the black and red dragons on the far side remained visible. Out of deference to the Emperor's divine blood there was one fewer of the dragons, but the largest was a banner forty feet long that ensured no one could forget where the power in the Empire lay.

He closed the shutters again and pulled on a clean set of grey trousers and jacket. Dressing quickly, Narin snatched up his stave from beside his bed, running fingers over the familiar smooth wood as he headed into the other room. The goshe lay on the bed in the same position he had been the previous day, his breathing faint against the sounds outside the quarters. Narin watched him a moment longer before turning to the door where Enchei had hung a slate the previous night. On it was a brief greeting and instructions that Mistress Sheti would be looking in on him occasionally during the day.

Most likely it wouldn't stop the man leaving if he woke, but Sheti was right that an Investigator – of all people – couldn't keep an injured man tied up in his assigned quarters. Politeness might surprise a street-fighter and make him think twice about escaping, Narin guessed, while a rope would be unlikely to stop him if he was determined.

'So who is the moon?' Narin asked the goshe softly. 'Is it you? Someone you answer to? Just what are you going to tell me when you wake up?'

There was no response and Narin shrugged, pocketing the piece of paper they'd found in the goshe's pockets the night before. He went to the stove on the other side of the room and opened the pantry cupboard. There was little left in there after Enchei's efforts the previous night so Narin contented himself with taking a swallow of weak wine before finding a twig to scrub at his teeth.

With one last look at the goshe, he slipped his stave through a loop behind his shoulder and ran it through until the flattened end nestled in a small pocket at the bottom of his jacket. Outside, the air was muted and still, the sounds of a city waking to the day softened by the mist. He guessed it was an hour after dawn as he headed down to the compound's high gate, greeting the other two Investigators also leaving.

'Narin!' the ebullient younger of the two called out. 'A bad morning for the early shift, eh?'

'Morning, Diman!' Narin said with a forced smile. 'And you, Nesare. Not keen on finding a half-eaten body before lunch then?'

Nesare snorted. He was a tall, willowy young man, but with an old head on his shoulders. 'You're as bad as Diman – worse, in fact, you're a native. There's shit-all chance any demon crawled out of the Crescent last night; it's rare enough in winter let alone spring.'

'Demons are always hungry,' Narin countered with a wink at Diman, 'well-known fact that – and souls taste just as good in any weather, the blood keeps them warm.'

'Pah, now you're just winding him up,' Nesare said. 'Keep it up then. Try that crap on your Lawbringer and see how it helps your appointment!'

They headed out onto the near-deserted streets, turning away from the Tier Bridge until the Imperial Palace appeared above the houses to dominate the view. As the sonorous clang of bells at the temple of Smith announced the morning hour, soon echoed by a hundred other temple bells across the city, they reached the great paved expanse of Lawbringer Square and the pale walls of the Palace of Law.

Grey gulls circled above the square, dozens of them crying and wheeling as though fearful to land. The three Investigators slowed and halted, his two companions glancing nervously at Narin. Up ahead was a figure dressed all in white, hands behind his back as though standing to attention, with an ornate black pistol-sheath at his waist. He was quite still, untouched by the movement all around him and looking directly at them – a Lawbringer, emissary of the Emperor himself and living embodiment of Imperial law.

Held cross-wise behind the Lawbringer's back was a white ash stave similar to those the Investigators carried. Few Lawbringers carried such a weapon and none could wield it so well as this one, but Narin still found himself resenting the sight of it. The majority wore swords; elegant and deadly weapons that were the symbol of their authority as much as a tool for punishment. But even here, in this place of justice and equality, some were above the rest.

Do you even know you do it? Narin wondered. *You don't deign to carry the sword of a Lawbringer; do you know how the rest of us see that? We just see the guns – always the guns and the reminder you're above us all. Lawbringer you've become, noble caste you've always been.*

A gust of wind brought a few drops of rain pattering down over them and that proved enough to stir the three into action once more. The other two Investigators bowed and made to leave, but Narin caught the arm of one and held him back. The young man frowned but made no complaint as Narin also bowed and at last the man in white spoke.

'Good morning, Investigator. You have business with Investigator Diman?'

Narin glanced at the man he'd held back. 'I do, Lawbringer – a moment only, if I may?'

Lawbringer Rhe inclined his head and adopted a statue-still pose of a man prepared to wait all day – so motionless he could have been one of the statues of their patron God, Lord Lawbringer, which looked down from all sides of the square. No wasted movement or instinctive questions – the man's ability to hold a position and fade into the background had always unnerved Narin. For once, however, he was thankful for his superior's unnaturally calm nature.

Narin had to remind himself that all of the Gods had once been mortal men and women. In the earliest days of the Empire a king and queen had found the secret to immortality and ascended into the heavens. Exactly how they did so remained the greatest mystery the Empire had to offer, but their closest cadre of advisers had joined them in the years to follow. Over the next centuries that passed others had also been granted their own divine constellations by the Gods, after achieving enlightenment through the perfection of some art or skill. Unflappable and a man of unswerving purpose, Rhe was considered by many novices and Investigators to be halfway to the stars.

'Diman,' Narin muttered quickly, 'you're stationed within the Palace still?'

The younger man nodded. 'Another moon still, why?' He was five years younger than Narin and still in training, so he spent half of the year on administrative duties.

'Have you heard any strange stories about the goshe in the last few days?'

'Goshe? I, ah, no – not that I recall.'

Narin nodded. 'If you do, could you tell me? I don't have anything more than that for you – only a rumour I don't want to share before I've got some sort of evidence.'

'Share? At all?' Diman couldn't help but look up at the motionless Lawbringer a few yards away.

'With anyone but him,' Narin said with a reassuring smile. 'I wanted to catch you before getting into the explanation.'

The look of relief on Diman's face was clear. Like most Investigators, his awe of Rhe bordered on reverence. None would dare incur the wrath of a man who had once fought his way into a warrior compound in Dragon district in pursuit of a noble murderer – disarming seven soldiers ordered to attack him before calmly shooting the criminal between the eyes as the man levelled a musket.

'Goshe. Right.'

With another bow to Lawbringer Rhe, Diman hurried away across the square to the jutting portico of the Palace of Law, leaving the two men facing each other.

'The younger Investigators still see me as some sort of hero then?'

Narin coughed in surprise. 'Ah, yes, Lawbringer. They all do, pretty much.'

'I had hoped that would fade,' Rhe said.

There was no expression on his face, just a detached calm that others saw as a cold aristocrat's indifference. Ever the investigator, Rhe viewed the entire world with a sober, analytical mind – never letting emotion cloud his conclusions.

A tall and muscular man, Rhe was not a native of the Imperial City. Once a noble son of House Brightlance, a major House under the Eagle hegemony to the north-east, Rhe's skin and pale cropped hair were dusted a faint grey-blue while his eyes were as grey and unyielding as steel.

He took a step forward, as light and lithe as a cat. Knowing the man's mannerisms after over a year of assignment together, Narin's eyes darted to the stave Rhe still held behind his back just as the Lawbringer brought it around with a crisp movement and tucked the weapon under his right arm.

'Goshe? You have a story to tell me?'

Narin nodded. 'More of a request really.'

'Noted.' Rhe nodded towards the street Narin had just come from. 'I have asked for the long patrol today, you can tell me as we walk.'

Narin tried not to glower. He knew perfectly well what the long patrol meant and why Rhe had requested it – an incident the previous week where his temper had got the better of him. They would spend the day on a slow tour of the city gathering news from every House guardpost and Lawbringer watchtower, which meant dealing with officials of every rank and caste. If there was any crime to be investigated in the city today it would be the chewed-on remains of people taken under cover of fog or murdered drunks, yet still Narin knew which task he would prefer.

'I did apologise to the man,' he muttered, feeling like a chastened child.

'Indeed you did,' Rhe said, 'and the words were all perfectly acceptable.'

'But my tone was not?'

The Lawbringer inclined his head. 'A child could have done better, Narin. That you thought the man an idiot was perfectly reasonable given the circumstances. That you failed to hide your opinion of a man in the warrior caste was foolish.' Rhe took a step forward, the smile fading. 'That you allowed such an opinion to colour your judgement remains unforgivable.'

Easy for you to say, Narin thought, ducking his head in acknowledgement. *Few men are above you.*

His gaze alighted on the pistol at Rhe's hip. The Lawbringer was third son to a lord of House Brightlance – a family of middling status among that nation's rulers. Though he had renounced his family and inheritance when he joined the Lawbringers, Rhe's caste remained and he could own a gunpower weapon. If Narin ever reached the same rank, he would still always be of the craftsman caste. It should be honour enough for someone of his low birth to be allowed a sword, apparently.

'So, the favour?' Rhe asked as he started off, indicating Narin should fall in beside him.

'I have addresses to check – I don't know for what, but I hope to discover a link between them.'

'Interesting. Does it take us far out of our way?'

He shook his head. 'The instructions seem simple enough, assuming I'm reading them correctly.'

'Then how could I refuse? I must trust the judgement of an Imperial Investigator if I am to evaluate it.' Rhe said in a level tone that Narin had to hope was intended as playful. 'Let us hope they're the addresses of palaces, to give you a little practice on that front too.'

Ah, humour. Maybe Enchei's right about him after all, Narin thought glumly. 'Thank you, Lawbringer.'

'In the meantime, some background information please. We have a long walk, no need to spare me the details.'

Narin took a deep breath. *All the details? Not with my judgement recently.* 'Of course. Tell me, have you ever spoken to a God?'

Rhe hesitated, surprise flashing across his face at the unexpected question. 'A strange thing to ask, even if half the novices would be keen to hear the answer. However – no, I have not.'

Narin nodded as they continued back the way he had come, heading for the Tier Bridge where they could cross onto the spur of land on which House Dragon's palazzos stood. The first address was not far from the other end of the bridge.

'Turns out, you're not missing much.'

*

The brass bell chimed. Kesh unknotted her fingers and rose from the bench, ignoring the nudge against her legs as the person beside her slid up into the end position. She had been there more than an hour and her legs were stiff, but Kesh forced herself to step purposefully forward. She'd watched some lurch from that seat and almost fall over the course of the hour, while others had spent what seemed like an age getting their balance before advancing – long enough that some had tried to take their place and further delayed everyone by sparking an argument.

With as much poise as she could muster Kesh walked up to the desk and bowed to the official sat behind it.

'Good morning, Mistress,' the man said, not rising but indicating one of the stools on Kesh's side. 'Please, sit as you wish.'

'Thank you, sir,' she replied as warmly as she could manage. After that damn bench, sitting was the last thing she wanted to do, but she had no wish to dismiss his courtesy and eased herself down onto the stool.

She saw the official was religious caste by his collarless coat – though not actually a priest himself, given his head was not shaved. Most high-castes would have expected her to stand and look at the ground the whole while. In the last hour of observing him, trying to fathom what sort of man she would be speaking to, Kesh had realised he cared little for caste stricture, but a lot for manners.

The official carefully laid his polished brass pen on the wood rack to his left and leaned forward, elbows on the desk's leather surface and fingers steepled. He was a small man, as most Moons were; well past his middle years and the tiny crinkles of his polished brown skin possessed a curious white sheen. Kindly eyes looked large in his face beneath prominent, bushy eyebrows.

'You are of the Imperial House?' the official inquired after taking in every detail of Kesh's face and clothes.

She shook her head. 'No, sir, the Harbour Warrant.'

'Of course,' he said with a smile, 'I should have guessed – that bench is designed to be uncomfortable, I often suspect. Only sailors are steady on their feet straight away.'

Kesh nodded. 'I served a few of my father's seasons on a merchant ship.'

'Ah, I thought you a bit young for a full term. So Mistress, what service may House Moon do you today?'

'I … I'm looking for advice I suppose.'

'Very well; don't believe what young men say after a few drinks, and never eat anything with more than eight legs. Will that do?'

She blinked up at him, mouth half-open in surprise at the thought that he was casually dismissing her. Only then did she spot the corners of his mouth twitch and realise this man of high rank was joking with her just as her mother would.

'Thank you, sir – I shall endeavour to keep those both in mind,' she croaked as she got over her surprise. 'There is, however, one more thing.'

'More?' He sighed theatrically, 'My dear, you are a demanding young woman!'

Kesh bowed her head again, attempting to hide the smile crossing her face. 'So I have been told, sir.'

'Did they mean it as a compliment at the time?'

'I, um, I really don't think so.'

A twinkle appeared in the man's eye. 'More fool them, they'll learn just like the rest of us had to. Now, what sort of advice were you seeking?'

Kesh's mind went blank for a moment, thrown by his unexpected manner – more as a result of his position than his age. Old men were just a different sort of fool most of the time, but senior House officials were said to be the greatest sticklers for protocol and status. Kesh was servant caste and used to being treated as such – higher castes would naturally treat her with gentle disdain at best, it was how they had been brought up to act.

'My mother and I, we run a guest house overlooking the harbour,' she explained at last. 'One of our guests has been missing a few days now and there is a debt on his room.'

'Missing rather than left without paying?'

'His belongings, a sea-chest and whatever's inside, are still in the room.'

'And he is a Moon?'

'Shadow,' she clarified. 'Master Estan Tokene Shadow.'

The official brightened. 'Well, that makes things easier,' he said. 'There are few enough Shadows in the city at any one time. If he is here on official business, he'll be easy to find in the rolls and if not, well, I suspect the chest will be of more than sufficient value? The Shadows are a funny lot, I've found. More than their fair share of wild adventurers from those parts.'

Kesh nodded. 'Certainly worth more – with whatever possessions are in it, far in excess I would expect.'

The official turned in his seat and attracted the attention of a pale young man in grey clerk's robes. 'Estian Tokene of House Shadow – please check the rolls for any man bearing the Tokene family name? And put it on the register in case we are notified about anything. Ah, Mistress – do you know his caste?'

'Craftsman or Merchant, by his manner – though he looked more like a mercenary.'

The official nodded to his clerk and the youth scampered off. 'Have you informed the Lawbringers that a man is missing?'

'Not yet, I have to cross the island to get home so I came here first.'

'See that you do so,' he said solemnly, picking up his pen and recording the details in an elegant script as he continued. 'Most likely your errant Shadow will turn up with a sore head later today. However, if he does not, my ruling is that a debt is acknowledged in your favour. Barring official business listed on the rolls, if there is no word of him by, ah – we are on the third day of Shield's Ascendancy, so let us say, by star's turn? If there is no word by the first of Pity's Ascendancy, the chest shall be brought here to be assessed and apportioned fairly. Your name, please, young lady?' He raised a finger, remembering she was not of House descent. 'Full name, that is.'

'Kesh Hinar,' she said hesitantly, reminding herself of the proper form to be used outside the Vesis and Darch Harbour Warrant. 'Ah, that is Kesh Hinar Vesis.'

'Home?'

'The Crow's Nest boarding house, the Highstrand in the Harbour Warrant.'

'It is done,' the official said with one final flourish of the pen, inscribing his name at the bottom before setting the paper aside. 'Any more advice I can offer you?'

Kesh gave him a small smile and got to her feet. 'No, thank you, sir. Your efforts are much appreciated.'

The official inclined his head in acknowledgement and signalled for the next person to come forward, while Kesh made her way out into the light of day again. Heading out through the open double doors, she stopped at the top of the steps and looked around. It was rare that she made her way to this part of the city. House Moon's district, the smallest in the Imperial City, was situated on the opposing spur of land from her home, across the broad mouth of the Crescent as it entered the Inner Sea.

As with the rest of the city, the district's architecture was dictated by Moon's homeland, far to the west and one of the most remote parts of the Empire. Traditional turf-roofed houses surrounded the fortress that served as the heart of the district, all sheltered from the coastal gales by jagged granite cliffs running unevenly along the outer shore. Steep, pitch-sealed roofs occupied the rest of the area, coloured pale greens and yellows by the lichens growing there.

Kesh walked down the steps to the cobbled ground below and paused before entering the flow of people. It was a circular junction of five streets, lined by carts selling wares and food fresh from the docks; a hub of humanity all turning about a verdigrised statue to Lady Chance. The Goddess had long hair swept back from her face, one half of which was covered by an expressionless mask, and carried a flail like a walking staff. Recalling the temple creed, Kesh's eyes were drawn to the half-dozen chains that trailed from it – variously tipped by blessings or curses.

The crack of sticks on the cobbled ground dragged her attention from the statue. Kesh watched the people spread almost as one to the edges of the junction as a tall man emerged from the left-hand road. He was dressed in Moon's own colours, a surcoat of white emblazoned with a black crescent, while a small conical hat identified him as a house servant of some noble family. He carried a switch of willow in his hand and struck the ground again with it, a rapid double-crack ringing out around the junction as a pair of covered litters advanced in his wake – each flanked by four armoured soldiers carrying muskets, their skin the same dusty-dark as the official's.

Kesh followed the rest and bowed her head respectfully rather than stare at the passing high-castes, though her eyes lingered on the rearmost litter once it had crossed the junction and the eyes of the guards were elsewhere. In their wake the locals resumed their day as though nothing had happened, but Kesh continued to stare after the small procession until it had turned the corner and passed out of sight.

The sight was common enough in the Imperial City, but Kesh's small corner of it saw few high-castes ever pass by. Those who came to the harbour did so in barges, eschewing the city streets when there were quicker routes for those who could afford them. At last she turned away and was about to push into the streams of people passing when something else caught her eye.

A flicker of movement in a shadow – a blur of white and rusty-red that seemed to drag her eyes directly towards it. She took a step forward and peered into the dim space below a cart selling pungent, spiced squid. Standing there, seemingly as oblivious of the scents of frying food above it as the cart's attendant was of it, Kesh saw a fox. The creature stared straight at her, unblinking and completely still now she was looking at it.

A shiver ran down Kesh's spine as she took a half-step backwards and made the sign of Lord Shield – hands together to form a diamond, fingers pressed against her lips.

'Shield defend me,' she whispered between her fingers, 'Knight guard me.'

The fox didn't move, concerned by neither the invocation of Gods nor a passerby crossing its view to walk around the back of the cart.

The cart's owner continued oblivious, deftly turning strips of squid on a hotplate before scooping them up in one movement and depositing them in a pocket of flatbread for a customer. The shifting footsteps around the cart still failed to distract the fox. It kept its gaze fixed on Kesh and her sense of foreboding increased, tales of fox-demons filling her mind. But then the fox broke the contact, for no reason Kesh could tell. It looked away then back at Kesh, long enough to show her it was not spooked, before darting into a narrow alley unnoticed by anyone but the young woman.

Kesh forced herself to swallow, suddenly aware that her mouth had gone dry. She took a few cautious steps towards the narrow alley, one hand pressing against the fold of her jacket to check her father's knife was still sheathed there. Life on board the merchantman had been difficult at the best of times and she'd been taught to use it on a rope or man with equal skill. What good it would do against a demon she didn't know, but just the presence of the weapon boosted her resolve. A mantra to Lord Shapeshifter on her lips, Kesh advanced towards the alley.

There was nothing there. Blocked a dozen yards down by a wall, there were two closed doors leading off it and the scattered debris found in any alley – but nowhere for a fox to hide.

'Maybe I'm going mad,' Kesh said to herself after a long while of looking.

'Eh?' said the man at the cart, half-turning to check if she was talking to him. 'Going mad?'

He wasn't a local, she could see – neither native to the Imperial City nor a man of House Moon as many in this district were. His skin was far paler than the official's deep dusty-brown, his face wide and features narrow in a way she'd never seen before in the city.

Some minor House, north of Moon's own lands?

The look on his face told Kesh he'd noticed her staring and she lowered her eyes, muttering an apology.

'Don't worry yourself, Mistress,' he said with a laugh. 'Ain't many of us in the city, I'm used to curious looks. I'm a Poisontongue, from the snow-line o' Kettekast – that's why I don't look much like most round here. My ancestors are the natives there, not the invaders who colonised the south.'

'It was still rude of me, I'm sorry.'

He shook his head. 'Better'n going mad,' he pointed out. 'What were you looking for there?'

'I … I thought I saw a fox.'

'Hah! Round here, during the day?' He shook his head. 'Not likely. Those evil little shadows keep clear of busy streets.'

'I know. That's what surprised me.'

He paused and glanced around him. 'You're serious, aren't you? Bastard things they are, I'd believe anything of 'em. Still remember when we found my cousin out on the snow one morning, miles from the village. The elders said they'd torn his soul out through his eyes – don't you go chasing after foxes, you hear me?'

Kesh nodded. 'Maybe it was nothing; I can't see where it would have gone.'

The trader hefted his cleaver, stained red with spice. 'All the same, you watch out. Keep to the main streets on your way home, case it got your scent. It comes back, I'll split it in two, I promise.'

Reluctantly, she turned away from the empty alley. The fox was gone, she'd get no answers here and there was a day's work to be done when she did make it home.

'First the Palace of Law,' Kesh reminded herself as she left the junction under the trader's watchful gaze, 'then home. Emari better have done her chores today, else she'll wish foxes had got her.'

CHAPTER 5

In the chaos that followed the revolution, the victorious Great Houses were more intent on territory than lives. Banditry and famine resulted, but while it was the Dragons who had started the problem, it was also one of them who chose to end it. Loyal to the Emperor he had served for decades, General Toro commanded his remaining Imperial forces out into the country to protect the beleaguered citizens from predation. Carrying only staves, many died, but the Great Houses viewed them as no threat and so the seed of the Lawbringers was sown.

From *A History* by Ayel Sorote

Narin looked back down the street, counting doorways to double-check they were at the right one. Lawbringer Rhe stood silent behind him, ignoring the curious stares of passersby as he waited. Finally, Narin was satisfied he was correct and rapped his knuckles smartly on the door.

'Who's there?' called a woman's voice from inside, followed swiftly by the howl of a baby.

'Servants of the Emperor's Law,' Narin called back in a loud voice, adding, 'If we could speak to you a moment?'

'Law?' echoed the woman, her voice tremulous even as it grew nearer. 'What's happened?'

The baby continued to cry, its wails accompanying the woman to the door. She pulled it open with fear on her face, soon looking past Narin to the imposing sight of Rhe behind him.

'Master Lawbringer, Investigator,' she said, curtseying as best she could with a large, red-faced infant pressed against her chest – its fists clamped around the long trails of hair that had escaped her scarf. 'I ... Ah, do you want to come in?'

Narin bowed in response. Though her white scarf declared she was servant caste, Investigators were expected to show respect to all.

'Thank you – there's no need to worry, you're not in any trouble.' He had to almost shout to make himself heard as the baby found new strength in its lungs and began to howl, but the mother heard enough and stepped back to admit the pair.

'How can I help you, Master Lawbringer?' she said once Rhe was inside, nervously looking from Narin to Rhe as though unsure which she should be addressing.

'My Investigator has questions for you,' Rhe replied, 'for the matter is his puzzle, not mine.' He paused then reached out his hands. 'Perhaps I might take the child while you speak?'

Both the woman and Narin started at the unexpected suggestion. The baby was crying still and showing no sign of stopping, but it was hardly seemly for a Lawbringer to be acting as nurse. That Rhe was unmarried, uninterested in anything bar the service of the law, meant Narin was even more startled than the child's mother.

'I will calm the child,' Rhe stated baldly and the mother wilted under his hard grey stare.

She meekly held it out and the Lawbringer scooped the baby up without a further word, holding the child up to his face to look it in the eye. With one arm supporting it, Rhe ran a callused hand over the baby's head and down its cheeks. The baby hesitated and stared up at Rhe, its cries faltering as though cowed by the uncompromising Lawbringer's face.

'Quiet now,' Rhe said in his usual stern tone. To Narin's surprise the baby did exactly that, eyes wide as it took in Rhe's cold-tinted skin. The Lawbringer looked briefly up. 'Ask your questions, Investigator. I'm sure the novelty of me will wear off soon enough.'

Narin blinked, momentarily dumbstruck by the sight. It seemed so ridiculous but there was no humour in his thoughts, only the clash of cold fear and hot elation at the thought of a child of his own.

Will I ever be able to hold my own child that way? Stars above, will I even see it? What I would give to look so strange, as out of place as Rhe does now.

'Narin?' Rhe said, nodding towards the mother.

The Investigator shook himself, fleeing from the burgeoning sense of panic in his chest as visions of Kine, child in hand, appeared in his mind.

'Ah, right – yes, questions. Ah, Mistress … might I ask your name?'

'Intail – Hetesh Intail.'

'I am Investigator Narin, this is Lawbringer Rhe.' He saw her eyes widen at the name, and her cheeks paled at the thought of such a famous man looking after her baby. 'How many of you live here?'

Narin looked around the small room. It was in one of the poorest areas of House Wolf's district, the house part of a long row of dilapidated narrow homes. There was a low fire in the hearth, barely more than embers, and a basket of muddy vegetables on a table in the centre of the room.

'Seven, all told,' Mistress Hetesh said nervously. 'My husband and eldest boy are porters on the dock. We share the house with a canal worker and his family – Essa, the wife, is at market with her daughter.'

Narin nodded encouragingly, seeing the rising fear in her eyes. 'And you were at home two nights past?'

'Aye, sir.'

'Did anything unusual happen that night?'

'Unusual? No, no I don't think so.'

'Anyone on your roof perhaps?'

Mistress Hetesh gasped. 'On the roof? Who would be on the roof? Can't you tell me what this is about?'

'Nothing at all?'

She frowned. 'Not that I ... Well, the strangest thing that happened was us all having odd dreams and waking in the night.'

'Waking? The whole house?'

'No, just me and my man,' she said with a shake of the head. 'The wind was bangin' a window; I must've not latched it properly. That's all I can recall – that and us both having fever dreams. Thought we were all getting sick the next day.'

'Because of the dreams?'

She hesitated. 'Them, and being so tired in the morning my son fair had to drag us from our bed. Whatever it was, it was gone by today.' She pointed towards the baby in Rhe's arms, still placid and content. 'My little one too, Ashar was so quiet that morning it frightened me – couldn't wake him at first, either.' She shrugged. 'Must've just been an ill wind though; he's been noisy enough today.'

Narin paused and exchanged a look with Rhe before continuing. 'Mistress Hetesh, do you have friends in the Dragon District or the Fett docks?'

61

She looked surprised at that. 'Dragons? No, no one from there. A few from Fett, though. Like I said, we share the house with a canal worker. Most o' his friends work that area – but they don't mix with the boatmen much, tight-knit bunch are the Crescent boatmen.'

Narin nodded in understanding. As a city native he knew how the barges and boats of the Crescent were traditionally run by a few dozen extended families from Fett. They protected their province with the ferocity of House Dragon's armies and could recite their boatmen ancestors with a similar pride.

Anyone foolish enough to ply a trade on the Crescent without Fett lineage or official House colours would likely end up drowned one morning – that or their boat would be holed and no craftsmen would agree to repair it. The canal was an entirely separate province in the small world of the city's boatmen, however. It ran north-south through the middle of the Thumb, that spur of land ending in the Harbour Warrant; a protected channel that could ferry goods to the city's largest harbour in a small craft.

'So no one at all in the Dragon District?' Narin confirmed glumly. Two of the addresses were in the low-caste areas of Dragon, but there seemed to be no links between them at all. 'What about goshe? Any contact with them? Your husband is not a member?'

'No, sir; my boy wants to train at one of their schools, but we don't have the money for such things. I had Ashar at their free hospital; midwife said he'd not turned right and I went into labour just as we got there to see a goshe doctor. She said they likely saved his life with their learning – even teaching some things to the midwives, she said!'

'Do you remember the name of the doctor?'

Her eyes widened. 'Is that what … ? But there was none of the witchcraft some folk say – they gave me medicine to help me sleep, that's all. The midwife said they were doctors, that they were more skilled than—'

Narin held up a hand. 'Don't worry yourself; we're just trying to cover every angle.'

Tears spilled from her face and the woman grabbed at her baby, taking him from Rhe's arms and hugging the child tight to her chest. 'My husband said not to go! He said not to trust the goshe, but I'd lost two! I couldn't bear to lose another baby, oh Gods – what've they done to him?'

'Nothing,' Rhe said sharply, 'Your baby looks healthy, do not fear.'

'But … ? Then why ask about goshe?'

'Membership was mentioned at one address we went to, use of the hospital at another,' he replied. 'We have a few disparate threads that do not yet warrant an official investigation, that is all. Until we know what is relevant, we must ask for all information that we can. It is not your place to draw conclusions.'

Narin turned to look at Rhe. The Lawbringer's face was totally expressionless. One woman they had spoken to had mentioned using the goshe hospital, but that was all. The link was in fact that three of the addresses had infants in them, nothing more, but that was the last thing they wanted to reveal to an anxious mother. The one where that hadn't been the case, neither of the men were sure they had actually gone to the right address – the brief instructions were too open to interpretation in the ramshackle street they'd been led to.

'Can you remember the doctor's name?' Narin asked more gently.

She shook her head at first. 'I was in a lot o' pain, I'm sorry. The young doctor was Pesher – dark-skinned, House Wyvern I'd have guessed – but once he examined me he called another. I don't remember his name; I barely saw him, but he seemed in charge of them all. Gave orders and they jumped to it so quick it was like they were puppets on string.'

'Pesher, I see. Thank you Mistress, we'll leave you now,' Narin said, heading for the door.

'That's all? I'm … I'm not in danger am I? From the goshe?'

Rhe shook his head as he waited for Narin to open the door. 'I see no reason to believe so, no. If there was a threat to your family, it is over – most likely it never existed and this is mere coincidence.'

The look on her face told Narin she wasn't much mollified by the response, but the woman dared not argue with a Lawbringer, certainly not one with Rhe's reputation, and she curtseyed again as the man joined Narin in the street. She shut the door quickly behind them, sparing only a glance around to see which of her neighbours were watching, and the two men started back the way they had come, heading for the main road that would take them back to their path.

The day was brightening at last, Narin realised. The early mist had long since faded, but as morning progressed the cloud was also breaking up. They walked side-by-side through the rutted, tree-studded streets that were intended to echo the forested homeland of House Wolf, on the very eastern edge of the Empire's south continent. Narin unconsciously rolled his shoulder as he went, to work the last of the stiffness from it, his mind trying to fit the pieces of what they'd learned together.

'What is your next move?' Rhe asked at last. 'Where now?'

'That's the last of the addresses,' Narin said with a sigh. 'We've some sort of connection, but what that is I've no damn idea.'

'Nothing that brings you closer to answering Lord Shield's question,' Rhe agreed. 'Who is the moon? I remember a myth I heard as a child, something about the moon being father of the stars – the lesser stars, of course, not the Gods.'

Without meaning to, Narin glanced upward. The cloud had not thinned enough to see the greater stars as faint grey dots, the constellations of the Gods that were visible on the clearest days. 'You think one man fathered all those children? No, it's impossible – the first two were pure-blood Dragons, skin as dark as anyone's, but that last had skin as light as its mother's.'

'Just so, and his caste-stain read servant caste. Whatever his parentage, whatever possible scandal there might be, they would have not marked it so had they been claiming a higher station – so what need could there be to send an assassin?'

'An assassin who only managed to make them feel a bit ill,' Narin added glumly. 'So there must be another purpose to the list, but what?'

Rhe was quiet for a half-dozen heartbeats. 'We have yet to earn that answer,' he said at last. 'All things in good time, Investigator. We will complete our duties for the day then visit this goshe free hospital tomorrow. As yet the puzzle is incomplete. If we shake the tree and something falls out, we may learn more of the shape of it. Until then we must be patient. The stars turn at no man's bidding, but turn they do.'

It was approaching midday when Kesh returned to the boarding house. Sheets were on the line outside it, lifting and falling in the breeze that ran in off the sea. The house was quiet as she trotted up the steps – the guests all away at work during daylight hours. Only their errant guest, Estan Tokene Shadow, had not kept honest hours during the few months of his stay there. He had said he worked at a tavern in Tale, the neighbouring district, when he couldn't find anything more lucrative. He hadn't explained what that had entailed and no one had wanted to ask, but it explained why he returned late and slept through most mornings.

Kesh ran her fingers down the billowing sheet before she pulled open the main door. It was damp, but had been out there a while. Her mother washed their linen on the pebble beaches of the Crescent, where there was less salt in the water than the sea. It meant a longer journey for each load, however, and most likely she would still be away with a second basket-ful.

'Emari,' Kesh called through the empty front hall, casting her eyes around at the floor to see if her sister had swept it as instructed.

The hall looked clean enough to her exacting eye, the long table scrubbed and the dozen stools pushed neatly underneath. They had five out of six rooms occupied, but took a regular trade from deck officers off the larger merchant ships who could arrive at any time and would not stand for any disorder.

'Emari, where are you?' Kesh called again after a long silence.

Again there was no answer so she headed on through the hall. Beyond that was the staircase leading to the upper floors and the kitchen, but as she reached the stairs Kesh could see the kitchen was dark – the shutters still closed, the door to the yard beyond shut. Clearly Emari wasn't out collecting eggs or tending their small garden, so Kesh grabbed the banister of the stair and hauled herself up to the third step in one hop.

Something caught her eye up ahead, beneath the window they'd been staring out of the previous day. Kesh went up a second step and faltered, slowing as a cold fist of apprehension closed about her gullet. There was a sea-chest angled against the wall ahead, wedged under the window-sill. It was old and solid; iron-bound wood with as sturdy a lock as Kesh had ever seen. And a thin brown hand caught in the leather handle.

Her breath caught, her legs faltering beneath her. Kesh's mouth fell open, to cry out or to scream, but only a tiny gasp escaped as she struggled up the remaining steps to the landing where the chest lay.

'Emari?' Kesh whispered as the clamouring screams of panic filled her mind. With hands shaking she crept forward, enfeebled by horror and disbelief. 'Emari, can you hear me?'

The little girl didn't move. She lay down the stairs, face pressed against the wooden floor of the landing with her legs tangled behind her and one arm outstretched – caught in the grip of the chest's handle. Kesh sank to her knees, keening faintly as she reached out a tentative hand to Emari's face. The young girl was quite still, but when Kesh brushed her face she felt warmth there still – then a pulse in her jugular that made hope surge like lightning up Kesh's arm.

'Oh sweet God-Empress of Light,' Kesh murmured as she gently slipped one hand under Emari's chest and disentangled her hand from the chest. 'Please, don't take her from me now – don't let her die. Lady Healer – bless my sister, I beg you.'

She lifted Emari like a doll. The girl was so thin and light she seemed to barely weigh a thing. Kesh turned her over and cradled Emari in her arms. Her eyes were closed, her cheek faintly grazed from the rough wooden steps but beyond that Kesh could see no obvious damage. Brushing her coarse black hair back, however, Kesh found a welt on the edge of her hairline – a bruise as long as Kesh's thumb.

'Wake up, little one,' she urged gently, stroking Emari's face with a mother's tenderness. 'Please wake up!'

Emari did not move. She lay limp in Kesh's broad arms, but just as Kesh's tears splashed on her chin, Emari's chest rose a fraction. Relief sparked more tears from Kesh as she realised Emari was still breathing – albeit shallowly and feebly. She was still alive.

'Emari!' she said again, louder this time. 'Emari, wake up!'

No amount of pleading could make a difference; the girl was as loose-limbed as a corpse in Kesh's arms. Kesh bent closer to her sister, suddenly fearful she had imagined the sight of her chest rising. She put one hand on Emari's chest, trying to feel the rise or fall, but in her anxiety pressed down on it instead. A small huff of breath brushed her knuckles as some air was forced from Emari's lungs and with it came a faint trail of greenish mist, leaking from Emari's mouth.

Kesh gasped and snatched her hand back as though the mist had stung her, but before her eyes it dissipated into nothing.

'What in the name of Jester is that?'

She stared down at Emari's expressionless face for a while, then pressed on the girl's chest again, but this time nothing more happened. She looked around at the stair and small landing where the tall window stood. Nothing resembling green mist was apparent, but the wooden floor around the chest was damp and greasy to the touch. Kesh looked up the stairs as though expecting to see someone looking down at her, then back at the dark chest that had dragged Emari almost to the grave. The empty stairway and strangely sinister chest seemed to spark a realisation inside her.

66

'I have to move her, get her to bed. No, wait – does she need a bonesetter?'

Kesh ran her hands all over the young girl's limbs, as gently as possible, looking for broken bones. After a while she could find nothing, no sign of injury beyond minor scrapes and that knock to the head. With a grunt she stood, Emari still in her arms, and gave the chest a hefty kick before heading up the stairs.

From inside the chest came the clatter of broken glass, shards rattling against each other as she pushed the chest out of her way. Kesh hesitated and looked down. She could see nothing, but out of caprice gave the chest a second kick, one that rocked it back a little.

More sounds of broken glass came from inside, but Kesh barely noticed. As the chest moved the lid jolted a fraction and a faint, green-tinted mist leaked through the gap. Half a dozen insubstantial trails spilled down the sides of the chest – each one seeming to continue on across the wooden floor like blind snakes seeking prey. Kesh took a step back up onto the stairs behind her. Her retreat displaced the air before them and the nearest trails curled forward in her wake, spreading and fading to nothing even as they followed her hurried footsteps.

'Stars above, what is that?' Kesh exclaimed. She looked down at Emari's face. 'Is it some sort of poison? Oh Emari, what's happened to you?'

She backed away another pace, wary gaze on the chest. The last of the mist trails dissipated and she was left staring at the bare wooden floor of the landing. It was a short, half-flight of stairs – Emari couldn't have fallen far even if she'd lost control of the chest right at the top of this section. A few yards, no more than three and a shallow incline to the stair.

Now she had time to breathe, Kesh felt the tears well up again. Emari had been trying to help, to bring the chest down so the room could be cleared for a paying guest.

'Oh Gods, I gave her the idea,' Kesh said in a near-whimper. 'I said we'd have to clear the room, get that chest out so another guest could take it. She was just trying to help. After all my chiding her for being slow about her chores she was trying to make it up to me.'

The thought felt like a punch to the gut and Kesh curled over Emari's helpless body as she sobbed, but with an effort fought back the guilt and the grief. Her sister needed her; that was all that mattered now.

'Unconscious or poisoned,' she said with new determination, 'she needs a healer. Healer's temple? No – the Gods forgive me, but I don't trust those old women and their needles. Master Tokene was a goshe, maybe they can do more.'

She closed her eyes and whispered a mantra to Lady Chance, hoping for a sign. None came but when she opened her eyes again her heart was more certain than before. The goshe were better healers than the Goddess' own, they tended solely to the body and did not trust in prayer.

'Lady Healer forgive me and bless me,' she whispered, 'the goshe are her best chance.'

Carefully, she picked her way around the chest as though it was a chained guard-dog and crept back down the stairs with Emari in her arms. Once in the main dining hall she hesitated and looked at the fragile bundle in her arms.

'The hospital's in Raven District,' she whispered. 'Emari – it's a long way, you need to hold on – please, be strong.'

Sheti held the tunic up to the light, turning it one way then the other to inspect her work. With a satisfied nod she set it down again and rubbed her hands together to warm her fingers. The afternoon breeze was chilly and, despite her cropped gloves, an hour of sewing on the walkway outside Narin's rooms was enough to leave her fingers cold and stiff.

'Something warming,' she announced to the salt-scented air as she stood, 'then the joys of an afternoon of cleaning.'

Easing open the front door to Narin's room, Sheti peered warily inside. The injured man had not moved, but with Enchei's dark utterances about the goshe's past, she found herself creeping around him all the same.

Once she had found tea and helped herself to the kettle keeping warm on the stove, Sheti made her way over to the goshe's bedside. She bent and put a hand on his forehead. He was cooler than when she'd first seen him – clearly the fever he'd been suffering through had passed. She set her tea to one side and tugged his blanket straight so it covered his chest once more.

'Last thing we need's you catching a cold,' she said to the goshe, patting his arm. 'Still, you're recovering and that's the main thing. You looked dead yesterday, now you could be just sleeping.'

The goshe gave an abrupt gasp, chest suddenly filling with air. Sheti shrieked and fell backwards as the man half lifted up from the bed in his effort to breathe in. The inhalation became a moan of pain as he instinctively tried to lift his bandaged arms. The left had been splinted as a precaution and bound to his tightly-wrapped ribs, so when he tried to move it he strained against both injuries. His eyes flashed open as the moan became a whimper and he sank back onto the bed, defeated by his efforts.

The retreat spurred Sheti into action and she returned to his bedside without another moment's hesitation.

'Hush now, stay still!' she urged the man, resting her hand lightly on his chest. 'You're injured, you've a cracked bone in your arm – ribs too.'

She saw him look around wildly, seeing nothing for a while. Eventually, his darting gaze found her and his eyes widened fearfully. He opened his mouth to speak but all that came out was a pained croak.

'Easy, you've been unconscious a few days,' Sheti continued, 'don't force it. Catch your breath while I fetch you some water.'

She jumped up and filled a clay cup up from the pitcher. The goshe wheezed and tried again to sit up when she offered it, but this time she slipped one arm behind his back to support him. Sitting on the side of the low bed, Sheti grunted with the effort of holding up such a large man. Before she put the cup to his lips she twisted herself around and manoeuvred one knee behind his back to prop him up.

'There we go. Hardly dignified but you're less likely to crush me,' she commented as she helped him drink.

Half of the mouthful spilled down his front as soon as Sheti took the cup away, but enough went the other way that she heard him sigh with something akin to pleasure.

'Now take your time,' she continued, 'there's no rush for any questions here.'

The goshe coughed feebly, enough to make him wince at his damaged ribs, but she could tell from the look on his face that he understood her.

'Right, shall we slide you back to the end of the bed there, prop you against the wall?'

The goshe grunted so she took it as assent and half-hauled him backwards until his shoulders were against the plastered wall at the head of the bed.

'Need …' the man wheezed, the effort making him cough once more.

'Take your time,' Sheti said gently, offering him the cup again. He drank as greedily as he could manage, then took three slow breaths to recover himself again.

'Need piss,' he said eventually.

Sheti laughed. 'Well, aren't you the charmer?' She stood and gave him an appraising look. 'You're not going make it to the outhouse, that's for sure. I'll fetch you a pot, that'll be a nice surprise for Narin when he gets home.'

To her intense relief, the goshe took the chamber pot in his one good hand with enough determination that Sheti realised he wouldn't need her help. She turned her back while he fumbled at the wrap covering his crotch and waited until he'd finished before retrieving the chamber pot and putting it to one side.

'Better now? Good. Right – introductions first. Despite the best efforts of some, we still live in a beacon of civilisation. My name is Sheti Antash, you're in the Imperial District – the rooms of a friend of mine, Narin. He's the Investigator who found you in the street a few nights back.'

The goshe looked blank as she spoke, face tight with puzzlement. Sheti waited a few moments and then cleared her throat pointedly.

'Now it would be your turn.'

'But ... I ...' The goshe fell silent and slumped even more heavily against the wall. He raised his one good hand, bruised and unwieldy, and turned it to inspect. It was a broad hand, tanned and marked with both grazes and older scars. The palm was rough, she knew, the hardened skin of a man used to hard work of one sort or another.

'Something wrong?' she prompted.

He looked up, mounting panic in his eyes. His mouth fell open but no sound came out as he stared up at Sheti. Turning as best he could, the goshe looked at the tattoos on his own shoulder. She could see his lips move slightly as the man read what was marked there, but the effort seemed to only drain him further.

'Can't remember your own name?' Sheti said, half in jest until the man flinched at her words. 'Stars above – your brains really have been scrambled, haven't they?'

'I ...' The man cast around with desperation in his eyes. 'I don't know. How can I not know?'

'Your skull almost got smashed open,' she said, trying to calm his alarm. 'Your mind's going to be more than a bit fuzzy for a while.'

'What? What happened to me? I can't remember anything!' His voice was wheezy and unsteady, the words coming out slow and rather slurred.

'Nothing? You know where you are?'

Slowly he nodded. 'You said Imperial District. I know what ...' The panic returned and he flailed at the blanket covering him as though trying to escape from whatever had affected his mind. 'Gods, can't remember my name. What've you done to me?' he gasped, hyperventilating as he pressed his free hand against his forehead. 'What's my name? Fuck's happened to me?'

'Hey now, calm yourself – you're hurt, remember?'

The big man only struggled harder, so wildly Sheti kept her distance – mindful that even an idle blow from his free arm could knock her down. He wrenched around and succeeded in throwing himself off the bed, thumping hard onto the floor below. Once there he seemed to deflate, his strength spent.

'Gods fucking damn. What's going on?' he moaned piteously. 'What's my name?'

'I don't know,' Sheti said, trying to quell her own sense of alarm. 'We're going to find out though. We'll help you find out – you hear me?'

She reached down and tentatively touched him on the shoulder. He twitched at the contact then settled and allowed Sheti to turn him onto his side so she could see his face again.

'Feels like my head's broken,' he groaned. The goshe took a few frantic breaths, jaw tightening as he tried to fight the confusion in his mind. 'Who did this? What's happening?'

'I don't know what happened to you, I swear it, but we're going to help you. My friend Narin is an Investigator for the Lawbringers; he's sworn an oath to help those in need.'

'Lawbringers,' the goshe coughed. 'I know 'em.'

'You remember them? Well that's good, maybe your memory's returning! What else do you remember?'

'I ...' He screwed up his eyes. 'Don't know.'

She could see his hand shaking, weakness and anger combined. His face was flushed now, the veins on his powerful arms clearly visible as instincts kicked in and he sought a way to fight what had happened to him.

He's a man of violence, Sheti reminded herself, *he's ready to hit out at anything.* She kept very still, her voice low as she spoke slowly to try and calm him down again.

'Very well, what about the Emperor – what's his name?'

'Sotorian,' he said without hesitation, 'first o' his name. Son o' Kenerian the Poet.'

She smiled. 'Now just be glad it was me here when you woke. If Enchei had been in my place, most likely he'd have told you Sotorian died a century past.'

He looked up, eyes wild. 'Enchei? Who's that?'

Sheti shook her head. 'Just some old fool who thinks he's funny. He's not important right now, getting you back into bed is.'

The goshe looked around at the floor, the tangled blanket around his legs and the bandages on his body. Sheti left him to it a while, not daring to move, and eventually fatigue and weakness took their toll. His shoulders slumped as the anger visibly drained from his body and he lay back with his head angled awkwardly against the wall.

'Shall I try to lift you?'

The goshe grunted so she stepped over him until she could crouch behind the man and slip her hands under his armpits. Pulling with all her strength, she could barely raise him, and with one arm bound to his chest the goshe could do little to help. Eventually, Sheti gave up and pulled over the clothes-packed sack Narin had given him for a pillow.

'How about we just stay here a while?' she said, slipping the pillow under his head. 'Nice and comfy on the floor.'

The goshe didn't reply so she turned to look at his face. His expression was completely blank, devoid even of the fear and panic she'd expected until she prodded his shoulder. Then it returned like a thunder-strike and he visibly wilted under the weight of it all.

'Hey now, give it time. Tell me more about what you do remember.'

'Remember?' he echoed in a rasping voice.

Hearing him, Sheti went to fetch the water again and he drained the rest of the cup in one go. The effort left him panting, but once he caught his breath the man seemed stronger already.

'What I remember? Don't know. Nothing, just an empty space in my mind. Not even glimpses – nothing at all!'

'Parents? Home? Childhood?'

Each suggestion only added to the strain and confusion on his face so Sheti fell silent again, unsure what else she could do.

'What's happened to me?' the goshe repeated. 'How can I not know who I am?' He raised his free hand and held it out towards Sheti.

'Don't remember anything – feels like I'm wearin' someone else's body. But how can I forget that, when I still know the Imperial City – still know the name o' the Emperor?'

Sheti shook her head. 'I've no answers for you, I'm sorry,' she said in a whisper, cut to the quick by the pained expression on his face. 'You've been unconscious for days, it must be that. The blow scrambled your brains, you'll need time to let it all unpick.'

He grunted and continued to stare down at his body. 'Head feels clear,' he muttered. 'I'm tired, I'm hurting, but my mind's clear. Just empty, there's nothing there. My body I don't recognise, these scars. Even the sound o' my voice – could all belong to someone else. I know people have tattoos on their shoulder, knew there'd be one on mine and what it says – but it means nothing, tells me nothing. I've no memory o' House Shadow, no idea if I've ever been there. Can't remember coming from anywhere. The tattoos could be fakes f'rall I know.'

He tailed off and Sheti couldn't find any words to reply. That last piece of news, Narin could break himself.

CHAPTER 6

One can only speculate what sort of single-minded obsession for order inspires a man to require every citizen of the new-formed Empire to be tattooed with their nation, family name and caste, but cometh the hour, cometh the madman. Uncle to the first Emperor he was, Imperial regent and architect of the present he became.

From A *History* by Ayel Sorote

The streets were busy as Kesh walked, limp bundle in her arms. Through the Tale Warrant and across the Spinner's Bridge over the Fett Canal. The current in the canal was minimal, protected from the tides of the Crescent and the sea by the artifice of its ancient design which meant only shallow-drafted barges could use it. At most times of the day there were dozens of canal workers and bargemen moving loads down the canal with their long-haired dogs barking encouragement.

Normally, the boisterous dogs would make Emari drag her to a halt, to watch them race nimbly along the barges. Kesh felt her eyes blur as she marched onward, every faint little huff of breath from her sister sparking both renewed fear and hope.

Into the Fett Warrant with its low, narrow houses and winding streets she went. The curious faces Kesh ignored, the concerned she shrugged off and marched onward. The intense, fearful expression on her face was enough to cut short all inquiries and offers of assistance. One young man trailed along behind her, trying to see what was wrong with the little girl Kesh clasped so tightly, desperate to help her in some fashion but unable to see how.

For a hundred yards she walked with the sad flap of his moccasins in step behind, but she refused to look back, refused to speak or acknowledge him lest the terror broke the dam in her mind and dragged her sobbing to the ground. At the border of Eagle District, that wall of tall buildings cutting across the streets where narrow-faced soldiers stared disdainfully down on the locals below, the young man fell away at last.

Though there was no restriction on entry into the district, Eagle's warrior caste were known to be imperious and aggressive. If they took an interest in Emari's plight, Kesh distantly realised, they would demand answers from anyone associated with her and a young man following the pair – suitor or husband, it might be assumed – would be first to answer their questions. There had been a flicker of relief in her heart when he dropped back and left her to her pilgrimage; less of a scene to attract attention and fewer distractions from forcing herself on, step after step towards the free hospital.

Her heart jumped as she spied the hospital, just inside Raven District, and she drove a path through the locals in the broad hexagonal plaza before it. The hospital was an imposing building, newly-built of pale granite but careful to conform to the ornate, layered style of House Raven's grander structures. Tiny, enclosed gardens of dwarf trees and rose-wreathed raven roosts stood at regular intervals around the plaza, while the statue of Duellist in the centre was flanked by fountains feeding great stone bowls where nobles would leave alms for the poor.

White pillars stood out beyond every wall of the hospital, extending the shallow lower roof into a veranda around the entire building. The three upper floors rose tall out of that, each pair of copper-bound shutters around the tall windows echoing the great shining double doors in the centre.

Raven's homelands were far in the remote east of the Empire; strung along the coastline and penned in by impassable mountains and the vast, demon-haunted forest of Shadowrain. Beyond those barriers civilisation could not reach. The Empire of a Hundred Houses ended there and Raven's lands were considered the edge of the world because so little was known of what lay beyond. The locals were all light-skinned with hair ranging from golden to black, identifiable by their prominent features and hooded eyes as much as by the fetishes, braids and jewellery they wore in their hair. Even by the varied standards of the Imperial City they were considered strange and unknowable; Imperial structures resting like a veneer on top of older tribal ties.

Kesh marched through the grand entrance and ground to a halt, swaying gently as she took in her surroundings. She was faced with a tall airy hallway, twenty yards wide and stretching away ahead of her until it reached some sort of central courtyard. All around her were people of all sizes and colours; bedraggled citizens huddled in tight groups while moving between them were black-robed goshe and doctors in sleeveless white. The people ranged from near-black-skinned Dragons, through the various ochre tints of Houses Iron and Salamander to the washed-out whites of Eagle and Leviathan. In the face of it all, Kesh found herself frozen in place, staring at the sight until one young doctor cautiously approached her.

'Mistress – the girl is hurt?'

Kesh blinked. His accent was strange, one she'd never heard before, though by his face he could have grown up next door to her without looking out of place.

'I … my sister.'

Without warning tears began to cascade down her cheeks and Kesh felt her hands shake. The doctor jumped forward and reached out towards Emari, but the gesture itself made Kesh recoil. Drawing Emari even tighter to her chest, Kesh glared like a wild thing at the man. He was no older than she, with muscular arms that bore the tattoos of a minor House under Ghost named Blackhare, but more striking was his caste-mark.

'You're warrior caste,' Kesh said abruptly, 'but you're unarmed.'

The man blinked at her before ducking his head in acknowledgement. 'A weapon is inconvenient here,' he explained, 'and frightens patients. I do not carry one while working.'

Kesh continued to stare at him, tripped by the sight of a warrior without weapons. A warrior's weapon was considered his soul. She had never before seen one without sword or gun on his person and the sight was enough that for a few seconds her sister's plight had disappeared from her mind.

When it returned, it was with a sickening jolt. 'My sister, she fell,' Kesh croaked, 'and … and I think she's been poisoned.'

'Poisoned? By what?'

She glanced warily at those closest, a pair of black-robed goshe who were far more the norm for their order – well-built men whose dark folds of clothing could conceal a variety of weapons.

'I do not know for certain,' Kesh said at last, knowing whatever risk there might be was unavoidable, 'but some strange chemical that leaked from a man's sea-chest – a man I think was goshe.'

76

'Goshe? Mistress, let me assure you—'

Kesh took an abrupt step forward, moving so close the doctor broke off in surprise. 'I accuse your order of nothing,' she said firmly, hands shaking with the effort of keeping a check on her emotions, 'but my sister saw him dressed as one and I know a fighter when I see one. I don't care if this has anything to do with the goshe – only that my sister's hurt and you are doctors. Please if there's anyone here who'd know about poisons or medicines that might be harmful to breathe, take me to them.'

The doctor stared at her in alarm, unsure what to make of her, but then he glanced down at Emari's slack face and something seemed to crumble inside him. He touched a cautious hand to her neck and felt for her pulse, nodding to himself after a pause that terrified Kesh.

'If anyone knows, it will be Father Jehq. Come.'

The doctor urged her forward and Kesh had no trouble finding the strength to match his hurried pace. Down the hall they went, past wooden partitions and open doorways leading to large whitewashed rooms, until they came to a smaller one alongside a closed, iron-bound door.

'First, sit – tell me exactly what happened.'

Kesh allowed him to usher her into the room. She sank onto a dark wooden bench just as the strength vanished from her legs, half-falling back onto it but caring only for Emari's limp body in her arms.

'I came home and found her on the stairs,' Kesh said, feeling help-less. 'A guest at our boarding house has disappeared, leaving behind a big sea-chest. She … she got it into her head to bring it downstairs while I was out and must have slipped. I found her on the stairs, not moving, with something like mist seeping out of the chest.'

'And you think she breathed it in?'

'Her neck's not broken, she took a bang on the head is all, but it doesn't look bad – not enough to do this.'

'You believe your missing guest is goshe?'

Kesh almost moaned in frustration. 'I think so. I don't know – I can't be sure. It doesn't matter, does it?'

'I'm just trying to work out what might be the problem,' the doctor said gently. 'If he's goshe, someone might know him – might know what he'd be carrying. Wait here; I will bring Father Jehq to you.'

The little girl's head thumped her shoulder gently as she slumped and almost without realising it Kesh found herself singing softly to

77

her sister. It was an ancient lullaby from Emari's homeland, one their mother had learned off a sailor when they took the child in. The tears fell hot and fast as she sang, all alone in the room – all alone with the cold, uncaring vastness of the Empire surrounding her.

How long she stayed there, Kesh couldn't say. A single moment stretched out for an age, then she blinked and she was not alone – there were two strangers facing her with the young doctor, neither dressed as he was.

The older of the two was a lean patriarch-type with stern eyes and a lined, greyish face; presumably the Father Jehq the doctor had mentioned. The white-haired doctor was dressed in nondescript clothes that gave no indication of his position or caste – Jehq could have been a clerk in some merchant's office but for the deference the other two seemed to show him.

The other man looked more like the reason folk went to healers – a heavyset local in goshe black with a blotchy, prizefighter's face and a sour scowl. He stood at the Father's heel like an attack dog; hands behind his back but ready to bite on command.

'I understand your sister is ill,' the older man said, peering down at Emari's slack face. 'Please, if I might examine her.' He glanced back over one shoulder. 'Thank you, Osseq, return to your duties.'

As the young doctor bobbed his head in acknowledgement and departed, Kesh reluctantly offered Emari forward for the man to inspect.

'You're Father Jehq?' she said. 'Can you help her?'

'My name is Jehq,' the older man said curtly, frowning slightly as she spoke his name.

Kesh realised he wasn't from anywhere near the Imperial City; though his command of the local language was excellent, it had slipped slightly when pronouncing names.

'I must examine her fully before I can tell you anything. You say she was poisoned – a goshe poison?'

'Or medicine,' Kesh insisted, 'I don't know what. She breathed something in as it leaked from a sea-chest – left by a missing guest at our boarding house. I, I'm not here to cause trouble or accuse anyone of anything, I just want my sister back.'

Jehq's pursed his lips before nodding abruptly. He gestured to his companion and the big man stepped forward to slip his hands underneath Emari's limp body. Jehq himself took hold of Kesh's shoulder as

78

though awkwardly trying to reassure her, but his words were far from comforting when at last he spoke, his grip strangely tight.

'You will stay here,' he commanded as Kesh felt the strength seep from her limbs and the fatigue of worry fill her. The older man bent down to stare her straight in the eye, no more than a foot from her face. Kesh found herself transfixed by his unblinking black eyes. 'I will take her next door to my study. You rest here, I will send for you soon.'

Drained of all her strength Kesh managed only to nod, but it was enough and the man straightened up again. Sparing her a brief final glance, Father Jehq turned and left, the goshe carrying Emari close behind.

Kesh watched them go through blurring eyes, shadows filling her mind as nervous exhaustion took hold of her. Jerking one elbow out to awkwardly catch the edge of an empty desk, Kesh barely managed to support herself in time as her head lolled and she sagged like a drunk.

Eyelids slipping closed, Kesh felt her knuckles press into her cheek as she tried to keep herself upright; every movement suddenly a struggle. With an effort she took a deep breath, sucking in as much air as possible before she collapsed back entirely, and the fog in her mind cleared a little. With that came the memory of Emari slumped on the stair and Kesh felt a jolt in her gut. She winced and fought to lift her head, her whole body so heavy the effort was enormous.

At last she did and looked around at the room she was in – a pair of desks and a small bookshelf. No papers or effects of any sort, just a blank room where she could rest, where she could sleep.

Sleep? Kesh almost screamed. 'How can I think about sleep now?' she muttered, hearing the exhausted slur in her voice as she spoke. 'Stars above, what's wrong with me?'

Concentrating, Kesh took another long, deep breath – then a second and a third. With each one the dull ache in her head eased and she found her strength returning – after a half-dozen, she managed to haul herself up onto her feet again.

Did he do something to me? she wondered. *Knight's mercy, it feels like I've been drinking all night.*

She lifted her arms up above her head, breathing heavily as though she'd been winded, and the fatigue eased a little more – enough for her senses to fall back into some semblance of order. The memory of Jehq's midnight-black eyes returned to her and Kesh shivered slightly, feeling the effect of his gaze like a shroud being drawn over her face.

'Hells,' she breathed as a chill prickled down her spine, 'he *did* do something to me.'

Without thinking her right hand slipped into her jacket and closed around the grip of her father's knife. Just as she thumbed the leather thong on the sheath, Kesh hesitated. There were two of them and she had no illusions about her skill with a blade – she was good enough to survive on a ship, but the Father's aide or bodyguard was as clear a fighter as Master Tokene had looked. Maybe she could catch him unawares despite feeling slow and sluggish, but most likely not and she'd only get one chance there.

Kesh released the knife again and looked around, taking a step towards the open doorway before halting.

Can't knock on the door now, can I? She turned to the window. *Maybe I can hear them instead.*

She leaned out of the window and checked left and right. Like the front of the hospital building, there was a gallery running down the whole flank of this part of the building – a sandy stretch of ground extending for twenty yards all around it before a six-foot wall separated the complex from the street-life beyond. Crucially there was no one in sight so Kesh slipped over the deep window sill and crouched down. Back against the wall she crept along it, keeping her head below window level. When she reached the next one along she paused, listening for voices, but they were faint through the closed shutters.

Must be the other side of the room.

She moved down the wall with a wary look around at the courtyard to check no one had spotted her. Reassured, she continued on and reached the next window, five yards further along. There she waited, hearing nothing at first. Just as she was wondering whether to stand and see if she could get closer, Father Jehq's voice came clear through the thick slat of the shutter.

'That man is proving a curse on us all, Perel – who'd have thought *Irato*, of all of the Detenii, would cause so many problems?'

'What do you want me to do?' asked a second man in a heavy growl, doubtless the bodyguard. 'The girl's dead, right?'

'This one? In her mind, yes. A small dose is all it takes to wipe the slate clean – her mind has been emptied entirely. There's nothing left of the child she once was or anything else. She'll stay like that until her body dies of thirst. Killing her will be a mercy.'

Kesh felt her stomach lurch at his words and jammed her knuckles into her mouth to stop herself crying out.

Emptied? Killing Emari would be a mercy?

She closed her eyes, a storm of terror unfolding inside her head, but somehow the voices cut through it all – adding to the maelstrom of horror and grief.

'I kill the sister?'

'No – let me do that, best we leave no sign of violence for anyone here to notice. You dispose of the bodies tonight; they're never to be found, you hear me? Good. Then this boarding house – Irato's sea-chest should have been rigged for anyone breaking into it. Tell Synter to clear up after her team properly this time around. Moon's Artifice is corrosive; if it's spilled enough to leak out of the chest, any further movement will likely set it off – but we cannot make assumptions.

'Her whole team keeps their eyes on the house – if it's not on fire by nightfall or the enemy are spotted, she does it herself, understand?'

'I will tell her so.'

Kesh tried not to gasp. *Mother! Mother would be home by now!* Without a warning she stood no chance, as little as Emari.

I have to warn her – I have to get there before they do! But how can I leave Emari? Kesh almost sobbed with helplessness. *How can I leave her here to die?*

The Father's chilling words had left her in no doubt about Emari's condition, but just thinking about fleeing left Kesh sickened. Her little sister was in the hands of men who talked about murder as though it was a mere detail – how could she abandon her? But how could she stay? How could she take the risk of trying to save Emari – when the old man had said she was beyond help and her mother remained in danger?

Kesh found herself reaching again for her knife, but caught herself just as her fingers touched it. She took a long controlled breath and stared down at the dirt underfoot. There was a weathered shard of pottery impressed into the ground right there, unremarkable in every respect, but she found her attention fixed upon it as the jangle of panic ran through her body.

Empress forgive me, I've got to go.

As soon as she thought the words, Kesh hated herself. At the back of her mind she screamed and raged, but the young woman crouched

81

below the window remained perfectly still, fighting the fury and fear as she tried to make herself move.

I can't take him – most likely even if that Jehq hadn't done something to me. I don't know if I can run, but if I stay I'm dead – Mother's dead, Emari's dead.

She closed her eyes and for a moment heard screams on the wind, men crying distantly from the roiling ocean. She'd watched sailors be washed overboard during her time on the merchantman *Piper's Lament* and done nothing to save them – unable to move lest she also lost her grip and was caught by the heaving waves. The captain hadn't turned the ship, had done nothing but watch them go under. There had been nothing more to do; no lines they could throw, no way to make up the distance or correct their path, but they had all felt like murderers once the storm subsided.

Shakily, she made her way back to the window she'd climbed from, then past it before straightening up. Kesh glanced back at the empty window, fearing she might see the brutal face of the bodyguard, Perel, staring back at her, but there was nothing.

She lurched back toward the plaza where she'd entered the hospital, heading for the gates that separated hospital grounds from the district beyond. After a dozen steps she started to find her balance again and almost broke into a run before she realised she'd only be attracting attention to herself. It was an effort to keep walking at a normal speed and not look back until she was at the edge of the plaza, but she did just that and only paused once she was in the shadow of a tall building. That one look was enough to spur her on. Half-hidden by the corner of the building, Kesh watched a man in black dart out of the hospital entrance.

At the foot of the steps below the polished double doors, he turned left and right like a man panicked. Kesh couldn't wait any longer – she ran, uncaring of who might see. There was only one thought in her mind now; saving her mother's life.

Kesh looked up and saw a break in the buildings ahead, the midday sun casting its light over the further buildings and bleaching their stone facades white. Her heart gave a jump – she was almost home, her mother was almost safe.

In the next instant something smashed into her shoulder and the world was thrown sideways. She flew across the rubbish-strewn street and into a shadowed alley, crashing into a jumble of abandoned, broken boxes. Stars burst before her eyes as she fell, landing heavily on her shoulder and crying out in shock and pain. Everything became a blur, sun and shadow slashed and whirled before her eyes as a second blow rolled her onto her back, then a rough hand grabbed her collar.

Kesh kicked out in panic, feet flailing wildly as she grabbed her attacker's wrist and tried to wrench free. His grip was iron-like. Kesh was strong and threw herself around in an attempt to break his hold, but she could do nothing and in the next moment she was lifted and hurled against a wall. She slammed into it with a stuttered howl, the impact driving the air from her lungs even as she cried out. Kesh fell to her knees, body ablaze with pain, and only the wall behind her stopped her from collapsing backwards.

'Led me a pretty dance, bitch,' Perel snarled. The big goshe stood over her and glared down, hate filling his eyes as he drew a long-knife. 'But it's all ended now.'

Kesh whimpered and curled up in a ball, but the goshe laughed and bent down to grab her by her hair.

'Crying ain't going to help,' he promised, dragging her back up to her knees.

Kesh didn't wait to hear any more. She slashed up with her father's knife and felt it bite into his inner arm. He released her and on the second pass she lunged for his throat, knowing she couldn't wait, but he was ready for her and caught the blow on his own weapon. Deftly slipping his free hand underneath her arm, the goshe grabbed her wrist and smirked, not even looking at his injury.

Blood dribbled from the tear in his sleeve, but if anything the wound seemed to have improved his mood and as he bent her hand back, Perel pursed his lips and made a kissing sound.

'Like it rough, eh?' he said with a broken-toothed grin.

Kesh wrenched her body back and stamped forward with all her strength, kicking the goshe square in the groin and at last eliciting a grunt of pain from the man. He released her wrist and backed off a step, his apparent amusement wavering only for a moment.

'Oh that's good – you're doing well, girl,' he laughed. 'Fancy another shot?'

To Kesh's astonishment the goshe pushed back a fold of his black robe and sheathed his long-knife, standing before her with empty hands outstretched.

'Come on then, you've earned a free swing. Help yourself.'

Knife held out before her, Kesh found her feet and stayed where she was, crouched low as she'd been taught – ready to move, despite the little space available in the alley.

'Come on, ain't got all day,' Perel said, beckoning to her. 'Think about me snapping that little girl's neck like a—'

He didn't get any more out as Kesh darted forward, cutting left and right in small, controlled movements. The first missed, the second caught the laughing goshe's palm and tore into the flesh, the third nicked him on the wrist. Kesh drove forwards, pushing inside his guard to jam the knife in his ribs, but Perel didn't try to back off. With his injured hand he swatted down into the side of her head and a blinding flash of light burst before her eyes. Kesh was driven down to one knee, knife almost falling from her hands before a second slap and flash of light sent her hand numb and the weapon fell.

Perel laughed and stepped back, in no rush to finish her off as Kesh groggily tried to keep upright. She blinked back the stars bursting darkly before her eyes and looked at her hand. A smear of scorched red skin ran across the back of her hand while her head rang with the impact of Perel's blow.

His throaty chuckle seemed to clear the fog from her mind, but it was replaced by an insistent sting from her hand and head. Realising she was unarmed, Kesh fumbled on the ground for her knife. Her hand seemed slow and uncoordinated, flapping against the knife's grip but refusing to grasp it. She managed to pick it up with her left but the contempt on Perel's face showed she looked far from threatening with it.

Kesh tried to stand but the effort made her sway and lurch backwards. The dim lines of the alley and the bright sky above seemed to distend and blur as she moved, the pain in her head waxing briefly until she found her balance once more. Beyond Perel, mere yards away, a thin strip of sun shone on the cobbles of the street – but it could have been a mile in her condition, with him blocking the path.

The brisk patter of footsteps suddenly came from further down the street, but Kesh only made out a flash of movement past the alley-mouth as she tried to cry out for help. The sound came out as little more than a moan, one that broke off as Perel drew back his hand threateningly. As he did so a flicker of light danced between his callused fingers – an ephemeral, threatening glitter that made Kesh realise it wasn't her scrambled senses. Her hand really was scorched, head too no doubt.

The realisation prompted a deeper fear inside her. This man was no mere thug or bodyguard but something worse – some sort of Astaren, with magic at his fingertips.

The goshe have warrior-mages? Kesh wondered dully. *How? How have the Houses allowed it?*

A streak of rusty-brown flashed down from the rooftop before she could make any sense of the sight, then a second from the other side. Wisps of white light seemed to follow them, faint in the daylight but distinct as they entered the building's shadow. Perel twisted with unnatural speed to slap away the first attacking shape with a whip-crack sound. There was a small explosion of light around the object and it was thrown to the ground. The second, Perel seemed to catch in a crackling ball of light, his expression contorted with rage in the bright flare of white.

As he held it there Kesh at last saw what it was and gasped – writhing in the cruel, searing fire was a fox, fur already scorched and teeth bared in a rictus of pain. She blinked and saw for a brief moment another shape surrounding it, some far larger creature with storm-blown fur and crushing jaws that similarly struggled against Perel's grip. An instant later it vanished and Kesh blinked away the stars bursting before her eyes, taking a moment to see the long furrows that had appeared along Perel's sleeve.

A third fox struck him from behind, racing into the alley along the ground and driving its teeth into the back of his knee while the wolf-spirit surrounding it raked its claws down his thigh. Perel let the second creature fall and turned towards the new attack, finally drawing his long-knife to stab it in the back. From up above came a piercing shriek that made Kesh flinch and reel from the burst of savage sound. Perel rocked back as though physically struck and staggered sideways before he caught himself. Through watering eyes, Kesh saw him recover a moment later and, long-knife at the ready, he hurled himself forward like a pouncing cat.

From a standing start the goshe jumped across the alley and up grabbing the gutter with his left hand and dragging himself up until he was above roof height, assailant still hanging from his leg. The fox standing there darted forwards at him, a russet blur of teeth that caught his face even as Perel drove a knife right through its side.

He dropped back down, sparks of lightning dancing over his knuckles and down the bloodied blade. His cheek was torn open and Perel touched his fingers to the wound, shock flourishing on his brutal features even as he staggered drunkenly back and almost tripped on the fox-corpses there. Behind him, at the entrance to the alley, came another sharp bark and he whirled around – knives drawn and ready to ward off a further attack.

None came. The remaining fox simply stared at him and for once he didn't move. The goshe wavered slightly and glanced up at the rooftop, wary of another attack from above, but no more of the lithe creatures jumped to their death. He was still watching for them when Kesh scooped up her own knife and rammed it with all her strength under his half-raised arm.

Perel coughed and shuddered under the impact. The blow drove him a step to the right and there he stood for a moment, impaled and shocked by the blow. Then Kesh whipped the broad knife out again and a gout of blood spattered onto the dark packed earth underfoot. The goshe wheezed, weapons tumbling from his hands. He tried to turn and Kesh hopped back, out of reach of his lightning-wreathed hands, but as he turned towards her she saw the agony on his face.

He didn't make it all the way round before the pain became too much and he crashed down to one knee. The man gasped for breath, chest heaving, but, as he exhaled, a fresh stream of blood poured out from the wound. Ashen-faced, the goshe pitched forward and fell, twitching once before he was still and the light around his hands winked out.

Kesh stared down at the body, then the weapon she'd killed him with. The blade was slick with blood and her hands started to tremble, but there was a tiny raging voice at her core that fought through the pain, confusion and horror to be heard.

Mother! I have to warn Mother!

She looked again at the corpse and suddenly was on her knees, vomiting up what little food she'd managed that day. Gasping for breath between heaves, Kesh cried out as convulsing bands wrapped around her stomach, but the voice in the back of her mind continued to scream. Panting hard, she fought through it and, using the alley wall to support her, forced herself back onto her feet. With shaking hands she wiped her father's knife on the dead goshe's back and returned it to the sheath inside her jacket.

The fox hadn't moved and she hesitated as she focused on the creature again. Before she could pick her way past the man she'd murdered, the fox bobbed its head as though bowing to her – unblinking gaze fixed firmly upon her all the while. With that, it turned and fled in a flash, vanishing from sight and somehow Kesh knew that by the time she reached the entrance of the alley, it would be gone completely.

Warn Mother! The voice in her head continued to shriek and now she obeyed, staggering forward for a few steps until she was past the body and she found her balance again.

She looked left and right down the street. Seeing no figures in black advancing on her, Kesh set off without daring to look back, arms tight across her chest and wincing at the pain in her head. The canal remained ahead, a sudden and familiar sight that she almost ran to. Once across the canal it was busy main streets all the way home and Kesh walked as quickly as she dared – head down, not meeting or even noticing any curious gazes she attracted. Of the foxes that had saved her, she saw not a trace.

CHAPTER 7

Peace remains a major advocate of the caste system in the Lesser Empire. Without acknowledging the Emperor as descended from Gods, and those who share his blood being above other nobles, it would be power alone that commanded authority and that would lead inevitably to war. Only an acceptance of the Emperor's moral authority keeps a check on the actions of the Great House nobilities. Only by accepting his primacy can they claim their own.

From A *History* by Ayel Sorote

Narin circled slowly, stave half-extended in an axe grip as he watched the other man give ground. The sound of his feet was muffled by the clatter of water on all sides, a steady thrum of noise that enclosed him in a world of his own.

He struck, surging forward as he snapped the stave towards the man's head. With impossible speed his opponent brought his own weapon up to bear and deflected Narin's with a sharp crack. The Investigator pressed on, swinging at the other man's knuckles as he edged right – then striking up at his arm.

His opponent whirled his stave down to catch the first then took the second blow on the other end. Holding it in the centre, he slipped his stave over Narin's and stepped inside his guard. Before Narin could retreat the man rammed the butt back into Narin's shoulder and hacked down towards Narin's face. The Investigator was forced to drop backwards to avoid the strike and ended up on his backside in the dirt.

'The edge of Dragon and the Harbour Warrant,' Rhe said casually as Narin picked himself up.

'Where I found the goshe? That's right,' Narin confirmed, readying himself for a second attempt. 'Why?'

He retreated to the edge of the marked ground where a channel of water flowed. They were in a training courtyard, one of several to the rear of the Palace of Law between buildings. At each corner stood a stone plinth supporting an ancient bronze statue – to the north, a phoenix taking flight, to the south a lion roaring.

East and west were the first of the Gods to ascend to the heavens – the God-Emperor and God-Empress, whose line stretched dozens of generations to the current Emperor himself. From each statue – the mouths of the beasts, a jug in the God-Empress's hands and the God-Emperor's drinking horn – poured water. Below each was a steel drum, each of which sang with a different pitch to the others as the water struck it

'Bodies were found there,' Rhe continued, darting forward and aiming a flurry of one-handed blows at Narin.

He beat them off, started forward then hesitated. Something of Rhe's balance told him not to move in and to demonstrate why, the Lawbringer dipped and extended his arm into a straight lunge. It was well short of Narin's chin, but he could see what would have happened had he been drawn in.

'Bodies?'

Rhe nodded just as Narin launched forward, smacking Rhe's stave aside and kicking at the Lawbringer's midriff. The bigger man angled his body as Narin struck and the impact was glancing. Riding it with ease, Rhe whirled around and smacked his stave into the back of Narin's calf – knocking him onto his back once more and calmly stepping back to allow Narin to struggle up.

'Burned bodies,' Rhe said at last. 'Burned in the open street after some sort of confrontation on the roof above.'

Narin paused in the process of levering himself up with the white wooden staff. 'On the roof? More goshe?'

'Perhaps. What is interesting is the burning itself. There is almost nothing left; though it was a cool night and no buildings were damaged, they burned so hot nothing useful remains.'

Rhe attacked lazily as he spoke, with slow and unhurried movements that forced Narin to react but still gave him time to process the news.

'Some sort of demon?'

'Or God,' Rhe pointed out. 'This was no natural fire.'

'The fire was what killed them?'

'There is no way to tell. It would certainly kill, but there was no flame-damage to the rooftops – only blood. More likely, the fire was set once they were dead.'

'Hiding evidence then – but evidence of what?'

Rhe shifted his grip, holding the stave in the centre once more and beckoning Narin forward. The Investigator copied him and moved to attack with shorter strikes of each end, watching Rhe for where he would counter-attack.

'We have only questions,' Rhe said as they sparred, clearly holding back as he warded Narin off, 'but still they tell us something.'

'If something needs to be hidden,' Narin said, kicking out at thin air as Rhe avoided his sudden strike, 'it tells us they have something to hide – more than that, even. The fire did not kill the victims, yet they were able or prepared to cover up their actions.'

'So unlikely a God.'

Narin grunted, too intent on defending Rhe's quickening blows to reply immediately. 'A God doesn't fear reprisals,' he agreed, 'but Lord Shield could have acted more directly than he did. He might not want his involvement known in this instance either.'

'Why leave a body at all then?'

Narin paused and realised Rhe was right. Surely a God could leave no trace if they wished? 'So a mortal. Astaren?'

'Quite a coincidence if so. The same area you find a goshe being chased by a God. If your man is an Astaren agent, why have they not found you yet? Or do we all ascribe too much to their mystical abilities?'

Narin grimaced. 'I'll ask them when I wake up with a knife to my throat.'

As Rhe made to reply Narin made his move, stepping in and hooking Rhe's weapon-arm. He turned into the Lawbringer and dipped his shoulder, dragging the bigger man over it even as Rhe tried to spin away. Narin drove his leg forward in anticipation and caught him just in time, using his hip as a pivot to haul the Lawbringer over and finally break his superb balance.

Rhe hit the ground hard, but he was moving even as he fell. Narin felt the man's stave behind his knee before he'd released Rhe and in the next moment he was pitched backwards with Rhe rolling on top of him, stave ready at his throat.

'Excellent,' the Lawbringer panted, a trace of colour appearing in the faint blue-grey tint of his skin. 'Few Lawbringers would have caught me that way.'

The Investigator grunted and mentally cursed – both at the elbow pressed heavily on his ribs and the Lawbringer's praise. Arms splayed wide, he felt like a turtle flipped on its back. Catching Rhe off-balance hadn't been enough to stop the Lawbringer finding a lethal opening.

Aren't you a good puppy, Narin? he thought darkly. *You get a treat for impressing master.*

'Narin!' yelled a voice from somewhere behind them. 'Narin, come quick!'

The two men turned to look even as the shout came again and Narin realised it was Investigator Diman calling. Rhe rolled to one side and Narin groaned as the weight on him was relieved. He lay on his back a moment longer, staring up at the sky, before he found the strength to haul himself upright once more.

'That'll be fun in the morning,' he muttered as he gingerly retrieved his stave and turned to face Diman. 'You called?'

Diman padded to a halt, his face flushed with animation but abashed in the face of the legendary Lawbringer. 'Investigator Narin,' he said formally, trying to present himself with the expected dignity after having sprinted around the corner. 'You asked me to keep an ear open for word of the goshe.'

Narin glanced at Rhe and nodded. 'And?'

Diman's face lit up again. 'And there's a woman just run into the great hall – bleeding and shouting all sorts! Some goshe just tried to kill her, she says, and murdered her sister this very morning!'

'Murdered? Where?'

'The bloody— Ahem, apologies, Lawbringer. At the Raven free hospital, so she says. She's, well she's scared and angry – yelling all sorts. Something about poison and foxes; I didn't stop to hear too much, just sat her down with someone to watch over her and said I'd come fetch you.'

Narin looked down at himself and dusted the worst of the sand from his clothes, aches forgotten but all too aware of Rhe's scrupulous gaze. A Lawbringer must be composed and serene; thoughts free of emotion and the cares of the world. Without warning Kine's face appeared in his mind – her smooth dark skin and easy smile.

I must be a Lawbringer, he realised, *and soon, if I'm to help Kine and our baby. Whatever shit I must eat as I deal with idiot noblemen, I must win Rhe's approval. Even if it means looking as soulless as he does.*

'Thank you, Investigator,' Narin said calmly. 'With your permission, Lawbringer?'

Rhe watched him a moment without blinking then inclined his head. 'A crime,' Rhe commented. 'It seems your instincts are as sharp as your throws. Lead on, Investigator – the matter is yours to pursue.'

They found her huddled in a side chamber of the great hall, one hand thrust inside her coat as she stared suspiciously at the faces around her. A young Investigator named Eperei stood a few yards away – a wary distance from the injured, wild-eyed woman who looked ready to hit out at anyone coming closer. Narin crossed the great hall that served as entrance to the Palace of Law, noting the glances Rhe's presence drew from many of those present. It was quiet in there; the avenues of slender pillars that ran down each side of the high, airy hall empty and echoing.

The whole building was built of pale stone and was austere in its adornments – the only colour being the yellow on the two dozen banners bearing the Imperial sun. Against all that, the young woman in muddied, blood-spattered clothes and a scorch-mark on her face was a stark contrast.

She sensed them approaching and looked up with fear in her eyes. From the way her hand was hidden he knew she had a weapon, but if half of what Diman had said was true he could understand the urge to have a blade close at hand.

'Mistress,' he said gently as he reached them, 'my name is Investigator Narin. I understand I may be able to help you?'

'Why not him?' she snapped, glancing at Rhe as the Lawbringer stopped a yard behind Narin. 'I need a Lawbringer, not his monkey.'

Narin inclined his head, trying not to rise to the comment. 'This is Lawbringer Rhe – he oversees all I do, however, I may be better able to help you.' He held up a hand to stop her instinctive retort. 'Please, right now that doesn't matter. Tell us both what's happened to you.'

She pursed her lips, body tense though he could see her left hand shaking. 'Here?'

'Somewhere more private, perhaps?'

Narin pointed back across the hall towards a wide stairway that stood behind the brass-fitted desk where a white-bearded Lawbringer supervised all those who entered. He had half a dozen young Investigators waiting on his command, ready to be directed towards visitors or sent to carry messages, while behind him the stairway led to a maze of offices that surrounded the Chamber of the Lawbringers.

'A room upstairs?'

She nodded and got to her feet with a grimace of pain.

'Do you need a doctor?' he asked gently, only to have her flinch at the word.

'Any doctor comes near me I'll cut his throat,' she growled.

Narin paused. Threats like that were not what he wanted to hear from an armed woman. From the scorch-mark on her head and generally battered demeanour, he didn't think she was anything more than a victim who'd fought back, but that was beside the point.

'What's your name?' he asked, standing in her path as she made to follow him towards the stair.

The young woman paused and squinted at him as though he was mad. 'My name? Kesh – Kesh Hinar Vesis. Why?'

'Well, Mistress Hinar,' Narin said, 'you're here in the Palace of Law now. There's no one going to hurt you, but we can't let you hurt anyone else either – understand me? If there's someone after you, they'll have to get past me first, and if they're having to take me down they're not watching Lawbringer Rhe properly, if you get my meaning. So let's go and have a talk somewhere quiet – but first, please take your hand off the knife in your coat. I don't want to have to explain anyone getting hurt by mistake. My superiors look down on that sort of thing and I've already got one unconscious man on my account this week, okay?'

Kesh's eyes widened, in her shock not realising how obvious she'd been about gripping her weapon. Eventually, she nodded and jerkily removed her right hand from inside her coat, revealing another blackened burn on the back of her hand.

'You sure you don't want a doctor?'

'Yes.'

Narin sighed. 'Very well. Diman, could you please fetch some clean water and a cloth? That is, if you wouldn't mind me cleaning your wounds, Mistress Hinar?'

She shook her head so he stepped back and directed her towards the stair, Rhe moving ahead of them and Narin falling in beside her. Kesh limped forward a few steps, eyes on the other faces in the hall still, then seemed to straighten and move with greater purpose.

'That's really Lawbringer Rhe?' she muttered, looking askance at Narin.

'It is,' he confirmed.

'Thank the Gods,' she said with a sudden rush of relief in her voice.

She almost missed her step as the tangled ball of fear and tension within her seemed to partially unravel, but when Narin put out a hand to steady her, Kesh withdrew like a scalded cat. Her hand twitched towards her coat again. Narin was careful not to react and Kesh caught herself in time.

'Don't,' she muttered. 'Just don't.'

Once her story was told the three of them sat in silence. Narin was lost in his own thoughts, Kesh in the emptiness of grief. What Rhe was thinking, Narin couldn't tell – not even whether the story had affected him. It prompted a memory of that morning, when Rhe had been holding the baby back in Wolf District. With a start, Narin realised it was loss he was feeling – a grief of his own at the child he'd most likely never hold. The Investigator lowered his eyes, feeling ashamed to be thinking of himself in the face of Kesh's truer hurt.

'You mother is safe,' he forced himself to say – dully repeating what she'd only just finished telling him. 'She will not return to the boarding house.'

Kesh nodded. 'I told her to run, to tell no one where and go nowhere I might guess ... in case ...'

Unfinished, her sentence told Narin everything. He dipped his head in acknowledgement. 'That's good, but I'm still worried. We cannot protect her if we don't know where she is.'

'She'll be here!' Kesh insisted fiercely. 'In the morning, she'll come! I trust Master Hamber, he'll give her the message true and make sure she follows. The goshe can't check every tavern and boarding house in the harbour; she'll be safe for one night and make it here in the morning. I couldn't take the risk of fetching her. I couldn't risk leading them to her!'

'You lost your sister and killed a man,' Rhe began suddenly. 'Encountered demons and ran halfway across the city – yet still you had the presence of mind to keep your mother safe. You are a remarkable young woman.'

Kesh scowled and flexed the fingers of her newly bandaged hand. 'Didn't run,' she said quietly, 'if I had, that bastard Perel wouldn't have got ahead of me.'

'Perhaps. It is just as possible he would have gone straight to your boarding house – or caught you on the run and not taken the time to do it quietly. It doesn't matter now – he is dead, you are not.'

'What now?'

Rhe turned to Narin and stood. 'Now, I will take my leave. This alley where you left the goshe's body – I think I can find it from your account. If I can find the body before his comrades do, or it is mysteriously burned to nothing, we learn something new. I will take some Investigators with me and pay the goshe hospital a visit afterwards – these doctors have some answers to provide.'

'Wait,' Narin said, 'perhaps you shouldn't.'

Rhe frowned. 'And why not? Mistress Kesh's allegations are serious and we are the guardians of the Emperor's law. It is our duty to investigate.'

'I realise that,' Narin explained, 'but they've had time to hide any evidence. What if they have removed the goshe's body already? Emari's too? The Father mentioned others, he might well have sent them on to cover their tracks – then we have merely the word of a lower-caste woman against high-castes.'

The Lawbringer was quiet for a moment. The law favoured the testimony of the higher castes, but for Rhe that usually meant that his word was tantamount to certainty given only the extended Imperial family were ranked higher. Rarely did he have to stop to consider such weighting the way Narin did.

'This remains your investigation,' Rhe said finally. 'What do you suggest?'

'That we wait, at least for the night. They don't know where Mistress Kesh is, do they? Her mother's fled the house; it'll be empty when their agents reach it. Could she not have fled with her mother rather than come to us? They might spend the evening searching for two women in hiding rather than one, content in the thought that it's merely a question of time and Kesh can pose them no real threat.

'Once we announce our involvement, they know we'll be investigating and can act accordingly. If we don't go to the hospital, they'll believe we know nothing of the plot yet – it might make them overplay their hand.'

Rhe gave a small nod. 'My first thought was to go there and find this doctor, yes. That would be simple enough for them to predict. If they do they would move Emari's body without delay and leave no evidence for us to discover.'

'Exactly,' Narin agreed, 'the Lawbringers bear the Emperor's authority – they know we wouldn't fear to march straight in and search the entire building.'

'So,' Rhe said slowly, 'we will outmanoeuvre them instead. I will go to this alley still, but with my badge of office concealed. If there is a body to find I can do it alone and unobtrusively. Our priority is to keep Mistress Kesh safe, and her mother too when she comes to us. Narin, that will be your task. Mistress Kesh needs protection and being surrounded by Investigators is as good a place as any, so take her to your home. That woman at your compound, Mistress Sheti? You've known her for several years now, you can trust her? Good. It might appear improper to have a young woman stay in your rooms alone and now is not a good time to invite gossip, so recruit her to the cause. I doubt any of you will be getting much sleep anyway and there is something there you should show Mistress Kesh.'

Narin gave a start. 'You're sure now's the time for that?'

Rhe nodded. 'She is a remarkable young woman,' he repeated, 'I have faith in her resilience.'

'What are you talking about?' Kesh demanded, 'what in Jester's name is going on?'

Narin turned towards her with a faint sense of dread in his heart. Rhe didn't wait for his Investigator to speak but turned and left the room without a further word. Once the door slid shut behind Rhe, Kesh repeated her question and Narin meekly submitted.

'This missing guest of yours,' he said hesitantly, 'this Master Tokene. I ...'

Kesh jumped up. 'What? You know where he is? Take me to him!'

'I can take you nowhere until I have your knife,' Narin said as gently as possible. 'First though, I think I should explain.'

Kesh opened her mouth to shout some sort of curse at him, then stopped and pressed her lips together so tightly they went white. 'Very well, explain,' she said in a restrained voice. 'I'm keeping the knife, though,' she added as she forced herself to sit back down again.

'He's no threat to you.'

'Good – that'll make it easier for me to cut off every finger and toe until the bastard tells me why my sister's dead. How do you know where he is? Did you arrest him?'

Narin grimaced. 'Not quite. He surprised me in the street a few nights back – I thought he was attacking me and I knocked him out, but he might have been looking for my help. I think he'd been thrown from a rooftop – perhaps by your fox-demons, perhaps by a God. Either way I'm charged with finding out what's going on, but no one's losing their fingers in the process. That's why I was fetched just now. He was dressed as a goshe and I asked to be summoned if there was any unusual news involving them.'

Kesh didn't respond, her gaze dropping to the table they had been sat around.

'I mean it,' Narin said in a warning tone, 'you try to use that knife on him and I'll break your hand before you do. Similarly, if he tries to escape or hurt you, I'll do whatever I must to stop him. So don't give him the excuse – give me the knife.'

The young woman glowered. For a while she didn't speak but eventually she looked up and nodded. 'I'm keeping the knife. I don't trust anyone right now, not even bloody Lawbringer Rhe himself, but I promise I'll not try to kill him. My word's as good as you're going to get. I'm no liar but there's no way I'm passing the night without a knife close at hand.'

She sighed and her exhaustion was clear to see. 'You'll just have to trust that I want answers more than I want to kill him. He's a goshe agent and probably a killer too, but he's not the one giving the orders. There's someone else to blame; maybe that Father at the hospital, but either way I want to know who and why before I watch them executed.'

Narin sighed. 'I suppose that's as good as I'm likely to get. Just don't expect your answers too soon; he's been unconscious since I dragged him home.' He stood. 'Let's go. If they're still looking for you, their next move might be to check here. Best we leave through a side door and get you out of sight as soon as we can.'

He paused and looked her up and down. Her shirt was torn and spattered in blood, while mud was smeared all the way down one trouser leg.

'Maybe a change of clothes first?'

The journey to the compound was fraught for them both. Kesh jumped at every unexpected noise and movement, and Narin was barely any calmer. The Palace of Law was an expansive complex, however; the spread of dormitories, courts, shrines and training grounds meant it covered a large area, so they easily found an unobserved door to slip out of.

In a borrowed coat and clean, albeit ill-fitting, shirt, Kesh waited in the shade of the doorway while Narin scouted the streets beyond. She was silent and tense even before she walked out at Narin's gesture.

Head covered with a married woman's scarf and hands balled into fists, she wordlessly followed him through a deserted alley in the opposite direction from where they were heading.

The afternoon had turned cool and grey, muting the city's colours and promising another night of fog in the Imperial City. As they reached the end of the winding alleyway, Kesh stopped and at last lifted her head to the view ahead of them. Past the pale stone buildings of the Imperial District, rising high atop a stark outcrop of rock thirty yards above the roofs below, was the Imperial Palace.

This close, Kesh felt its presence like a strong wind blowing into her face and she took a pace back at the sight. The Palace was a vast building, built long before the first Gods had ascended to the stars, that she knew, but up close – barely a hundred yards from the nearest of its cold white columns and curved roofs – it became an entirely different prospect.

More than a mile long and seven oversized storeys high in the central block, the Palace complex appeared to be carved entirely of ice by the hands of giants. The adornments that hung from its huge pillared flanks seemed mere foolishness – a vain attempt to stamp man's authority on a creation the world of man had inherited from a dead race. There was an organic sweep to its lines, the pillars reaching up like trees, the stepped roofs all gently curved.

'I've never been so close to it before,' she muttered. 'Gods – look at it!'

Narin hurried back to her, impatience in his face as he followed her gaze. 'The Palace? Haven't you lived here all your life?'

Kesh nodded, swallowing as she did so and unable to tear her attention from the gigantic, unnatural edifice. 'Never come to this part though.'

'Why not? Weren't you even curious as a child?'

'Of course, but …' She gestured towards the Palace, then at the grand granite buildings skirting the outcrop of rock ahead. 'Look at them, this half of the district's not for the likes of me. You don't get much of a sight of it from the west, the streets are too narrow, and Crescent-side it's sheer cliffs with little to see. We were scared to come this close, didn't think we were even allowed east of the Knight's Path Avenue. A few of the older boys claimed they'd gone up to the Gate of the Sun or one of the grand temples, but no one ever believed them. And once I was older … well, I'm just servant caste. These streets aren't for my sort.'

'Because of your caste?' Narin said in a strangely stern way, as though she'd committed some breach of etiquette.

Kesh nodded, suddenly wary of him. The Investigator radiated anger and disapproval. For a moment she found herself wanting to put her fingers around the grip of her knife, but then he turned away.

'Come on,' Narin snapped, 'we need to keep moving. You can marvel at your betters another day.'

Rounding the sprawl of the Palace of Law they avoided the busy streets where shops and stalls were established, keeping to side-streets that ran in parallel. The Investigator set a brisk pace but it was one Kesh was happy to match, every casual glance from passersby enough to send a jolt of panic through her chest. Unbidden, her thoughts returned to Emari – the little girl's face as it had been in her arms, asleep but indefinably less her sister than when she'd watched the girl sleep before.

Thin tears began to trickle down her face, but Kesh angrily wiped them away before the glowering Investigator noticed them – knowing it would draw unwelcome attention and not wanting to show the whole Empire her pain. That was a private thing, something to be jealously guarded until she could be with her mother again; the only one who could feel the same loss that ate at Kesh's heart.

It didn't take them long to leave behind the towering grey stone buildings of the Imperial administration and noble families. Abruptly, they came to a rougher district – still smart by the standards of the Harbour Warrant, but lacking the ornamentation of the various palaces and lesser palazzos on the eastern half of the island. The buildings were stone and wood now, fenced compounds with pitch-sealed overhanging roofs that met their neighbours at the corners to create arches at the end of each side-street.

The people were more normal too, dressed to work rather than compete with their peers and walking with purpose instead of slow, haughty indifference. Kesh followed Narin closely, the man walking with the assurance of someone who knew those streets well, of someone close to home. She was just about to relax as they turned a corner and Narin headed for an open compound gate, when a voice called out across the street towards them.

'Investigator!'

They both stopped, Kesh's hand diving for her knife even as she turned. Narin had moved even faster, whipping his stave from his back and bringing it up to guard position in a heartbeat. But no attack came, only an amused sound.

Kesh narrowed her eyes on a man leaning against the wall of the compound across the street, local-born by his face. He wasn't a goshe – no, he wasn't dressed like a goshe – but even she had to admit it was a strange disguise for a goshe agent to adopt. The stranger was not much older than Narin, she guessed, but slim and wearing a grey sleeved cape over an expensive-looking tunic, britches and tall patterned boots. The cape looked like an academic's robe, but the rest screamed high-caste, however muted the dark green tunic was compared to what some noblemen wore. The man shifted position slightly and just inside his robe she glimpsed the ornate handle of a rapier – noble caste then, unless he was a strangely traditional-minded warrior caste.

'Investigator,' the man repeated. He pushed himself off the wall and offered them a small bow. 'Might I have a word?'

Narin was frozen to the spot for a moment, then recovered himself and lowered his stave. He bowed low, watching the man carefully, as Kesh belatedly knelt, head dipped enough that her chin touched the hand that refused to release the knife inside her coat. Both glanced behind them as though this was a ruse of some sort, but no assassins appeared and reluctantly Narin advanced towards the speaker.

'My apologies, sir, but I am on urgent Lawbringer business.'

'Oh come now, make an exception,' the man said cheerfully. 'I'm here in friendship and I'll only take up a moment of your time.'

Narin glanced back at Kesh and gestured for her to keep close. 'Sir, do I know you?'

'Not yet, but you will.' The man tilted his head, making a show of looking at Kesh. 'I think we'd both appreciate this word to be in private however.'

'She does not leave my side,' Narin warned, fingers tightening on his stave. 'If this is a private matter, it must wait.'

'Doesn't leave your side, eh?' the man inquired with a small smile. 'Now that's curious. I'd have not said she was really your type.'

Kesh glanced at Narin, confused, but saw in his frown the Investigator was similarly puzzled.

'I assure you, sir, it is nothing of the sort.'

The man shrugged. 'Didn't think so. A bit pale for your tastes, eh?'

To Kesh's surprise the comment seemed to make Narin flinch as though he'd been stung by a hornet. Her gaze drifted naturally down to the stave he held and something told her Narin was struggling not to strike out at the man, high-born or not.

'Your meaning, sir?' Narin demanded coldly.

The smile remained on the man's face. He was handsome in an aristocratic sort of way; clean-shaven, with pronounced cheekbones and narrow nose that gave him a delicate air, but there was a hard edge that stopped him from looking some court fop.

'My meaning being that it is a personal matter we have to discuss.' He pulled a silver cigar case from inside his cape and brandished it like a declaration of peace. 'But I'm in no rush. Please, see to your young lady first – I would not want to interfere with official Lawbringer business after all. I'll just wait here and enjoy a smoke, come out any time.'

Narin's face darkened more, but he was caught in indecision and had no response to the man's words. Kesh shifted her feet and he turned sharply, stave still raised, before catching himself and lowering the weapon.

'Very well,' he muttered sourly. 'Come on.'

With one final look at the stranger he ushered Kesh inside the compound and dragged the gate shut behind him.

'What was that all about?' Kesh said as Narin checked around at the empty courtyard. A pair of speckled chickens scratched at the ground at the far end, but there was nothing more to see there.

'I've no idea,' he said distractedly, 'but the last thing we need is a scene of any sort.'

He looked up to the right just as a middle-aged woman emerged from one of the rooms onto the walkway overlooking the courtyard. Relief flooded across his face. 'Mistress Sheti, is all well?'

The woman nodded, fixing Kesh with a hard stare before she replied. 'All well,' she declared. 'Patient's awake, but more'n a bit confused.'

'Awake?' demanded both Kesh and Narin in the same breath. He shot her a look and reluctantly Kesh closed her mouth again.

'He's awake?' Narin repeated. 'Good, maybe we'll get some answers. Is Enchei up there?'

Mistress Sheti sniffed. 'They're talking now; Enchei's performing some heathen magic on him, it looks.'

'Right – Kesh, please go with Sheti. Enchei is a friend of mine; he knows as much as I do and he's not as feeble as he looks. You'll be safe around him while I deal with whoever it is out there. Okay?'

'Wait here?' she asked in surprise. 'What sort of protection is that supposed to be?' Panic at being left with strangers flared briefly inside her, but then she remembered who else was in his rooms and hate quickly supplanted it.

'Enchei is as good as me,' Narin assured her, 'and it'll only be for a few minutes, I promise. You are quite safe. Half of the quarters here belong to Investigators.'

'Fine, if you say so,' Kesh said, hand still on her knife.

'Thank you. Sheti, no one is to stab anyone – especially her,' Narin ordered, pointing at Kesh. The woman on the walkway gave a start at that, but nodded readily enough. 'Good. Kesh, I don't know what's going on in there; I don't know how he'll react when he sees you, but please – don't do anything without me, okay?'

The young woman found herself biting down on her lip at the thought, but she nodded in agreement. The knife would stay close at hand in case the goshe tried anything, but she didn't want any sort of commotion to draw his friends.

'Thank you.' He looked back at the gate, where the nobleman was waiting. 'Now let's find out what this fool wants.'

Narin closed the gate behind him and spent a long while checking the street beyond. There were a few people within sight, but only the strange nobleman looked out of place and eventually he crossed the narrow street to face the man again.

'Who are you? What do you want with me?' Narin demanded, forgetting any semblance of protocol as the man's words came back to haunt him – *a bit pale for your tastes.*

He kept his stave in his hand, unsure what sort of threat was coming but not wanting to face it unarmed. *Does he know?* Narin wondered as cold dread filled his gut. *How could he have found out?*

'Now then, Investigator,' the man said sternly, 'this might be a private matter, but there's no need to be rude.'

Narin bit back his reply, remembering Lawbringer Rhe's words earlier that day. With an effort he swallowed his anger and inclined his head respectfully. 'My apologies, sir. You've caught me at a difficult time, a delicate and dangerous matter.'

'In which case I shall not delay you long. The young lady is a witness?'

'Something like that.'

The man nodded. 'Very well – my name is Ayel Sorote of the House of the Sun.'

He paused to let his words sink in and Narin felt the dread in his stomach increase. Technically, Narin could describe himself the same way; he was born into the legal domain of the House of the Sun and remained a lifelong inhabitant of the Imperial quarter, but only high-caste people would do so. Master Sorote was either noble or Imperial caste and as a result, could doubtlessly destroy Narin's life with a word.

'My Lord Sun,' Narin said hoarsely, belatedly dropping to one knee.

'No need for that. On your feet, Investigator. Prince Sorote will suffice.'

Screaming hells! Prince? Narin thought as he obeyed. *He's not a nobleman, he's royal family! The bastard's Imperial caste, blood-relation to the Emperor himself!*

'How can I serve you, Prince Sorote?'

Sorote watched Narin's face with a faint smile, affecting a thoughtful air. 'How indeed?'

'I ... I don't understand.'

'Tell me about Lawbringer Rhe.'

Narin frowned. This was about Rhe? 'He, ah – he's the most devoted servant of the Emperor's law I've ever met. All the Lawbringers are dedicated, but Rhe is more than that – there is no place in his heart for anything else.'

'A hard man to please?'

'I suppose so,' Narin said awkwardly, desperately trying to work out what was going on. 'He is exacting in all he does and demands perfection from those around him. He's difficult to please, certainly, but doesn't refuse to praise and when it is given, you know it is properly earned. My dream has always to be a Lawbringer, to serve the Emperor, and Rhe makes me better in all I do.'

'Does he indeed?' mused Sorote, 'That is good to hear.'

'My Lord, might I ask why you're asking me this?'

The man shrugged. 'I was curious to hear how you spoke of him – rather formally, it appears. I've heard good things about you, Investigator Narin, interesting things.'

'I don't understand, sir,' Narin said quietly, suppressing the urge to grab the man by the collar and shake him like a rat.

'You have friends in high places, you have an interesting future ahead of you – a protégé of Lawbringer Rhe is not destined to walk the streets for the rest of his career, certainly not one with political connections.'

'Lord Vanden Wyvern,' Narin said dully. Clearly there was rumour of his patronage in higher circles than Narin had imagined.

'A generous man, so I hear,' Sorote continued, 'with a beautiful young wife. The man must have hidden depths; one must assume so, to have found a bride such as her.'

'Lady Kine is from a minor warrior caste family, I believe,' Narin said through gritted teeth. 'And Lord Vanden is my friend.'

'Of course, my apologies,' the high nobleman said soothingly, 'I did not mean to demean him. You saved his life, I believe?'

Narin nodded. Hating the lie, the false heroism, he tried not to speak it himself whenever possible.

'And still modest with it I see – seven men dead by your hand, wasn't it?'

He shook his head. 'The guards had killed several before they died.'

'It remains impressive none the less,' Sorote countered, 'marking you as a man with a future – an ideal man to pair with Lawbringer Rhe.'

'Rhe's abilities far outstrip my own,' Narin said. 'I have improved under his tuition, but it was luck I survived that ambush on Lord Vanden, while Rhe is an astonishing fighter. With a sword in hand I doubt there are many in the Empire who could stand against him.'

'And what's the count of those who've failed to? Thirty? Forty? Some are starting to wonder if men of the warrior caste are committing crimes just to test themselves against him.'

'I have not kept a count, but I doubt it is so high. As for criminals in the higher castes, it's not my place to comment there. I do my duty by the Emperor's law.'

'Of course, my friend, just idle gossip. So, you are a loyal friend of Lord Vanden. The Wyverns are a powerful House, prideful but good to their friends. I'm glad a man of your skills has earned such patronage, the doors it opens for you will be significant.'

'I want only the chance to earn my position,' Narin said firmly. 'Lord Vanden asked for me to be assigned to Lawbringer Rhe, it is true, he told me so himself, but I made it clear to him I wanted to earn my badge alone. I convinced him that the prestige of being apprenticed to Rhe was reward enough.'

'Most honourable,' Sorote said smoothly, 'given how I'm sure Lord Vanden was willing to share everything he possessed with you.'

Narin's hands tightened. 'He was more than generous to me.'

'Indeed he was!' The nobleman beamed abruptly. 'However, I have observed that House officials are fickle in their generosity. Sometimes they can wake up of a morning, look over at their wife beside them, and suddenly decide to make an enemy of their friends. Stranger things have happened in this life. It is a treacherous world we live in, Investigator Narin.'

'I don't follow you, sir.'

Sorote raised his hands in a gesture of submission. 'Nowhere to follow; just a man idly thinking aloud. But I do see a great future for you, given the right assistance, and I am also a man of influence. If you find yourself looking elsewhere for patronage, there are others who admire your devotion to the Emperor. They might be willing to assist one also working for the betterment of the House of the Sun. Certainly, such a man's loyalty is not for sale, I realise, but we are all prone to our fancies. If the day comes when you find life amid the teahouses of Dragon District not to your liking, do remember you have an acquaintance at the Office of the Catacombs – a modest, but ancient corner of the Imperial household.'

Narin tried not to gape at the man, just as he fought the urges to crack his smirking skull or flee for his life. *The teahouses of Dragon District?* There had been enough insinuations up to that point already, but that had sealed the deal. This man knew about his relationship with Kine. This man could destroy his life without even trying.

Whether he wanted access to Lawbringer Rhe – a man who could one day lead the Vanguard, ruling council of the Lawbringers – or something entirely different, he'd followed Narin. The Gods alone knew how many times, how long it had been, but he knew enough.

Dead or damned, Narin thought hollowly. *Whatever he knows, it's enough to mean I'm his to be used or Vanden's to be murdered.*

'You've made your point,' Narin muttered.

'Yes, I rather think I have.' Sorote offered him a shallow bow. 'Now I shall leave you to your urgent business, Master Narin. I wish you luck with your investigation and should you ever need my assistance … Well, we may run into one another again. Good day.'

CHAPTER 8

The Greater Empire lasted almost a millennium before it was overthrown by a united strike of three Great Houses, now called the Ten Day War, and became the Lesser Empire. That the mere downgrading of an adjective is deemed sufficient to express the catastrophic loss of life incurred in those days is a stain on the souls of all historians.

From *A History* by Ayel Sorote

Kesh ascended the stair quickly, intent on confronting the man responsible for her sister's death, but as she neared the door she faltered. The woman, Sheti, waited for her in silence, fingers interlocked as though to stop herself wringing her hands. The sight drained Kesh's resolve further as guilt blossomed in her heart. She looked nothing like Kesh's mother, Teike, but they were both middle-aged natives of the city – it could have been her mother's apron the woman wore, and her clothes as well except for the more generous proportions of Sheti.

'Mistress Sheti,' Kesh said with a small curtsey. Formality came uneasily to Kesh, but it was preferable to an awkward, apprehensive silence.

'Your name is Kesh?' Sheti inquired gently. 'I'm pleased to meet you. You, ah, you're caught up in whatever this is too?'

Kesh's face tightened and she gave a curt nod. 'You have Master Tokene Shadow in there?'

The name elicited a blank look from Sheti. 'Mebbe,' she said. 'He claims not to know his own name, but he's certainly of House Shadow.' She hesitated. 'That's what his tattoo says, anyway.'

'He doesn't know his own name?' Kesh demanded, a spark of anger awakening in her belly. 'And you believe him?'

'I believe my friends,' Sheti said, 'but I've reserved judgement.' She held out her hand. 'Please, give me your knife.'

'What? No! There are people trying to kill me,' Kesh almost shouted. She pointed at the half-open door beside Sheti. 'Friends of his are trying to kill me – one of them cornered me in an alley and almost …' Her voice dropped and she looked down at her hands, one now bandaged. 'I barely got away alive, I can only hope my mother got my message and escaped our house in time.'

'Then you only convince me more of his honesty,' Sheti said firmly, hand still outstretched. 'I've been watching over the man for most of the day. If he had anywhere to go – anyone to go to or anything to hide from – he'd have managed it, injured or not. I'm not going to stand in the way of some goshe assassin if he wants to escape; I like my blood where it is, thank you very much.'

Kesh didn't have anything to say to that, but under Sheti's determined look she felt herself wilt. The set of the woman's jaw was all too familiar and before she'd even realised it, Kesh was reaching for her father's knife. She pulled the weapon from her coat pocket and stared at it.

Uncle Horote would be angry, she thought distantly, realising a quick wipe was all she'd thought to give the blade. Its surface was spotted and streaked with half-dried blood, the metal stained red-brown and the leather grip tacky under her fingers. *He always said to keep it clean, always clean.*

Horote had been a close friend of her father's, the man who'd taken Kesh under his wing as she saw out the rest of her father's term of service, rather than give up the boarding house they'd bought with his bond money. He was still on the merchant line now, first mate on a fast cutter that did the spice run to Sight's End. She held the weapon out and Sheti took it delicately between forefinger and thumb.

Of course Horote wouldn't be angry, Kesh corrected herself. *I'm alive, that bastard goshe isn't – Horote would bloody well be proud. Remember that, you stupid girl!*

'Thank you,' Sheti said as she bundled the weapon up in her apron. 'Shall we go in now?'

Kesh followed her into Narin's living quarters. One half was taken up by a stove and table while on the right was a low bed and a battered pair of captain's chairs. A lean grey-haired man lounged in one, a bowl of milky liquid in his hands, while a larger man, apparently naked bar his bandages, occupied the bed. She stopped in the doorway, hardly daring to go further as the younger man's battered face looked blankly up at her.

It was him, there could be no doubt. Kesh found herself holding her breath as fear and rage clashed inside her, but then she noticed the change about him. Master Tokene Shadow it was, but something was changed about him.

They had spoken little during his stay at the boarding house – the guests would come and go as they pleased and he hadn't been one of those looking for a substitute family. Tokene would eat with the rest only occasionally and never lingered to talk to either Emari or Kesh. In her memory he moved with purpose, always moving and always alone even in a crowd.

But there he lay, propped against the wall and looking up at her with a faintly pathetic look of hopefulness. Gone was the swagger, the arrogance and self-assurance. Gone was the sense of purpose, too – the man now looked lost, and without it he was diminished.

'Irato,' Kesh muttered, to herself more than anyone else. 'That's what they called you.'

'What?' demanded the grey-haired one, pushing himself to his feet. 'You know his name?'

Kesh nodded. 'Who're you?'

'Enchei – friend o' Narin's.'

She turned to look him up and down. He was clearly fit and strong for his age, but the wrong side of fifty and had hardly ever been anything impressive. Only a little taller than Kesh, her designated protector wasn't even armed.

'You're Enchei?' she said scornfully. 'If this man's friends send another assassin after me, you're going to keep me safe?'

He grinned, quite unruffled by her disbelief. 'Mebbe,' he replied. 'Most folk tend to underestimate me – I guess that'll go for assassins as well.'

'Who're you?' the man in the bed asked. 'What did you call me?'

Kesh turned to face him. The goshe hadn't moved from where he was. For a moment she debated what to do – whether to snatch up a kitchen knife or go for the long-knife lying under the foot of the bed – but in the end she did neither. As great as her hatred was, she wanted answers now; the moment for wrath had gone and in its place was a numb emptiness.

'You think I'm buying this memory loss rubbish?'

'Who are you?'

Kesh lunged forward, but before she could grab his throat the old man had caught her arm in an immovable grip. She swung around to try and batter him away, but his arm was as hard as oak when she slammed her fist down onto it. Kesh gasped in pain as she flailed and tried to haul her arm free, but it did no good. After a few moments more she stopped and sagged, drained by her efforts throughout this long day.

Enchei didn't release her straight away, but used his hold to turn her around so he could look Kesh in the eye.

'Believe it or not, it's true.'

'How in hell's crater do you know that?'

He paused. 'You a pious girl?'

'What? What's that got to do with anything?'

Enchei shrugged. 'I've learned a lot over the years, picked up some tricks some priests might disapprove of.'

'The Gods weren't what kept me alive today,' Kesh said angrily, jerking her arm out of his hand as Enchei relaxed his grip. 'It was a pack of bloody demons that saved me, so I just got a lot less pious.'

He cocked his head at that, looking curious. 'Sounds like a tale worth hearing. In the meantime though, you'd probably call it heathen magic. I can't look into his mind or anything, but there are spirits in this world that can brush the surface at least – tell me if anything's happened to him. This man's been poisoned, I can tell that much, and it's torn up his memory something proper.'

'Poisoned?' Kesh said hollowly, recalling what she'd overheard at the free hospital. 'A poison that took his mind – is it called Moon's Artifice?'

Enchei frowned. 'Sounds like you know more than me. I've never heard that name before, what is it?'

'It's what he,' Kesh snapped, pointing at Irato, 'had in his bloody sea-chest – it leaked out and poisoned my sister. His friends murdered her when I took her to the goshe hospital. They said her mind was gone and they should just kill her.'

'Sister?' Irato echoed in dismay. 'Friends of mine?'

She saw now he was exhausted and dazed, uncoordinated as though drunk and feeling the weight of her glare like the heat of a fire. Kesh edged closer towards him, glad she had him off-balance and determined to exploit it.

'Recognise the name Perel? Father Jehq?'

He shook his head miserably, pressing the fingers of his free hand against his temple so hard the skin around them went white. 'I can't remember anything – the more I try, the more it hurts.'

'You think I care how much it hurts?' Kesh demanded, 'I'd gladly cut the answers out of you if I could!'

His hand dropped back down to his lap. 'Right now I'd let you,' he said, 'if I thought it'd do any good. I don't know what else to say. I just don't remember, I'm sorry.'

'Sorry?'

She lunged forward again, caught this time rather more gently by Enchei who wrapped his arm around her waist and patiently held on until she stopped straining against him.

'You think sorry's good enough? My sister's dead, your friends sent assassins to kill my mother – I didn't dare go there myself in case they saw me. I had to send someone else to warn my own damn mother that she had to flee for her life! But you're sorry?'

Kesh sank down to her knees, supported only by Enchei as the strength suddenly drained from her limbs.

'Right, enough of all that,' Enchei said briskly, lifting her up and manoeuvring her into the seat he'd been occupying. 'You're as exhausted as he is, famished too I'm guessing. Revenge doesn't come on an empty stomach, I've found; you need your strength for it. Sit here a moment and I'll fetch you something, okay?'

Kesh managed a nod as she slumped in the chair, eyes still on Irato but too tired to feel much of her earlier hate. When Enchei returned with a wooden bowl overflowing with stew she wasted no time in filling her belly.

As Kesh ate, Sheti took the other seat and Enchei pulled a stool from under the table, positioning it in the middle of the room so he could watch both the closed door and her.

'So Moon's Artifice is a poison, eh?' he commented while Kesh was draining the last of the stew.

She nodded, too busy to reply.

'And most likely Irato here was carrying some – would explain all the glass Narin found in the street, then.'

'What street?' Kesh asked.

'Somewhere in the Dragon District, he heard a noise and thought

Irato was attacking him. Turns out he'd fallen off a roof while fleeing something.'

'Fleeing what?'

Enchei snorted. 'Mebbe a God if you believe they're easy to run from; more likely one o' your demons I'd guess.'

'More than one,' Kesh corrected after a moment's pause. 'The man they sent after me – the bodyguard of Father Jehq – he killed several foxes with ease. He wouldn't be running from just one.'

Enchei inclined his head to acknowledge her point. 'The question is – what would matter so greatly to a tribe of demons that they're willing to lose so many vessels in the pursuit of it?'

'Vessels?'

Enchei nodded. 'Those foxes aren't the demons; it's what's inhabiting their minds. The demon's harder to kill than just cutting the head off a fox, but it doesn't mean they'll waste the bodies without good reason.'

'Enchei, how is it you know all this about demons?' Sheti interjected.

He grinned. 'People round here would think the place I grew up was pretty backward. We had temples to the Gods, but it was remote – where the mountain line met the shore. Places like that, you'll get demons and spirits o' all kinds. Without shamans they'll circle your village like hungry wolves around a herd of deer. In a city they're much rarer and they keep clear mostly, but they've no fear out in the dark wilds.'

'You're a shaman?' Kesh asked in disbelief.

'I was a hunter, then an army scout,' Enchei countered, 'but I got the sight sure enough. I can read the spirits and hear the demon-voices on the wind. Blasphemy or heresy don't mean much when some spirit's got a mind to feed on your soul or creep into your mind.'

'What's all this got to do with me?' Irato broke in, still sounding weak. 'A demon did this to me? A God? Why would I be carrying a poison that could destroy my memory?'

'I'm guessing that's not what it's for,' Enchei said, 'doesn't sound a whole lot of use for that, not without raising suspicions. If it was just one dose you kept to shut folk up, witnesses or whatever, I could see it, but enough to poison a little girl with what you left at home too? It leaked out of his sea-chest, you said?'

Kesh nodded. 'There was a lot I think, Emari fell while trying to take the chest downstairs, I heard the broken glass inside it. There must have been enough inside it for dozens of people to be dosed.'

Footsteps came from the walkway outside. Before anyone else could move, Enchei had casually risen and slipped his fingers around the grip of a large kitchen knife left out on the table. 'Narin?' he called.

'It's me,' the Investigator confirmed, ducking briefly at the open window to glance in before he reached the door beside it and came in. 'All good here?'

'Just getting acquainted,' Enchei said with a small smile. 'You?'

Narin glanced guiltily back towards the closed gate of the compound. 'I've no idea. Think I've just been threatened, but with the upper classes who can bloody tell?'

'Ready for some good news then?'

Narin looked surprised at that but he nodded readily enough, closing the door behind him and propping his stave against the wall as he surveyed the faces in the room. 'Been ready for days now,' he muttered.

'Mistress Kesh there might have found your moon, of a fashion anyway,' Enchei said cryptically. 'If you're still interested?'

'What? You didn't mention that at the Palace of Law,' Narin said, rounding on Kesh.

'I only just remembered, it's what they called the poison that took Emari's mind – Moon's Artifice,' she said hotly, staring him down until Narin remembered himself and backed off a shade. 'Maybe his mind too, if you believe your friend here.'

'Gods! Yes, you're awake!' Narin exclaimed, clearly distracted enough that he'd not even had time for his thoughts to catch up with events. 'Wait, what about your mind?'

'He can't remember anything,' Enchei supplied. 'Not his name, where he came from, what he was doing out on that street or who his friends are.'

Narin hesitated, staring at Irato as though a hard look would change matters. The muscular goshe matched his gaze but could say nothing further, pained helplessness on his face. 'Nothing?'

Irato shook his head.

'He's not lying, I'm sure,' Enchei added.

'So that's what Lord Shield meant,' Narin breathed after a long moment of thought.

'Shield?' Irato croaked. 'What's Lord Shield got to do with this?'

Narin glanced at Sheti and Enchei. 'You haven't told him?'

'I thought it best he hear everything from you,' Sheti said firmly, 'and now seems as good a time as any.'

The Investigator grimaced, as though the idea made him feel physically sick. 'Everything?' he echoed. 'Stars above, I don't even know where to begin.'

Curls of orange cloud flecked the western horizon of a darkening, striated sky. The Gods shone bright in the evening light – the Order of Knight slowly wheeling through its allotted month of dominion. Shield remained in ascendance and there were a few days more before star's turn, when Lady Pity would assume her place at the fore of the Order's nightly march across the sky. Behind the Gods only a handful of other stars were visible yet, the sky still not fully dark after sunset.

'You know,' Enchei said as he and Narin looked up at the night sky, 'when I first got here, the world seemed to make more sense.'

'Here?' Narin looked around. The compound was peaceful and still, but the city beyond, with its markets and gambling dens, was often chaotic and incomprehensible to most. 'How's that then?'

Enchei pointed up to the stars. 'It's Shield's Ascendancy across the Empire, everyone knows that and everyone lives by it. But you try living somewhere distant. You live by the Imperial calendar and you know the date, but it doesn't look right from where you are in the world. Shield doesn't look ascendant when you're in some far corner of the Empire, Pity does.' The grey-haired man shrugged. 'Just saying; the known world turns around this city. You look inward from the edges, things looks different.'

Narin shook his head. 'Not much makes sense to me right now.'

Enchei offered over his pipe and Narin took it, drawing in a long breath of the silky-smooth smoke.

'Even without this damn goshe and a dead little girl, I'm lost at the moment.'

Enchei gave a fatalistic shrug. 'How about this Prince Sorote of yours? Ever heard the name before? The Office of the Catacombs means nothing to me.'

Narin shook his head. 'But there are dozens of small fiefdoms surrounding the Imperial court, some ancient or extinct, others just names for some minor royal trying to carve themselves a little piece of power around the court. With the Houses always ready to go to war with each other, someone needs to broker between them I suppose, but what one wants with me I've no idea – except he was asking about Rhe.'

'Makes sense. Lawbringer Rhe's star is burning bright. He's already a presence in the Forum, so how long before he's on the Vanguard Council itself?'

'What's that got to do with me?'

'Rhe's got a reputation – one that doesn't sound like he's willing to help the politicking and quiet deals that run this Empire. But if you're right there at his side and this man's got dirt on you, you're valuable and vulnerable in equal measures.'

'I'm a bloody Investigator!' Narin protested. 'What use could I be to him?'

Enchei held up a finger to correct him. 'Currently,' he said, 'currently an Investigator – but not forever. Prince Sorote's investing in the future, to my mind, wants to get his hooks in nice and deep in case you ever become useful.'

'So why mess around? He could have come out and given me a choice – not as if there was much I could do about it. The rumour alone would be enough for Vanden to have me killed.'

The older man took his pipe back and puffed appreciatively on it as he idly looked around the still rooftops and nearby streets, watching for any sign of trouble. 'You've got a future ahead of you,' he said eventually. 'It's a way off but some men think decades in advance. He might not think he's the only one.'

'What do you mean?'

Enchei grinned. 'Seven men dead, a lord saved and you helped into a position many Investigators would cheerfully kill for. You're a lucky boy there, some might wonder if it's more than luck. If Prince Sorote wants you as a plaything, he's got to be careful you aren't already someone's toy.'

Narin stared blankly for a moment before realisation began to creep over him like a cloud's shadow. 'He's looking to see if I'm a plant, if the whole thing was engineered to win Lord Vanden's trust.'

'I would be, if I hadn't seen your prowess first hand,' Enchei said with a smile.

'And if it was all a set-up, there's someone powerful behind it, Astaren even.'

'Aye; Imperial caste power-broker or not, Prince Sorote won't want to get his fingers burned. He comes to say hello and make a few allusions, but not actually threaten you ... . well, if you belong to someone, you mention it and he gets a whisper in the ear to back off. Royal family don't tend to get killed so easily after all, not without a fuss, and anyone running your operation won't want to draw attention to their games.'

'Bloody madness,' Narin sighed. 'And yet I'm left wishing I did have a handler to make him go away.' He paused and cocked his head at Enchei. 'Fancy playing the role to get him off my back?'

'Could be a good thing, in the end,' Enchei said, pointedly ignoring the question. 'People who do stupid things like falling in love with a married woman above their station go one of two ways. Either they die pretty damn quick or they know someone who can help them fix it. Until this afternoon, you only had one of those options to hand.'

Narin gave a start. 'What? Submit to him? Become his pawn for whatever game he's playing? I have the oaths to uphold! I can't just betray the Lawbringers like that!'

'Oaths are fine when it's just your life on the line,' Enchei said with a sour expression, as though the words tasted unpleasant to speak. 'Put someone you care about in the mix, it gets tricky. Mebbe wait until you find out what he wants, and what he can do for you, before you make any decisions.'

Narin opened his mouth to argue then seemed to think better of it. He looked away, his shoulders slumped. 'Fine,' he muttered. 'Since you've got all the answers tonight, what about these burned bodies we've found in the streets?'

Enchei frowned. 'Easier than carrying your dead home, mebbe?'

'Eh? But why do it at all?'

'Didn't you hear Kesh's story? That goshe had lightning at his finger-tips – was strong enough to jump to roof-height from a standing start.'

Enchei nodded towards the closed door, behind which Irato slept. Beyond it, in Narin's bedroom, Sheti had gone with Kesh to help wash the rest of the blood and dirt off before changing into something clean for the night.

'Your man in there – don't know if he knows it or not, but he's the same. He's been altered I reckon; some mage has made a weapon of him.'

'So they don't want to reveal their weapons?'

Enchei shook his head. 'They don't want to reveal they've got weapons. Tell me, what'd happen if the goshe started producing guns and any Astaren found out?'

'They'd be slaughtered,' Narin said slowly, 'in the night, with no warning. That's the law; no one would dare do such a thing.'

'Exactly. Since the Ebalee Trading Company got obliterated, no one'd be fool enough to think they could keep it hidden. But – what if they had mages doing something similar for an elite cadre? You can't leave your dead behind; absolutely *can't* if it means you might get the full force of the Empire's Astaren hunting you down. Gunpowder weapons are the one piece of Imperial law no Great House would compromise or hold back on. Imagine what they'd do if you threatened the power of their Astaren.'

'So they burn their dead – even if the Great Houses do investigate, there's not enough left to point whatever suspicions they might have at the goshe. Could easily be Astaren doing the same thing. No one wants to leave their secrets for the enemy to find.'

Narin looked around. Suddenly he felt very exposed out there under the stars. That it was Lord Shield looking down on them wasn't enough comfort. The Gods had greater things to occupy their time than watch mortals for every moment, even mortals they'd taken an interest in.

'What you're saying,' he began slowly, 'is that they're not going to stop – that there's nothing they won't do to hide their secrets?'

'Aye,' Enchei nodded. 'There's too much at stake. Good thing you weren't followed home eh?'

Narin turned to Enchei, hoping to see a reassuring grin on the man's face, but the eccentric foreigner looked deadly serious now – a sight that chilled Narin more than the cool night air.

'You think we were?'

Enchei made a non-committal noise. 'Don't know, but I bet they're working hard to find out one way or another.'

'And that doesn't worry you?' Narin snapped, trying hard not to shout.

The older man shrugged. 'Ain't trying to kill me.'

'You think they'll leave witnesses?'

Enchei grinned. 'Everyone underestimates a man o' my age. They'll be more worried about you and Irato.'

'Why don't I find that encouraging?' Narin wondered grimly.

''Cos you ain't a fool.' Enchei knocked out his pipe on the wooden rail they had been leaning on before turning to the door. 'Come on. If they do come it won't be until the whole city's gone to sleep. There'll be another heavy fog tonight I reckon, perfect for nasty little deeds. Gives us some time to choose our ground a bit.'

'It does?'

'Aye, you've had a few good ideas about making these rooms more secure, just in case,' Enchei said. 'What with you being the one in charge and all. You've just told me what to do and here I am following orders.'

Narin looked around one final time and shivered. He was all too keen to follow as Enchei pulled open the door and headed inside, the quiet cold of the night suddenly too much to bear.

As darkness descended, the lights of the Gods dulled. Faint dabs of white in the sky, they illuminated a ghostly blanket of fog that rose up from the waters of the Crescent and spilled across the city. With her Starsight, Synter watched the fog's gradual creep through the city's streets. Looming through it all was the Imperial Palace, its white walls picked out by the blackened iron gas lamps that burned on only the grandest buildings.

To her twice-blessed eyes, the city was at its most beautiful at night – a monochrome etching of heart-stopping intricacy. It had always been a pleasure for her to haunt these streets at night, untouched by the cold and embraced by the myriad shadows.

She turned her head slowly, wary of attracting the attention of any demons that hunted them. Perel had killed several of the foxes before his arrogance got him killed – they would be keen for revenge, but weakened by the losses. Foxes were the best hosts, their preferred minds, but cats and rats would also serve when times became desperate – and they were indeed growing so.

They're feeling the loss of their lodestone, Synter remembered, *and it festers like a wound in their heart.*

The demons' nightmarish soldiers would be scuttling through the empty streets of the Thumb, Synter guessed; desperately hunting for the scent of a blessed goshe or the girl who'd escaped Perel. They'd not pick up Synter's trail, she'd made sure of that, but they were enough of a danger for her to remain vigilant.

Few people would venture out now the fog had come – their super-stitions were justified by the array of horrors she'd encountered over her years, but in turn the demons had long since learned to fear the light in its various forms. A prickle ran down her neck as she saw a shape moving stealthily in the dark, then a second in parallel. Crossbow in hand, Synter watched the advancing goshe agents for anything following them.

Even to her eyes it was difficult to make out the net of killers slowly closing around the quiet Imperial compound. Two full teams; all slaved to the mind of a leader and chosen to be expendable. Some Investigator and a young woman, whether or not she could handle herself, should prove little trouble for the dozen fighters, but they could take no further risks and it was best any losses did not prove disastrous. Eyes blessed with Starsight were the only advantage these goshe possessed, but it was one unlikely to be discovered on any corpse they left behind.

Even if the attack causes a scandal and the Lawbringers close down the hospitals and Shures, they'll find nothing.

A flicker of movement caught her eye and Synter pressed the butt of her crossbow into her shoulder as she tracked it down, but then realised it was just an errant scrap of cloth twitching in the breeze. She relaxed her arm and continued to scan the streets and rooftops.

Come out to play, little foxes, she called in the privacy of her mind. *Come and find out if I'm as easy to take as those fools, Irato and Perel. Come dance in the starlight.*

CHAPTER 9

One curiously persistent piece of folklore from Kettekast has, through Imperial trade and travel, spread to the far reaches of the Empire. The shadow-demons known as Detenii, whether real or not, now haunt the dreams of children from all parts with claims they creep into bedrooms at night to steal souls. Over the years these whispered tales have taken on a life of their own and many murders committed by thieves are blamed on these demons.

From *A History* by Ayel Sorote

Narin looked around the room, then back to the door he expected to burst open at any moment.

'This is the extent of your plan?' Kesh demanded at last. 'Sitting quiet as bloody mice so they don't notice us?'

He shook his head and opened his mouth to speak, but faltered after only a few words. 'We're not …' Narin sighed and his gaze dropped to the white shaft of his stave and the banded leather gauntlets that protected his hands. 'I hope no one's coming, I don't think they are.'

'But?'

He shrugged and looked at Enchei. 'Best we don't make assumptions.'

'And what about him?' Kesh continued, pointing at Irato. 'You so sure of his story you're happy for him to have a weapon? What if everything comes back to him when he sees his friends?'

Irato shook his head. With food in him and the chance to stand up straight, his strength had started to return. His mind might be shocked and dazed by it all, but his body was recovering the balance and purpose Narin would have expected from some sort of elite fighter.

'Nothing to come back,' the goshe said wearily. 'It's gone – not hidden behind some door in my mind.' He scowled and looked down. 'All I got left is the knowledge I got your sister killed. All I got's atoning for that. Maybe I'll figure something else out after this is over, but that's tomorrow's problem.'

Narin paused. In all honesty he didn't know for sure whether Irato was telling the truth. Despite Kesh's own account of the goshe doctors and Enchei's confidence, the Lawbringer at the back of his mind reminded him of the risk. Words could be misconstrued and the aging tattooist had a remarkably cavalier attitude to life.

No doubt I would too, Narin reflected, *if I was so hard to kill.* His thoughts were dragged back to that night when they'd saved Lord Vanden and all that followed. A knot of anxiety began to twist in his stomach but he fought it down, determined to focus on the problem at hand.

'Lord Shield didn't think he'd be getting answers once Irato woke. Might not be quite the same, but only a fool refuses to trust what evidence he has. Irato's going to be the least of our problems.'

Behind him lay the remains of a quick meal. None of them had felt much like eating, but Enchei had insisted and they'd all forced down the broth and noodles he'd provided. The room was illuminated by a pair of candles, their light flickering across the faces of the four of them. Sheti had returned to her room before they ate, ordered out to keep her safe, and a heavy chest pulled up behind the door after she'd gone.

The window's shutters were fastened shut, Irato's bed wedged up at an angle against them to stop anyone bursting through. The bedroom they'd left vulnerable, the window shutters slightly ajar and the room dark. Every piece of porcelain Narin owned was concealed beneath the window there and a tripwire fixed across the middle of the room, with another strung across the doorway. Narin had decided against letting the other Investigators in the compound know anything. Narin was a better fighter than his colleagues after two years of Rhe's training and he was unwilling to drag inexperienced Investigators into a fight with armed elites, quite aside from letting them see too much of Enchei's skills.

Arrayed at their feet were a variety of weapons, mostly those Irato had been carrying. The injured goshe had, with some assistance, pulled on his boots and now sat in a chair facing the barricaded window. A long-knife rested on his thighs; his hand seemed to know it and slip comfortably around its grip, though the ease of that seemed a surprise to Irato.

He was still in poor shape physically; weak after days without food, deep bruises and lingering pain in his bones. It was clear to see that the man he'd previously been was no stranger to hurt, however. Just the prospect of violence had sparked a wakening inside the goshe – his limbs understanding it even if his mind was still reeling.

Irato had been quiet since they returned, apparently cowed by Kesh's presence as much as he was struggling to accept the gaping hole in his mind. Narin suspected Father Jehq's assertion that Emari's memory was gone for good had actually helped on that path. Any sort of explanation, any point to start at, was perhaps better than none. The scars on his body showed he had not been a pampered man and Narin could only wonder what hard truths would be beyond him to accept.

What Narin hadn't expected was Irato's meek response to Kesh's anger. None of them had – even the big goshe seemed startled by it. It didn't seem likely guilt had played much part in Irato's life, but it seemed genuine enough when displayed on his face that afternoon. Narin looked at Enchei and couldn't help wonder how a soldier buried the guilt and horror of battle – whether a conscience was something that could scab over and scar as the years went by. Without his experience, was Irato's conscience or soul as exposed as a child's again?

We're both adrift, Narin realised as he watched the man. *Life's suddenly not making as much sense as it should. His path might be the longer, but we're both struggling to even find the right direction to take.*

As much as he tried, Narin couldn't banish his fears for Kine from his mind. Time and again he found himself staring at an enamel brooch placed unobtrusively beside the window. It was a simple design, a yellow humming-bird on a pale blue background, not even Wyvern in origin, but for that very reason Kine had given it to him as a reminder of her. The more he stared at it, the more he almost felt the electric touch of her coffee-dark skin on his own, almost caught a faint trace of her sweet perfumed scent on a phantom breeze. He looked away, for the first time in his life desperate for a drink of something strong to try and drown out the questions in his head.

Opposite Irato sat Kesh, bolt upright and barely able to keep still as she stoked the fires of her hate. No doubt the balm-smeared burns on her forehead and hand helped there, despite her insistence they weren't troubling her. Of all of them, she seemed the most sure they would be attacked and the long hatchet that had been among Irato's

121

weapons never left her hand. The weapon had a slim, curved steel head, built to hook or chop with savage speed. Narin had never seen a weapon like it; it was a far cry from the cold elegance of a warrior's sword. The hatchet was all functional brutality, stained a dull black to avoid the moonlight, but far more suited than a sword to the confined space they had chosen.

By contrast to Kesh, Enchei appeared calm and serene with Irato's spare long-knife to complement his own slim blade. More strangely, he wore his long coat still and cut an odd figure on a stool in the centre of the room – coat swept back to be clear of his feet and knives loose in his fingers.

'Narin,' Enchei said softly, causing all three of his companions to jerk at the unexpected sound, 'how's that shoulder of yours?'

The Investigator blinked in surprise. 'Shoulder? Almost good as new, just a little stiff in the mornings.'

'Aye well, that happens to boys of your age,' Enchei smirked, 'best I give you the talk about girls soon eh? Anyways, glad the shoulder's better.'

As Narin frowned, Enchei raised his eyebrows and nodded towards the door, motioning for Narin to stay where he was. The Investigator turned, eyes widening for a moment before he remembered himself. He moved slowly and brought his stave around to the left-hand side of his body. The ceiling was not so high that he could swing it properly, but there was room for a diagonal strike at anyone coming through the door.

The two men had first met playing dachan, a game which employed carved sticks four feet long that resembled very slim paddles. It was no coincidence that the strokes used resembled sword-blows, nor that the sport had appeared in the wake of the House of the Sun's warrior caste being outlawed by the victorious rebel Great Houses. The game had piled on strength to Narin's years of stave training and in his hands the tapered edge of the traditional Investigator's weapon would shatter bone with ease.

Enchei rose and faced the door to Narin's bedroom, one foot on the cross-piece of his stool to kick it back and out of his way. He gave a barely-perceptible nod just as Narin heard a small sound from the room beyond that door, the muffled crunch of some clay cup breaking. In his peripheral vision Narin saw Kesh edge forward and Irato push up from his chair, pain briefly showing on his face.

122

Without further warning the bedroom door crashed open, only to wedge hard against a knife Enchei had driven into the floorboards. A man in grey barrelled through, collided with the immobile door and lurched sideways just as a second bang echoed through the small room. The chest that had been pushed up against the outer door rocked back, jolted far enough by the impact that a second blow slid it half-over a second dagger Enchei had set there.

Narin tensed, ready to strike at the first person to force their way through as the tattooist threw himself into the grey-clad intruder. Enchei slapped away the goshe's short-sword and slammed his dagger into the man's ribs hard enough to knock him over. Blood sprayed up as Enchei jerked the weapon out and slashed left with his longer blade. Pinning a second attacker's weapon against the door Enchei cut at his face then kicked him in the midriff with shocking speed.

Narin never saw the second man fall, his view obscured as one made it through the main door. He smashed down at his first glimpse, moving so fast they were barely out from behind the door when the stave struck. The black-masked figure wore no armour and Narin felt the arm snap on impact. The goshe stumbled sideways, almost dropping the mace he carried as he fell back against the stove. Another took his place and Narin struck again, forcing that one back into those behind while the first yelled something unintelligible.

Suddenly a flash of light burst around the mace head and Narin realised it wasn't a weapon at all but some sort of lamp. The second masked face lunged forward again, long-knives thrust out towards Narin, but the Investigator had the longer reach and drove forward faster than the other could counter. The wooden staff's snub tip crunched into the goshe's face before his blades could deflect it, knives sliding uselessly down the haft as Narin connected and the goshe's nose shattered.

The man with the mace made no effort to attack – on the contrary he hung back, injured arm hanging useless at his side while another two goshe charged in and Narin was forced to retreat. To his left, Enchei still held the bedroom door – blades flashing through the dull candlelight with unnatural speed. Another man moved in to match him and the pair traded blows, three quick clashes of steel that looked like a stage-fight. From nowhere the goshe's throat burst open, white skin and shocking red blood tearing open through the black cloth without Narin seeing the lethal blow fall.

He called a warning as one man swung down at Enchei's back, but the tattooist turned as the sound left Narin's mouth. Long-knife raised, he caught a high blow then twisted back around to ward off another from the still-dark bedroom doorway. Somehow he caught both, although Narin could only prod forward with his stave to keep his own attacker back.

A second burst of light came from the mace-like lamp, leaving purple traces across Narin's vision as he lunged again to create an opening for Kesh. The nimble woman had dodged around him and she buried the hatchet's head into the goshe's wrist as Narin's blow was deflected. Without pause Kesh drove her knife into the man's neck and he fell with a cut-off shriek.

Narin glanced over to see Enchei run one man through while taking a slash on his forearm at the same time. Then the strange purple light pulsed once more – and the next moment everything went pitch-black.

Irato blinked as darkness filled his eyes. He heard Narin cry out and reel from the shock of blindness, but then Irato opened his eyes again and found he could see. The room had become an etching in black and white; shadows and outlines unfolding before him while the candle's light remained an orb of white. Kesh and Narin both hurled themselves backwards, falling as they flailed blindly and tripped. Enchei continued to fight, unaffected by the tidal-wave of night that had swamped the room. The tattooist hurled his long-knife towards the main door, looking like he'd discarded it until another goshe fell with the blade buried to the hilt in his throat.

Enchei retreated into the centre of the room, his own knife held ready as the next came for him. Somehow he seemed to slip inside the goshe's guard – twitching away the man's blades with his own and a casual slap of the palm. He punched the man left-handed in the ribs and Irato heard agony in the man's cry. In the next moment Enchei had stabbed him in the neck and dragged the body around to use as a shield.

White-outlined droplets of blood arced around Irato's vision and at last his sluggish mind seemed to snap back into movement. He saw the nearest goshe advance on Narin, looking to finish the stricken Investigator off. Irato lurched forward and the goshe flinched, stopping dead as he realised Irato wasn't blinded like the rest.

'You?' the goshe called out, astonished enough to drop his guard.

Irato faced him, almost close enough to touch. The recognition was clear despite the goshe's mask, but to Irato it meant nothing. All he felt was a cold sensation, like ice water slipping down his gullet. The pain receded, his injured limbs and aching head faded from his awareness as he faced a man he'd perhaps once known.

'Irat—' the goshe said, but got no further.

Irato looked down and saw he'd thrust forward with his long-knife. He blinked at the weapon, the savage movement seemingly ingrained and entirely natural to his body. He jerked the weapon clear and the goshe fell with a sigh of air expelled from his punctured sternum.

'Irato?'

He looked up. The man with the strange pulsing device was staring straight at him, but Irato was more interested in what he held in his remaining hand. Whatever it was, it had apparently drained the light from the room and blinded Narin and Kesh. He'd almost felt the change in his eyes as the sceptre had activated; every corner, fold and seam picked out in the perfect black and white of some arcane night sight. Part of him wanted to marvel at the beauty of it, to wonder at this next mystery of his life, but a deeper instinct took over.

Against the shades of greys and star-lit edges of everything in the room, the head of the object was a black hole in the world. No texture or depth, he could see nothing except an empty space on the end of a length of wood carved with some sort of swirling script or decoration. To look at its head made his eyes swim and ache, but a hungry fascination had taken hold of him and Irato found he couldn't tear his eyes away.

I'm one of them. I see as they do – I really am a killer.

'Traitor!' the man barked and Irato could hear his sudden fury over the clatter of Enchei's continued struggle.

Irato looked down at the knife in his hand as Enchei grappled with another goshe, turning in a circle as though performing a frenetic dance before his partner crumpled and another took his place. He had the knife back behind his head before he'd even thought about what to do next.

I'm a killer, he thought distantly, the rush and chaos of the fight pushing the horror of that realisation to the far recesses of his mind. *I was just like them, a murderer in the night.*

He threw the knife with a strength he didn't know he had and it thudded into the goshe's throat before the man could react.

But even a killer can choose, Irato thought as the goshe slumped back against the far wall.

For a moment the goshe was propped up, then his knees folded and he sank, sceptre slipping from his fingers. It fell awkwardly; the butt thumped against the floor and tipped to one side, the head falling with the crack of breaking glass. In an instant the darkness was gone, sucked back into the night as though the Gods themselves had wrenched the veil away.

There was a strange still moment as the remaining goshe hesitated. Enchei didn't. He whirled with his knife leading the way and took down the two inside the door, then stood stock still in the centre of the room as those remaining outside fled. With blood spattered down him and ragged tears in his sleeves where blades had sliced through the leather, Enchei finally relaxed and let his weapon lower as the sound of running feet clattered away outside.

Blood pattered from the blade to the floor as two still-living goshe squirmed and wheezed at Enchei's feet. He assessed them with a glance and crouched beside one, pushing back the man's cloth mask for a moment to inspect the injury underneath. After a moment he shook his head and, with a perfunctory motion, opened the man's throat the rest of the way.

He looked up as Narin and Kesh drunkenly got to their feet. The pair were still disorientated by the unnatural darkness that had enveloped the room, but Enchei ignored them as he cleaned his blade. Irato looked at the scene of carnage that now surrounded them. In a matter of seconds it had become a slaughterhouse. He did a quick count and saw eight dead, maybe more hidden by the open doors.

So I'm not the only one with secrets, Irato thought as Enchei sheathed his knife and picked up the strange sceptre.

'Well,' Enchei declared, a fierce grin on his face as he sucked in air to catch his breath, 'that was interesting, wasn't it?'

'Interesting?' Narin said in a choked voice, staring at the blood on the end of his stave. 'That's what you'd call it?'

Enchei shrugged and turned the sceptre over in his hands. Irato heard the chink of glass within the dull iron-like orb on the end and a few pieces dropped onto the floorboards at Enchei's feet.

'Different, then,' Enchei countered. 'We certainly learned a thing or two.'

'Stars above!' Kesh exclaimed. 'You sound like Jester's very own.'

126

Enchei gave a dismissive shrug. Once adviser to the first Emperor, Lady Jester had been a master politician renowned for her callous and dispassionate advice. The expression was used as a rebuke, but clearly Enchei didn't object to the comparison.

Irato saw Kesh's hands were shaking, Narin's too. The Investigator in particular had paled, as though most likely he'd not killed anyone before. It was probably the most violence Narin had ever witnessed and all the more shocking for the speed of it.

Irato looked down at his own hands, one still in a sling and the other empty after he'd killed a man from across the room. The rough, broad palms and blunt fingers seemed perfectly still.

I really am a killer – but I can't even bring myself to care about that.

The weight on his mind returned and Irato awkwardly eased himself back down into a chair as the first shouts of alarm echoed up from the courtyard below.

What sort of man was I? Do I even want to know?

Narin emerged onto the walkway and looked around the courtyard. Lamps shone from the windows that opened onto it and someone had lit the large iron lanterns on the courtyard wall. He'd had to pick his way over the smears of blood that now stained the wood underfoot, each one of the dead goshe having been dragged out into the courtyard. On the roof were Investigators with crossbows, watching for more goshe, and a half-dozen more stood at the gate keeping the curious faces of locals away. The men and women at the gate carried halberds – none looking comfortable with weapons they rarely trained with, but the threat was enough for the moment.

White figures stood over the bodies of the goshe; Lawbringers of various ages with Rhe and a bald, grey-bearded man at their centre. The two were talking quietly, Rhe pointing at something on one of the bodies. When the other man glanced up towards Narin, he realised with a jolt that it was Law Master Sheven – a member of the Lawbringer's Vanguard Council.

The Law Master motioned for Narin to join them and he felt a sinking feeling. Casting around for an excuse to put off the inevitable questioning, Narin alighted upon the blood staining his sleeve. It hadn't been there after the fight, but Enchei had shown no interest in being the hero of this savage little event and again staged matters to cast Narin as the lead.

He gestured to the stained jacket and Sheven nodded, dismissing him with a curt hand motion. Relieved, Narin escaped inside – back to the relative safety of his bloodied and wrecked rooms, where Irato and Kesh had been ordered to remain.

'They want to question me,' he hissed to Enchei.

The tattooist was sat at the table, ignoring the mess as he calmly stitched one of the gashes in his coat's sleeve. Enchei's knuckles were scraped raw with a neat cut between the middle and index, but he still worked the fat needle comfortably enough. Through the damaged leather Narin could see the dull gleam of steel, metal plates sewn into the material to serve as armour.

'Of course they do,' Enchei said, not looking up. 'You just fought off two teams of goshe, no surprise they've got questions.'

'So I just pretend, yet again?' Narin slammed his palm down on the table to demand Enchei's attention. 'I can't keep doing this! You can't keep asking me to lie to my superiors!'

'Why not?' Enchei said in a mild voice. 'Where's the harm?'

'Where's the harm?' Narin gasped, 'I'm pretending to be a hero! That first time I explained it as luck – we took them by surprise and got lucky, but Rhe's been training me hard this past year. He knows exactly how well I can fight and he knows damn well I'm not this good.'

He looked back to where Kesh and Irato both watched them. The young woman had calmed after the fight, had recovered from the shock better than he had, if Narin was honest, and Irato seemed unaffected by the violence. Neither was looking forward to the interrogation they'd be getting, however.

'First things first,' Enchei said. 'Practice is different to a fight to the death and Rhe knows that too. Secondly, you didn't do it alone. We all four of us took them down one by one – working together and restricting how many got in the room at any one time. That's plausible enough; you're an Investigator, I've had a term in the army and so has Irato, according to his tattoos. They weren't attacking novices here.'

'And it's better than the alternative,' Kesh said, joining them at the table. 'Which is?'

She gave him a look as though he was simple. 'Them killing us all. I'm happy with a bit of lying compared to that.'

'I still have to explain it, though,' Narin insisted. 'That's not an easy thing when they're trained to catch out liars.'

'So deal with it,' Kesh said with a fierce look. 'You want to swap problems with me, fucking help yourself and I'll tell the old men what they're expecting to hear.'

Narin didn't reply as her eyes glistened with tears. Kesh refused to submit to them but he could see the fight in her face, and it wasn't one she was willing to lose.

'I'm sorry, I didn't mean to ...'

'I know,' she said in a small voice, 'I wasn't blaming you, but please – I'm exhausted. I need to sleep; I need to see the morning and my mother safe. I can't mourn Emari here, like this. I can barely stay on my feet.'

He ducked his head in acknowledgement. 'You're right. Enchei, you sure we'll be safe here?'

The tattooist glanced towards the bedroom where he'd secreted a few choice items from the goshe before the first Investigator had a chance to search the bodies. There wasn't much, but the strange sceptre and a bag of some unknown powder he'd pronounced worth hiding were now safe inside a drawer. Safer for all involved if there was no word of dangerous magics that might reach Astaren ears, and a pinch of the powder burned in a pan had showed it wasn't mere illegal gunpowder the goshe carried.

'Sure? No, but compared to you walking the streets to get back to the Palace of Law, I'd risk it. They won't try again – they don't have the capabilities to attack us here. Well, maybe they do, but I doubt there's many like Irato and our friend Perel. This lot certainly weren't. For all that they recognised Irato, they didn't fight like elites with sorcery at their fingertips.'

'They wanted to do it quietly and had the fire-powder to hide any evidence,' Kesh said with a nod. 'They're still scared of attracting the wrong attention.'

'As are we,' Enchei said, staring meaningfully at Narin. 'More'n a few of us have secrets to keep hidden, so go and tell some pretty lies, Narin.'

'I, ah, dammit. You'll be the death of me yet, old man. Okay, I'll go, I just need to change my jacket first,' he muttered.

Narin went into his bedroom and looked around at the broken remnants of pots on the floor, shutting the door behind him out of instinct. After the evening they'd shared, he felt ridiculous wanting privacy as he changed clothes, but it had been half a decade since he'd last shared quarters with anyone.

He was a man of few possessions and the room, though modest in size, was all the more empty without a bed. The shutters had been boarded up, despite the fact he knew there were guards in the street beyond, but there were still broken fragments of porcelain scattered across the floor. Looking around him he felt the sudden warmth of relief that he hadn't died leaving such a small impact on the world.

The sum total of my possessions, he thought sadly, *a handful of broken cups and a few stained jackets. The one good thing in my life is a child I can tell no one about.*

Orphaned towards the end of his childhood, Narin had been an outsider among the novices when he'd entered their dormitories – caught at an age between foundlings and those high-castes who'd chosen the calling as they came of age. Being half a step out of place was an old and familiar coat for him, the fact that he might die unremembered by all a long-feared thought.

Unexpectedly, his strength seemed to abandon him and Narin sank to his knees. A sudden chill ran through his body and he wrapped his arms around his belly.

'Lord Shield,' he whispered, too quietly to be heard in the other room, 'do you know you've entrusted this to a fraud?'

Narin bowed his head, not praying exactly but for once hoping fervently the Gods were listening to him.

'I don't have the strength for this; I can't even fall in love without screwing it up. How am I supposed to claim I'm a hero now? How am I supposed to uphold the law and oaths when my whole life is a lie?'

He knelt there a dozen heartbeats or more before the mantle of despondency lifted slightly. Narin looked up at the faint trace of starlight creeping through the boards over the window. His thoughts went inexorably to Kine, the flash of white teeth when she smiled – as secret as the starlight through those boards, for Wyvern women would always hide a smile from their prideful menfolk.

We argued about it once, Narin recalled. *That first time I realised I loved her. She smiled and turned away, hid her mouth. I could hear her laugh and I wanted to see her smile. I took her hand to pull it away and in that first touch I knew.*

He looked around at the room again. Now it was just a room to him, familiar perhaps but it told nothing of who he was, of the life he led. The realisation gave him strength again – these meagre possessions couldn't sum up a life. Perhaps some lord or merchant prince could see their life in their estates and goods, but it was not the Lawbringer way.

I am my oaths and the love I bear, he declared in the privacy of his mind, *those I protect by my duty whether or not I ever know of them. No one can take that from me. If I could leave all this behind, have my memory cursed for the liar I am but run away with Kine, would I?* He nodded.

The merchant warrants across the sea, the trader towns and trade corridors where no Great House ruled – someone there would value his training and not care about scandal. There he could still serve the Emperor's law and build a life of his own.

'But until then,' Narin declared, rising and swiftly removing his jacket as he went to retrieve a cleaner one, 'I have a duty still; to my friend, to Lord Shield – and to Kesh and a little girl who deserved better.'

CHAPTER 10

The Ten Day War saw House Dragon troops assault the Imperial Palace itself and ended when the Gods themselves incarnated to face the attackers down. Many have suggested they were unwilling to interfere at all, but were forced to by the ensuing chaos. Without the sanctification of the Imperial line, the Houses looked ready to fight to the death before permitting their rivals to take over. Given the weapons at their disposal, the possibility remains chilling.

From A History by Ayel Sorote

Narin hurried back outside and down into the courtyard. Half the Lawbringers had left, he discovered; most likely the older ones to their beds, the younger to command the guards on the gate. Rhe remained with Law Master Sheven, both men now holding lanterns from the courtyard wall.

'Investigator Narin, please join us,' the Law Master intoned in deep, sonorous voice. 'We were just admiring your work.'

He was a burly man with red-tinted skin and a gentle twinkle in his rusty-brown eyes. Like Rhe, he had elected to join the Lawbringers as a young man, but for Sheven it had been a case of being unsuited to life in the religious caste. Narin had only spoken to him once before, but with his unusual background, wrestler's build and warm sense of humour, Sheven was one of the better-known Law Masters. Stories of men such as him were told year after year to an awestruck audience in every novice dormitory.

'It wasn't my work alone, Law Master,' Narin said, glancing at Rhe's impassive face as he spoke. 'I would never have survived without help.'

'Impressive none the less,' Sheven said. 'Eight dead assassins surpasses your previous feat of arms.'

'That was luck alone,' Narin blurted out, 'Lawbringer Rhe knows my skill with a stave is unremarkable by his standards. I was lucky that other night, and tonight was more good planning than heroism.'

'You forced them to come one by one,' Rhe said levelly, 'that is good planning. Killing each one rather more so.'

'I did not kill them all, not even most,' he protested, feeling Rhe's cold aristocratic stare like ice on his skin. 'Enchei served a term in his army, the goshe prisoner too, and Kesh is no helpless girl.'

'That is where it gets interesting,' Sheven said with sudden intent. 'The prisoner fought at your side against his own? Forgive me if I'm wrong, but isn't that unusual?'

Narin ducked his head. 'He, ah, is not strictly a prisoner. He cannot remember what side he was on. The ... the circumstances in which I found him have affected his memory – it's unlikely he will ever remember the man he was before.'

'But still he fought and killed his own?' Before Narin could reply Sheven raised his hand and made a dismissive gesture. 'No. I don't want to know the details, explain no more.'

'You don't?'

The Law Master's face hardened. 'This was an attack on a Lawbringer compound – such a thing is unprecedented in itself, but Lawbringer Rhe has raised a worrying possibility.'

'I make no accusations, Law Master,' Rhe said in his usual stern manner. 'Nor could I accuse anyone at present – I wish to be clear on that.'

Narin looked from one man to the other in puzzlement. 'I'm sorry, sir, I don't understand.'

'Narin, how sure can you be that you weren't followed here? Given the story Mistress Kesh told us, how certain can you be?'

'I, ah,' Narin hesitated, noting the lack of detail in Rhe's words. 'Given what she said, I suppose I cannot be certain.'

'But if someone like the goshe who attacked her – Perel, I believe? What if one like him had seen where you'd gone?'

Narin shook his head. 'They'd have dealt with me easily enough,' he said, thinking it through. 'Kesh was attacked in broad daylight – the man had little fear of acting alone, but to attack a low-caste woman in a quiet street is one thing, assaulting a Lawbringer compound something different entirely.'

'Agreed,' Rhe conceded, 'but coming to your door would not be so great a risk when most here would be out working or asleep.'

'I still don't understand,' Narin said.

'An alternative remains,' Sheven interjected, lips pursed with distaste. 'As much as I hate to admit it, Lawbringer Rhe has made a sensible case. That you were followed is possible, but as I understand it this man Perel was a highly skilled veteran. Why then did they wait hours to attack and send younger goshe to finish the job?'

He pointed down to the bodies and Rhe crouched beside one to better show Narin what they meant.

'Gods above, I hadn't noticed that,' Narin breathed as Rhe removed the mask of the nearest. Pale in death and throat gaping with an angled cut that had severed the jugular, the goshe was less than twenty years old.

'Kesh described Perel as a seasoned fighter,' Narin muttered, a sickened feeling filling his gut as he realised quite how young the dead goshe was. 'Irato's certainly older than me. This one's little more than a child.'

He tilted his head to look at the tattoos on the youth's shoulder. It told him little. The man came from House Rain peasant stock, a major state within the domain of Moon, but aside from that he bore only the goshe's small glyph.

'They are all young,' Rhe said, 'bar one I'd expect to be the leader, who was still younger than you. All from House Moon's district – tattoos for Rain, Moon and Shadow.'

'So most likely not an elite team, just goshe who attend the same Shure sent on a mission?'

'The implications of that alone will cause chaos,' Sheven said. 'Evidence that the goshe send out their own as assassins; this is enough to warrant a full-scale investigation of their entire hierarchy. I must now speak to the Vanguard Council and ask them to decide how we approach the matter.'

'But right now we're more concerned with the other implication,' Rhe added. 'The question of how they found out where you lived – how they even knew to look for you.'

'You suspect our own?' Narin gasped and shook his head. 'Surely not?'

Rhe inclined his head. 'We must not ignore the possibility. You put the word out that matters involving the goshe should be referred to you, and Kesh's entrance to the Palace of Law was hardly clandestine. If the goshe have agents inside the Palace, they could pass your name without needing to do anything suspicious.'

'The idea is abhorrent,' Law Master Sheven declared, 'but we cannot be sure. Lawbringer Rhe asks that I order him to take charge of the investigation – given that you are at the heart of this, it is a natural choice. However, this investigation shall be closed by my name – the details kept secret even from our own and I will not ask Rhe to report until he is satisfied. No Lawbringer can order him to break a Law Master's order and we may be able to lure out the spy as a result.'

Sheven patted the hilt of his sword as he spoke, a large scimitar in the style of House Salamander, his homeland. Though his long beard and what hair remained on his head were both light grey, Sheven still looked a fearsome fighter to Narin's eyes.

Definitely not suited to his caste, Narin thought as he saw the flash in Sheven's eyes. *Let's hope he remembers we need answers before he kills anyone asking questions.*

'First of all,' Sheven continued, glancing at Rhe, 'I must speak to my peers. If we're to act against the goshe and investigate the hiring-out of assassins, it will need to happen quickly.' He inclined his head to both of them. 'Lawbringer, Investigator.'

Both Rhe and Narin bowed as the Law Master swept away, a pair of Investigators detaching themselves from the guards outside to follow in his wake.

Once Sheven had gone, Narin took the opportunity to properly look at the guards standing on the rooftops of the compound. In grey robes made pale by a haze of lamp-tinted fog, they looked like avatars of the Gods. Narin felt a prickle on his neck as he remembered Lord Shield's stern, unyielding presence and could well imagine them to be that God's emissaries.

No such luck, Narin thought with sour humour. *Even if his order counts as some holy charge, it was a bloody cryptic one. I'll be standing here a while before Shield sends his avatars to protect me.*

He looked up. The Order of Knight was half-obscured by cloud and only two of the six constellations that turned around Knight's own were visible. Lady Pity was gradually moving towards ascendancy, when she would lead the charge across the night sky for her allotted ten days – while Lord Lawbringer himself, his week of ascendancy over for another year, trailed well behind.

'If you've finished praying?'

Narin flinched and realised Lawbringer Rhe was staring at him. 'Eh? Praying?'

'You were staring at the Gods,' Rhe pointed out, 'so either you were praying or preparing yourself to tell me the truth. I am prepared to accept either.'

'The truth?' Narin spluttered, a cold feeling building in the pit of his stomach. 'What do you mean?'

Rhe didn't speak immediately, he simply stared directly at Narin with his usual dispassionate intensity. 'Do not take me for a fool, Narin,' he said quietly. 'As befits an Investigator perhaps, your skill at lying is poor.'

He raised a hand to cut Narin off as the Investigator opened his mouth to defend himself.

'Wait, do not speak. Untruths are part of our world – we hunt criminals after all – but tell me an outright lie now and I will think less of you. Please wait until I am finished.'

Narin hesitated then closed his mouth and nodded, brow furrowed in confusion.

'Thank you.' Rhe looked down at the bodies at their feet, each one with the sleeve of their right arm torn to reveal the tattoos on their shoulder. 'We have known each other for almost two years. I have observed and trained you to the best of my ability, I know you better than you perhaps realise. I have taken a number of details on trust – ones that I would consider outlandish coming from another person – but I know I am not being told everything.'

There was a long pause. Narin looked down at the bodies and shook his head. 'I don't know what to say.'

'Start by telling me this – are you, by whatever means or compulsion, in the service of another master?'

Narin's eyes widened, his thoughts immediately turning to his strange encounter with Prince Sorote. *Gods, how could he …? No, that's not what he's talking about – and anyway, he's asked me to do nothing as yet.*

'No, I'm not – why would you ask?'

'I have seen you fight and I have been in both formal duels and street-fights. If these truly are goshe-trained assassins you should not have survived and certainly your little group would have taken casualties. I cannot believe they would send out novices and all of these could have been attending a goshe Shure for five years or more.'

136

'I ... I cannot say,' Narin began. 'You know my skills better than anyone else – I know this just as I know I have a duty to you and the Lawbringers. But such secrets I have are not mine alone.'

Rhe gave a curt nod. Without warning, he started off towards the wooden stair that led towards Narin's rooms. The Investigator blinked in surprise, but had no choice other than follow Rhe up the steps to his front door. The Lawbringer entered without announcing himself and past his shoulder Narin saw a flicker of surprise cross Enchei's face as the tattooist glanced up from his repairs.

In one fluid movement Rhe drew his white stave and whipped it around at Enchei's face. The tattooist threw his head back and the weapon's snub tip flashed past his cheek, but Rhe wasn't satisfied and swung again.

Narin raced forward, but couldn't reach the Lawbringer in time. With no more space to retreat into, Enchei could only raise his arm to defend his face. A resounding crack echoed out around the room, a moment before Narin reached Rhe and shoved the man away.

'What in Jester's name are you doing?' he yelled at Rhe. 'Have you gone mad?'

Rhe lowered his stave and fixed Narin with his usual cold statue-stare. The sight was chilling, even to Narin, who'd seen it before – Rhe's ability to fight with shocking speed but return to emotionless and near-motionless in a heartbeat.

'I have not.' Rhe said as he turned toward Enchei. The aging tattooist cradled his forearm, grimacing. 'I wished to test a theory.'

'By breaking the man's arm?'

Rhe shook his head. Before Narin could say anything more the Lawbringer started abruptly forward, feinting to one side of Narin then buffeting past as Narin reacted to the movement. Off-balance, Narin couldn't stop the bigger man as Rhe drove past him and brought his stave down on Enchei a second time – striking at the very same spot, one that could kill a man unable to defend himself.

Again the tempered wood thwacked down into Enchei's forearm loud enough to make Narin flinch, but this time Rhe kept his arm outstretched and the weapon remained pressing down on Enchei's raised arm.

The two men matched gazes for a moment then Enchei twisted his hand around the stave and moved it away from his face. 'You've made your point,' he said sourly. 'That does still hurt.'

'What's going on?' Kesh demanded from behind Narin. He turned towards her, as bewildered as her for the time being, but they were both ignored by Rhe.

'Why are you still here?' Rhe demanded. Enchei frowned then released the stave and Rhe smoothly returned it to the loop behind his back. 'You should have left by now.'

'Would've looked suspicious if I'd run off,' Enchei said, returning to his sewing with one final rub on his forearm. Narin gaped – either one of those blows could have broken his arm.

'Last thing I needed was a reason to make a bunch of Lawbringers suspicious – or be chased through the streets by Investigators who've seen me go. We didn't get them all and the last one that runs, in my experience, is the bugger who gets shot.'

Rhe turned abruptly and sought out Irato. 'What about you? Are you … changed?'

Irato blinked back in confusion, but Enchei replied for him. 'Aye, he is – doesn't remember it, but he's no natural.'

'Am I going to have a covert war on my hands?'

'With the goshe?' Enchei sniffed. 'Not by my doing. I ain't here under orders.'

'What the fuck're you both on about?' Kesh snapped, almost shoving Narin out of the way as she stormed up to Lawbringer Rhe. 'Why did you hit him? I thought you had rules about attacking unarmed men?'

Rhe inclined his head. 'I doubt he can ever be considered unarmed,' he said by way of explanation, 'but you should have guessed the half of it already. You saw him fight, correct?'

Kesh hesitated. 'I did.'

'Then you must be able to draw some conclusions.'

'Mebbe,' Kesh said with more than a little reluctance. 'What's that got to do with anything?'

Rhe leaned forward, almost close enough to kiss her, and at last Kesh seemed to remember the man's reputation. She took an involuntary step back.

'It has everything to do with it. The Lawbringers are charged with upholding the Emperor's law. I have a crime to investigate – several, in fact, and the presence of Astaren affects everything. Witnesses are harder to interview when they've all been kidnapped and imprisoned in some secret dungeon, criminals harder to catch when they can walk through walls or erase a man's mind.'

At the mention of Astaren, Kesh paled. Whatever she'd guessed, Narin knew that voicing the word changed things. Even he, Enchei's friend and confidant, had felt a frisson at the very mention of the name: Astaren – the elite warrior-mages of the Great Houses.

Men and women who were living weapons, from whom even demons fled. The God-Emperor and God-Empress, the first of the Ascendants, had discovered secrets from a time before mankind and used them to conquer half the known world before ascending into the heavens. Thereafter the Imperial regent, brother of the first Emperor, had conquered every accessible part of the map in the name of his young nephew and imposed the strictures of his nation on his new empire, creating the system of Great Houses still in existence.

It was the Imperial Astaren that had carved the empire from hundreds of small nation states and five centuries ago it had been a new breed that broke the Emperor's power, while the attention of the Ascendant Gods slowly turned beyond mortal concerns. Only after the Emperor's own had been slaughtered did the Gods step in, realising at last the Great Houses were about to destroy one another in a struggle for power. And so the Emperor's position was retained – forever weakened, forever subordinate, but remaining an unbroken blood-line to the greatest of the Gods.

'You really are one of them?' Kesh asked quietly. 'Not a soldier at all?'

'The Ebalee Trading Company,' Rhe said suddenly. 'Did you ever do anything like that?'

His words cast a pall over the room. Even Narin, already used to the unspoken idea, felt a chill at the reminder. That was the flip-side of the Astaren. They were the destroyers – unmatched and unstoppable through the known world. When Great Houses went to war, the Astaren were sent in first. They hamstrung armies and burned crops, stirred up insurrection and inflicted terror with impunity. They were the preservers of the present, the immovable rock against which change broke.

'Well? Did you?' Kesh persisted.

'Don't be soft,' Enchei said. 'It was the Dragons who destroyed Ebalee, everyone knows that and they don't even bother to deny it.' He raised his pale hand. 'I look a Dragon to you?'

'But you'll have done something similar?' Kesh said. 'Astaren have slaughtered towns, murdered children – softened up entire nations for invasion. Folk say your magic's learned from demons and that's the price you pay for it.'

They all turned to Enchei but he said nothing until he had finished the last stitch of his coat and slipped his arms through the repaired sleeves. Once his coat was on Enchei sat back down and looked around at the four faces staring at him.

'What do you all want from me?' the greying man growled. 'You hear a word and you think you know what it means? Astaren's just a name for a dozen different types of magic. You reckon daft stories told round a fire's got bloody anything to do with the truth? Piss on the lot o' you. You know nothing.'

'Enlighten us,' Rhe said.

'Why? It's my business – my life. I learned long ago how to keep a secret.'

'You're a renegade, not under House orders?'

Enchei sighed and stood up to look Rhe in the eye. The Lawbringer was significantly taller than Enchei, broader too, but Narin realised size would mean nothing in a fight between the two. You didn't need to be the biggest when mage-priests had altered your body and taught you the secrets of their craft.

'There won't be anyone running in here after me, if that's what you mean.'

'And what happens if some spy tells his Astaren master?' Rhe asked. 'I doubt even Sight's End contains as many Astaren as the Imperial City. Even a Lawbringer must acknowledge the dominant power in this city is the House Dragon garrison. So why are you still here, playing your games with us mere mortals?'

'You know nothing,' Enchei replied, slowly and deliberately. 'And I've got just as much to lose as the lot of you – more so in fact.'

'Really? Because they're trying to kill me!' Kesh snapped as she moved around Rhe to face Enchei. 'They *have* killed my sister and they're trying to kill my mother, so what in Jester's name do you have to lose that I don't?'

'More,' Enchei said flatly. 'And that's all I'm saying. You want to know about Astaren – here's one piece for free. They don't brag, they don't exaggerate and they don't get into pissing contests. Those who do, don't live long.'

'And which sort live to go grey?' Rhe asked.

'The ones who're good at staying alive. Make no mistake though, I ain't afraid of dying. I've lived with a death sentence over my head for years now and when I go, none of you want to be nearby when I do. You want to see what a spiteful old shaman's got ready for anyone who kills him? Best you do so from a distance.'

'Yet you remained here,' Rhe mused, 'risking exposure when you could have disappeared into the night.'

Enchei shrugged. 'I said I wasn't afraid to die and I ain't – but I also like what life I do have and Narin's been a good friend over the last couple years. Most friends I ever had are dead; the rest'd likely kill me as soon as they set eyes on me. What span I've left, I don't intend to spend it always on the run while I leave friends behind to deal with whatever trouble they're in.

'The measure of a man's in the choices he makes, choices he's willing to live and die by. If the Dragons are taking an interest and my presence'll only add shit to the storm, I'm gone like a ghost on the wind. In the meantime this old man's still got a few tricks up his coat-sleeves, so how's about you stop worrying and never breathe a word of this to anyone, hey?'

Rhe didn't comment. Narin glanced at Kesh and Irato and saw neither had anything to add – not that the goshe seemed to have much to say in any situation. For a man Kesh had described as an arrogant thug when at her boarding house, he had proved almost meek since he'd woken. Whether or not his brains had been scrambled, Narin had at least expected to hear the man's voice more.

An effect of the poison? Narin wondered suddenly. *Seems a pretty drastic way of making a man docile, but there's something there all right. What about if it's given to babies or children rather than a grown man? Would it still make them more willing to obey orders? And who'd notice a personality change in a newborn? Seven hells, how long have they been doing this? The goshe order has been around since before I was born! Are they building an army right under the noses of the Great Houses?*

'Enough of this,' Narin blurted out, causing all eyes to be turned in his direction. 'We can worry about Enchei's past if we survive the next few days. There's something else I'm more interested in right now. Kesh, the poison was called Moon's Artifice, yes? At least two of the assassins out there, I saw their tattoos – they're House Rain and Irato's tattoos say House Shadow.'

141

'What? You think someone's engineering a coup?'

Narin turned abruptly. 'Irato, what do you think?'

'Me?' The injured goshe blinked up at him. 'I don't … How would I know? I can't remember anything. I …' He tailed off, looking anxiously between Kesh and Narin as though one of them could provide the answers.

'Kesh – does he act like the man you first met?' Narin asked.

She frowned at both of them. 'Not really, but if I got thrown off a building I might be subdued too.'

'True. Irato, get up.'

The goshe struggled to his feet, wincing with his free hand pressed against his ribs.

'Sit back down.'

Irato did so, puzzled at the orders but uncomplaining.

'Enchei – sit.'

'Fuck off.'

Narin smiled grimly at Kesh. 'Yours is more obedient than mine.'

'What are you saying?' Rhe interjected.

'That Irato's quiet and obedient – not what I'd expect from an arrogant assassin who's been made into a killing machine. So what if they're all like that, all happy to follow any order without question?'

'En masse they would be a disciplined, fearsome army. Do you believe that's what they're building?'

Narin nodded as Enchei joined in. 'And once they're fully under control, they're marking 'em with Rain or Shadow tattoos, ready for a coup against House Moon?' The tattooist whistled appreciatively. 'At least the bastards are ambitious then. House Moon might be relatively weak, but I doubt their Astaren are.'

'And if they had a thousand like Irato?' Narin asked. 'Or more? How many have been poisoned with this? Have agents like him been poisoning children at birth for decades, readying them for when they needed an army? How many across the Empire train in Shure run by the goshe?'

'Tens of thousands,' Enchei agreed grimly. 'Enough to hide the obedient soldiers within their ranks. Maybe even enough to deal with House Moon's Astaren if they knew what they were up against – but you know what prevents all-out war these days? It ain't the Gods, not really. It's uncertainty – not knowing what the other Great Houses

142

have in reserve. Everyone's heard of the Stone Dragons tearing apart whole armies, but if you think those armoured monsters are the only thing they've got in their arsenal you'll get dead quick enough.'

'So where do the fox-demons fit into all this?' Kesh pointed out.

Narin sighed. 'I didn't say I had all the answers,' he said, 'but we might be running out of time to find them.'

Rhe turned towards the door. 'You are right. Earlier you asked me to be circumspect and you were right to do so.' He glanced back. 'The time for that has passed – come.'

CHAPTER 11

It took seven years for the Great Houses to formally ratify the existence of the Lawbringers as protectors of the Emperor and overseers of his law. It took twelve years until a Lawbringer was permitted to make an arrest on House Dragon sovereign soil, despite the treaties they had signed. For a long time, blind and fearless obstinacy proved the greater force and likely it will outlast the laws of men too.

From *A History* by Ayel Sorote

The first light of dawn illuminated a low fog that filled the Imperial City's veins and arteries. From a balcony, two figures viewed the near-empty expanse of Lostwind plaza. The older of the two warmed his hands around a tall cup of pale red tea that steamed gently in the cool morning air. Opposite them, occupying one side of the hexagonal plaza was the goshe hospital; its windows dark this early, while white-cloaked figures advanced towards it like vengeful ghosts. The only sound was the muted croak of ravens from their many roosts across the district.

In the very centre of the plaza was a statue of a man facing west, carved from the same pale local stone as the hospital. The figure was twice the height of a normal man and stood atop a plinth of similar proportions, fetishes engraved into his long hair and detailed in gold. Similarly gilded was the swept hilt of his rapier and grip of his sheathed pistol. The statue watched the horizon where the divine constellations appeared in their endless pursuit around the world; legs slightly apart and knees part-bent as though ready to leap from its plinth.

'I met him once, did I ever tell you that, Synter?' the elderly man said, nodding towards the statue.

'Duellist?' his companion asked. She turned to face him. 'When was that?'

144

'Not long before his ascension,' he replied. Father Jehq sipped his tea while the white-clad Lawbringers arrived at the gate of the hospital, near-silent behind the curtain of fog. 'It was one of his last duels. I was too young to be present at that of course, but I knew what was going to happen.'

'You knew his opponent?'

Jehq inclined his head. 'My uncle. The man had trained for years; he spent a decade living like a monk after becoming champion of House Darksky – living and training at the soldier's temple here solely for the chance one day to give insult to Kiro Raven.'

Synter smiled and patted the long-knife at her thigh. 'If he'd just waited a few years, we'd have trained him.'

'Oh no,' Jehq said with a shake of the head. 'He founded the goshe, I suppose – created the training school that I turned into the Order – but he would have deplored the teaching of noble arts to commoners such as you.'

Her smile widened. 'Maybe for good reason,' Synter said, 'given what we're going to do to his precious noble castes.' She shrugged. 'So he survived? Survived a fight with the man soon to become a God?'

'By then Duellist had no taste for death. He had moved far beyond that; no doubt it was why the Gods took an interest in him. Technically, the duel was a draw, if memory serves.'

'A draw?'

'They drew first blood together,' Jehq explained. 'Uncle scraped a shin while Duellist pricked his ribs. They both knew who had the killing stroke, but it was a draw and my uncle retired in glory to retell the duel a thousand times to his eager students.'

'I hope this isn't just a late revenge,' Synter commented, 'upon the God that bested your beloved uncle?'

He raised an eyebrow at her and Synter pursed her lips, smothering a smile. Jehq watched her as she returned her attention to the Lawbringers already forcing their way into the goshe hospital. Her skin was ghostly in the dawn twilight, pale blue eyes as arresting as the grace with which she moved.

Women have always been my weakness, Jehq thought to himself. *It's fortunate I never met one like her in my youth. Who knows what foolishness I'd have managed trying to impress her, not realising the attempt itself would have been my downfall.*

145

He was strong for his age, he knew, but in recent months had realised she saw him as an old man rather than an elder and teacher. With their varied arcane Blessings they had staved off the advancing years, but now he realised it was all a delay – nothing more, despite the ancient magics they had unearthed so many years ago.

'Perhaps that's all it is,' Jehq said, joining in her joke. 'My travels and research, all the lives we ruined as we created you Detenii – it was all to show the newest of our Gods the true worth of House Darksky!'

He sighed and shook his head. 'Even now I still cannot fathom it. That was the pinnacle of my uncle's life, the moment he worked so hard for. Perhaps he never even believed he could best the man, but just hoped one day he could match him and win glory.' Jehq made a dismissive gesture. 'A lifetime of work and who remembers his name now?'

'You.'

'And after I'm gone?'

'I thought that was the point. You'd be able to remind Duellist of his name.'

Jehq's face softened. Unsuited to much expression, it barely changed as he spoke. 'And have the other Gods think me gauche? Now *that* would mean a wasted life.'

The Lawbringers disappeared from view, heading inside the hospital, and the pair fell into thoughtful hush once more. The sight of the Emperor's servants invading their domain reminded Jehq of the news Synter had brought – a worrying and puzzling report they had argued through for an hour until one of his guards brought word of Lawbringers in the plaza.

Irato's alive, he mused yet again, knowing his companion was still wondering over the same exact detail.

Alive and turned against us. I didn't see that one coming, I must admit.

It still didn't make sense. He didn't disbelieve Synter, he knew better than that, but he'd known Irato for years. The man was a blunt instrument at times, a good team-leader and excellent fighter, but nothing more than that. He had been one of them for decades now; had enjoyed the skills he'd been given more than the power it brought. Why throw away the reward he knew he'd receive soon?

Synter, now her I could imagine turning on us, given the right reward, he realised, looking askance at the lithe woman who commanded the Detenii – a name appropriated from the shadow demons of House Moon folklore.

She's bold enough to switch sides, but not Irato. His flaw has always been failing to consider the other path.

'The doctor's dead?' Synter asked. 'Do I need to do anything there?'

Jehq shook his head. 'He was fetched to attend at the asylum, to dress the wounds of an inmate. Somehow the patient got free and throttled him; Osseq was buried quietly in the grounds.'

'Good, it's bad enough that girl knows your face.'

Jehq gestured across the plaza ahead of them. 'A modest risk, there are Shure in every district of the city. It will take the Lawbringers days to search them all and discover I'm at none. Irato's betrayal brings more complications, but the safehouses are cleared and none were raided.'

'What about the artefact? That's still safe?'

His face tightened. 'It is. I'm glad we took the precaution of keeping its location from all you Detenii for fear of demons tearing it from someone's mind. Normally I would move the artefact on general principle, but where to? The foxes are scouring the city for it and whatever happened when we lost Irato attracted all sorts of attention. Even getting it to the island is risking too much exposure.'

'Mother Tereil sent you word?'

'Pallasane.'

Synter scowled at that, just as Jehq had himself when the messenger had reached him. Each of the Elders, the goshe's secret ruling circle, had a specific remit. Mother Tereil's was surveillance of the city; a network of informers and more arcane methods to keep a wary eye on their various facilities and the city in general. As a result, she was a woman Jehq spoke to often. On the other hand that malevolent dwarf, Father Pallasane, was one they rarely saw or heard from. To most he was merely a madman locked in a tower on the wind-swept outer cliff of Leviathan District and sometimes Jehq wished it were so.

The interior of Pallasane's tower was a mesh of interlocking cages and distorted mirrors, a madcap spider's lair only he could adequately navigate, but from there he listened to the voices of demons on the wind, the distant call of Gods and spirits. How much he understood Jehq had never been sure, but the volume and intensity of voices told enough in this instance.

'Are the Gods getting involved?' she growled. 'Damn him, I should have followed those novices in and killed Irato myself. There's no telling what damage he could bring down on us.'

'Or they might have killed you,' Jehq pointed out. 'We didn't know he would be there – you only caught that fragment from our agents as they were dying and we still don't know what went on exactly.'

'Don't remind me!' she continued, barely keeping her voice down in her anger. 'Our Lawbringer agents got sloppy and that's put us all in danger. I'll cut their balls off for that.'

'We can worry about them later. Firstly, what does Irato know?'

'More than enough! Places for them to raid or watch all over the city – the asylum, Pallasane's tower – the base of operations for most of you Elders, the colony too! The lairs we can abandon easily enough, but we can't destroy the evidence in every facility before they're raided. Only the asylum is rigged that way.'

'Do we bother trying to?'

Synter gaped at him. 'What do you mean? If the Lawbringers find what's inside some, the only question's how quickly they arrest every goshe they can find – and that's the best outcome. If some bastard Astaren gets word then everything collapses around our ears; the Great Houses all declare war on the goshe and anyone with the mark's on a death list for the rest of their life.'

'What happens to the cattle doesn't interest me,' Jehq said calmly, 'only how our plans are affected. Tattoos are simple enough to erase for those who matter.'

'If Irato's given them everything he knows it's more of a question of what we can salvage rather than how the plan's affected.'

He turned to face her. 'That's the key, and exactly what I cannot fathom. If the foxes caught him, they'd have torn out his mind and left a lump of barely-breathing meat at the side of the road. If the Lawbringers arrested him, why turn on us at all? They've nothing to hold over him; no threat he'll fear and no gaol that could keep him.'

'So what then?' she asked tersely. 'A reward? He's hardly one for luxuries or wealth, never has been. He's no family, no legacy or anything like that to work for.'

'Could that be it? The offer of such a thing?'

There came a bark of laughter from Synter, a clipped sound that put Jehq in mind of a fox's cry. 'Hah! Marriage and an heir? Irato's never given two shits about that. He was born a gutter rat, but he never pined for a nobleman's life.'

'The Lawbringers are being used by someone else then? With or without their knowledge – Astaren? Demons?' He shook his head. 'But surely it would have to be a higher order of demons than the fox-spirits? And I find it hard to imagine Astaren using the Lawbringers, they have their own methods.'

Synter went still. 'It doesn't matter,' she said in the measured voice of someone realising there was only one path to take. 'Either we're entirely compromised, or the Lawbringers have no understanding of what they've stumbled over.'

'So either we're dead or free to continue,' Father Jehq continued hesitantly. 'Perhaps you're right. Speculation does us no good. Gods or high demons can destroy us at will; it's out of our hands. I'll put a team to watch over the artefact, someone we can afford to lose. That's the prize for all involved – if it's taken, we walk away and the goshe fade into history. If we find no one watching it by tomorrow evening, we move it to the colony.'

'And while we wait, the goshe are already half-compromised by the attack so we should use them while we still can. The Shure master in Moon District – they'll go to question him so maybe he'll get a chance to kill whoever's leading the investigation. The Lawbringers must be a pawn of someone or something unknown and the best secrets are those shared sparingly. There may be only one of them who fully knows what the purpose is here. We may slow whatever pursues us by killing their agent within the Lawbringers and if the Shure master dies in the process, the trail ends there.'

Father Jehq was quiet a long time. The grainy light of day now filled the plaza and seemed to thicken the fog as though the air was suffused with the cold white breath of some pagan god. The insistent rasp of squabbling ravens cut the air, but could not penetrate his thoughts.

'To buy time we must construct a story to explain it all,' he said by way of agreement.

'Easy enough,' Synter said with a shrug. 'We've got a woman and a man, oldest story in the world. All our novices came from the same Shure and the Shure master's taking the fall, so he and Irato were competing over the same woman. Men have killed for less than that and it isolates the rest of the order.'

'It buys us a day or two,' Jehq clarified, 'but prejudices against the goshe will remain. Opinion will turn against us soon enough, it's simply a question of how long we can stave that off. I'll have high-caste members of the An-Goshe council go to the Lawbringers and deny everything. That will make them hesitate before publicly accusing anyone and give us time to spread our version.'

On the other side of the plaza, a handful of white-cloaked figures filed out of the hospital entrance. There would be an extensive search still to come, no doubt, but a quick investigation of the principal offices and private areas of the hospital had turned up nothing. Father Jehq smiled inwardly at the change in their manner, the child-like eagerness they had displayed as they forced their way in – only to find they had been anticipated and their quarry was gone.

'Our numbers might be sufficient to proceed to the Ascension,' he said at last, his words barely audible as though he hardly dared to dream. 'It would be a risk though, even if we used every goshe and stolen mind in the city.'

'But we have enough?' Synter pressed, suddenly animated at the idea. 'If this is our only chance, we can't turn away and not even try.'

'But the risk!' Jehq gasped. 'How could we prepare in time? How could we assemble them all without drawing notice? We'd have none at all to spare as guards. There would be …' He tailed off, unable to even express what was now flashing through his mind.

Synter shook her head. 'It wouldn't be perfect, it would be vulnerable – but if we succeed, no Great House or demon would dare move against us. The Gods themselves would preserve us and given the choice between risking it and walking away entirely, I'd rather have tried.'

'And so the moon will rise,' Jehq said hollowly, straightening and looking up to the shrouded sky as though her words had given him renewed strength.

'The moon will rise,' Synter echoed, fierce determination on her face. 'Get the Elders ready. For better or for worse, the Empire stands on the brink. Time to spin the coin.'

They bumped to a stop at a deserted slip of wharf and the bargeman hopped nimbly out. His long oar slipped easily from its rest and a trail of water from the Crescent glittered in the morning light as it fell to the wooden walkway. Just as they had emerged from the grey shadow of the Mason's Bridge, on the north shore of the Crescent, the sun had crested the hills east of the Imperial City. The water around them, layered with mist, had taken on a diffuse golden glow and their bargeman had broken into song to greet the day. The other boats on the Crescent, carrying the first of the day's trade, had taken up the song in the next heartbeat – an invocation of the God presently in ascendance that made the hairs on Narin's neck stand on end.

He'd heard the song often enough; every resident of the city had heard the bargemen's songs – a rousing reveille to start the day and chase away the spirits of the mist, a softer lament as dusk fell and they prepared to abandon the waters once more. This time it was different for Narin. Now he felt Shield's gaze heavily on his shoulders, though the God's constellation had passed by several hours earlier – and there was no comfort to be found there.

A second barge followed them and slipped easily into the neighbouring slot, its pilot tying up with two deft flicks before his boat had even come to rest. Rhe disembarked with an imperious look around the near-deserted dock. There were several barges tied up for the night, while a pair of sea-going ships occupied most of the wharf space. At present they were observed only by a pair of sailors on watch and a handful of servants in white scarves already about their daily tasks.

'You know where the Shure is?' Narin asked as he followed Rhe off the boat.

Rhe turned, watching their companions disembark before he replied. 'I believe so,' he said, 'but Lawbringer Shoten knows the district better than I.'

The other Lawbringer was a tall, lean man with long, flowing limbs and a serene air, while by contrast the Investigator hovering in his lee was a wary, sharp-eyed youth. Both were tanned of skin – not nearly so dark as Kine's rich ebony, but enough to show they were not local stock. The pair were certainly not House Moon or their major subordinate, Rain, so Narin guessed they were part of some lesser House under Moon to know their way around the district.

'The Shure is just behind the dock,' Lawbringer Shoten announced, one hand resting on the long hilt of his sword. He pointed off to the right towards a large non-descript building. 'Two streets away; we can cut down that alley.'

Rhe nodded and handed their bargeman a square steel token inscribed with his own name – payment to be redeemed at the Palace of Law – and instructed them both to wait. That done he set out in the direction Shoten had indicated. Narin fell in behind, allowing the other Lawbringer to stride forward and walk alongside his peer.

At least this one's not a nobleman, Narin thought sourly. *Think I've got enough of them messing up my life for the moment.*

He felt foolish and childish almost as soon as he thought that. The lack of sleep had not improved his mood, nor the fruitless search of the free hospital, but Narin knew perfectly well that Rhe was being generous in the freedom he allowed his Investigator. At least he was being trusted and listened to rather than lectured at – as no doubt some Lawbringers would have done, once there was blood spilled.

He glanced at Shoten's Investigator as they crossed the cobbled ground of the docks. Clearly new to his position, the young man trotted in his master's wake like a frightened puppy, eyes on the ground. His name was Orel, or so the brief introductions had revealed, but all Narin had got from him was a bob of the head and no actual words. In the presence of the great Lawbringer Rhe, Orel had no voice, it seemed.

Into the alley and across a market street they went, the four men attracting a few curious looks from the inhabitants of the district – mostly dusty-dark Moons in stained brown labourer's coats. Rhe and Shoten kept their eyes ahead, the pair seeming to compete to appear the most calm and controlled, while Narin tried not to compulsively check every doorway and alley.

The last of the mist had fled under the sun's assault, but his fears hadn't gone with it. For the bargemen, the dawn heralded a return of the mortal realm. It was the water that brought concealing fog and its lowest depths housed predatory demons more than willing to eat humans. Possessed foxes might steal a man's soul, but there were many kinds of demons and some were monstrous hunters rather than incorporeal horrors.

Narin found himself hardly able to summon the childhood fears he'd once possessed. Now the demons were men, not monsters, and his fear was reserved for more adult things. The aristocratic tones of Prince Sorote echoed in his ears, the electric touch of Kine lingered on his skin. Both provoked a different sort of fear inside him; very different flavours to the terror of blood and steel he'd experienced during the night, but just as real.

It was almost with relief that they came upon the goshe training house, nestled unobtrusively at the end of a narrow street. It was a single-storey construction built to blend in to the moss-topped houses of Moon District, but obvious for the long bank of sliding panels flanking a red-lacquer double door that all opened out onto a surrounding courtyard.

The building was fenced on three sides and extended a little way back, but the room at the front occupied half its area and was where the goshe fighters trained. One red-bordered wooden panel was open and through it Narin could see a man sitting in the centre of the training hall.

He was a Moon by the colour of his skin, the grey of his cropped hair accentuating its dusted appearance. Dressed in a dark tunic identical to those the assassins had worn, the man had his eyes closed and some sort of spear across his lap – a broad-headed weapon Narin realised was a bill, a peasant's tool converted for battle. Here, they cared little for caste, but clearly paid attention to the implements their pupils might already be used to.

In another life, he said inwardly, *I might have been one of you.*

He slipped his hands behind his back, feigning a respectful pose while freeing his stave, ready to draw.

Lawbringer Rhe strode up to the open doors and stepped through them. The Shure master made no sign of noticing them and it was only when all four had entered the room that he deigned to open his eyes. As he and Rhe regarded each other, Narin checked around the room. In the low morning light it was dim without lamps. Racks of weapons stood at regular positions on the walls; alternately wooden ones for practice and steel-bladed for something more serious. The Shure master was alone, but one of the doors leading off from behind the man was ajar. There was an altar-like table set against one end, flanked by weapon racks. Covered by a dark red cloth edged in silver, the table held only a small ornament – a stylised silver tree from the base of which a stick of incense burned.

'You are the Shure master?' Rhe asked.

The man looked away from Rhe before answering, scrutinising each of them in turn before finally locking his eyes back on Rhe and speaking. 'I am.'

'Your name?'

'Master Nemeke.'

'You know why we are here?'

The Shure master didn't reply.

'You gave the order?'

Again there was no response, but Nemeke didn't break eye contact with Rhe.

'Who instructed you to do so?'

At that the Shure master tilted his head slightly. 'Instructed?' he repeated dully.

Is he drunk? Narin wondered, *or a man who knows he faces execution?* He glanced at Orel, but the young investigator didn't notice, so intent was he on the aging man in the centre of the room.

'You claim this was a personal dispute?' Shoten broke in.

Nemeke kept his gaze on Rhe. 'The order was mine alone.'

'You freely admit ordering an assassination, but not that it was under instruction from another?' Rhe clarified. Lawbringers were empowered to pronounce guilt and carry out sentences under the law, but rarely was it so simple. 'This is a capital crime – you will be executed unless you were coerced into this affair.'

'There was no other,' he said with finality. 'The girl was a temptress, she turned our brother against us. She had to be punished.'

'What?' Narin demanded, taking a step forward. 'What rubbish is this?'

Rhe glared at him but it was too late and the Shure master's attention locked onto Narin, eyes widening with slight surprise at who had replied.

'You were party to the betrayal?'

'What betrayal? She barely knew your man. There was nothing between them!'

'She is the cause,' Nemeke insisted, 'and by assisting her, you, Investigator, are also to blame.'

The man's eyes betrayed him, flicking slightly to one side. As the door behind him began to open, the world seemed to slow to Narin. His hands refused to draw his stave; his feet were rooted to the spot. All he could do for that long, tortuous moment was watch the door open and the light catch the tip of a steel point.

Crossbow, he thought uselessly while some part of himself raged at his body to move, to dive out of the way or do something to save his own life. *He was drawing me out!*

A thunder-crack split the air and Narin shuddered involuntarily. A black spot appeared on the door and threw it backwards, closing on a falling figure behind. The shock made him breathe again and suddenly Narin could move, slipping his stave from the loop on his back.

'I am goshe,' Nemeke declared. He jumped to his feet and snatched up his weapon in one movement, eyes fixed on Narin. 'I will die a warrior.'

Behind him, black-garbed goshe raced into the room – three— five of them, armed and heading for Narin.

'No.' Rhe said in an almost bored voice.

As Nemeke turned towards Narin, Rhe lashed out with one foot and caught the man behind the knee. The blow made the man falter and Rhe made up the ground between them in a split-second, hammering down at his head with the discharged pistol. The blow dropped Nemeke like a stone; he crashed to his knees then pitched face-forward, already limp, while Rhe hurled the pistol at the next attacker.

Lawbringer Shoten charged in the wake of the throw, sword drawn and cutting down at the nearest. Narin didn't wait to watch what happened as a masked figure with long plaited hair swung an axe towards his head. He dodged backwards and chopped down with his stave. The hardened wood thwacked crisply against the goshe's forearm and jerked the weapon from its hand. A second whip-crack blow caught it on the side of the face and Narin felt it shatter its cheekbone.

Two more lunged at him with spears, but before they could run him through Rhe had arrived. The Lawbringer forced his way between the two goshe with a flurry of swift blows. Deflecting the spear-shafts of each, he planted a kick in the ribs of the larger and caught the other round the head with his stave. The goshe staggered and he hammered the butt into its shoulder, jerking the spear free. Before the other could react he'd struck up and caught them on the chin, snapping the hooded head back. A final *coup de grâce* across the shoulders of each and the first sagged to their knees, the other crumpled and went still.

Off to Narin's right, Lawbringer Shoten dispatched his second goshe as they traded blows with Orel and then all was suddenly silent. Only one was still upright – the smaller of the spearmen who'd been driven to their knees. The goshe's head was bowed, shuddering under the effect of Rhe's blow, before they tore off their mask and vomited over the floor.

The Lawbringers hesitated. It was a woman, barely out of her teens, with a raised welt on her cheek from where Rhe had struck her. For a moment no one spoke or moved but then she seemed to recover herself and looked up at Narin.

'I die a warrior,' she announced as she pulled a dagger from her belt.

Rhe started forward, arm reaching back to hurl his stave, but it was too late. The woman never took her gaze off Narin as she wrenched the blade across her throat. Blood cascaded out across the pale wooden floor of the training room and, a look of momentary agony on her face, she pitched forward. Rhe ran forward and put one foot on the knife in her hand as he turned her over, but it was immediately clear that the wound was fatal and he stepped back.

'Gods,' breathed Orel. 'They would rather die than be taken, but they're just low born!'

Narin didn't dare look at him, for fear he'd break his stave over the youth's head.

You think cutting your own throat's reserved to the higher castes? he wanted to scream at Orel. *All you need's the guts to do it – guts I doubt you have.*

'The goshe welcome all castes,' Rhe said, as though in explanation to Orel. 'Do not assume anything.'

Narin watched the blood spread out from her prostrate body, pooling around her head like a dark halo. It was the first time he had seen such a thing and, though the horror of suicide left him sickened, Narin's mind lingered on the look on her face as she had done it. There had been a perfect moment of purpose in her face; of calmness and resolve that was its own horror.

Narin shook his head and kicked away the nearest of the weapons at his feet. The plaited goshe was motionless at his feet and when he rolled the body over he felt a jolt in his stomach. Another woman, her cheek crumpled inward and her eye a bloodied ruin. His chest tightened at the realisation, his hands shaking as he tried to feel for a pulse. For a moment there was nothing other than the twitch of his fingers against her throat, but at last he felt something pulse weakly under her skin. It took a long time for a second beat, but at last he felt it and looked up with a sense of relief.

'She lives?' Rhe asked, standing up again from where he'd been crouched at the Shure master's side.

Narin opened his mouth to reply, then realised all was still under his fingers. He looked back down again and adjusted the position, but still there was nothing. It hit him like a punch to the gut. He turned her face so he could see the undamaged side of it and was stuck by the delicacy of her features. Skin not so dark as Kine's, but for a moment Narin saw his lover's face superimposed on the dead woman's and he

156

almost moaned at the thought. Kine was no soldier, but if her husband discovered she was pregnant by another man, Wyvern tradition dictated she should be garrotted.

'She's dead,' he whispered, head bowed.

Rhe grunted. 'She was armed, you had no choice.'

He looked up, eyes wide. 'That's supposed to make me feel better? Look at her, she's barely old enough to be married and now she's dead.'

'And that was her choice.' Rhe frowned at Narin. 'I had not thought you so squeamish as this.'

'Squeamish? I just killed a woman!'

Rhe glanced towards the half-open doorway where the first goshe was sprawled. Face covered by a mask, Narin saw that one was similarly slight of build. 'Most likely so did I, but their sex makes no difference.'

'You really think that?' Narin gasped.

'They were trained to fight,' Rhe said simply, 'taught to kill just as high-caste women may be instructed in the arts of pistol, spear and dagger. There is no dishonour in death, only the killing of those unable to defend themselves.'

Narin felt deflated by his disbelief. From the faces of the others he could see he was the only one to even be given pause by such a thing.

'Not all of us grew up thinking that way,' he muttered. 'Not all of us grew up in your world. Where I'm from, women don't get much chance to fight back. Only cowards hurt them.'

Rhe inclined his head. 'Most noblewomen do not choose to learn how to fight and the Gods themselves have decreed violence upon them to be a crime equal to heresy, but these goshe were not such women.'

Narin turned away, knowing he'd not win this argument – knowing Rhe could not even conceive there was an argument to be had.

'Are any of them alive?'

'One at least,' Rhe said, looking down at the larger goshe he'd rendered unconscious. 'The Shure master is dead, but I suspect he would have told us nothing anyway.'

'This one also,' Shoten said from the side of another, pressing a cloth against his opponent's wounded shoulder. The goshe he knelt over appeared to have passed out from the pain. 'They were after you, Investigator Narin,' Shoten continued. 'Why?'

Narin blinked. 'I ... I don't know. What he said didn't make any sense; he was trying to determine which of us knew Kesh the most.'

'And you revealed yourself at the first opportunity,' Rhe observed sternly. 'Yet again your rashness almost proves your undoing.'

Narin ducked his head at the admonishment, realising the mistake he'd made. After all this time in Rhe's lee, he should have known better.

'The man takes all the blame on his own shoulders, isolating the crime to this Shure only – that I understand, but wanting to kill Narin specifically?' Shoten left Orel to continue ministering to the injured goshe and stood to give Narin a curious look. 'But why would they believe killing you could affect the investigation? Is there information you have withheld?'

Narin found himself backing away. 'Of course not!' he protested, but his words seemed to have little effect.

'Investigator Orel,' Rhe said as he went to fetch and reload his pistol, 'watch these two while we check the rest of the building.'

He didn't bother to holster his gun once it was reloaded, merely wiped a trace of blood from the brass decoration and cocked it as he headed for the half-open door.

Narin followed dumbly, sparing one last look at the woman he'd killed without even trying. The street behind them, through the open panel, was completely empty – the gunshot had cleared it quickly enough. A slanting shaft of sunlight cut across the street and down through the open wall section to settle on the tip of the axe he'd kicked away. The sight made him hesitate as though it was a message from the Gods.

She wanted nothing more than to kill me, he thought numbly as he headed through to where the assassin had been waiting for the Shure master's signal. *Obedient to her master's word, she didn't care for any other reason. Just like Irato, these bastards had made her a slave to be used without regard. For all the goshe's claims of equality and brotherhood, they're no better than the noble castes. All they want is control and they'll tear out your mind if that's the cost.*

He tightened his grip on his stave, feeling a cold resolve steal over him.

No. The goshe are worse – high-caste folk just want to keep the Empire the way it is; safe and unchanging. As it's always been, as they've always known it. But these goshe, they don't want anything to change, not really. They just want to be the ones at the top – they see all that's wrong with the Empire and they're just envious.

He felt it as a shock, the realisation of what he was feeling. It was hatred – pure and unadulterated. His upbringing within the ordered

158

Imperial District meant he rarely experienced such strength of feeling, but now hate filled him. These people who had tried to murder him, these people who played games with lives and sent their assassins out after newborns – armed with a poison that stole who a person was.

And now they've declared war on us all. So be it – I know a man who seems to know all about war in all its cruel colours. Time I learned more than dachan from the old bastard.

'What now?'

Enchei looked up from the blade he was sharpening. 'Now?'

Kesh stood and gestured around at the small room she, Enchei and Irato occupied. 'Now! Narin's been gone for hours. How long do we have to sit in this room and wait to be killed?'

Enchei shrugged and went to the door. He removed the steel bar he'd wedged behind it and pulled the door open. 'You want to go, help yourself.'

'Preferably without being killed.'

'Ah.' He nudged the door shut again with his toe. 'In that case, stay put. Waiting won't kill you and being bored's better than the alternative.'

'Easy enough for you to say; they're not after you!'

The older man grinned. 'True.'

Kesh waited a moment then gave a snort of irritation. 'That's all you've got to say? We can't even go to the Palace of Law? Surely we're safer there than we are as sitting ducks in here.'

Enchei nodded. 'Certainly. Hey, Irato, you awake?'

'Yes.' The goshe sat up, a flicker of discomfort on his face. He'd removed the sling from his left arm so presumably the pain continued to subside – his body recovering unnaturally quickly after Lord Shield's intervention. 'What is it?'

'You're a goshe – tell Kesh how you'd kill us all if you were the one planning it?'

'How would I ...' Irato tailed off at Enchei's level look. He thought for a moment, eyelids flickering slightly as though rediscovering some lost part of his mind. 'I ... I would wait. Kesh wants to move somewhere safer – anyone would – but you're vulnerable out in the open.'

'Exactly. At the Palace of Law you're safe, but you'd never make it that far. Those people clearly don't care about taking losses, but they'll only get one shot.'

'They lost eight when there weren't guards here,' Kesh realised, 'now there are twenty-odd Investigators surrounding the compound they'd need their elite troops to get us.'

'And that's a display they don't want to put on while the whole city's watching,' Enchei said. 'So they wait for us to get anxious and move you. Losing another five as a distraction while they put a crossbow bolt through Irato and you, that's a sign the goshe are serious about traitors. Losing fifty or some elites with secrets they don't want to share in a full-scale assault, that's a sign they've a small army to call on and House Dragon might have something to say there.'

Kesh dropped down into a chair. 'So what then? I just sit?'

'Unless you'd prefer to scrub the bloodstains out of the floor?' Enchei suggested.

She scowled at the jibe, hands clasped together as she tried to stop herself fidgeting. 'Empress forgive me, that might actually be preferable to sitting around,' Kesh said, giving up her effort to compose herself. 'Go fetch a pail of water then, a brush for yourself too. I'm not doing it by myself, I'll tell you that for nothing.'

Enchei nodded and rose to head out onto the walkway. 'Mistress Sheti should have something we can use.'

He closed the door behind him and the room became abruptly silent. Kesh looked up and saw Irato staring blankly at her. The room was lit by a lamp despite it being day outside, the window shutters now nailed shut. The bruising on Irato's face looked sickly in the meagre light, the right-hand side of his forehead still swollen after the fall that had started all this.

'What are you looking at?'

Irato turned away and lowered his gaze. She watched him obey with a mixture of pity and contempt. *Caught in his own form of slavery. I hope the man he once was had time to realise what was happening to him.*

She shook her head. As much as she still wanted to hate Irato, Kesh was too tired to feel much and he cut a pathetic sight when left to his own devices. It wasn't that he was consumed by misery or loss; certainly he was affected, but when left alone the man would simply sit and stare, not so much grieving as emptied. Removed from the world around him, Irato was drained of his self – less than human somehow, more like an animal. His deeds were not expunged, but the creature sitting in front of her wasn't quite the same as the one she hated.

Right now, all Kesh wanted to know was that her mother was safe. Now the secret was out, now they knew Irato was here, surely there would be no purpose in killing her? She had to hope. Kesh could identify Father Jehq, could recognise the man at the heart of whatever was going on, and for that she was marked for death – but her mother knew nothing of use. Even taking her hostage seemed an unlikely prospect.

'You just going to sit there, then?' Kesh called, for want of something better to do.

'What should I be doing?'

She looked him up and down. He was wearing the same blood-stained trousers and shirt he had been all night.

'You could change your clothes, wash the blood off your hands maybe?'

Irato looked down and seemed to notice the streaks of blood on his skin for the first time. He looked around for a helpless moment before Kesh lost patience.

'Oh for Lady Pity's sake – there's a washbowl in the other room,' she said, pointing to the door to Narin's bedroom. 'Take a shirt from there once you're clean, then run a cloth and whetstone over your weapons.'

The goshe ducked his head and started off towards the bedroom, awkwardly tugging at his shirt as he went. Kesh's gaze fell to the discarded grey coat and leather armour on the floor. Even with the continued threat and his gradual recovery, it hadn't occurred to Irato to put them on again.

'What are we going to do with you?' she muttered, more to herself than Irato but he still stopped in the open doorway, head caught halfway through hauling his shirt off.

'What do you mean?'

Kesh pinched the bridge of her nose, feeling the lack of sleep dig its claws a little deeper into her head. 'You don't seem so capable by yourself. Might just be the shock, but whatever's in that Moon's Artifice has really turned your head inside out.'

He turned to face her. 'What are you going to do with me?'

'Me?' Kesh snorted. 'You're twice my size, there's not much I can do to you.'

'But your sister …'

'What about her?' she snapped. 'What?' Without meaning to she jumped up and squared up to the muscular assassin. 'What about my sister?'

161

'It's my fault,' Irato said simply. 'Whether or not I can remember, I'm to blame.'

She bit down her automatic response and took a deep breath. 'It sounds like what happened to my sister is the least of your crimes. I don't know what Narin intends to do about them, but he's the one who'll decide what happens to you.' Kesh looked away. 'You're not my concern.'

Irato seemed to sag a shade. 'I understand.'

Kesh hesitated, not for the first time struck by the sense that he was playing her – but if he was, Irato was the finest actor she'd ever met. *And what's the point? If he had information on the goshe, Rhe would offer him a deal in a heartbeat – this is too momentous to care about one man's crimes.* She eyed the lean lines and scars of his powerful arms. *And how hard would it be for him to get away? The guards are all looking in the other direction – if he runs, he'd make it, most likely.*

'Do you really not care what happens to you?' she said at last.

For a moment, confusion flickered across Irato's face. Then he turned and fetched one of Narin's shirts from a drawer and pulled it on, buying himself a few moments to think.

'I don't know,' he admitted finally. 'I don't know who I am any more.'

'What's it like?'

He grimaced. 'Like there's a hole inside me. It doesn't hurt, there's just nothing there. Like a block of ice in my stomach; it feels cold and numb rather than painful.'

'What do you want to do?' Kesh asked, watching the fatigue and incomprehension play out on his battered face. 'About the goshe, about all of this?'

Irato shrugged and returned to where he'd been sitting. He ran his hands over the scored leather armour he'd been wearing that first night, seemingly finding it both alien and familiar at the same time. 'What does anyone want to do with their life?' he said, eventually setting the armour down. 'What do you want?'

'To live it,' Kesh declared fiercely. 'To find my mother safe and well and go home. This isn't my world, the Empire I live in.' She gestured to the bloodstains on the floor and the weapons on the ground beside Irato. 'You're welcome to it.'

'Is it my world if I can't remember any of it?' Irato wondered.

'You've still got skills. Narin and I'd likely be dead if you hadn't defended us. The Empire's got enough uses for a man like you.'

Irato was silent for a long moment. 'What if I don't want that?' he said slowly, as though even attempting to decide something for himself required great effort. 'What if I don't want to be the man I once was?'

'You don't even know who you were!'

'Does it matter?' he said simply. 'I was a killer – friend of killers. You say I'm never going to remember who I was, and maybe that's for the best. Maybe that's the shape of my soul; but maybe the world made me a killer. Either way I'll never know that man – never think his thoughts or live his life. Maybe I get a chance to be something better, something more than a plague on this world.'

Kesh stared at him for a long time, trying to make sense of the clashing emotions inside her. Part of her was desperate to help his wish come about; to satisfy a cynic's secret yearning that the world was not all terrible, despite everything that had happened. But the cynic was also suspicious, and the black flame of grief still screamed for the man's blood – a distant but urgent shriek at the back of her mind.

For some reason her thoughts went back to her father, of the cheerful man she'd waved goodbye to on his last voyage. It had been only a few years ago, but it now seemed a lifetime – two lifetimes. Everything before the loss of Emari, just a few days ago, was now another lifetime, while the seasons she'd spent on the merchantman had changed her just as irrevocably.

Father would want to help him, Kesh realised. He had been warm-hearted and generous, sometimes to a fault. The cynic at the back of Kesh's mind spoke in her mother's voice, but her father would have been glad of Irato's wish to put his past behind him.

Emari too, she realised, *daughter of a different father – isn't that what he used to call her? No guile, little sense half the time, but they'd be the ones laughing in the sun while Mother and I kept a weather eye open.*

'To get that chance,' she said hesitantly, 'you'll probably have to kill again – you realise that? These next few days you'll be faced with those friends of yours, I'd bet. They'll have to die or you'll never have time for peace.'

Irato's face was chillingly blank as he responded. 'If that's the price, that's what I'll pay.' He opened his mouth to say more but hesitated until Kesh frowned at him. 'I can't bring your sister back,' he said slowly, 'and I can't make you forgive me, I know. But I'll see you safe through this or die trying. I owe you that much at least.'

'Don't make promises you can't keep,' Kesh said, hating herself for the slight waver in her voice. 'My mother's lost one daughter already and I'm the only one who knows what your friend Jehq looks like. They'll want you dead as a traitor, but if they find out I know more than you, I'll be top of their list.'

Irato seemed to bow under the weight of thinking for himself, of making decisions without someone to prompt him, but after a few heavy breaths that made him wince at his cracked ribs, he looked up again.

'That's the price,' he said with a determination she'd not heard from him before. 'Whatever it takes, I'll do it.'

Kesh nodded. 'Your injuries improving? Good – then get your weapons clean and once the floor's been scrubbed, get that armour on,' she ordered and pulled her father's knife from her jacket, draped over the back of her chair. 'It's been months since I properly practised with this and we're both going to need to be ready for what's to come.'

CHAPTER 12

Among the wars, plots and disasters that litter the history of the Lesser Empire, one stands out as particularly significant – the fate of the Ebalee Trading Company. Their reach spanned the empire, their power was vast, but not so great as they assumed. When House Dragon discovered they were manufacturing guns in secret, ostensibly to protect islands they had settled in the far west, the result was a slaughter that dumbfounded even the other Great Houses. The error is unlikely to be repeated.

From *A History* by Ayel Sorote

Narin and Rhe returned by boat to the Palace of Law, their prisoners trussed and limp in the belly of the small barge. There was barely space for all of them, so the bargeman was forced to perch at the very back of his craft while he rowed, but he made no complaints. If he'd even thought to, the faces of his two conscious passengers would have kept him silent. Rhe was as cold and detached as always, Narin thunderous and glowering.

The rest of the Shure had been empty – conspicuously so. Only those looking to kill Narin had remained; whether the rest had been instructed to keep away or had simply caught wind of last night's events, they couldn't say. Narin refused to believe every man and woman who trained at the Shure in Moon – or any of the others across the Empire – were all thralled to the order's rulers in some cruel, arcane manner, but they had no way of knowing how many were.

And what of those who aren't? Are they innocent in this, or do they know what's going on? Are they complicit and all the more to blame for choosing to be part of it?

He shook his head as his gaze travelled down to the nearer of the two insensate figures.

165

No – perhaps one or two, but the rest must be ignorant. Lots of people want to join for just the reasons I might have in another life. I've never heard of someone being turned away by the goshe – not all can have been poisoned as a child, can they?

The goshe were both young, they all had been. Men with down on their cheeks, women with the slimness of youth making them hard to distinguish from the majority. Boys and girls, really – probably unaware that they were mere living tools, but all the more dangerous for it. They would not question, nor hesitate nor regret.

Or would they? Would they see those they killed for years to come, tormented in dreams they cannot understand, plagued by orders they cannot resist?

Narin found himself biting down on his knuckle, feeling the shudder from striking that woman echo up his arm again. The crisp swipe of hardened ash through the air, the faint flutter of his sleeve and the surge through his body as every muscle worked in unison to deliver its power.

It was a killing blow – that's what dachan has taught me. To put everything into a stroke, to take strength from every part of my body and channel it. On the court it means speed, a strike that might win me the game. But I've long known what dachan was created for, why Investigators are encouraged to play it. And now I'll hear the crack of bone in every point. And now I realise my body's been trained to glory in every blow, to take pleasure in the killing strokes.

Lawbringer Shoten and Investigator Orel remained at the Shure, awaiting a party of Investigators sent in their wake to seal the place off. Narin was glad Rhe hadn't wanted to wait. They had doctors at the Palace of Law – Gods, some even trained at the goshe hospital perhaps – and these two needed attention as much as interrogation.

The problem of Kesh and Irato remained at the forefront of his mind. They were now imprisoned at the compound, secure given the guards on the gate and roof, but to stay there indefinitely? Should they be moved to the Palace of Law? Out in the open, how skilled would an assassin have to be when they feared neither death nor arrest?

The Crescent was busy now; they passed dozens of boats as they skirted the northern edge of the Imperial District. This shore of the island was rocky and unwelcoming, consisting of small jagged beaches beneath sheer cliffs or blank, slime-coated walls of ruined buildings. The ruins were merely walls, mostly, relics of when there had been garrisons and fortifications sheltering the otherworldly presence of the Imperial Palace from attack.

Once they had rounded the lonely spur of island known locally as Demon's Point, the barge turned and headed for the canal dug into the heart of the island hundreds of years previously. The traffic on it was exclusively Imperial functionaries of one form or another, passing a wide stone wharf at the edge of the Palace and branching off down a smaller off-shoot towards the Palace of Law. Narin had never stopped at the Imperial Dock; rarely did he travel by barge at all and certainly no one of his caste would think of using that half-deserted dock.

He knew folk joked that one had to be warrior caste just to row the Emperor's private barge, but the truth wasn't so different. The servant castes who worked in the Palace came from only certain families, breeding with all the exclusive and regimented attention of nobility. Like the bargemen of the Crescent, Imperial servants jealously protected their small niche in the Empire and remained dismissive of all those outside it.

At the Palace of Law, half a dozen young novices were waiting on the dock to receive them. One must have caught sight of Rhe as they approached, Narin reasoned, but when the barge slid neatly into the grey brick dock it was eager voices rather than hands that greeted them.

'Lawbringer!'

The cacophony of excited voices rendered any message entirely garbled, but the youths fell silent when Rhe raised a hand.

'You,' the Lawbringer said, pointing at the eldest. 'There is a message for me?'

The youth flushed with pleasure and bobbed his head. 'The Vanguard Council are waiting on your arrival – you're to attend them at once.'

'Why?'

'The goshe,' was the reply, 'they've sent a delegation! Their leaders arrived almost an hour ago; they're in with the council now and waiting on you, sir.'

Rhe nodded curtly. 'Narin, see to the prisoners then follow me. I want them with a doctor and under guard. Novice, do you know the names of those who've come?'

The young man shook his head. 'No, Lawbringer, but they're high born – came in full ceremony too, litters and heralds all the way to the gate someone said.'

'Have they come to deny involvement? What else could they have come to say?' Narin asked as the novices began hauling the prisoners from the bottom of their barge.

'We shall have to see,' Rhe said at last. 'Attend in the gallery when you are done with these two. It is what they don't say that may prove the most valuable.'

Narin followed the second of the goshe out of the boat, glad to be standing on firm ground again. 'The manner of their denial?'

'Everything that is unsaid. Consider yourself in their position. What would you say if you truly knew nothing, had nothing to hide and were appalled by last night's events? It is hard to forget all you know to play a part – the direction of what they want us to believe may reveal what they already know. Keep that in your mind as you hear their words and decide what is missing – decide why it might be missing and what it tells you.'

Narin bowed and Rhe turned away, marching swiftly toward the Hall of the Vanguard. He walked in the unconsciously poised manner of a nobleman, one elbow bent so his hand rested on the polished pistol butt he had used not long ago to shatter a man's skull.

The Investigator shook himself, realising he was staring with the rest of the novices as they watched their idol stride fearlessly away.

'Come on,' he said gruffly, 'hop to it, all of you. There's work to be done.'

The Hall of the Vanguard, ruling council of the Lawbringers, was a great domed chamber at the heart of the Palace of Law. Having seen his prisoners into the care of the resident doctors and left under heavy guard, Narin hurried through the maze of passageways to reach the hall before much was said. There were half a dozen entrances to the gallery that overlooked the hall, each one flanked by white stone statues of an armed Lawbringer, while glorious colours poured through the narrow entrances from the stained glass of the dome beyond.

One of the few parts of the Palace of Law to bear the grandeur one expected from a palace, the hall was built to seat the five hundred appointed Lawbringers around the walls while in the centre was an enormous oval stone table at which the Law Masters presided. Above it all was a dome structure built of iron and stone, segmented so that fifty long, slender windows ran from the rear of the gallery to the golden spear that pointed straight down from its apex.

As Narin slipped through to the wooden benches of the gallery, the sun came out from behind a cloud and the chamber was filled with

168

a dazzling spray of colours from the images of the Gods arrayed on the glass above. The voices below momentarily stopped as scarlet and orange slashes from Lady Jester's robe erupted across the room, even the Law Masters of the Vanguard made to pause by the riot of colour that filled their sombre chamber.

At the north end was a huge throne large enough for two men to sit side by side. Built of black stained oak and inlaid with gold and gems, the back was a single curved column fully fifteen feet high. Bearing the Emperor's personal sun emblem in gold at the top, it was reserved solely for his Imperial Majesty on ceremonial occasions. Right now Lawbringer Rhe stood before it, carefully keeping apart from the object itself, but the sight itself was enough to make Narin pause and he doubted he was the only one struck by it.

Opposite the throne stood a lesser chair, but still ancient and impressive – the seat of the Lord Martial of the Lawbringers, leader of the Vanguard Council and the only one of them permitted by the Great Houses to bear a military title. Down each side were eight more chairs for the Law Masters of the council. Narin could see the distinctive broad shape of Law Master Sheven in one of the nearest seats, but to his surprise the members of the Vanguard present only occupied one side of the table. Opposite them were men and women in a variety of dress. They could only be the leaders of the goshe.

'Quite a mix, eh?' whispered a voice in his ear.

Narin jumped at the unexpected sound. His mouth fell open as he turned to see Prince Sorote sat just behind him, a small smile on the minor royal's face.

'Close your mouth,' Prince Sorote muttered, 'it's hardly dignified.'

Narin blinked. 'What are you doing here?' he whispered back. 'How did you … ?'

Sorote wore a long white cape over his clothes, but it wasn't exactly anything mimicking Lawbringer garb. Instead it was emblazoned with a stylised sun and, just to make the point clear, Sorote wore the gold-braided collar that announced he was Imperial caste.

'Titles are rather wasted on you, aren't they, Investigator?' Sorote said, still smiling, as he looked back to the table in the centre of the room. 'No, don't worry about formality, bit late now and you're busy. If you need any help working out who's sat down there, by the way, please do just ask.'

'How did you get in here, Prince Sorote?'

'There's no law to preclude members of the public from sitting in on open discussions here, that's rather the point of the Forum isn't it?'

'But still ...' Narin gestured around to indicate Sorote was the only person present not to be in the employ of the Lawbringers somehow.

Sorote shrugged in a way that reminded Narin rules didn't often apply to members of the Imperial caste. The minor prince put a finger to his lips, bidding Narin be quiet. He obeyed reluctantly, knowing the time for questions was later. Rhe had wanted him to be present for this and he could worry about Sorote afterwards.

Down on the floor of the chamber, Rhe finished giving his account of the events at the Shure and the Lord Martial leaned forward in his chair. Rehn ald Har was an archetypal Lord Martial – stern and white-haired, but strong enough to cross staves with the novices when he chose. He was a Wolf by blood; pale skinned with startling red-tinted eyes, but he had lived his whole life in the Imperial City and was utterly devoted to it. What he would be thinking after the events of the last night, Narin could hardly imagine.

'Thank you, Lawbringer,' ald Har announced. 'You may retire.'

Rhe bowed and retreated to a seat out of Narin's view, beneath the gallery. Once he was gone attention turned to the five members of the goshe delegation. As Sorote had suggested, they cut a strange group in any circumstance. Their apparent leader was a nobleman, of House Wyvern, no less, according to the orange emblem on his robe and deep brown skin, while a local female merchant sat on his right and a young man of the religious caste on his left – not a priest, given his clothes, but displaying devoutness by the tattoos on his shaved head and austere black clothes. With a start, Narin saw the young man had similar eyes to Lord ald Har and realised he too was a Wolf.

Of the other two, one was what Narin expected of the goshe, a burly middle-aged man with the stiffened red collar of a warrior caste, while the last was the biggest surprise of the lot. Almost separate from the rest and furthest from the Lord Martial sat a woman with jet black hair swept down over one side of her face and gold braid on her collar. She was strikingly beautiful, with light coffee-coloured skin suggesting mixed parentage, a rare thing for any high-caste, let alone an Imperial. She contrived to lounge in her hard oak chair, content to remain a distraction for the room rather than lead any conversation as would be her right.

'Her name is Kerata,' Sorote continued quietly. 'Not highly ranked within the horde of my cousins, but unmarried still – scandalously, given she's well into her twenties – which gives her significant influence with suitors. Uninterested in the games of court I'm told, but now it's clear why.'

Narin nodded, eyes still fixed on the woman.

The goshe count royal family among their members? That they brought a Wolf before Lord ald Har is unsurprising, but to reveal a royal family member as one of their own – are the goshe that desperate?

'Honoured members of the Vanguard Council,' the Wyvern nobleman began, rising to speak for all of the goshe. 'Let me first say we are equally appalled at the events just related to us. The Shure master in question is not well-known to me, but I had believed him to be a good and honest man, quiet but dedicated.'

As the nobleman spoke, Narin was struck by the contrast between his and Kine's voice. Both had strong tones of home in their accent, but the nobleman's seemed to mangle the Imperial dialect, merging sounds in a deep, baritone rumble where Kine would carefully pick her way through each and every syllable.

'However, it only strengthens our purpose today; that of ensuring no conflict between the Lawbringers and goshe arises.'

None arises? Narin wondered. *Does last night not bloody count?*

'Avoiding conflict is not our concern, Lord Weyerl,' Lord ald Har declared in a firm voice. 'We are the guardians of the law in this city – it is for the goshe to adhere to this law and in recent days, they have not. Consequently, the Lawbringers will act.'

The nobleman, Weyerl, inclined his head.

'I apologise. I did not intend to state otherwise. I meant to say only that crimes committed by members of our Order do not mean the Order is criminal. Ours is not a strict hierarchy; while we have gathered the members of our ruling body, the An-Goshe, before you now, the goshe do not exist in the way a Great House might.

'We meet on an infrequent basis as matters require, but our contact with our brothers and sisters is mostly when attending a Shure.'

Weyerl spread his hands in a politician's gesture of humility as he continued. 'Our positions are principally ceremonial – what authority does exist within the Order resides in the master of each Shure rather than the An-Goshe.'

'Your point is noted. Have you anything further to state?'

Lord Weyerl bowed his head. 'I wish to reiterate our guiding principles, if I may, to confirm the position of our ruling body. The goshe is a brotherhood dedicated to personal betterment, strength of mind and strength of body. We are not a mercenary force of any form and require our members to swear an oath to conform to the Emperor's laws. Beyond that, we came here merely in the assumption you would want to speak to us after the events of last night. These acts have terrible ramifications for the Order and we will only preserve what reputation we have left by giving you every assistance.'

Lord Martial ald Har returned the Wyvern nobleman's bow and turned to where Rhe sat. 'The investigation is to be conducted by Lawbringer Rhe and so I turn matters over to him.'

A murmur of anticipation seemed to run around the Investigators and novices assembled on the gallery. A public interrogation was a rare thing, most especially of high-born individuals.

'Lord Weyerl,' Rhe began gravely as he reappeared in Narin's view, 'when were you first informed of these events?'

Weyerl folded his hands together and remained standing as he spoke. 'A runner came to the gates of my home around dawn. It is no secret within Dragon District that I am a member of the goshe, so the master of the Shure I attend did not hesitate to contact me. How he heard I do not know, but city rumour seems to have carried the news far.

'I sent messages to my colleagues here,' Weyerl said as he turned slightly left then right to indicate those beside him, 'and we met within the hour, realising the gravity of the situation. We agreed we should come straight to the Palace of Law and wait on your convenience rather than be summoned.'

'These are all the members of your ruling council?'

Weyerl frowned slightly at the term, having been at pains to downplay their power, but he did not argue the point. 'All the members within the city, yes.'

'Which of you has jurisdiction over the free hospital?'

'None of us.'

'There is another who does?'

'Jurisdiction has never been necessary,' Weyerl clarified. 'The free hospital in Raven District is still a Shure with a master. The training there is merely of a different form to most Shure. My colleagues and I would only ever interfere if such a thing was requested by members of the Shure.'

'The name of the master for the free hospital?'

'Addenalai.'

Rhe paused a moment, perhaps having expected to hear the name Jehq as Narin had. 'Father Addenalai? And where is he presently?'

Weyerl pursed his lips. 'Assuming what I heard is correct, you arrested him last night.'

'Do you know why?'

There was a fractional pause. 'I do not. I have been told the Shure was searched and its doors locked, that is all.'

'But you come here to preclude the possibility of a conflict rather than demand an explanation? You are a most restrained man.'

The goshe inclined his head. 'Self-control lies at the heart of our teachings. Whether instructed in science or the martial arts, one is a danger to those around one without control.'

'Tell me about the master in Moon District,' Rhe said, moving away from the topic as though they were merely exchanging pleasantries.

'I … I do not know him. I have been told Shure Master Nemeke was a teacher who commanded great respect among his pupils, but that he had a personal dispute with a former member of his Shure.'

'Oh? And that was?'

'One Estan Tokene of House Shadow.'

'Do you know the nature of the dispute?'

Weyerl shook his head. 'Only that it was over a woman, nothing more.'

'You said former member?'

'I am told Master Tokene ceased attending the Shure after an argument with the Shure Master – one that involved threats.'

'From both sides or just one? Surely a Shure Master possesses your remarkable calm?'

Weyerl merely blinked at that. 'We are all human, we are all fallible.'

'Do you know what the argument was about?'

'No. However I do know Master Tokene has been involved in other disputes. He has been described as paranoid and erratic, prone to drink and bouts of aggression. He was for a time treated at an asylum run by the Order, afflicted with an imbalance of the mind, but after the argument with Master Nemeke he disappeared and has not been seen since. It is the opinion of the goshe that we have failed him and still consider his care our responsibility.'

'Most noble of you,' Rhe said in a level voice. 'Is this a common thing – to show such care for the more erratic and aggressive members of your Order?'

'We attempt to care for all who need it; that is a founding principle of the Order,' Weyerl said carefully.

'So an aide at the free hospital named Perel, he is also your responsibility?'

The nobleman blinked. 'I, ah, I do not know the name. If he is … we have many working at the free hospital, I know only very few of them. If there is a man of that name there, I'm sure the Order would embrace him also.'

'Would your responsibility extend to his attempted murder of a young woman on the orders of a doctor there? One Father Jehq, I believe.'

The pause was slight, but Narin was listening for it. 'We cannot be held responsible for a man's crimes,' Weyerl said stiffly. 'A man's actions are his own and the Emperor's law must be upheld.'

'I'm glad we agree there. Do you know the whereabouts of Father Jehq so we can question him directly?'

'I do not – I know the name only. I have never met him, but I find it difficult to believe he could order such a thing.'

'Why not? You've never met the man.'

'He is a healer, not a killer – and why would he order his aide to murder anyone? What possible motive is there?'

'Motive is my concern,' Rhe declared. 'In the meantime, put the word out that he is to turn himself in for questioning immediately.'

'Do you have evidence for this?' Weyerl asked. 'You believe Fathers Nemeke and Jehq acted in collusion? On whose testimony? This woman's?'

Rhe paused. 'I note you assume it was the same young woman in each instance. As a matter of fact it was, but let us return to the principal matter at hand – the assassination attempt committed last night at an Imperial compound by at least ten members of the House Moon Shure.'

'Ten?' Weyerl asked pointedly. 'I had only heard that Nemeke sent his most easily swayed pupils to murder a young woman. I had assumed that meant two or three of the youngest members who, regrettably, are often more focused on the martial disciplines and obedience than the spiritual ones that accompany them. Might I be permitted to inquire why the woman was at an Imperial compound in the first place, and how she survived if there were ten attackers?'

174

'She was not alone there – the young woman had impressed upon us a fear for her life, having arrived at the Palace of Law bloodied and bruised after the first attack on her. Furthermore, Investigator Narin took a number of precautions against attack and, as official record will testify, is not a man unfamiliar with being outnumbered.'

Narin winced, not daring to turn his head and see what Prince Sorote's reaction would be to the assertion.

'It was this Investigator's own rooms,' Weyerl asked with studied confusion on his face, 'rather than this secured premises?' He gestured to the great hall they currently stood in and Narin heard a mutter from all around the gallery as others wondered the same thing.

'She was not under arrest,' Rhe said, 'and she was concerned that associates of Father Jehq might assume she had come into our care and seek her here. As last night has shown, the more fanatical among your Order are not dissuaded by any authority.'

'But no assassins would breach the Palace of Law, surely?' Weyerl insisted. 'So why remove her from its safety?'

Rhe did not respond immediately – instead he gave the nobleman a long look before turning to Law Master Sheven. Whether he got any sort of response from the Law Master, Narin couldn't tell.

Prince Sorote nudged Narin's elbow. 'As much as I'm enjoying the show, why is Weyerl pressing our famous Lawbringer on this?'

Narin scowled, but forced himself to face the man. Before he could speak, Rhe finally replied to the question.

'There was a concern that her attackers had some sort of assistance from demons, that she might not in fact be safe from all assaults on this Palace.'

Prince Sorote and Weyerl gasped in the same breath, as did most of those watching. Despite the man's dark skin, Narin thought he could detect a flush of anger in Weyerl's cheeks. But as the nobleman spluttered and blustered about the increasingly farcical nature of these claims, Sorote's attention became only more fixed.

'Demons?' he whispered.

Narin didn't respond, but Sorote jolted his elbow once more, pointedly this time, and repeated the word. With a sinking feeling, Narin explained.

'Lawbringer Rhe is misrepresenting the facts,' he whispered, 'rather than accuse them outright of conspiracy.'

'The goshe within the Lawbringers,' Sorote said in a knowing tone. 'It would cripple you, to accuse your own.'

'What did you say?'

The Imperial nobleman smiled smugly at him. 'I deal in information, whatever form it comes in. I've known for a while there are goshe within the Lawbringers – I could provide you with a few names even, if you wish. That you suspect their allegiance is with the goshe rather than the Lawbringers, however, I find interesting.'

Down on the floor of the chamber Lord ald Har rapped a smooth-edged stone on the table top, a fist-sized chunk of rock that tradition dictated was used as a gavel in this chamber. Almost immediately the muttering voices subsided, but Lord Weyerl's clear voice filled the gap.

'Lord ald Har – now we have accusations of demon-worshipping thrown at us? It seems to me this is at best the ravings of a handful of disturbed individuals – at worst your Lawbringer has naively allowed himself to be swayed by an orchestrated attempt to discredit the goshe Order!'

'You will lower your voice,' the Lord Martial replied coldly, 'and calm yourself before you level accusations you cannot rescind.' The old man had half-stood in his anger – but it was not reserved solely for Weyerl, given the glare he afforded Rhe.

Narin found himself leaning forward in anticipation. The credibility of the Lawbringers was the Lord Martial's highest priority, he knew that. With the Emperor only a titular figure and the Lawbringers existing on sufferance of the Great Houses, their authority was a precarious currency.

While it certainly wasn't the existence of demons that was in dispute, Narin couldn't think of any plausible account of humans acting in collusion with them. At best there were only brief, isolated instances of possession that bore little resemblance to current events.

'Lawbringer Rhe,' ald Har continued, 'your allegation is grave. Do you have evidence to support it?'

'I am investigating the allegations of others,' Rhe replied with a respectful bow to the Lord Martial, 'I make no such claims at present, but merely explain my actions in calming a frightened woman who wished her location to be a secret from those trying to kill her.'

'Others?' Weyerl echoed, seizing upon the word. 'What others? Have you Master Tokene in your custody? Or were you bringing the girl to her lover and Nemeke had her followed all the way? Is that where this madness comes from? Two disturbed lunatics whose madness the Lawbringers have foolishly believed and encouraged?'

'The only individuals I have in custody are those arrested at the free hospital, and none are mad that I am aware.'

'Then I demand they are immediately released.'

'Demand?' ald Har growled. 'You do not make demands in this place!'

Weyerl bowed just as Rhe had done. 'My apologies – I request they are released, unless you have other testimony to support such fanciful claims?'

At Narin's side, Prince Sorote suddenly gave a purr of pleasure. 'You've got this supposed madman,' he whispered to Narin, delight clear in his face. 'He's the one making these claims, isn't he? Stars above, what secrets can he tell – could you take down the entire goshe Order?'

Narin pursed his lips. 'And your interest in all this is?'

'Oh please, do you think I would be sitting here if I was a goshe agent?' Sorote muttered scornfully. 'I'd offer to show you my tattoos if I thought it would prove anything, but credit me with a little more grace than that, my friend.'

'I'm not your friend.'

Sorote tensed at the anger in Narin's voice. 'Perhaps not, but a little civility would still be appropriate, *Master* Narin. The look on your face tells me you're far more out of your depth than you realised yesterday – just how far I wonder? I smell secrets here. When Lawbringer Rhe himself makes false claims before the Vanguard Council, the stakes must really be high in this game. Just remember that he's the golden boy of the Lawbringers and a nobleman too – you're neither. If a wave comes crashing down on you all, might be you want to have a friend able to throw you a lifeline.'

'And I should trust my future to the good graces of an Imperial prince I barely know?' Narin asked. 'Hoping he's not just readying me for a fall?'

Sorote's smile faded. 'You've readied your own fall,' he said sharply and rose to leave. 'I could discredit your investigation right now should I want to, but I'm not your enemy, despite your obvious misgivings about my caste. You would do well to remember that, Investigator. Until we meet again, Master Narin.'

CHAPTER 13

*To observers of the politics of court there is one marked oddity in these deli-
cate and ephemeral dealings. The lords of Leviathan are rare presences and
their islands far less populous than any other Great House, yet when they
are present, the respect they are offered borders on the painstaking. Without
the economic or apparent military power to warrant this, one must wonder
what marvels and horrors those seafarers have encountered as they plumb
the ocean depths.*

From A *History* by Ayel Sorote

It was not long before Lawbringer Rhe had finished questioning the
goshe's leaders. They left without fanfare; stiff thanks offered by Lord
Martial ald Har and Rhe, curt bows from the goshe – with the exception of the Imperial woman, who merely swept out the door without
waiting. The entertainment over, most of those watching from the
gallery filed out, discussing what they'd heard in urgent whispers.

Before long there remained only three men in the chamber below:
Rhe, standing regally at the Emperor's end of the table, Law Master
Sheven, and ald Har, head bowed and leaning heavily on the opposing
end as though old age had rushed upon him. Narin stayed where he
was, unsure whether to go or stay, but Rhe's attention was on the Lord
Martial of the Lawbringers alone.

They stayed that way for a long while, long enough for Narin to
be sure the room below was empty. Finally, there came a deep rumble
from the throat of Sheven.

'Did they think bringing an Imperial here would cow us?' the bearded
Law Master growled. 'Are they so certain of their position?'

'It means we must take care before we proceed, my friend,' ald Har
replied wearily. 'They brought her as a warning and it served its purpose.'

178

'What? You can't be serious, Lord Martial!' Sheven said furiously.

Ald Har raised a hand to cut off his colleague's protests. 'The warning is what it is; I cannot choose to pretend it does not exist.'

'It does not change the law!'

The Lord Martial smashed a fist down on the stone table. 'Do not lecture me about the law! You think I could forget it so easily?'

'Then this changes nothing,' Sheven said in a more restrained voice. 'Lawbringer Rhe's investigation exists under my purview – you cannot order me to cease matters simply because it may lead to all strata of society!'

'Have I asked that?'

Sheven hesitated. 'No, but ...'

'Then do not put words in my mouth, old friend,' ald Har advised. 'Now – this investigation is closed by your name. Rhe will pursue it without providing account to any other than yourself. I will trust you have sufficient reason to do this and I shall not ask why, but the fact remains – this may tarnish Imperials and nobles. The royal family may be vast, but the Emperor values the station even of those he does not know by name. Delicacy is called for unless you would enjoy being summoned to the Imperial Palace. Am I clear?'

Sheven grunted, his fiery nature blunted by the man's words. 'As you command, Lord Martial.'

'Thank you. Lawbringer Rhe, what resources will you need to pursue this matter?'

Rhe took a long breath and a brief blaze of scarlet from the stained glass above illuminated his pale face. 'I could employ every Lawbringer, Investigator and novice we have; search every Shure and hospital belonging to the goshe without finding the man I seek. And so I ask for nothing.'

'Nothing?' Sheven and ald Har echoed together.

Rhe inclined his head. 'As you have recognised, it could be damaging to the Emperor and society as a whole if we blindly tarnish the names of all goshe. What is served by acting as though a conspiracy exists when our evidence is a single unverified account?'

Narin gave a cough of surprise at what his uncompromising mentor had just suggested. He'd always thought Rhe would let the Empire burn in the name of the law.

Are we all prisoners to our caste after all? Even Rhe?

The Lord Martial looked from Sheven to Rhe, but neither man seemed willing to provide an explanation for the apparent turn-around.

'We are all servants of the Emperor's law,' ald Har said at last, his tone making it sound a warning as much as a reminder.

'And I intend to see his justice done,' Rhe replied with a bow, 'but how I go about it must be mine alone. The Lawbringers may be better served if I act alone.'

After a long pause it was clear from the Lord Martial's face that he recognised the sense in Rhe's words. They all knew the death-sentence that awaited any Lawbringer abusing their position, so ald Har chose not to speak further. Trusting the judgement of his long-time friend, he turned and left without another word.

'And now?' Sheven asked, looking up at the gallery.

Narin glanced around, automatically guilty at having witnessed such a scene though he knew they had all been aware of his presence. From his position, Narin could see the gallery was clear and gave Sheven a nod to confirm they were alone.

'Now I must go,' Rhe said evenly. 'I have prisoners to see to.'

'Is there nothing I can do?'

Rhe's grey eyes levelled at the Law Master. 'Pray our suspicions do not come true – but even that, I fear, will do no good.'

Narin trotted down the stair that led to the ground floor of the Palace of Law. He emerged into a busy corridor that ran all the way around the circular council chamber and for a moment watched the flow of humanity. Men and women of all ages crossed his path, unmindful of the graceful vaulting and ornate clerestory windows above their heads. Stone carvings of a sun with four golden rays extending from it were all around. The iconography of Imperial service that could be seen through this district was nowhere more heavily repeated than here.

The Palace of Law contained several distinct wings, including a large walled-off section that housed courtrooms and a small corps of Imperial-sanctioned lawyers, bolstered by a contingent from the Great Houses. That lay to the east of the Hall of the Vanguard, with the gaol and execution ground toward the shore of the island, facing the high towers of House Eagle across the waters of the Crescent.

As he started off down the corridor, Narin found himself glancing out towards the great open doorway at the Noble Courts. They were a pair of square buildings four storeys high and surrounded by flying buttresses in the alternating shapes of four Gods; Lord Lawbringer, Lady Magistrate, Lady Pity and Lord Monk, all presided over by a towering statue of the God-Empress.

Despite the time he had spent here over the years, Narin had never lost that slight thrill of the grandeur of these white stone buildings. The temple-like courts and chambers that demanded quiet reverence, the statues and carvings throughout – all in the unearthly presence of the Imperial Palace, as imposing and unchanging as a mountain. Today, however, Narin found himself hunching his shoulders, the presence of all the Gods more than he wished to bear. He felt them watch him with hawk-like scrutiny and wondered – how long any man could endure the attention of Gods?

Passing through a hall lined with Imperial flags, he was woken from his thoughts by an unexpected yank on his arm. Narin flinched, half-reaching for his stave, before he realised who had caught hold of his arm – Diman, his neighbour at the compound.

'There you are!' the younger man gasped, 'I've been looking all over for you.'

'What's wrong?'

'Nothing,' Diman said hurriedly. 'Quite the opposite I'd guess. Got you another visitor, and not a bad-looking one either!'

Narin scowled at the Investigator and the young man's face fell. 'Right, yes. Anyways, she's waiting at the shrine on the second floor – under escort of course.'

Narin felt a flood of relief. 'Gods, Kesh's mother!'

He clapped a hand of thanks on Diman's shoulder and broke into a run for the stairs. Wide stone staircases flanked a central block at the heart of the palace wing that looked out over Lawbringer's Square. Broad enough for seven men to ascend together, the staircases led from opposing directions onto the first floor hall and similarly grand steps took him up to the upper floor; a less public area of the palace where half of the city's Lawbringers shared offices.

He skidded around a pair of clerks and almost collided with a tall Lawbringer, drawing a cut-off curse from the woman as Narin clipped his ankle on the steel-shod end of her scabbard. Half-limping, he called an apology as he turned the corner and continued on towards the shrine to Lord Lawbringer that stood at the end of the upper hall.

Three arched doorways separated off the space, but it was all open to the traffic of passing Lawbringers and Investigators as they went about their daily duties.

Ahead of him Narin saw a pair of elderly Lawbringers bow respectfully to the statue of Lord Lawbringer facing down the hallway towards him. At the sight he clattered to a halt, remembering the level of respect required for the shrine, whether or not it occupied a through-route for all the offices on the south face of the palace. He paused at the arched doorways, bowing to Lord Lawbringer then scouting around for his new visitor among the dozen or so people within the shrine's bounds.

For a moment he didn't see her, but then a figure in a dark blue dress stepped out from behind one of six stone tablets that bore the Lawbringers' oaths. From her stance as much as anything, Narin recognised the woman as Kesh's mother – hands clasped anxiously, but back straight and face rigid in defiance of the world. He hurried over and fear flashed across the woman's face until he bowed to her and spoke.

'Mistress Hinar?' Narin inquired as gently as he could. 'Teike Hinar?'

A wave of relief seemed to break across her face. 'Merciful Gods. It's true – my daughter's here? She told you to expect me?'

'She did – your daughter's safe,' Narin said as calmly as he could.

'Take me to her!' Teike demanded. 'Please, I must see her!'

'Mistress, please, we must talk first.'

'What? What about?'

Without warning the woman took a step forward and looked about to grab Narin by the throat as bristling indignation took her over. Behind her, a novice assigned to attend her drifted forward, anticipating a confrontation, but Narin gave him a look and he backed off, retiring to a discreet distance.

'Mistress Hinar,' Narin continued, 'matters are not so simple – please, trust me and spare me some time first.'

'Are you a bloody fool?' Teike snapped. 'I've just spent the night in hiding – one of my daughters has been murdered! You expect me to wait and listen to you? I want my daughter, *right* now – I need to know she's safe. Kesh said there were people looking for us, that they'd killed Emari and were looking for us too!'

She took a deep breath, one that threatened to shake loose the tears of grief and fear that threatened beneath the surface.

'I don't know what's happening,' Teike continued quietly. 'The message gave no details, but right now I do not care. Do you hear me? I came here thinking I would be murdered in the street; I almost didn't come at all. Whatever's going on, whatever's happened, I don't care. The city can burn for all I give a damn until I see my girl's safe and well.'

'She's safe,' Narin insisted, 'under guard by a friend of mine, but I can't take you to her.'

'Why in Jester's name not?' she snapped, almost shouting directly into his face. 'What's going on?'

'Please – lower your voice,' Narin said stonily, well aware of the looks they would be receiving from every Lawbringer nearby. 'I am trying to help you, but my power to help Kesh is dependent on my position here and creating a disturbance in the shrine of Lord Lawbringer hampers that.'

Teike flushed with rage and glared around her, but managed to get control of her emotions and nodded.

'Very well,' she said, and allowed him to guide her past the shrine towards the long bank of thin windows beyond, where the sill running all along the wall was deep enough to sit.

'Now first – I don't believe you are in any danger now, but your daughter still is,' Narin said in a quiet voice. 'I cannot take you to where she is hiding because almost certainly it is being watched and once inside you will not be able to leave again. She'll be vulnerable out on the street. There is a band of professional killers after her.'

'Why? What in Pity's name could she have done to deserve that?'

'Nothing,' Narin said with feeling. 'It was just bad … terrible luck, for Emari and then for her.'

'What happened? How did Emari die?' Teike gasped, doubling over all of a sudden as though Narin had punched her. 'How did my little girl die? Where is her body?'

'I don't know,' Narin admitted, 'but I will tell you everything I can. Now, do you remember your guest who went missing? Master Tokene Shadow?'

Behind the tears, her face hardened. It was no different to the look he'd seen on Kesh's face the previous night – just as she stabbed a man in the throat. Narin took a long breath and began to recount her daughter's story.

*

183

The big man sidled down the street towards her, a long battered coat down to his knees. He squinted and frowned at the ground as he went, chancing only brief glances up to navigate before lowering his head once more to let greasy strands of hair hang across his face. It only accentuated the stoop Kodeh often seemed to walk with, burdened by the weight of his massive arms and fists the size of hams.

The black-skinned Dragon drew no curious glances here in Tale, but still the man felt vulnerable, Synter could see. Without armour or mask, without most of his usual weapons or the cover of night, Kodeh clearly felt exposed within the foot-traffic of the Fett Canal towpath.

Too stupid to realise his clothes are his protection, Synter joked to herself, scanning his appearance to ensure there was nothing that would give him away. A grubby black neckerchief was tied around his bull neck, almost invisible against the man's dark skin, while on his feet Kodeh wore hempen sandals rather than his usual heavy boots.

At least he remembers his roots well enough, she thought, smiling inwardly. *I don't have to worry about him being too proud to look peasant caste and get noticed by some observant Lawbringer.*

Overhead, a pair of seagulls resumed the screaming calls she'd had to put up with all morning. Synter glanced up and scowled, resisting the urge to fetch a crossbow and put a bolt through each bird's tiny brain. Instead, she shifted in her seat and continued to work her knife over the carcass before her while the seagulls peered down at the bloody mess on the table.

'Needed to get your hands bloody today?' Kodeh commented as he joined her. To one side of Synter was a battered brass samovar, polished as lovingly as any temple effigy, and he helped himself to a tall cup of black tea.

'I can't sit out here all day without something to do,' Synter replied, putting the slim knife down a moment to re-roll one sleeve up again. 'The cook's not much of a butcher anyway.'

Kodeh looked past her, through the open window into the empty eatery beyond. It wasn't open for business yet so they were safe to talk.

'We all use our Blessings in different ways, I guess,' Kodeh muttered, wrinkling his nose at the half-dismembered pig carcass.

They were considered low-caste beasts, pigs, and not fit for any noble table, but that was one detail the low-born Synter was glad to put up with. Kodeh drained his cup and set it down before sitting with his back against the wall so he could look both ways down the canal with minimal effort.

'Good news, I take it?' she said.

Kodeh nodded with a grunt. 'Building's intact, guards still there – your watchers likewise. If it's under surveillance, it's by someone better'n me.'

'Or more unnatural,' Synter muttered. 'And that's saying something, so the whores of Arbold tell.'

Kodeh grinned wolfishly. 'Never trust a whore,' was his only reply.

'Uttir was here not long ago, said Father Pallasane reported the same,' Synter commented. 'Though what that truly means, buggered if I know.'

'That stunted fuck's about as unnatural as I ever saw,' Kodeh said, 'including the soldier-demon we took down a few nights back. Not much'll slip past his paranoia.'

'So it's time to commit – throw the bones and see what happens.'

'Aye, sir,' Kodeh confirmed, gaze still roving up and down the late-morning passersby. 'Waiting on your order.'

The weather had become overcast since morning, a chill in the air that hadn't been there earlier. It came from the mountains to the north-east, Synter knew – she'd lived in this city long enough to taste the cold air off House Eagle's icy heart. A promise of heavy fog to come, she guessed.

'A good omen, for them who believe in 'em,' she said, tilting her nose up to the sky. 'Cold air coming in.'

'Aye, fog tonight – thick enough for Mischief Night itself,' Kodeh agreed. 'What tricks do you fancy playing on our betters, then?'

'Quiet ones,' she warned. 'The An-Goshe just claimed last night was an isolated incident. We don't want to contradict that if we can help it.'

'When the fuck do they order us around?'

She shook her head. 'They don't – they got their orders just as we got ours. Too many eyes on what we do right now, it's not our way.'

'Nor was being betrayed by our own,' Kodeh growled, fingers tightening into a fist. 'What do we do about him?'

'We've got a handful of slaved minds left from the Moon District Shure – only three, but enough to justify the An-Goshe sending a message to the Lawbringers later today. If they're warned a few remaining rogues are out for Irato's blood, we mebbe get another throw of the bones before they realise we're cheating.'

'You think they'll get to him?' Kodeh hawked and spat noisily on the

185

cobbled ground beyond the eatery's decking. 'Nah, you'd need dozens to kill Irato now.'

'Mebbe they get lucky, mebbe it's cover for us to act instead.' She shrugged and finished her work, casting one final glance at the seagulls in case they risked grabbing a piece. 'Either way, he's not given away our locations yet. He's no fool, seems he's playing his own game and buying us time. Mebbe forcing us to act – Father Jehq's been worrying like an old woman this past year, bad as the rest of them.'

'Time to push new blood through?' Kodeh said with a gleam in his startling eyes. 'Give the old blood a bit of an airing?'

Synter put her knife down and dragged over a bucket to scrub the blood from her forearms and hands. 'Don't underestimate them,' she said, 'they gave us the Blessings – you can bet they held some back for themselves.'

'Then what?'

'We lead them. None of us have the knowledge to perform the ritual, but they're too timid to do anything 'less we force the issue. Might be I could turn some to our side, but you want to risk getting it wrong?' She shook her head. 'No, for the moment the Detenii remain the sharp end we're meant to be. Be as the seagulls,' she added with a theatrical flourish.

'Eh? Seagulls?' Kodeh glanced upward where the gulls watched the bloody remains with hungry eyes. 'What about 'em?'

Synter smiled. 'Too spiteful even for demons to try and possess, so the stories go; and bold enough to snatch food out o' your hand if you're not paying attention, but these two haven't moved. They're watching me sure, but they're not stupid enough to risk it and nor should we be. Enough blood'll be spilled before this is over, but I've got other work planned. So track down the team leaders. I want them all here at dusk for orders.'

'You're the commander,' Kodeh said with a note of scepticism as he heaved himself up out of his seat. 'You're the one the teams are loyal to, though, so when you give me the word ...' He let the suggestion of treachery and murder hang unspoken.

She nodded. 'I know. We're just not there yet.'

'And the artefact?'

'We keep watching. Send someone into the building come nightfall; they go in and report back to somewhere neutral. If there's a higher order in this game, we need to know. Someone expendable, though. I don't know about you, but I don't fancy having my soul ripped out through my eyes and flayed by some demon-prince with a grudge.'

When Narin was finished, Teike remained silent and very still. He watched her process his words, unsure what else to say and painfully aware he'd been of little comfort. He'd been careful not to tell her everything, not to share Enchei's secrets or anything else that could only prove dangerous for all concerned, but she still knew more than the Lord Martial of the Lawbringers now.

'What now? Fanatics, demons, poisons that steal a man's mind … What now for Kesh?'

Narin didn't speak at first. She looked up, unashamed of the tears lingering on her cheeks, and waited for a response. Her scarf hung loose around her neck, the length of white cotton a mark of her caste as much as something to tie her hair up with.

'Now we find a way to get her to safety,' he said and tentatively reached out to put a hand on her arm. 'I'll protect her with my life,' he added with conviction. 'That is my oath.'

He pointed at the standing tablets around the statue of Lord Lawbringer, arranged in the shape of the God's constellation – points on the stone floor connected by a groove that described the pattern of the stars.

'"Protect the innocent",' he read from the first of the tablets, '"punish the guilty". That is what my life's devoted to. Lawbringer Rhe's too, and he will be beside me in all I do.'

'"Weigh in judgement the souls of the accused",' Teike said in response, pointing at another tablet. 'Do these goshe even have souls? Are they no better than demons – worse indeed, worse than those fox-spirits who seem to have a claim on my daughter?'

'"Seek truth in all things",' a new voice declared, prompting them both to flinch and look up to where Rhe had silently approached. '"Fear nothing bar failure". "Embrace pain as the price of service". "Carry the Emperor's light into dark places". Soulless or not, Madam, they will be held to account.'

Rhe stopped and fixed Teike with his stern, unblinking steel gaze. 'Mistress Hinar – you have my sympathies for the loss of your daughter.'

'Thank you, Lord Lawbringer,' Teike said in a choked voice, even her proud bearing affected by the man's regard. 'But sympathy won't bring Emari back,' she added, 'and I don't even have a body to bury. See my other daughter safe, Lawbringer. Stop these murderers and see Kesh safe.'

Her last words were spoken as nothing more than a whisper, but Narin felt them drive home like icy needles into his heart. If Rhe was similarly affected he gave no sign, but the Lawbringer bowed to her in response.

'Come, Narin.'

CHAPTER 14

One under-appreciated cause of the Lesser Empire's permanent state of detente is naked belligerence. The boldest and least subtle of the Great Houses, House Dragon's ongoing primacy within the empire in part results from being, in the opinion of some, humourless savages who will go to war over nothing irrespective of the casualties. Not to this writer obviously, I hold nothing but the highest esteem for our benevolent protectors, but the cost of overthrowing them is acknowledged by all.

From A *History* by Ayel Sorote

Back at his home, Narin and Rhe greeted the Lawbringer overseeing the compound's guards. Hetellin was only a year or so older than Narin and the two knew each other well, having almost grown up together in noviciate dormitories and classrooms. Tall and slim, such was the newly-raised Lawbringer's pride in his position that he never removed his hand from the pristine sword hilt at his hip, even as he bowed.

'Lawbringer Rhe,' Hetellin said formally.

Narin bowed to his superior, knowing Hetellin was a stickler for such details, but his attention was caught by something else entirely. On either side of the gate, watching the street while Hetellin and Rhe spoke, were a man and a woman in Investigator grey – both tall with pronounced features, one dark haired, one silvery-blond. They each carried staves in their left hand as one might expect, but each also wore a double-holster strapped across their belly – a pair of slim pistols nestling inside.

Noble-born, Narin thought to himself. *The goshe aren't the only ones who can deploy their high-caste members.*

'Lawbringer Hetellin,' Rhe acknowledged. 'All has been quiet?'

'Just so, Lawbringer,' Hetellin said. 'The only movement has been that tattooist friend of Investigator Narin's, leaving and returning not long ago.'

He spoke with such a note of distaste that Narin had to force himself not to smile. Of course Hetellin would not like Enchei's attitude, the vague disregard he had for authority that bordered on disrespect.

'Did he say where he went?' Narin asked. Given he was heading in to talk to his friend, it hardly mattered, but he knew Enchei would have delighted in needling the dour Lawbringer and Narin found himself adding to that instinctively.

'He declined to.'

'Oh – declined? So he wasn't just out fetching supplies? He does like to pick over the morning catch at the markets.'

'He brought no food,' Hetellin confirmed frostily, 'and was not gone long enough to be at work.'

Narin nodded, his best expression of understanding on his face. 'They don't give him many shifts; the poor man can barely earn an honest living. His work is excellent, but of course he came late to the House of the Sun and his status is low.'

'One would not know it by his attitude.'

'Narin, perhaps you should go inside and speak to your charges?' Rhe suggested pointedly. 'I will deal with matters out here.'

'Of course, Lawbringer,' Narin said, mentally cursing himself. He bowed low to the two of them and advanced on the gate.

In his way was the dark-haired woman, a House Raven warrior caste, and she gave him an unfriendly look as she stepped out of his way. He inclined his head to her, careful to be polite having already earned Rhe's disapproval, but relishing the sniff of distaste at moving for a lower-born man.

Once inside, he saw several doors were propped open despite the cool afternoon and faces peered out at him from them – more guards, he realised – but it was a woman's voice that called to him before he'd crossed to the steps leading up to his room.

'Narin – Investigator!'

He whirled around to see Mistress Sheti hurrying over, a thick shawl wrapped tight around her shoulders and a look of relief on her face. 'I heard what happened at the Shure, are you hurt?'

He shook his head, realising a smile had crept onto his face at the sight of her. After a morning of goshe, Imperials and stern-faced Lawbringers, it was a pleasure to speak to someone normal for a change.

'I'm fine,' he reassured her, 'they were no match for Rhe. How are you?'

Sheti frowned. 'How do you think? Men tried to kill you last night. There were dead bodies out in the courtyard half the morning!'

'I know, I'm sorry about that – I never really expected it to happen, in truth.'

'And what now? Has Kesh's mother been found?'

'She's safe and at the Palace of Law.'

'Oh thank the Gods,' Sheti gasped. 'That poor girl's grieving enough – go tell her the news.'

Narin nodded. 'I will. Are you sure you're okay?'

'I'm fine, my boy – shaken up is all. We all are. I think you've forgotten not every resident here is an Investigator!'

'I've not forgotten,' he said, feeling a pang of guilt all the same. 'How many are left?'

'Just me, bar the Investigators who were woken and put straight to guard duty. The rest were escorted out with their heads bare so no one could mistake them for your friends upstairs – a strange precaution, that. I heard the Lawbringer say they're not allowed to return tonight, not unless Rhe gives permission. Do you think he will?'

Narin shook his head. 'Tomorrow, I hope.'

'You've something planned?'

'We need to do something,' he said with a nod of agreement. 'We can't just sit here and hope it'll all work out.'

'So, what?' She raised a hand. 'No, wait; I don't want to know – I've heard enough already. If it's all the same with you, I think it best I keep clear unless you need something of me. Go explain matters to your new friends up there; they're the ones without a choice here.'

Narin gave a weak smile. 'You've got a point there. I should be trained for this sort of thing, but even I'd prefer it to be someone else's problem. I'm far enough out of my depth as it is.'

'Rubbish,' Sheti said, only then remembering they were not alone in the courtyard. She blushed and lowered her eyes, adding, 'if you don't mind me saying, Master Narin. You've told me often enough – being a Lawbringer's all you ever wanted. You'd never walk away from them even if you had the choice.'

'Doesn't mean I'm happy with the choices I've got,' Narin said in a glum voice. 'Ah, you're right. This is all I've ever wanted – the chance to prove myself as a Lawbringer. I'd just hoped for an even chance when the time came. I can't even tell my superiors everything, for fear of what trouble that might bring!' He shook his head. 'But to let murderers win? No, I'd rather die than turn away.'

Sheti caught his hand and squeezed it, giving him a warm smile then nodding towards the stair. Narin left without a further word, but he was heartened by the strength of the resolve inside him. He took the steps two at a time and, with one look at the guards squatting on the shallow sloped roof on the opposite side of the compound, went to his own door and rapped his knuckles on it.

'It's me,' he called, feeling foolish as he did so, 'it's Narin.'

'So it is,' Enchei said from behind the door, accompanied by a scraping sound as some sort of bar was removed. 'Fresh from your latest escapades I hear.'

'Gods, has the whole city heard?' Narin wondered as he slipped inside the dimly lit room. The air was thick, with the doors and windows barred; too many people in close confinement, too many men and women killed in there the previous night.

'Ripe in here, eh? And yes, most of the city will've heard by now – the news has reached the markets and everyone knows how gossip goes through this city like bad shrimp.'

Narin wrinkled his nose. 'Smells like gossip in here, then.'

'Was worse before we cleaned,' Kesh said with a grimace.

'Aye, never got used to it myself after years of soldiering,' Enchei said darkly. The grey-haired man seemed lost in his memories for a moment then shook the mood off. 'I guess cleaning ain't why you're here.'

'No – but I've got some good news at least,' Narin said, brightening as he turned to Kesh. 'Your mother's alive and well, Kesh – demanding to see you of course, but I've persuaded her the Palace of Law is the safest place for her at the moment.'

'You spoke to her! She got my message?' Kesh jumped out of her seat, delight spread across her face. 'When can I see her?'

'When your life isn't in danger!' Narin said, almost laughing at the change in her manner. 'Soon, just as soon as we can get you out of here.'

'Well? What're we waiting for?' Kesh demanded, looking round at the three men. 'Can't your Investigators escort us there?'

Narin's smile wavered. 'No – I don't know, but I don't want to risk it.'

'What? Even now, in the middle of the day?'

Enchei put a restraining hand on her arm. 'Kesh, lass – he's right. You're at your most vulnerable out in the street. These goshe don't care if they die getting to you and Irato. You know they're slaves to the will of others.'

'Oh, so suddenly you're an expert in assassination too?' Kesh snapped, rounding on him. The look on Enchei's face was stony but it barely blunted her anger at him.

Enchei didn't rise to the provocation and kept his voice level. 'Why don't we listen to Narin's plan?'

The Investigator nodded. 'They'll be watching us – not too closely I guess, but enough to see anyone leaving this place. There'll be an ambush ready somewhere on the road to the Palace of Law, ready to spring when it's clear what route we're taking.'

'So, what? We run and take our chances? You fetch a team of horses?'

'We do it on our terms. I've been thinking – the leaders of the goshe came to the Palace of Law to deny having any part in this. They said it was just a rogue temple-leader with a grudge against Irato,' Narin nodded towards the former goshe who was silently watching them all, 'making vague claims that you two were having some sort of affair.'

'Us?' Kesh spluttered. 'Me and him? Are you insane?'

'They needed something half-plausible to buy them time,' Narin explained hurriedly. 'No one believes them, but they needed to say something in their denial – that's all. Their real reason was to show us the faces of their leaders, a nobleman and an Imperial amongst them. They're threatening us with what we might find as we investigate their Order – who we might end up having to arrest, but two can play that game.'

'What're you on about?' Enchei asked in a wary voice. 'Oh, I don't like the sound of where this is going.'

Narin glared at him. 'I'm not saying it's perfect, but they're scared – so why shouldn't we take advantage of that?'

'They're scared the Great Houses are going to get involved,' Enchei said carefully. 'We don't exactly want to encourage that either, do we?'

'What threat do we have over them? Nothing – they're not worried about us killing their enslaved soldiers, all they fear is exposure of their secrets!'

'Exposure, yes – and we all know whose scrutiny they want to avoid,' Enchei growled. 'The same attention I don't need, you don't need – none of us do. There are Stone Dragons on standby in this city all year round, more than any of us can handle and reinforcements likely just a day or two away.'

He pointed in the rough direction of north. 'You bloody Lawbringers. You don't get it, do you? You operate on sufferance, only so far as it pleases the Dragons! The Imperial City's inside House Dragon's sovereign territory; they're the power here and they'll bloody do as they like if they get a sniff of what's going on.'

'No reason we can't use fear of them to direct the goshe though, is it?'

'Isn't it?' Enchei grabbed Irato's arm and dragged the big man forward. 'Show him; show Narin what you found you could do this morning.'

Irato scowled at being dragged into the argument, but didn't say anything as he obliged. Blue-white sparks began to dance around his fingertips then became jagged, writhing lines twisting and curling malevolently all over his palm.

'Just like the one that attacked Kesh,' Enchei added, 'and we're working on what else he can do. What else he might have to help keep the rest of us alive. But if any Astaren see that, they'll take him and cut him open like a dog on an altar – me too. You and Kesh, you'll get taken for interrogation and have a short, painful life before you disappear into the sea.'

'You finished?' Narin asked quietly.

'Hah. What's happened to you today, boy?' Enchei exclaimed. 'Been spending too much time around bloody Lawbringer Rhe? Suddenly fearless of consequences, are we? Or did you just lose your soul same way Rhe must've?'

Narin scowled, shook his head, trying not to think of the woman he'd killed. 'I've lost nothing, but either we take control and make them play on our terms or we lose. That's what today's taught me. There's no way out of this except by winning, so that's what I intend to do.'

'How exactly?'

'I've one final card to play – I think now's the time for it. I think this Father Jehq, or whoever he reports to, is really in charge of the goshe. The leadership they sent to us are simply their influential members, useful just for that purpose and there to take the blame if anything goes wrong.'

Enchei hissed with realisation. 'So you're going to reach out to an influential friend of your own and hope that doesn't blow up in your face? Boy, that's clever and bloody stupid all in one tidy little package.'

'Right now I think we're running out of options, don't you?'

'And if your friend ain't so friendly? These lords of Wyvern can be like that, I'm told.'

'I saved the man's life, remember?' Narin said firmly. 'I'm sure he could do me this one favour and if there's any time to ask it of him, the sooner the better, no?'

'And you're just off to ask him that, eh?'

Narin shook his head. 'No, my friend – I need someone to check I've not got the worst luck in the world. That he's not another nobleman under the influence of the goshe. Right now we've no idea just how far their power spreads.'

'What're you saying?'

The Investigator smiled. 'I'm saying I'm not going to ask him for help – *we* are.'

With Enchei dressed as a servant, grey hair tied back so his face was clearly visible to any watchers, he and Narin left the compound without incident. They took a direct route to the Crescent and hired a boat to take them across, circumventing the Tier Bridge and its cramped markets on either shore.

'The Fett Canal,' Narin ordered the boatman when he asked their destination.

His words caused Enchei to nod briefly as he watched for faces on the receding Imperial Island shore. They could go directly to House Dragon's dock – indeed, it would be a shorter journey – but best not to alarm the goshe yet. Lord Vanden Wyvern's palazzo was a modest affair in the centre of the district, but it would be easy to misinterpret their destination.

The main Dragon dock was almost directly across the Crescent from where they were – to the right of that was a walled fortress of black stone that stood above any other in the district. The fortress was a central block topped by a pair of slender towers that shone with eldritch light and flanked by square barbicans on a perimeter wall. There the most powerful man in the city lived, Lord Omtoray Dragon, with a standing force of five hundred warrior-caste soldiers and no doubt at least as many servants to serve in the famously opulent Halls of Silk and Gold.

If the warrior-mages of House Dragon's Astaren were to be found anywhere in the Imperial City that was a man's best bet; some secret corner the courtiers and power-brokers were politely excluded from. To see Narin head towards that would probably panic any enemy into doing something rash – and it was too early for that.

With the practice of a lifetime, the boatman steered a path between a pair of barges, both decked out in House Dragon's colours, a huge roaring maw on the larger's prow. The tide was turning, running out from the mouth of the river on the far side of the island, but they made fair time as he rowed up alongside the island shore until they were almost at Temple Island.

Far smaller than the Imperial Island's three-mile span, it was no more than two hundred yards at its longest and had been colonised by a dozen temples as ground apart from the authority of any Great House. A single bridge connected it to Dragon District and it was here that their boatman cut across the flow of traffic on the Crescent, the barge gliding neatly into the small artificial harbour at the mouth of the Fett Canal locals referred to as the lagoon.

Once inside, two canal men hopped up from where they lounged until Narin gestured he wouldn't be needing passage onward. The two men disembarked and headed past a stack of crates being loaded onto a barge. Narin looked around and saw a fair number of dock workers waiting for work despite the hour. Clearly, trade was slow at the moment, something that could perhaps be ascribed to the House Dragon soldiers stationed on the far side of the small oval lagoon.

Wearing formal cuirasses emblazoned with the dragon of their home-land, the black-skinned soldiers carried both longswords and solid, brass-chased muskets. The party of four men and one woman all wore the red collar of the warrior caste – high born and clearly unused to the guard duty they considered this to be. The labourers steered well clear of the soldiers, knowing the slightest askance look could result in a beating, and even Narin – safe at least from unprovoked violence – quickly turned away.

'Looks like they're reminding the city who rules here,' Narin muttered, eliciting a grunt of agreement from Enchei.

'Aye, sure it's all smiles and laughter in Eagle District,' his friend added. 'You can bet the Dragons are reminding every district that borders Eagle of that. Probably marching troops up and down the public thoroughfare too.'

'Are they trying to start the war early?'

Enchei shrugged. 'Ah, it's mostly show. No doubt there'll be some duels, but this is neutral ground and the Houses won't let it go beyond that. When that Eagle warship disappears from outside the harbour waters though, then you'll know things have got serious.'

The small lagoon was sheltered from the tides of the Crescent by enormous stone blocks sunk into the riverbed. The canal beyond was unnaturally still – a calm and regular curve of green-tinted water marking the border between Dragon and Tale districts on one side, Fett and Cas Tere on the other. At the far end, where it met the Inner Sea, the canal was sheltered by a seawall built before the Greater Gods had ascended – allowing shallow-bottomed canal barges to travel right into the harbour in almost any weather.

Narin disliked travelling that way, as the canal passed under a section of the city known as Coldcliffs, a multi-level expanse strung across two high cliffs. Built out of the same unnatural white stone as the Imperial Palace, both buildings pre-dated any recorded history – but there the similarities ended. The Imperial Palace had been easily adapted for human habitation, possessing freshwater wells and all the usual requirements, albeit on a scale to house many hundreds in luxury. By contrast, Coldcliffs was near featureless aside from its gently curved roof and the four curling ramps that connected its two levels.

There was no ornamentation or detailing to be found anywhere, no walls to deflect the surging sea winds, no drinkable water except brackish rainfall. Throughout the city's history it had been a slum, a sparsely-populated refuge of criminals and the poor that most Lawbringers felt was a stain on their souls, but never managed to change.

Narin and Enchei walked a short way down the towpath to enter Dragon District through a grand, red-lacquered archway – sinuous reptilian bodies wound around each pillar. It led onto the public thoroughfare that cut all the way through the district to the Tier Bridge, one of only two streets in Dragon District where the colours and arms of rival Houses would be tolerated.

They set off at a brisk pace, pausing only to bow to a patrolling Lawbringer as she passed them. Narin didn't know her name; she was one of perhaps a hundred women to have reached that rank and her face was only vaguely familiar. Most were neither locals nor those orphaned into the Lawbringers. They tended to be high-born women who had been trained in arms but cared more for justice than battlefield

197

honours, frequently proving themselves the most driven and dedicated of all Lawbringers.

As Narin bowed, he saw the pistol holster under her coat and the red collar that declared her caste – marking her out as a fighter, as opposed to one of the untrained, who would wear a silk scarf instead.

'Is that adhered to, really, in times of war?' he asked Enchei once they were well past the Lawbringer.

'You mean if she had a sister wearing a high-caste scarf?' Enchei scowled. 'Depends whether or not you think people are bastards whatever caste they're born into.'

'Well? You fought in wars didn't you? Did you ever …?'

The tattooist pursed his lips as he considered the question. 'I probably ain't the right one to ask, but when I commanded troops I soon let 'em know what I'd put up with. Other officers didn't give much of a shit, but when you're sacking a town or city there's not much order to be found whatever your intentions. The warriors adhere to it mostly; they're taught rules of warfare their whole lives so they don't have to think much. The low-born, serving military terms; depends on their sergeants, but sure, oftentimes it's respected.'

'You were an officer first, or as a result of … ?' Narin asked cautiously.

'Aye.' Enchei hesitated a moment before he continued. 'A result. Served a good few years in the army one way or another. Never had a head for the other work. You want someone to travel halfway across the world without being seen, I'm your man. You want someone to spend years cultivating sources and using their arts to manipulate nations without falling asleep because he's fucking bored by the whole thing, best find someone else.'

Narin shook his head. 'I still find it hard to imagine – it's not that I don't believe you, it's just …'

'Whole point, ain't it?' Enchei said, smiling at last. 'My homeland, they never wanted roaring monsters like the Stone Dragons to strike fear into the hearts o' their enemies.'

'Homeland? You said you were born on the Otornen shore, House Falcon.'

Enchei patted him on the shoulder. 'I say a lot o' things,' he chuckled, 'don't mean any of them is true. You should know that by now.'

'Is your name really Enchei?' Narin said sharply.

'It is now,' the older man replied, upping his pace to move on ahead of Narin. 'And that's all that matters, my friend.'

After the pale stone and white-painted buildings of the Imperial District, there couldn't have been more of a contrast here. The buildings were lower and darker, all painted with reds, oranges and yellows. Every gutter overlooking the main street was finished with stylised dragon-heads and banners hung over almost every window and doorway. Some bore prayers of invocation in the flowing script of the Dragons, on others Narin read savage exhortations to war or denunciations of House Eagle. Some were recently posted, he was sure, but Narin had walked these streets long enough to know the fervour and brutal strength of will that this nation and its vassal states possessed.

It didn't take them long to reach the streets given over to House Wyvern, first amongst House Dragon's vassals. Unlike most of the subordinate states, Wyvern occupied several streets of the district and ignorant observers would consider the sudden wash of blues and sharp-peaked roofs a note of defiance from that quarter. The truth was less dramatic, though; Wyvern's links to the Dragons pre-dated the Empire and only a mixture of geography and pride had kept the two nations separate.

Turning off the public thoroughfare the two men found themselves facing a crowd of people that almost blocked the street. The dark-skinned, powerful Dragons comprised the greater number, but Narin could see that their attention was taken up by two Wyverns – tall and relatively slender men on a raised platform. Their heads were shaved and each had trails of blood and sweat running down his scalp; this was a strange and savage game peculiar to the Wyverns, fought with razor-tipped lashes.

It looked like a duel to Narin's eyes, but the combatants wore black neckerchiefs over the leather collars protecting their throats, indicating peasant caste. Only then did Narin notice the bookmakers waving fistfuls of white and red slips, the deep voices of Dragons calling encouragement or shouting additional bets instead of the solemnity of a duel. The two combatants wove and ducked through a whip-crack storm of their own devising, pausing only to disentangle their weapons before resuming their deft small slashes.

Working their way around the crowd, the pair were forced right up against the house-fronts to get past. Pillars marked the boundary of the Wyvern quarter, tall boles painted sky-blue with reptiles writhing around them. The Wyvern streets all centred on an open patch of ground where great jagged slabs of rock had been dug into the ground to form a sort of pen. Within, Narin knew, were more stone slabs that created a makeshift set of tunnels for an actual wyvern transported from the western desertlands. As they neared it, Narin felt a prickle of excitement as a shape moved within the pen, drawn by the noises and scent of blood on the air.

He went closer, drawing Enchei in his wake. The wyvern was a dusty brown colour, fading to white on its belly, while its darting tongue and the frill of spines around its neck were a bright, startling blue. The creature raised itself up on its hind legs, crooked wings touched to the ground for balance; standing the height of a man before it dropped back down again.

'Come on,' Enchei said, nudging his elbow. 'You can think about the pretty wyverns later, eh?'

They crossed the broad square to a grand building on the far side, one of four palazzos occupying a corner of the square. Their destination was the oldest of the four, lacking the scale of decoration that the other three possessed, but they all bore grand porticos set in a cut-off corner that faced in toward the wyvern. Only three floors in height and possessing an air of fading grandeur, the palazzo still had a pair of guards on the door so Narin had to push ahead of his friend to prevent a scene.

The guards were both as tall as Lawbringer Rhe, but wiry like the fighters they'd just passed. Their hair was styled in long twists of blue cloth to echo the spike frills of their House's emblem, tunics topped in steel collars painted the red of the warrior caste. They carried tall, broad-bladed spears that were traditional weapons in their homeland, but still had pistols sheathed at their waists. The pair gave curt bows when it became clear Narin was intending to enter, more out of cautious courtesy than anything else.

'Master Investigator,' the elder of the pair called in the common tongue, 'how may I aid you?'

'We come to speak to my friend, Lord Vanden. I am Investigator Narin.'

'Both?' the man couldn't help but ask, one eyebrow rising at Enchei. Servants wouldn't normally be admitted by the main door, whoever their master was.

Narin inclined his head. 'I wish him to give testimony to the Lord Wyvern. He is home, I trust?'

The guard's cheek twitched, but he did not say any more as he opened the door to accompany them inside. It was dim within; two arrow-slit windows admitting little light into the hallway beyond. As his eyes adjusted Narin looked up to where he knew he would see another guard on a mezzanine, this one carrying a fat blunderbuss for use on anyone forcing their way through into the tapered hall.

'This way, Investigator,' the first soldier said, indicating an audience chamber down the hall. 'You may wait here.'

Without waiting for a reply the soldier continued to the end of the hall and pulled the door open just as a servant bustled through, having heard the main door open.

'Investigator Narin for the Lord Vanden Wyvern,' the soldier stated.

'Thank you, sir,' the servant replied smoothly. 'The Lord Wyvern will be delighted; I will take them straight up. Investigator, it has been weeks since you last visited us!'

Narin smiled, trying to wipe the nervousness from his mind. 'Good to see you, Breven, you're keeping well?'

The servant bowed. 'Yes, Master Narin, you honour me by asking.'

Breven was a greying man who'd been looking that way for decades, Narin suspected, seemingly having cultivated the look of a discreet, experienced lord's servant early in life. Though he was more than familiar with the expressions and mannerisms of Wyverns these days, Narin still found Steward Breven a closed book. Kine reported that the man ran the entire palazzo around Lord Vanden, whatever the proud nobles and warriors of the household might think.

'And the Lady Vanden?' Narin found himself asking, barely able to restrain the words.

'The Lady Wyvern's radiance is ever burgeoning,' Breven said as he led the way up to the formal reception rooms, 'as Master Narin will surely agree when he greets her.'

Narin felt a jolt at that. *Kine is with her husband?*

Many political matches spent little time together and Kine was surely going to avoid her husband as much as possible now she was pregnant. He steeled himself to keep to his station around them both and remain beyond touching distance of Kine as much as possible. The last thing he needed was some familiar gesture to betray them both.

He glanced back at Enchei who gave him an unfriendly grin. 'Radiant, eh?' the tattooist said. 'That sounds like the Lady Wyvern sure enough.'

'Indeed, Master Enchei,' Breven said a shade curtly, unable to object to Enchei's presence but making clear from his tone the tattooist should be silent at least. 'The Emperor himself complimented the Lord Wyvern on it this very week.'

'Complimented?' Narin croaked.

'On the Lady Wyvern's radiance,' Breven continued. By his tone Narin could tell Breven considered the matter relevant to his master's standing at court – and thus something to be broadcast widely – rather than simple gossip.

'Emperor Sotorian singled her out, saying to the court at large that only a good husband could produce such glowing beauty in his wife.'

Narin almost choked – a constricting band of fear around his chest. *Kine's glow pointed out to the whole of court?*

In his distraction he scuffed his foot on the stair and stumbled. It was only Enchei's quick reaction that stopped him from tripping and falling, but Breven was careful not to notice.

'That was kind o' the Emperor,' Enchei said, filling the silence while Narin reeled from the news. 'O' course, might be any House Iron nobles there took it as a rebuke, given their habits, but the Emperor wasn't meaning them I'm sure.'

'Quite,' Breven agreed, 'it would take a jaded soul to read so pure a sentiment that way.'

Narin didn't trust himself to comment, but he was relieved the Emperor had been making a deliberate point. Kine's smile appeared in his memory, the faint flush that appeared in her cheeks when she was happy.

She's carrying my child and so happy the Emperor himself noticed!

Part of him wanted to cheer, to crow to the entire city, but instead he clamped his jaw shut and tried to focus just on putting one foot in front of the other.

'Investigator Narin and servant,' Breven announced as he reached the top of the stair and opened a broad double-door.

Strains of music broke off at the announcement, the high notes of a lyra hanging momentarily in the air as they were admitted. As he bowed low, Narin caught a glimpse that could have been a classical painting; the lord reclining while his lady sat on a stool before him, lyra resting at her feet and bow still poised before it.

'Narin!' called Lord Vanden with evident pleasure, 'Narin, my good friend!'

At that Narin straightened, while the lower-caste Enchei remained where he was – kneeling, hands folded at his chest.

'Good afternoon, Lord Vanden,' Narin said, forcing himself to smile and keep his eyes fixed on the man advancing towards them.

Lord Vanden was small and portly compared to most Wyverns, with skin a far lighter brown than his wife's and a genuine smile that was just as unusual amongst his race when greeting outsiders.

He wore a long embroidered silk coat; beautifully worked in blues and greens with half a dozen wyverns fighting eagles. In a fit of self-deprecating humour, the wyverns gripped over-sized dip pens in their claws, the exaggerated nibs like axe-blades. In a fierce warrior culture he was smaller and weaker than his peers, but maintained his position because competent administrators were a rarer commodity than killers.

'And Master Enchei too, I see,' Vanden replied. 'Come, stand – you are also welcome in my house.'

The tattooist stood but was careful to bow again in thanks. 'You honour me, Lord Wyvern.'

'The honour is mine!' Vanden said, embracing Narin heartily and offering his hand to Enchei. The tattooist took it in both hands lightly, bending to almost kiss the imposing gold rings and ornate bracelet of office Vanden wore.

'Might I ...' Enchei hesitated, head still bowed so the nobleman could not see his face. Narin saw Enchei's lips move in that pause and tried not to give a start as he thought a faint glimmer of light flared in the tattooist's eyes. 'My Lord, might I be permitted to speak a blessing?'

Lord Vanden frowned, hand still clasped in Enchei's. 'Over me? Ah yes, I remember Narin telling me of your pagan beliefs. No, do not – it would not be appropriate.'

He looked up at Narin, who tried to look apologetic. The Investigator stepped forward and placed a hand on Enchei's shoulder. The tattoist immediately released the hand.

'Forgive me, Lord Vanden,' Enchai said in a contrite manner. 'My ways are all I have to thank you for your gift, which proved most opportune.'

They had not been able to pretend Enchei had served no role at all in saving Vanden, so the pair had downplayed it instead and allowed Vanden to buy Enchei's silence for a sum modest enough to support the notion.

'You both participated in my rescue,' Vanden said a little stiffly, but not obviously offended, Narin was glad to see. 'You both are welcome here and deserving of more than the small thanks you would accept.'

He gestured to the cushioned stools arranged around the grand chair he'd been sitting in. 'Come, join me – Breven, fetch wine and food for my guests.'

Without waiting, Vanden swept back to his seat and Narin followed, at last meeting Kine's gaze. Kine respectfully inclined her head to him and he bowed again, not so low this time so he caught the brief delight shine through her pristine make-up once her husband was facing the other way.

'Lady Vanden, I trust you are well?' Narin said as he approached a stool and waited while the two nobles sat. His tongue felt thick and awkward in his mouth as he spoke to her, trying not to grin like a fool just because they were back in each other's company.

'Perfectly so, Master Narin.' Kine hesitated as she looked closer at his face. 'But what about you, Narin? You look tired and bruised – Knight protect us, were you caught up in this disturbance we've been hearing about?'

Narin nodded. 'I fear I was at the heart of it but, a little fatigue aside, I am fine.'

'Is it true?' Vanden asked eagerly as his wife paled. He leaned forward in his seat, hands tightly gripping the armrests. 'Assassins broke into your home?'

'They did, hunting a young woman who had seen the face of a criminal.'

'And she was in your home?' Kine said coolly.

'Escorted by several others, Enchei here included,' Narin said hurriedly. 'We suspected they would be keeping a watch on the Palace of Law and hoped we had moved her without being observed.'

'And the scum didn't realise who they were messing with, hah!' Vanden crowed. 'I could have told them not to bother – to turn them-selves in rather than cross blades with my saviour.'

Narin found himself colouring at the man's words. Undeserved as they were, Vanden was genuine enough in believing it was Narin who had killed his attackers.

'I was fortunate enough to not be alone,' he muttered, 'and with time to prepare in case anything did happen.'

'The, ah, the matter is resolved then?' Kine asked. 'You are not still in danger, are you?'

Narin cleared his throat and tried to sound confident. 'Not quite, my Lady, but I come to ask your husband a favour – one I believe may go some way towards bringing it to an end.'

'Then it is granted!' Vandan declared expansively. 'Whatever my friend needs, he shall have.'

'Thank you, my Lord.' Narin bowed again to try and hide his relief. 'The young woman in question, I believe there are more criminals hunting her, waiting for her to leave the compound.'

'I heard it was the goshe?' Vanden said. 'Is the whole Order involved or were they hired killers?'

Narin shook his head, mindful of Vanden's position. The last thing they could afford was any great interest from the military powers, as Enchei had pointed out.

He's a nobleman like any other, Narin reminded himself as Breven returned with a tray of glasses and small bowls of delicacies. *Whether or not he calls me friend, he trades in power and favours. Any hint that this is more than a criminal matter and he'll know who would appreciate hearing that ahead of the pack.*

'A small criminal element within the goshe,' he said eventually, waiting until Breven had served his lord and been dismissed again. 'Limited to one Shure training house – the Shure master is now dead, but there are others still at large.'

'Well I'm hardly surprised, the goshe've been ripe for exploitation by criminals for decades,' Vanden surmised, sitting back again. 'The Lawbringers are an enclosed culture, modelled on the ways of the warrior caste, after all. It imposes the order and discipline necessary for such training. To offer all castes and trades that, disparate people handed skills of violence, I'm surprised such a thing hasn't happened sooner.'

'Indeed, Lord Vanden,' Narin replied smoothly. 'I suspect the Vanguard Council are increasingly coming to that opinion too.'

'Good – high time they took a firmer hand, but how is it I can help you?' Vanden cocked his head. 'I can't imagine the other Houses would like Wyvern troops being the ones to investigate every Shure in the city now!'

Narin smiled. 'No Lord, I suspect not. However, these criminals will naturally shy away from a confrontation with troops. I intend to make a break from the compound using the guards as a diversion. If the criminals do attack even a large body of Investigators there will be significant bloodshed – if the Investigators draw them away, however, it buys us time to run for the Crescent and cross. If we can trick them we might be able to prevent a fight entirely.'

'You want to come here?' Vanden asked with a frown. 'Have a detachment of Wyvern troops waiting to ward off any pursuit?'

'And safe haven for the woman in question. She is young and frightened, her sister is dead because of this matter and I have promised to see her safe.' *I just have to persuade Kesh to stay safe. That'll be a harder one to sell.*

'Naturally,' the nobleman said with a thoughtful nod. 'Perhaps not the Dragon dock though, just in case there is a confrontation. Lord Omtoray would not appreciate that, tensions as they currently are. If just one man with House Eagle blood draws a weapon in such a public part of Dragon District … well, there may be official ramifications quite aside from warriors taking matters into their own hands.'

'We came via the Fett Canal just now,' Narin suggested. 'There were soldiers there already, perhaps that would be best?'

'Yes – I can assign men for that easily enough. Let me instruct my captain to do so and brief him on what to expect. When do you intend to do it?'

'Just before dawn, as the darkness is fading. There shouldn't be anyone on the streets to get in the way or get hurt.'

'Dawn it is,' Vanden declared. 'They'll think Lady Trickster herself has it out for them!'

Narin swallowed and smiled weakly. 'Let us hope so.'

CHAPTER 15

The five Lesser Gods of each Order remain in ascendancy for ten days; each Order rules the heavens for sixty with the last ten commonly styled a 'dark week' where none is in ascendance. These things we can observe ourselves yet between the light of facts, the shadow of argument may remain. The dark week tells some that more may yet be raised to Godhood but I prefer a different interpretation. Instead of being a prize dangled for all to reach for, I see the dark weeks as a reminder by the Gods that they do not see all – that sometimes, we can rely on no one but ourselves.

From *A History* by Ayel Sorote

Synter fought the urge to grab the man and shake him like a dog. Instead, she wrinkled her nose against the acrid smell that constantly surrounded him and took a careful step back. There was a virulent green liquid in the jar he carried and experience told her to be careful of everything in this room.

'Tell me what you could manage?' Synter said carefully. 'We need to be prepared, there's no time to lose.'

'Were I to lower myself to such things,' replied the tall, skeletally thin man with naked distaste, 'all you ask and more. One of the Moon's Artifice variants would serve, but I will not provide it, precisely for the reason that we never used it in the first place. No matter how careful you might be, it will lead back to us if used on adults.'

'Father Polagin, you must – for the future of us all.'

With the care of a fastidious man Polagin replaced the brass cap on the jar and returned it to its rack. He turned and moved around to the far side of his long work table, pausing by the oil lamp before he sat. It was on a low wick and cast deep shadows over the Father's workshop, his gaunt face looking ghastly in the dim light.

'Must?' Polagin echoed at last, narrowing his eyes at her. 'Why *must* I do anything you ask?'

He wore a long black robe, stained in a dozen places on the sleeves and waist, but somehow failing to look unkempt still. Instead of weapons there were pouches and vials hanging from his belt, but Synter reminded herself he was far from helpless.

'This is our only opportunity,' she urged, putting her hands on the worktop and leaning forward. 'If we don't now, the chance could be lost to us for ever.'

Synter had changed her clothes since giving Kodeh his orders and now wore a close-fitting grey jacket, stiffened by overlapping steel plates sewn into the cloth. Her weapons and mask lay in a non-descript bag at her feet.

'You do not know that, Synter.' Father Polagin gave a little shake of the head. 'You always were over-eager and impulsive as a student.'

Synter bit back a retort and instead looked around the man's workshop, hoping for inspiration to persuade him. They stood in the lowest levels of an orphanage run by the goshe, one of two that took in foundlings abandoned on their doorstep. Most of the children were taught a trade of some sort, the intelligent ones given clerking skills and employed to look after the economic interests of the goshe – properties, investments and bequests the order had accumulated over the years.

The very best of them, the most loyal, were given additional training – shown the hidden face of the world by the Elders and made into weapons for their secret purpose. The Blessings were a range of magical alterations to body and mind – unearthed in secret or stolen outright from demons – that elevated their elite to the ranks of the Detenii. It was the Detenii who were entrusted with Moon's Artifice and the purpose behind it, but it was the Elders alone who knew the fullest extent of their plan.

'Impulsive? No, not really. You just never liked the fact a woman was the best student you ever had.'

'Watch your tone with me, girl,' Polagin snapped.

'No, I don't think I will. If I was impulsive, I'd have put this knife through your chest by now,' Synter said plainly, brandishing a long-knife in the weak light. From the look on Polagin's face she knew he hadn't even seen her draw it.

'And I'd gladly kill you,' she continued, 'but you're still useful to me – just as you all need me. Year after year I see you Elders getting older and more frightened, time catching up with you despite all your Blessings and schemes. So the way I see it, we still need each other and the goal remains the same. I don't have the skill for the final ritual, not enough to be sure, and none of you are going to survive the next few days without me.'

Unexpectedly, Polagin laughed, a cold and grating sound. 'You think us so feeble? With all the Blessings we have given you, with all the power that made you more than normal mortals – you still think us weak ourselves?'

She shook her head. 'I think you're old. The Blessings have no cure for age, you've only staved death off a decade or two. Only success in our plans can achieve that – right now we're at war and that's a young man's game, or in this case, a young woman's. Our bargains still hold true, but if you don't start doing what the fuck I tell you we're all dead.'

'And what do you suggest to save us from ourselves?' called a voice from her right.

Synter whirled with her knife already moving, knowing them to be alone. Just as she had her hand back to throw, darting trails of light appeared around the fingers of her free hand as the shadow of a battered bureau unfolded to reveal Father Jehq, wrapped in a black cloak and faintly smiling at her surprise.

'One Blessing you Detenii will not get,' he added, 'as useful as it might prove. I learned that lesson the hard way.'

'How long have you been there?'

'Since before you came. Now – as you are so certain we are old and slow, perhaps you might put your surprise aside and tell us what we should be doing?'

Synter carefully sheathed her long-knife again and let the lightning playing around her fingers dissipate into nothing. 'We need to act,' she said firmly, 'now – tonight.'

'By poisoning the city?'

'If you heard everything,' she said with a trace of defiance, 'you know exactly what I mean.'

'And you just expect us to trust your judgement, now at this most delicate of times?' Polagin demanded. 'Jehq, the girl is mad – I told you she was never up to commanding the Detenii.'

Jehq didn't speak at first. Head cocked slightly to one side, he observed Synter with a strange, intense look as though staring into her soul. She bore the scrutiny in silence, fighting down her mounting impatience.

'Not mad,' he said at last, 'and certainly no fool. We chose well I think, even if we do not like the result. This is the job we gave her, after all.'

'What? Have you lost your wits?'

Jehq shook his head very deliberately, gaze not leaving Synter. 'Do you deny it, Polagin? Did you not share the same instinct as I – to run and hide, lie low and let the Lawbringers pick over this mess until it is safe for us to act once more?'

'That is prudence, not fear.'

'Perhaps.' Jehq's expression told a different story. 'We will do as you suggest, Synter. When do you need us to be ready?'

'We will do no such thing!' Polagin roared. 'Have you now assumed control of the goshe, Jehq? We are equals – that is at the heart of everything we have done. Our circle has no leader, it never has!'

Synter caught a slight nod from Jehq and readied herself. The white-haired man turned abruptly towards Polagin and stalked towards him, hands appearing from the folds of his robe – empty, but still threatening. Polagin reacted accordingly and retreated a step while he prepared for whatever was coming. In the next moment Synter chopped into his neck with her long-knife and hot, dark blood spurted across workbench.

A heave of final breath came from Polagin's ruined throat and sprayed blood down his front. The tall man shuddered and slumped over the workbench, feet scuffing on the stone floor as he kicked his last. Jehq didn't wait for his friend to die but spread an open palm over Polagin's face as though administering a benediction. A brief flash of blinding white light erupted from Jehq's palm. By the time Synter's Starsight had activated then receded again, Polagin with quite still.

'He was my friend. I would not have him suffer unnecessarily.'

Synter dipped her head in acknowledgement, knowing he wouldn't want any comment from her.

'It seems I am committed now,' Jehq continued, 'so what else do you need?'

'Authority,' she replied after a moment's thought. 'My night's barely started; I need to give several sets of orders before I return here.'

Jehq nodded and reached inside the neck of his shirt. From underneath it he pulled a scrap of metal covered in twisting lines that shone like oil in the lamplight. 'This will convince any other Elders that you act under my authority; they'll not oppose you unless you do something outrageous.'

'I need to move the artefact tonight,' she said. 'Mother Terail or Father Pallasane – either of them will notice when I do.'

'One is pragmatic,' Jehq said with a shrug, 'the other quite mad. They will not object to boldness on our part so long as they are informed and summoned to participate. I will assemble those who can be trusted; you mean to use the island sanatorium?'

'Yes.'

'I will have them there in time. Kill Stass and Lox, they are the ones most likely to object and demand any decision is made in committee. All your Detenii are ready to move?'

'Close enough.'

He nodded towards the door. 'Then go. I will have your poison ready in a few hours.'

In a quiet, mouldering corner of the Shier Warrant on the city's eastern extremity, Kodeh slipped through the dark streets with the stealth of a cat. The ground rose under his feet as he headed east and the mist seemed to fade away behind him as he ascended.

This was a quiet corner of the city at night, Shier a poor district when compared to others. It was home to labourers and factories now, mills on the river bank and smallholdings in grounds that once had housed the palazzos of Imperial nobles and warriors. Little light came from the buildings around him and all was dark under a starless sky, but that was how the black-skinned Dragon preferred it. He wore his usual clothing now he was about business and moved with greater purpose, eyes ever scanning for wisps of white or some darting pale fox.

'Kodeh,' called a voice from the shadows above him, 'you're clear.'

The big man grunted and glanced behind him. A dark figure, dressed in concealed armour just as he was, followed him up the street. He kept watching as more detached from the shadows around him and slipped down from the rooftops nearby. All told there were another six of them – hooded and masked. In his Starsight they looked like demons, eyes shining bright from behind a dull, expressionless mask.

So the children of this city call us, he thought humourlessly. *They're about to learn there are worse things than the Detenii, though.*

'Good,' he said once the seven were assembled in front of him. 'Last bloody thing I needed was to pick up a tail on the way here.'

'A fox-tail eh?' commented one. 'Appropriate I guess.'

Kodeh narrowed his eyes at the one he thought had spoken. 'Who's that?'

The figure gave a small bow of the head. 'Atash, sir.'

'Well, Atash – I don't know what shit Irato let slide, but you're playing by my rules now. This whole team needs to impress me, so any more dumb jokes and I'll gut you, got it?'

'Aye, sir.'

'Good.' Kodeh turned and continued on up the street, his new team falling in around him. 'Let's get off the street then I'll brief you all.'

The Shier Warrant was as old as any in the Imperial City, once rural estates separate from the villages on the Crescent's shore. Rogue towers remained along with scraps of wall, lending the district a dismal air that had doubtless helped the settlement of newer districts to the west. There was another reason, however, and Kodeh made directly for it, the ground gently sloping up towards the highest point in the city.

There the cliffs looked out along the eastern coast and an ancient tower had been converted into a lighthouse to help the navigation of the sandbanks and small islands in the bay beyond. Beside that was a grim building the size of a Great House palazzo, but different in every other way. A high wall surrounded a large courtyard, the top lined with twists of jagged wire, while on the far side of the yard loomed a block of dark stone three storeys high. From the street it appeared deserted; unlit and silent over the sigh of the sea-breeze drifting in over its stone walls.

Then the breeze waned briefly and Kodeh heard something else. A moan cut through the air; faint, wordless cries that could have been an animal in pain, punctuated by clipped shouts from somewhere distant – certainly human, but equally as unfathomable.

'I fucking hate this place,' Atash muttered from behind Kodeh.

The big Dragon spun around and grabbed Atash by the throat, slamming him into the nearest wall and ripping his mask from his face. Atash was a Wolf, Kodeh discovered – eyes so pale in Kodeh's Starsight that they had to be yellow. His nose was uneven and scarred, giving the man a slight sneer to the lip even when he found a blade two inches from his left eye.

'Not one more word, get me?' Kodeh growled. 'No jokes, no bitching, no nothing except what's necessary.'

He felt Atash tense a moment, clearly wondering if he could draw his own weapons in time, then relax again. The man nodded as best he could and Kodeh released him.

'Shift.'

He went to the large gate set into the courtyard wall and took hold of the large iron ring that served as handle. There was no lock, but he felt it solid and secure under his touch until he'd imperceptibly squeezed the underside of the ring's mounting, variously twisting, pulling and pushing on the ring until a quiet clunk came from the other side.

They entered the courtyard and Kodeh closed the gate behind them, resetting the lock and heading out across the bare earth yard towards a door. On the ground were a handful of discarded children's toys, with more on view in an open chest beside the far door – heaped inside without care to keep them out of any rain. The building itself had plain, arrow-slit windows all down the inside and a double-height coach-house door at the furthest corner.

This time Atash kept his mouth shut until they were through into the building beyond, where they were greeted by a middle-aged woman carrying a lamp. She had clearly just got out of bed and stood barefoot, rumpled clothes pulled on and a blanket around her shoulders, but what Kodeh noticed first was a trio of livid red scratch-marks down one cheek. The hallway itself was almost bare, a barred doorway on their left, a heavy, battered chest with a large lock on the right.

'You need me?' the woman asked briskly.

'One of the crazies almost got you, huh?' Kodeh said, pointing to the marks.

'A patient became distressed,' she said firmly. 'They're not always so easy to restrain – but I rather doubt you're here to help me with that, Kodeh.'

In the distance, a howl seemed to echo out from elsewhere in the building – sounding louder now they were inside.

'True, Mother Eyote,' Kodeh agreed. 'But I am here to make your life easier. We've come to take some crazies off your hands – and some coffins if you've got 'em.'

'You can keep your hands off my patients,' she said curtly before pausing. 'You don't mean the patients, do you?'

He grinned and stepped to one side so he could look at his team as well. 'I don't mean patients. We've got orders – the artefact's being moved in the morning and we need to set up a few distractions throughout the city to keep everyone looking in the other direction.'

Mother Eyote gave him a sceptical look while his team exchanged looks and Atash smothered a curse.

'I thought we would be keeping a low profile over the next few days. Unleashing horror and death on the city might not be in keeping with that.'

'So long as they're nothing to do with us, we're fine,' Kodeh replied. 'We need the Lawbringers busy, the city in uproar.'

'Why the coffins then?'

''Cos you're going to dope our horrors up – as much as you can. Give us enough time to leave 'em across the city and be well away before they wake up.'

She shook her head in disbelief. 'Whose mad idea was this? It's a bit bloodthirsty for Jehq or Terail. Is Pallasane giving you orders now?'

'Synter's order,' he said, adding, 'on Father Jehq's authority. We're committed now, but with the attention of the city on us we need a bit of theatre.'

'Theatre isn't the same as mass-murder,' Eyote said with a resigned sigh. 'But perhaps she's right, we're too far gone now.'

'Aye – you'll be getting word from Jehq soon, though given what Synter's planning I think they'll be orders to stay until the moon's ready to rise.'

She nodded and went to the chest against the right-hand wall. Beckoning over the nearest of the Denteii, Eyote set the lamp down on the ground and knelt beside the chest. The feet of the chest were just high enough to slip her fingers underneath it and after a moment she found the correct spot and pressed a button.

'Pull,' she ordered the Detenii. Together they hauled one end of the chest around and as they did so a section of floor sank as some counter-weight moved in the wall.

'Kodeh, follow me – the rest of you, go to the coach house. We have no coffins, but there are crates in there. Empty them and there'll be enough space. Bring the coach out into the yard and we'll be waiting for you.'

The others jumped to obey, leaving Eyote alone with Kodeh. She gave him an appraising look as she retrieved her lamp and started off down the steps that had been revealed.

'Have you ever seen them?' she asked, nodding towards the underground room at the far end of the stair. Kodeh shook his head.

'It's not pleasant,' she warned him. 'For Pity's sake, don't touch anything and don't get close! And remember some have a greater reach than you do, so don't make assumptions.'

She descended into the gloom below and reluctantly Kodeh followed. He knew exactly what lay down there the casualties of their forbidden arts, for whom the Blessings had proved curses.

CHAPTER 16

He dreams of late summer – the sun a smile's gentle warmth on his skin, the air heavy with scents both sweet and sharp. Striated clouds fill the southern sky, turning pink in the early evening light. The palazzo is larger in his dreams; it looms as imposing as the Imperial Palace when he approaches the open gate. Tall soldiers in blue watch him enter from the shadows, faces hidden by steel masks like the prow of a ship and muskets darkly gleaming.

He ascends a rich, carpeted stair. The walls narrow as he climbs and the light fades to shadow around him, but then he emerges into a grand reception room with a bank of archways leading out onto a terrace. Long hanging cloths keep the room cool; diaphanous strips of linen decorated by paintings of exotic birds drifting in the desultory breeze. The terrace beyond it is a blaze of light, white marble catching the last of the daylight and reflecting it inside.

He blinks and turns away, realises he is not alone and drops to one knee.

'Master Narin,' she calls from the far reaches of the room, distant through the shadows in his eyes until he blinks away the terrace's lingering brightness. 'Please, rise. We remain in your debt and will not have you kneel here.'

'Lady Vanden,' he hears himself say, standing once more.

There is a woman beside her, one Narin does not recognise. A bodyguard he guesses; warrior caste by her blood-red collar but dressed in the easy luxury of a noble rather than a soldier's uniform.

'Come, Master Narin, we are friends now. Address me as Lady Kine.'

A spark runs up his spine as he bows his head in acknowledgement, hoping she cannot see the flush of pleasure on his face at such informality.

She has turned away by the time he approaches to stand uncomfortably before her. Legs tucked underneath, Lady Kine is curled like a cat upon a divan, upright and elegant. She wears a dress of yellow with orange script-like embroidery swirling diagonally down. Her brown arms are bare and

216

perfectly smooth, slender golden bangles hanging loose on each, while her long dark hair curls down over her chest. Beside her on a rosewood stand is a lyra, the bow discarded casually on the other end of the divan.

'Siresse Myken,' she says in a honey-sweet voice that he feels like a blow to the chest, 'you may leave us. I am quite safe.'

The warrior-woman bows, eyes never leaving Narin all the while. Siresse – he finds himself surprised by the term, having never heard it used formally. Warriors are normally referred to by military rank, but remain knights by birth and female warriors are dubbed Siresse rather than Lady, as they would be as the wife of a knight.

'Come, Master Narin,' she says once they are alone, 'sit with me.'

He awkwardly eases himself into the grandest chair he has ever used, one of four arranged for high-castes attending the lord or lady of the house. She snaps a fan open and cools her face with it, her mouth hidden from view as he thanks her gracelessly.

'My husband sleeps,' she explains, gesturing to the enormous gilt chair beside her divan. 'His wound troubles him still.'

Under the gentle regard of her almond-shaped eyes, Narin feels transfixed – suddenly panicked that he is alone with a high-caste lady. His mind goes blank as he wonders what conversation he can make with a woman of refinement, but with a twitch of her fan his anxiety evaporates. He finds himself watching it silently, entranced by each lazy movement.

'He recovers,' Lady Kine continues, 'but slowly. The doctor has given him something for the pain. He tells me that wounds to the stomach are slow to heal, but this one will in time.'

Narin seems to jerk awake. Her knowing eyes tell him that she is aware of Lord Vanden's true injury, then he chides himself. Of course she is aware – how could a wife not be that her husband lies castrated in their bed?

'I am glad,' he says with gruff shortness.

'My apologies,' Lady Kine replies, 'you are a busy man and came to call on my husband, not be bored by pleasantries from his wife.'

'No!' he says anxiously. 'I mean – no, you do not bore me, my Lady. Quite the opposite, I ah …' He tails off, realising he should have not spoken that way and terrified he has acted in a forward or offensive manner towards a married woman.

The fan snaps down briefly. 'I am glad,' she says softly, the hint of a smile on her full lips before once more concealed.

'I, ah, am … also glad.'

'Then you will sit with me a while longer? I would hear the tale of my husband's rescue, if you care to tell it.'

Narin frowns at the memory. He has told the story a dozen times or more. In his mind he half-wonders if in fact he was the one to save Lord Vanden, but then the hot sense of shame fills his mind.

'My apologies, Master Narin,' Kine adds, seeing his reaction, 'I should not have asked. I am used to the presence of warrior castes whose honour rests on their feats of arms, but I should have realised a Lawbringer does not see violence in that way. You are not trained to kill but to protect others, I know the oaths.' She pauses, then adds almost shyly, 'I admire that, the desire to protect and uphold the law rather than fight and kill.'

He bows his head, unsure quite what to say in response but filled with pleasure that such a beauty might admire him.

'Tell me about yourself instead,' Kine suggests. 'Your parents, your life.'

'My life?' he asks hesitantly. 'It is unremarkable, I'm afraid, not fit for your company.'

'Still I would like to hear more about you,' she presses. 'You were born into the Imperial House?'

He nods. 'My parents too, I have lived here all my life.'

'You look happy,' Kine says, 'you are very close with them?'

Not even realising he had been smiling, Narin nods. 'I was. They're both dead now. White fever took my father, my mother died of a tumour a few years later.'

'Tell me about them.'

The warmth in her voice surprises him, but he finds himself opening his mouth to speak without hesitation. It has been years since he's even mentioned them and never has he spoken of the love of his early years; of his father's principles and admiration of the Lawbringers, of his mother's gentle way and boundless generosity.

In the dormitories and training yards of the Lawbringers he would never have thought to mention such things, but now he finds himself talking. For the first time in years he finds himself wishing they were still with him, that they could know him as the man he has become. In the presence of this high-born woman he barely knows, he feels that love again and it fills his heart.

Narin felt a hand on his shoulder, shaking him awake. Startled, he flinched away and flailed for a weapon until his alarm subsided. He rolled over and despite the dark saw it was Enchei standing over him.

218

The tattooist gestured for him to stay where he was and Narin grunted in response, fumbling at the blanket tangled around his waist.

'Is it time?' he asked eventually.

'Close. I let you sleep as long as I could.'

Across the room from Narin, Irato also stirred – then sat up, wide awake already.

'Gods,' Narin muttered, rubbing a hand over his face. 'I feel still asleep, or drunk mebbe.'

Enchei raised a small porcelain cup. 'Here, drink this.'

'Coffee?' Narin scowled. 'Nasty foreign muck.'

'It's either that or a slap round the face.'

Narin accepted the cup and struggled into a seating position while Irato stood and stretched, briefly loosening his muscles before pulling on his jacket and leather armour.

'Bright and eager to go?' he asked the goshe.

'I've had more sleep than you,' Irato pointed out, 'and less chance to be out of here.'

One by one, the goshe strapped on his weapons. First a pair of long-knives went into sheaths on his thighs, crossbow bolts in pouches over each, then a pair of hatchets slid up his back to rest in custom-made slots. A stiletto went into one boot and blowpipe in the other, while a pouch of darts and punch dagger slotted onto one spaulder. Lastly, he strapped his small crossbow below the hatchets before pulling on the intentionally-ragged coat that hid them all and looking expectantly up at Enchei.

'Sure you're ready, then?' Narin croaked, just about prepared to try putting his feet on the floor and start finding his boots. 'Not forgotten anything there?'

'I am.'

'Trickster's cold heart – what bell is it?' groaned Kesh from the far side of the room where she'd curled up beside the warm iron stove.

'The dawn bell will be rung soon,' Enchei said.

'You sure?' she peered over at the shuttered window. There was no dawn light yet peeking through.

'I'm sure. We should be ready to move.' He went over as she sat up and poured another cup of coffee from the copper pot on the stove top. 'Here, this'll wake you up.'

'Bugger that,' Kesh said, yawning once before rising. 'I don't need coffee when someone's going to try to kill me. How about a weapon?'

Enchei grinned and pointed to a bag on the table. 'Help yourself.'

She investigated the bag as Enchei lit a candle and put it on a brass stand to cast some sort of light over the room.

'You're as bad as Irato,' Kesh said, her voice tinged with wonder as she inspected the contents of the bag. 'Are these all yours?'

'Some – I borrowed a few. I thought you and Narin might both want something extra.'

'I'm fine with my stave,' Narin said as he pulled on his boots and stood to slip his arms into his grey Investigator's jacket.

'Here,' Enchei said, tossing over a bundle. 'Don't argue, just bloody take them.'

Narin unwrapped it to discover elbow-to-knuckle leather gauntlets, a vest-like shirt with thin plates of metal sewn into it, and a sheath containing a pair of daggers.

'Will this do any good?' he asked sceptically as Kesh was handed a similar bundle.

'Mebbe, mebbe not. The shirts go under your clothes, so get that jacket off.'

Enchei withdrew a short-sword from the bag and slipped it from its sheath as though intending to demonstrate his point.

'In a fight, hands and arms get cut easily, while a knife in the belly's an easy way to kill. Your head's still vulnerable, but such is life. These might give you a second chance, so wear 'em.'

'What about you?' Even as he said it Narin realised under his clothes Enchei looked bulkier than normal.

'Got something similar,' the tattooist said gnomically.

Enchei sheathed the short-sword again and strapped it cross-wise across his back. A long-knife was attached to one thigh and he pulled his dark leather coat on over it all so only the rounded pommel of the short-sword was visible. As almost an afterthought, and much to Narin's surprise, he also dropped a sling and a handful of pebbles into a pocket.

'A sling?' Narin commented as he put on the shirt and belted the knives to his waist. 'Isn't that a farm-boy's weapon?'

'Easier to carry than a bow,' Enchei said, 'and so long as you can use it right, deadly over the same range. And trust me; I'm a good shot.'

'If you say so. Did you sleep?'

'I caught enough. You all ready?' Enchei cast a critical eye over his companions, adjusting the lie of Kesh's daggers as she tightened one vambrace.

Narin nodded and led them out onto the walkway, unable to resist a nervous glance around as he did. They went down into the yard below where a dozen grey-cloaked Investigators stood waiting. The air was cool with fog, but it was thinner than Narin had expected and from the walkway he could make out the dulled white bulk of the Imperial Palace in the distance, seemingly catching the dawn light before the rest of the city.

'Lawbringer Hetellin,' he said to the man who approached them, offering him a respectful bow. While he didn't like the man much, Hetellin was about to risk ambush for their sakes and had made no complaint about the plan proposed to him.

'Investigator, you are all ready?'

'We are. Thank you for agreeing to this.'

'We stand between the innocent and harm,' Hetellin replied stiffly. Above, the first hint of dawn was creeping through the clouds and the low toll of the bell from Smith's temple here on the island announced the dawn hour.

'Aye well, don't forget to remove your hoods before the crossroad,' Enchei added. 'You're to distract harm, not take half a dozen crossbow bolts from it, remember?'

'I know my place in this. Will you need help climbing the rear wall, old man?'

Enchei grinned and stuck out a hand. 'Be safe, Lawbringer.'

Hetellin ignored the gesture and turned to the gate. 'Hoods on, we go now.'

At his word, the cloaked Investigators slipped hoods over their heads, hiding their faces in shadow while the gate was eased open and they headed out. Beyond the gate Narin knew there was another party of Lawbringers led by Rhe, ready to clear the way to the Palace of Law. Enchei shook his head and headed in the other direction, making for an open doorway to another Investigator's quarters.

'It'll take not much more than a minute to reach the crossroad,' Enchei said as his three companions filed in behind him. 'That's the best ambush point; any sensible assassin would set the trap there.'

'What if they decide not to do the obvious? Attack them before they take their hoods off?' Kesh asked 'Or they guess what we're about to do?'

'It's obvious because it'll work best,' Enchei said dismissively. 'As for them guessing – there's a reason we're running for the Crescent once we're over the back wall!'

'And if we run into trouble?'

'Irato and me're in the lead, you two five yards behind so if anyone tries to block our path you don't run straight into us. They'll be after Irato first, remember, so if we're surrounded you just run for any gap you see and head to the water. The boat's waiting to cast off and if we're following we'll shout as we come. If not, don't hang around. Remember, they were novices that attacked the compound, but the elite'll be around too so don't get into a fight if you don't have to.'

He opened the back door of the quarters and headed out into the communal garden, dusted grey by the light of impending dawn. A short ladder had been placed against the wall already – four steps only, but enough that they'd be able to clear it and swing back down.

'Me first, Narin you're last, got it?' They all nodded. 'Right, time to see whether they've bought it.'

With a few steps' run-up, Enchei scaled the wall and lowered himself down on the other side with barely a sound, Irato following a moment later. Narin moved forward to assist Kesh over, but she brushed him aside and followed the example set.

Narin had to stop himself from laughing, remembering belatedly that she'd served a season on a merchantman and was likely more agile than he. Then he realised he was all alone in the darkness and glanced up. Lord Shield's constellation was obscured by shadowy cloud – even the Gods were not watching over him.

He scrambled over the wall as fast as he could, all the while expecting a shout or crossbow bolt to break the quiet.

'All wearing hoods,' Jaril said aloud. 'A feint, or are they daring us to act?'

The tall, sharp-featured Eagle glanced at his companions across the dark room. Eman and Loram, the pair from House Ghost, shared a look that told Jaril nothing, while Jerg kept on staring out the window, watching for signals from their lookouts, Kissen and Calt.

'A dare,' suggested the last of them, Trai. The Moon slipped his black mask down over his dusty-brown face and rose, ready to leave. 'We can't afford Irato to get to safety – he must be withholding what he knows until then.'

Jaril nodded and stood. 'Jerg, give the signal to attack.'

'Wait!' Jerg called, turning in the other direction. 'Signal from Calt – movement, four figures.'

'They're going east – Eman, Loram, move!' Jaril snapped, pointing at the window. The pair didn't hesitate, one then the other diving out of the window with just an anchor-rope to slow their fall.

'And us?' Trai asked, one hand on his crossbow.

'Jerg, you stay here in case they're both diversions – signal Calt to attack and Kissen to hold. Trai, with me.'

Jaril slipped down his mask and mentally cursed as he ran after Eman and Loram. The last member of his team, Calt, had a dozen thralled goshe to command, but scattered around the eastern streets and they'd already lost that many to this damn traitor and his handlers. He just had to hope they'd slow Irato down long enough for the Detenii to catch him.

Narin had barely touched his feet on the ground by the time Enchei was off into the haze of dawn mist. Down the side of the nearby compound, he turned east into a tangle of smaller buildings where the narrow side-streets would give them cover from crossbowmen. Irato was on his heels and Kesh not far behind, both carrying drawn blades. He ran to catch up with Kesh, tugging his stave free as he went, and they followed Enchei into the confined shadows. The tattooist ran with a light, delicate step from building to building, checking around each corner and swapping sides of the streets frequently.

Behind them, Narin kept expecting to hear shouts or cries break the dawn hush as the Investigators were attacked, or their ruse was discovered. But all was quiet – only the morning calls of seabirds punctuated the sounds of the city before it was properly woken. His heart hammering in his chest, Narin couldn't accurately judge how long it had been since they'd scaled the wall, but the city remained silent. The air was still and the cold salty tang of the sea filled every street.

In what seemed like no time at all they were at the edge of a broad avenue dimly lit by ancient, tree-like gas lamps turned low after the midnight bell. The faint light of the lamps was only a diffuse glow through the mist, but without sun or stars to light the way, they made a difference. The avenue wound a path north-east from the Tier bridge to the sprawl of palazzos of nobles and merchant-princes south of the

223

Imperial canal. In the shadows of a small, steep-roofed house Enchei paused, peering out across the yellow-lit avenue searching for danger.

'See him?' Irato muttered at the man's side, indicating somewhere a little further up the street. He slipped the small crossbow from behind his back and cocked it, dropping a bolt into the slide.

'Aye, waiting for us to get out in the open.'

'Plan?'

'You wait for my word.'

Enchei didn't expand on his order, only fished his sling out from his pocket and stepped back to give himself some room. Narin edged backwards, unable to see where Irato had pointed but giving Enchei space to swing. It all happened in a second; one moment the tattooist had slipped a stone into the pouch of his sling, the next he'd whirled it twice and released.

As a loud crack echoed out across the street, Enchei broke into a run across the street, rolling his forearm as he went to loop the sling around it. Kesh was about to follow when Irato put a hand out, checking her to keep her behind the corner of the house. They watched Enchei sprint across the cobbled avenue towards a side-street in the lee of an inn. As he reached halfway there was the thunk of a crossbow and something darted out from the shadows to strike his midriff. The impact drove him a step right, but barely slowed his charge and in the next moment he'd reached the street, short-sword drawn and slashing down.

There was muted crash and a thump of something hitting the ground. A moment later, silence – followed by a hoarse call of, 'Come!'

Irato leading, they ran as fast as they could to the darkened side-street where Enchei had disappeared. Narin felt his breath catch as they went into the light, a band of iron around his ribs until they reached the dark side-street and were standing over two dead goshe.

Narin could only see the face of one, hood dislodged by Enchei's killing blow. The other had had his throat cut, a loaded crossbow at his feet, but as Narin looked closer he realised the man's black hood was torn and bloody above the eye.

'They were just novices,' Enchei said, turning away to scan the side-street they were now on.

'You're hurt,' Kesh said, reaching out instinctively towards him.

'It's fine,' he said distractedly.

She exchanged a look with Narin, who was similarly alarmed. 'There's an arrow in your stomach,' Kesh pointed out.

Enchei gave a snort and swatted down at the wooden shaft protruding from his gut. The shaft snapped and fell to the ground. 'Didn't penetrate,' he added, fishing in his pocket for a second stone before freeing his sling and loading it. He didn't let the weapon hang, but kept the leather pouch pinched in his fingers.

'Come on.'

With that he started off again, Irato loping along behind him like a wolf. Kesh shook her head in disbelief but made no argument. She scooped up the loaded crossbow and followed, with Narin close behind.

The streets on the far side of the avenue were broader, affluent middle castes occupying the properties leading down to the Crescent. There was no gas lighting there, only the white gaze of the Gods and dawn's first glow, but still they were more exposed than before. Enchei upped his pace, knowing the boat station they were heading for was not far now.

Without warning, a pair of black-garbed figures broke from cover and smashed into Enchei, knocking him sideways. Irato almost ran straight into the nearer of the two and only just managed to block a slashing blade with his crossbow. The weapon was smashed from his hands, but won him time enough to draw his long-knives.

'Move!' Kesh called, raising her crossbow. Irato threw himself to one side and she fired in the next moment, but his attacker also twisted away and the bolt only grazed his spaulder. Narin ran in while Kesh hurled the crossbow and Irato attacked from the other side. The goshe let the crossbow bounce harmlessly off him before calmly retreating under a flurry of blows.

Behind, Enchei dodged the other goshe's lunge, somehow guiding the arm away as he dodged left. Before the goshe could recover Enchei had hauled on his wrist and punched the man's shoulder. The goshe gave an abrupt cry, but in the next moment Enchei hammered a right hook into the goshe's throat. The blow lifted him from his feet and threw him into the wall behind, already limp.

As the goshe fell like a discarded toy, Enchei hurled himself at the back of the remaining goshe. He kicked the man in the back of the knee and grabbed his arm to pull him off-balance – buying Irato time to bury a long-knife into each of the goshe's armpits. The man went rigid, then fell limp when Irato whipped the blades out in a spray of blood.

'We just found the elites,' Enchei said. He tugged the sling from his finger and pocketed it, drawing his short-sword instead. 'There'll be more of them.'

'The water's not far,' Narin pointed out, seeing the ground was starting to slope gently.

'Good, come on.'

Enchei ghosted off through the dark again, not bothering to stop at each alley and street entrance as he went now. Irato stayed a moment and nudged up the mask of the goshe he'd been fighting. It revealed the face of a man in early middle-age; originally from House Ghost, Narin guessed, with pale greyish skin and jet black hair.

There was no change in expression on Irato's face, clearly no recognition there, and when Kesh hissed 'Move,' he jumped forward without a moment's hesitation.

The three of them ran together, Enchei pausing for them to catch up before they all crossed into a street that led directly to the Strandway, the thoroughfare lined with shops and stalls that skirted the shore of the Crescent. On the far side of that were various small jetties where many boatmen would berth for the night, it being a route regularly patrolled by Lawbringers. From the Strandway there was no sound beyond the lap of waves and the gentle thud of boats against the wooden jetties.

The sky was lightening steadily, the mist-laden air grainy and washed out. Even the colours of House Dragon's flags on the far side of the Crescent seemed dull. Narin caught the scent of wood smoke on the breeze and the clack of shutters opening. The city was waking. There was no traffic on the Crescent yet, the waters dark and forbidding to Narin's eye, but he could see lamps marking the entrance to the Fett Canal upriver which gave him a spark of hope.

'There,' Enchei said, pointing towards the nearest jetty. 'Our boat.'

Narin looked over the man's shoulder and realised he could just make out a shape aboard one barge, a man hunched over perhaps.

'You sure?'

'Aye. Right, we make a run for it – Irato, you lead the way just ta be sure, I'll be last.'

With that he gave the big goshe a shove and Irato was propelled out into the street. He sprinted towards the barge as its owner sat bolt upright at the sound and grabbed his oar. Kesh and Narin went together; little more than two dozen paces to cover, but Narin felt his neck prickle cold as he waited for a shot that never came. Then he was in the barge and grabbing one of the spare oars, ready to go.

He barely registered the terrified face of the young boatman as he took in their weapons and the blood on Irato's face, hands shaking as he fumbled with the rope that tied the boat up. The barge was barely big enough for five. Enchei appeared and hopped in. The boatman pushed away with his long oar and they started out towards the far shore.

'Here,' Enchei said, dropping a handful of silver coins at the feet of the boatman. 'In case we need to run on the other side.'

He didn't take up a paddle straight away but turned and crouched, facing backwards with sling in hand as he watched for pursuit. Not seeing any, he grabbed an oar and added his strength to their efforts.

'Are we clear?' Narin asked, resisting the temptation to look over his shoulder.

'I, ah,' Enchei hesitated, 'damn – no!'

Narin heard the man drop his paddle and turn again. The barge wobbled briefly as he stood to whirl his sling, then jerked as he released. Narin didn't hear a connection and Enchei went for another shot, then a third before returning to paddling.

'More'n half a dozen of 'em,' he reported, driving hard into the water. 'I got two, but they're in boats now – we need to get across fast.'

He glanced behind him. 'What's your name, friend?'

The young boatman gulped. 'Sen, it's Sen.'

'Keep your head down lad, we'll see you through in one piece.' The tattooist patted the young man on the shoulder, then used him for balance as he stood and hurled another stone. This time Narin heard the crack of it striking, followed by a distant splash.

A black bolt darted across the grey waters on their right; well clear of the barge, but enough to make Kesh flinch all the same. Narin glanced towards it and saw the bolt swallowed up by the water, then the faint impression of something larger gliding beneath the surface. A few moments later there was a distinct bump against the underside of the boat as something large brushed it. Enchei cursed under his breath and briefly trailed his hand through the water, muttering some sort of mantra or invocation.

After that he felt nothing, but Narin found himself keeping his eyes just on his paddle, focused only on getting to the far side as fast as possible. They were crammed together, his knees pressed against Kesh's back so he had to time every stroke of his oar to avoid scraping down her shoulder.

227

Despite Enchei's sporadic rowing they made good time crossing – the weight of five people off-set by the fact they were all rowing hard. The goshe took a few more shots with their crossbows, but couldn't aim as well as Enchei and their best efforts fell just short.

Narin chanced a look back, the dull dawn light enough to show him the flanks of two pursuing barges while a third trailed behind. 'They're turning,' he called to Enchei. 'They giving up?'

Enchei glanced back. 'They've seen the soldiers,' he corrected, nodding towards figures watching from the stone wall of the canal's entry lagoon.

The morning was now bright enough to make out the blue liveries and distinctive shape of soldiers ready to fight. There were six of them; each one warrior caste and carrying a musket at the ready. Any open confrontation would go in their favour, Narin was sure, and the goshe had clearly concluded the same – either that or they didn't want to fight so openly.

'They're heading into Dragon District,' Narin realised. 'Damn. They're not breaking off, they mean to ambush us on the streets instead.'

'Better'n facing down muskets in the open,' Enchei agreed. 'Right now they're panicking – it looks like Irato's made a deal with House Wyvern, most likely he knows everything about their little scheme and is about to tell. He gives that to some Wyvern lord, they'll bring in the Dragons soon enough and then the goshe are as good as burned to a crisp.'

Narin looked back to the Wyvern soldiers, four men and two women all in identical armour. 'Precisely what we were trying to avoid. Looks like they're more desperate than we hoped.'

'So we ease their fears,' Enchei said. 'That's why we've got a backup plan. Tell the captain here thanks but no thanks – we don't want a fight on the streets of Dragon District any more than they do.'

'We don't?' interjected Kesh. 'There's more soldiers there than anywhere else, isn't that our best chance?'

'Sure, but they'll be asking questions later. Questions some of us won't survive. Kesh, you should stay with them, you'll be safe – the rest of us got to keep on.'

She shook her head violently. 'Think I'm going to run out on you now? Not a chance.'

Enchei gave a snort. 'Thought you'd say that, but I'm serious. You can hold your own, I know, but you're the only one who's got the choice so think again, for your ma's sake.'

Kesh was quiet a moment. 'No,' she said at last, as they slipped into the lagoon, 'I'm not hiding from this. Emari's dead because of them, I'm not walking away.'

'As you wish.'

The boatman guided them neatly into one of the narrow lagoon berths and hopped out to tie up, careful to bow to the approaching soldiers first.

'Investigator Narin?' one of the women called. He looked up and saw she had four gold bands on her left shoulder, a captain. 'I am Captain Venten, I have orders to escort you—'

Narin raised a hand to cut her off. 'I'm sorry; we've had to change our plans.'

'Change?' she said coldly. While Narin wore no indication of his caste, he didn't carry a gun so he could be fairly sure she outranked him. 'I have my orders from Lord Vanden.'

'And I'm sorry,' Narin said quickly, before her anger could mount, 'but our pursuers have seen you and they want to kill this man very badly.' He indicated Irato, who instinctively lowered his eyes as the soldiers all glared at him. 'We fear they'll be desperate enough to ambush us on the streets of Dragon.'

'Let them!'

Narin ducked his head, trying to hide the frustration on his face as he resisted the urge to shout at her. He could tell from her face she'd go looking for the goshe to confront them, whether or not Irato was nearby, unless he could persuade her not to. Battle was a warrior's whole life and purpose – any potential threat could only be met with a brutal demonstration of their own prowess.

'I do not care for their lives,' he said carefully. 'I have no doubt they would be slaughtered, but as you are bound by your oaths, so I am bound by mine. I would be remiss in my duty to encourage any sort of confrontation on the streets of this city, not least at a time of great tension. Please, let us continue on down the canal – your very presence has frightened them away, and by that you have already performed the service I begged of Lord Vanden.'

Captain Venten was silent a moment, her jaw clenched tight as she considered her position. A warrior's position and honour also depended on the lord they served, *their* wishes and needs. Narin had no doubt that as tensions with House Eagle increased, instructions would have been issued to every warrior under the Dragon hegemony.

'We will accompany you,' she declared, stepping back to allow them to head to the shallow barges on the other side of the canal gate. 'Lord Vanden's instructions were to see you to safety. The manner of that is yours to choose.'

A canal worker jumped forward to untie his craft, seeing they were in a rush and not foolish enough to negotiate a fee while under the watchful gaze of soldiers.

'Captain, if I may,' Enchei broke in, kneeling before her while the others got into the barge. 'Our intention was to lose them in the Coldcliffs slum, but with an escort of soldiers we would be conspicuous and Law Master Sheven has instructed Investigator Narin to avoid any confrontation wherever possible.'

Venten paused a moment longer before making a dismissive gesture. 'Very well, if you are determined to flee like cowards our place is not beside you.'

Narin bowed again to her, happy to take the insult if it meant he got his way. 'That is my intention, Captain.'

'Get out of my sight then,' she snapped and turned her back, her soldiers following suit.

'Thank you, Captain,' Narin added as they pushed off, knowing he'd get no response.

The water was near-still on the canal ahead of them and as they went Enchei grabbed a pair of poles from berthed barges, handing one to Irato. The bargeman, a whiskered man who only came up to Irato's shoulder, just pushed all the harder on his own pole.

They slipped away in silence, all of them watching the right-hand bank as the sleepy fringe of Dragon District glided briskly past. With awnings, doors and windows painted the colour of blood, dragon statues and gargoyles all roaring defiance and faint curls of mist in the streets between, it was a far from comforting sight. Only the speed of their combined efforts gave Narin any heart. They settled into a steady clip that their pursuers would be hard pushed to match through the narrow side-streets of Dragon, certainly without attracting attention, so Narin made himself consider the path ahead instead.

More than a mile away, nestled between two tall outcrops of black granite, the ghostly white shape of Coldcliffs stood high against the lightening sky. Its slanted roofs rose to five peaks across the undulating building, the sharp rear slope streaked green and grey by lichen.

'Are you sure about this?' he said quietly to Enchei.

The older man nodded and pulled a key out from under his shirt. 'You get 'em through and down the north steps. I arranged for a surprise for our goshe friends – in case they looked like they'd be coming after us hard on Dragon's streets.'

'Surprise?'

'While I was out yesterday,' Enchei explained. 'I've met a few o' the bully-boys who've run Coldcliffs these past few years. Hard not to, when the price o' room and board includes tossing out drunks. They were more than interested to hear some gang o' hired knives were planning on making a move there this morning. Think they might have something to say about anyone flashing weapons on their alleys today.'

Narin grimaced as he pictured the local toughs ambushing skilled killers, but there was little he could do about it now. Coldcliffs was a tangled mess of squalor and crime that the Lawbringers had never managed to tame and the thieves and murderers Enchei had duped were far from vulnerable innocents. Right now that chaotic, unmapped interior of shacks interspersed with stone towers rising up to the ceiling seemed like sanctuary to Narin.

Trying to navigate the place was difficult enough – to pursue someone across it without being ambushed or becoming lost for an hour, nearly impossible. And close to the northern set of oversized steps cut into the bedrock? Enchei's home, a place the goshe knew nothing about.

'Someone get me a drink,' Synter muttered, hauling her boots off and sinking back into the chair she'd dragged out of the eatery. 'Something strong.'

Her second, Uttir, grunted and heaved himself up again. The man smacked his lips at the thought, stirred into movement by the idea despite his fatigue.

'Getting some sleep, me,' Uster said with a shake of the head, tugging the ties in his long grey hair free. ''Less you want me on first watch?'

Synter waved him away and the man offered her a half-joking salute as he headed inside. The rest of her team, one short now Kodeh had taken Irato's command, followed him at a twitch of her fingers. She fumbled briefly at the straps across her chest to loosen her armour and unhitched it with the weapons still attached, struggling out of the tangle as Uttir returned with a bottle and two glass tumblers.

'This'll do,' Uttir muttered, depositing them on the table before dragging his coat off and sitting opposite Synter. Like Uster, he was from House Iron and had a wild mane of dark grey hair as they all seemed to, old and young alike. While Synter poured them each a generous measure of what smelled like whisky, he fumbled at his tobacco pouch to fill his pipe.

'Straight from the old country,' Uttir commented, raising the pipe, 'and the best you'll find within a hundred miles.'

He glanced around to check they were alone then ignited the tobacco with a crackling burst of fire from his fingertips. Synter snorted at the childish display and the man shrugged. He was the youngest of the team; still new to the Blessings of the Elders and revelling in his abilities. Synter remembered she'd done exactly the same.

'Am I going to have a problem with the others?' Uttir asked, keen to move the conversation on. 'They can't be happy, Uster especially.'

'They're fine.'

Uttir thought for a moment. He was a handsome young man, tall and muscular with an easy smile and beguiling grey eyes. That had almost been enough to stop her promoting him to her team – complications like that were the last thing she needed when hers was supposed to be the best of all the Detenii. But then she'd realised it would have been stupid to pass him over. Uttir was skilled and clever, and having the best at her side was all that mattered, now more than ever.

'They're not looking to be a second,' he concluded. 'They're all waiting for their own team.'

Synter inclined her head and took a big swallow of whisky. It was good stuff; a smooth warmth sliding down her body like the welcome hands of a lover. 'Price of having the best in my team, they won't stay. Too good to keep.'

'And me?'

She shrugged. 'The Elders say you're the best they've seen in a while. When the time comes, if you want your own team it'll be yours. If you want to stay second, one day my place will open up.'

'Assuming we're not all dead by then.'

She nodded and finished her drink, pouring them both another without even asking the man.

'Assuming we're not all dead,' Synter echoed.

She raised her glass to the brightening sky. Above the houses across the canal she could just about make out a constellation in the east, six stars darkened by the low dawn sun before it climbed and they became near-invisible. She paused a moment, trying to recall which God's constellation it was: three above three, the upper ones following a slant.

'Play us a tune, Lady Piper,' she called softly, 'give us a fitting fanfare to the coming day.'

'Huh, long's she does it quietly,' Uttir added, glancing over his shoulder towards the constellation she addressed. 'I need a few hours' sleep before we go shift the artefact. Spreading plague and murder is tiring work.' He drew on his pipe again and eased his feet up onto a nearby stool. 'Aye, but tomorrow's going to be quite a sight. Especially when Kodeh's little secrets wake up.'

'With luck, they'll be out until evening,' Synter corrected. 'City'll be in chaos by then if Father Jehq's done his work right.'

She stiffened, then lowered her head to the tangled pile of boots and armour at the foot of her chair. Carefully, she set her glass to one side.

'Uttir,' Synter said in a soft voice, 'your crossbow to hand?'

The man frowned at her, puzzled. He shook his head and nodded toward the interior of the eatery. 'Inside. Why?'

Synter picked up a boot and tugged it on. 'Go fetch the others, now.'

'What is it?' he asked as he rose to obey.

'I've just seen an old friend,' she muttered, glancing at her discarded glass of whisky as though it was making her hallucinate. 'Bloody Irato – the man's just gone past on a damn barge!'

'You're fucking—' He turned to see a canal barge bearing four or five figures swiftly away.

Without another word he darted inside, calling orders to the team in a hoarse whisper.

Synter didn't waste any more time. Once her other boot was on she hauled her armour up over her head and tugged the straps tight with a practised hand. Aware day was coming, she swept up her ragged grey coat to hide her weapons, leaving the forbidding black mask where it was, and started off down the towpath, her team clattering along behind.

Did he see me? Why would he come this way? Has he gone mad to risk it? She shook her head. *I'll get my answers when I cut them out of him.*

CHAPTER 17

Some of my more craven colleagues fail to note the fact that the Gods were not always raised for the same reasons. The majority, it is true, were granted Godhood for finding enlightenment through perfection of their chosen calling. This remains an example to us all without pretending it was true for all. Our world is a dangerous place and our Gods first needed a power-base; entirely sensible to my mind and that is a characteristic more could aspire to in this life.

From *A History* by Ayel Sorote

Narin watched the waves roll in off the Inner Sea, catching the first rays of sun to break the clouds. White spume rose up off the ancient, slime-coated barrier that protected the canal from the incoming tide, while pale slashes in the swell indicated the sandbars to the east so prized by the city's fishermen.

A shiver ran down his neck. The power of the wind and water surged towards them while the cliffs were a slanted shelf of black rock twenty yards above their heads. The canal barrier was low against the water, the incoming tide driving the level up so the barrier seemed only two feet high – a pitiful defence against such an expanse. Perched on the great jutting cliff was Coldcliffs but, from underneath, Narin could see only the very edge of the unnatural white stone structure. It pointed out toward the horizon like a ship's prow, parting the incoming breeze as it struck the land.

He looked around at his companions. Kesh seemed similarly affected by the sea and looming rock, while Enchei was more intent on watching for sight of their pursuers around the long curve of the canal. Irato and the bargeman both poled towards the harbour entrance with long, powerful strokes – the larger man still looking absent and detached from events while the smaller twitched and huffed with fear enough for both.

There were slipways for canal barges to enter the walled harbour so goods could be taken directly up to cargo ships, but their destination was just ahead of them – a shelf at the base of a zigzagging stair cut into the rock itself that led up to the base of Coldcliffs. It was a steep climb and difficult to get goods up, so at this hour Narin guessed the only obstacle would be workers descending for a morning shift.

'Take the barge on into the harbour,' he said to the bargeman. 'As far as you can. Might be it'll look like we went for the Harbour Warrant – Kesh's home ground.'

The bargeman nodded, keeping his silence in the face of armed passengers and their pursuers.

'Any of you know your way around Coldcliffs?' Enchei called from the back. He had his sling out again, having expended a stone just before they reached the cliffs as their pursuers appeared on the towpath.

Narin shook his head, as did Kesh. 'You're not coming with us?'

'I was going to slow 'em down on the stair,' the tattooist replied. 'It's a good spot to hold them off, but there's no point if you're going to get lost in the meantime.'

'We take our chances together,' Kesh declared, 'we've come this far well enough.'

'No,' Narin said, almost surprising himself with the determination in his voice. 'Best we buy some time here.'

'You volunteering to be killed?' she asked sceptically.

He shook his head. 'No, but I'm not the one they're after. We need to get you two to safety and Enchei knows the way – that leaves just me. Irato, give me your crossbow once we're on dry land.'

'You can't stop them all,' Enchei warned, 'they're too quick.'

'I only need to make them hesitate – a shot or two to make them duck back down and think they're being ambushed. They'll stop and think for a few more seconds. That gives you some extra time. If they want to keep on chasing me, fine. I'll head into the slum and hide, give me an hour then I'll meet you all at Enchei's rooms.'

'You know the way?'

'Not through Coldcliffs, but I'll find my way out. I can't believe the locals would knife an Investigator, not for no reason and the Gods themselves know we're not worth robbing.'

'What if you're taken?' Kesh asked.

'Then I'll hold out an hour,' he said firmly. 'Long enough for you to move elsewhere.'

All eyes turned to Enchei. The older man looked unhappy with the plan, but he said nothing to refute what Narin had said. After another glance back he nodded grimly.

'Don't take any chances, you hear me? And don't be a hero. If I was them and I caught you, I'd have something on hand to dose you with. Last thing they'll want is a yelling prisoner to carry away and knocking someone out's difficult to get right. Get it slightly wrong and they die – get it right and they're concussed and make bugger all sense anyways.'

Kesh raised an eyebrow. 'Sometimes your knowledge worries me, old man.'

That prompted a grin from Enchei. 'Aye, you'n me both. Point is, don't get caught, but if you are, don't think you're gonna hold out for ever. You put up too much resistance, they'll tear your mind out sure as a demon got its claws into you. Then there's nothing left to rescue, hear me?'

Narin nodded. 'No being a hero,' he said with what he hoped was a wry smile. *Not with a child I want to meet before I die,* he added in the privacy of his own mind.

Enchei pointed past Narin. 'We're here.'

They disembarked and watched the bargeman waste no time in heading off into the harbour. Narin looked up at the giant's stairway above them and was put in mind of a ziggurat's tiers leading up the slope. Cut into the solid black rock, each step was almost a yard deep and slightly angled to let the rain or ocean spray run off.

The outer side of the steps was a rough chest-high wall, enough to deflect the worst of the wind and hide them from anyone below as the stair doubled back on itself. Before they started up the first set Irato pulled his crossbow from behind his back and cocked the weapon, handing Narin three bolts from the pouch on his leg.

'Climb with us,' Enchei suggested, 'pick your spot at the top – not so far to run alone that way.'

They set off at a brisk pace up the first few flights and met no one at first, then a trickle of black-shirted, barefoot labourers started coming the other way for work on the docks. By the fourth flight, Narin felt himself properly start to tire, the shirt Enchei had given him weighing him down as he pushed up from one step to the next. Glancing over he saw Kesh labouring as well, keeping her head down and attention on the treacherous rock underfoot.

Their footsteps echoed worryingly loud to Narin's ear, but there was nothing he could do about it and just keeping his footing was enough of an effort as he started to tire. The only pause Enchei allowed was an occasional glance over the wall at the flights below. On the fifth, with three more to go before they reached the top, the pace really began to drop away. Enchei checked over the edge again and growled a curse as he unwound his sling.

'They're following, pick up the pace.' He pulled out one of his remaining stones and let the sling extend to its full length as he judged the angle he'd have to throw at. 'Kesh, Narin – fast as you can, I'll catch up.'

Lungs aching, Narin didn't respond other than to suck as much air in as he could before starting up the next set of steps. Irato hesitated, unsure whether to stay, but Enchei said nothing more as he hurled the pebble down as hard as he could. It struck stone with the crack of a pistol-shot and Narin flinched at the sound but didn't look back, willing his feet to move faster as fatigue took hold.

They passed another pair of labourers, warily rounding a corner in case they stumbled into a skirmish between House soldiers. Narin caught a glimpse of one, a young bearded man, whose eyes widened suddenly just as Narin reached them. A cold stab of fear entered his stomach and he slipped his fingers around the grip of his knife, but in the next moment Irato sprinted up the steps past them – ragged coat flapping in the strengthening breeze as he turned to face them.

'They're gaining.'

'Not helping,' Kesh gasped from beside him, 'just move.'

Narin grunted in agreement, pretty much all the effort he could spare, but Irato obeyed Kesh without a moment's hesitation and turned to go on ahead.

With two more to go, Enchei caught them up – breathing hard but far from the shaky-kneed exhaustion Narin was feeling. He accompanied them one more flight, then a cry of alarm from the next spurred him on ahead. As Kesh and Narin wheezed around the corner their hearts sank – two men blocking the path up, with one pointing a hatchet at Irato.

'We're being pursued,' Enchei was explaining hurriedly, 'men with knives after us.'

237

The pair of thugs exchanged looks. Both were young and scarred locals; one significantly bigger than his friend, but the smaller bore the greater number of gang tattoos on his bare arms. That one went to the wall to look down, a cleaver in his hand in case Irato tried anything. He had to stand on tip-toe to see properly over it, but when he did he jerked back as though stung.

'They're comin',' he growled to his comrade. 'Dozen or more – three flights down.' He waved towards Irato and Enchei. 'Go, all o' you. Senten, send word to the rest.'

'They're tough,' Enchei warned as he passed, one hand under Kesh's arm as she staggered up the last stretch. 'Trained killers.'

The smaller man nodded, not bothering with bravado in the face of such numbers. He turned to follow but then paused as he saw Narin stop at the top and fumble with the crossbow as he tried to fit a bolt. Using the corner as cover, he rested his left arm on the stone wall as best he could to steady his aim.

'You mad, law-man?'

The Investigator shook his head, still too tired to speak. Eventually fitting the bolt in the groove he readied the weapon with shaky hands, taking great heaving breaths as he waited for the goshe to come. The thug watched him with an inscrutable expression, but once it was clear Narin was going to face them alone he went to the wall again and looked over.

'Last flight,' he said quickly. 'Coming fast.'

'Thanks,' Narin muttered. He felt a strange sense of guilt that he was thanking a criminal, but the man had already disappeared up the half-dozen steps leading into Coldcliffs itself.

A figure rounded the corner and Narin slipped his finger onto the trigger, making sure they were wearing goshe clothes before firing. The bolt caught the masked goshe square in the chest and knocked him backwards, crashing into one following close behind and both falling to the foot of the steps.

Those following darted back, anticipating another shot at any moment. Narin dropped the end of the crossbow to the ground and ratcheted back the string as fast as he could, one eye watching the foot of the stair for the goshe to return fire. The weapon's catch clicked into place, sounding ominous as it echoed down the stone stairway. After that there was a moment of complete silence. The goshe would have heard the sound of him reloading and that made them hesitate a few heartbeats longer. Tough they might be, Narin had just proved they weren't invulnerable and they knew that the first to run round that corner was getting the same.

A face peered briefly around the corner, a woman's face with hanging black hair. Narin brought the crossbow up almost in the next moment and she ducked back as he took aim.

There you go, take a moment, he thought, fatigue and fear provoking a manic light-headedness in him. *Decide amongst yourselves, who's coming first?*

At the foot of the stair the goshe he'd shot squirmed feebly. Narin ignored him and the tentative hands that reached out to drag him back into cover. One heartbeat of uncertain quiet turned into two, then three and four. At last the woman eased around the corner again and Narin pulled the trigger without thinking, knowing he couldn't let her line up a shot. She flinched back and the bolt glanced harmlessly away, but Narin barely registered that as he abandoned the bow and raced for the last stairway.

The precious moments of standing had let him recover enough to sprint that last stretch. In seconds he found himself staring wildly around at an alley no more than two yards wide, just the space between two piecemeal shacks opening out onto something resembling a street. He ran forward and looked left and right, registering nothing at first. Then he realised there was a child squatting in an alcove between two shacks off to the left, staring straight at him while it defecated into a bucket. No more than five or six, its sex impossible to determined behind the grubby clothes and grease-smeared cheeks, the child pointed towards another alley with one finger.

Realising he didn't have time for questions, Narin just obeyed the child's directions. Hoping he'd find the gang member around the corner there, he rounded to find himself presented with just three curtained doorways and two more alleys branching away. An old woman squinted up at him and jabbed a thumb towards the left-hand of the alleys so again Narin did has he was told, aware the goshe would be up the stairs by now.

He raced forward, still not seeing anyone he recognised but content to lose himself in the unfathomable, lawless tangle that was Coldcliffs.

*

Synter reached the top of the flight ahead of the rest of her troops, blades drawn and lashing out as she rounded the corner. The walkway was empty bar a discarded crossbow. She bit back a curse and headed up the handful of steps that took them into Coldcliffs itself. The stink of refuse and mud hit her like a slap around the face as she came out onto a narrow street and looked left and right. Their Blessings varied in effect, but the Hunter's Nose was one that remained active throughout the day and it was startling to be able to smell a slum as its stray dogs could.

At least they're interested in what they smell, Synter thought privately.

She strode forward towards a young girl who had frozen in the process of wiping her behind.

I can't even follow his scent through all this – doubly useless. Let's try the old-fashioned way.

'Which way?' she demanded, putting the point of her long-knife to the girl's neck. 'Quick or I cut your throat.'

Wordlessly the child pointed down the dirt-packed street to Synter's right. She removed the blade and turned to her troops emerging from the alley. The Eagle, Jaril, had four of his team left and five thralled goshe – most still masked despite the brightening day. Her own team had just grabbed whatever they had to hand, but each would be dangerous even unarmed.

'Three teams – Uttir, you Uster and Frayl take one of the thralled and go left. Caric and Ushernai, and you,' she pointed towards one of the thralled goshe at random, 'we'll take right. Jaril, you and the rest spread out through these alleys in case they're holed up nearby. Head towards the exits and hold there as long as you can without attracting House or Lawbringer attention.'

She set off without waiting for a response, the three she'd chosen falling in behind. Weapons ready, they trotted down the street scanning left and right for their quarry – Synter all too aware they couldn't check all of the houses and alleys without giving Irato plenty of time to escape. It was bright inside Coldcliffs compared to what she'd been expecting, the white stone roof largely resistant to the combined effects of smoke and time. A stratum of sunlight streamed in over the shacks like the incoming tide, interrupted only by occasional buildings above one storey, while smoke from the communal fires was swept briskly away by the breeze.

The street curved left and forked, the left path heading deep into the heart of Coldcliffs and the right towards the soaring, wind-swept view over the Inner Sea. Faces appeared at half the windows she could see as she hesitated there, mostly locals but already she'd seen faces from four or five other Houses too.

At her side, Ushernai still looked out of place, the big man from Leviathan unusual anywhere apart from their sparsely-populated district, but dark-haired Caric would have only needed to dirty his clothes to fit straight in. No one approached them down the street, the handful of passersby immediately turning tail at the sight of them. Gesturing left, to head into the centre of Coldcliffs, Synter kept her eyes on the path ahead – trusting her men to watch their flanks.

The distinctive thunk of a crossbow discharging made her dart to one side even as she turned to follow the sound. She saw Ushernai reel, a bolt in his upper-arm, while the thralled goshe gave a cry and darted into a nearby alley. As he disappeared from view, there came a clatter and scuffle of feet while Ushernai's growl of anger echoed around the enclosed street.

'Shit,' Synter muttered as she plunged after the thralled man.

Caric stayed where he was, covering his comrade while the pale giant checked his wound. In the alley there was a flurry of noise as she hurtled around a corner, knives raised but barely able to turn the wild lunge of some long weapon. Before her attacker had the chance to react Synter knocked it loose and chopped into the man's neck so hard she almost severed his head. Blood sprayed across the alley and cut a scarlet arc across two men driving daggers into the goshe she'd been pursuing.

Before they could withdraw their weapons she was on them, stabbing each simultaneously. She kicked the first off her blade and brought that around to open the throat of the second even as her first victim began to cry out in pain. He fell backwards, dragging the goshe with him. She didn't bother checking if the thralled man was still alive, stabbing down into the first attacker's heart before retreating back to the street. All around her she heard running feet, some ambushers fleeing alongside the locals most likely, but she didn't want to wait in case it was reinforcements.

Back in the dim street she found Ushernai wrapping a binding around his bicep with practised movements. Caric watched him with one eye, hatchets at the ready, but the Leviathan clearly needed no assistance until he gestured for Synter to snap the wooden shaft.

'You're good?' she asked once there was only an inch or two of wood protruding from his arm.

Ushernai nodded, a slight wince crossing his near-albino pale face as he flexed his fingers. Clearly, the result satisfied him and with a shake of his white hair the Leviathan's expression turned to his usual savage glower.

Synter retook her place at the front and upped the pace, not wanting to give their attackers time to regroup. The street seemed to darken as she headed deeper into the slum, further from the open outer edge that was only punctuated by a supporting pillar every thirty or forty yards. After twenty paces the street seemed to end abruptly, a handful of alley-entrances and open doorways clustered around a stone trough of filthy-looking water. Over the shacks she could see a tall stone building marked with gang colours; old and filthy like everything inside the slum, but more permanent than anything else they'd seen thus far.

'Reckon they're holed up there?' Caric said, seeing her look.

Synter shook her head. 'Too obvious. Irato's more likely to find a hovel next to it and watch us attack the tower.'

'How do we find him in all this?'

Synter went to the nearest shack and grabbed its patchwork wooden wall, shaking it hard. The wall rattled and bowed, but didn't fall entirely. 'We're better on rooftops,' she said by way of explanation, 'so maybe we can cover the ground better that way. Keep clear of ambushes more easily, anyway.'

'They'll hold me?' Ushernai asked, casting an appraising look around at the ramshackle structures.

'Keep to the walls, not that most have much in the way of roofs anyways,' Synter said. 'We play to our strengths – the locals'll pick us off one by one if we get lost in these alleys.'

Ushernai grunted and gripped Caric by the shoulder, nodding toward the wall behind him. Caric nodded and sheathed his weapons, making a cradle of his hands to boost the big man up. Even with the head of a crossbow bolt embedded in his arm, Ushernai got up there easily and balanced at the corner while Synter and Caric jumped up after him.

Synter glanced around. The air seemed clearer up here, the filth and stink of the slum less all-embracing as the clean sea-breeze rolled overhead. The streets and alleys unfolded before her, a madcap maze that no longer constrained them.

'There.'

She pointed off to the east, past a fat tree-trunk-like pillar that spread a dozen branches up to meet the undulating ceiling and support the level above. The two men followed her finger – a pair of pillars, these ones slender and arched inward. It had to be the eastern exit of Coldcliffs, the bottle-neck that was their last chance to catch Irato. Synter broke into a staccato sprint across the houses, quick little steps along walls and long strides to cross each alley.

Away to her left she heard a crash of splintering wood and steel ringing on steel, but in moments she was past the commotion. The distance between her and the stairway cut into the bedrock seemed to evaporate with every passing step, the tight network of tiny houses providing her with a free path all the way across. In a matter of minutes she had reached it and dropped back down to the packed earth that covered the ground.

There was an open stretch of ground around the arch, on the north side of which stood a solid-looking tavern; dirty brick walls framing an open front where the bar was hidden behind shutters. A thin trail of smoke rose from its chimney, almost immediately whipped away by the breeze. Three long tables stood in front of the bar, penned by roughly-built walls intended to keep the breeze off, and at the nearest sat five men – all armed and heavily tattooed with swirling gang markings from shoulder to wrist.

Synter raised a hand to tell her comrades to hang back and advanced towards the men, carefully looking around just in case Irato was hiding in the shadows somewhere.

'The fuck you think you're going?' the largest of them called, a broken-nosed lump as wide as he was tall.

There was a tint to his skin that didn't seem to match his features and Synter guessed he was mixed-race rather than some House she didn't recognise. Most likely that meant he was doubly-tough in the eyes of the rest, given the disdain most felt towards anyone not of pure blood, but still she sheathed her weapons as she approached.

As one, the men rose but their leader also motioned for the rest to wait, clearly not wanting to look like he needed backup to deal with a woman. 'You ain't welcome round here.'

Synter looked him up and down. A nail-studded club the length of her leg dangled from his pudgy fingers.

'And here was me looking for love,' she replied eventually. 'Doing so in all the wrong places yet again.'

'Oh you'll get more'n enough o' that from us,' he said with a fat grin crossing his face.

Synter sighed. When men were trying to look tough in front of a woman, they were pathetically predictable. His mind distracted just for a moment, the man was still grinning like a hero of virility when she planted her boot into his crotch hard enough to lift him off his feet.

The man gave a strangled squeal and Synter caught hold of his club just long enough for his brain to catch up with what had happened. He briefly tried to wrench the club from her grip, but in the next moment the pain properly hit him and he stumbled backwards, spewing vomit down his front.

With a deft yank Synter turned him back around and grabbed him by the scruff of his oversized neck. That her hand couldn't reach far around it proved immaterial as fingers as strong as a steel vice pinched into his flesh. With little apparent effort she held him upright between her and the rest of his men.

Synter drew a long-knife and put it to his throat in case any of the others got ideas, but they were all frozen with surprise.

'Now boys – give me answers and I might let you all live,' she announced breezily as Ushernai and Caric moved up beside her. 'Who hired you all?'

There was no response other than the big one puking again. She wrinkled her nose – ah yes, he'd shit himself too.

Maybe I kicked him a bit harder than necessary, she reflected. *Ah well.*

'I haven't got all day,' she warned them, slicing a shallow furrow into the man's fleshy throat. Blood sprang out of the wound and she saw one of the men flinch at the sight, another grabbing his shoulder to hold him back.

'This your dad?' she asked, looking at the one who'd flinched – one of the youngest there but still marked as the rest were.

The man nodded.

'Then start talking now or say goodbye to him.'

'We weren't hired,' the man blurted out, gaze on his father until he reluctantly dragged it up to meet hers. 'We heard you were making a move on our turf is all.'

'Who heard?'

244

'Dunno, the Knight just gave the order to ambush anyone coming in force.'

'Knight?' Synter said. A cold feeling slithered down her spine even as she realised the man wasn't talking about the Ascendant God, Lord Knight, but some self-aggrandising criminal.

'He runs Coldcliffs, no one gets a knife round here without his say so.'

'Well your Knight got played for a fool. We're not moving on you, just got a bit of business with the people we chased in here. You know if they're coming this way?'

The man shook his head, glancing at his fellows but getting nothing of use from them. 'Don't know nothing about that, we just got told to wait here. No one's come this way.'

Synter thought for a moment. The fastest way to get her blade off his father's throat was to say their quarry had already run down those steps – but the truth came easier than a considered lie. If they hadn't come this way they might still, but she didn't know her way through the slum and doubted Irato did either. If they'd made some sort of deal with this Knight, most likely he'd be leading them through and seeing to his payment personally.

'Take him,' she said, shoving the big man towards his son, 'and get out of my sight or I'll gut the lot o' you.'

They didn't need telling twice. Two of the gang members tentatively approached to grab their leader and help him away, while the others fled. In moments they were alone there, any bystanders having run at the first sign of violence. Synter turned to Ushernai and Caric.

'You two wait here; find yourselves a nice corner to hide in. Most likely they were never coming this way, but I want every exit covered.'

'And you?' Caric asked.

'I'll head for one of the others, see if I can sniff our man out – or that bloody Investigator. If they've split up he might be lying low.' She raised her voice. 'Someone here must be keen to earn some coin! I've gold nobles for anyone who leads me to my traitors!'

With that she walked off, heading for an alley broadly in the direction of the north stairs. No voices spoke up so when she reached the alley she leaped back up onto the nearest sturdy-looking building and set out, this time at a slower pace. Moving almost silently, cat-like and predatory, she headed out across the slum, the glimpsed face of a local man in Investigator robes fixed firmly in her mind.

There was no direct path across the slum for Enchei to follow. Even worse, the irregular network of tiny, winding streets had changed since last he was there. Some houses had sprouted smaller off-shoots like parasites that cut right across their path, others were missing entirely. He could tell what rough direction they were moving in, but several times they'd been forced to double-back as the street ended abruptly or swung off in a new, unexpected direction. As more and more of the locals went about their morning they became enveloped in a fluctuating hubbub of raised voices, barking dogs and crying children – a chaotic cacophony that masked any sounds of pursuit.

'How much further?' Kesh gasped from behind him, still suffering from the draining scamper up the stone steps outside.

'Not far— Hells!' Enchei skidded to a halt as he rounded a corner to come face to face with a pair of black-clad goshe. Kesh slammed into the back of him while Irato barrelled on and was almost impaled by an alarmed knife-swing.

'Here!' bellowed one, 'They're here!'

Both were Ghosts, pale-skinned and agile, and Irato was forced to desperately parry a flurry of blows from the one who'd almost caught him. Enchei left him to it and went for the other. The man stopped shouting and moved to meet him, swinging an axe at Enchei's ribs and forcing him to stop dead. The axe head scraped harmlessly across Enchei's side while he grabbed the goshe's arm and hauled sideways. Using the arm as a lever Enchei dragged the goshe off his feet and slammed him face-first into a wall that shuddered under the impact.

Not giving the goshe time to recover, Enchei smashed an elbow down into the top of the man's shoulder and felt the socket pop. The axe slipped from his enemy's grip and Enchei chopped savagely into the side of his head.

On the other side of the alley, Irato had been driven back against a house – still warding off his opponent's blows but barely stopping the lightning-quick slashes. Only the presence of Kesh stopped him from being overcome; she was not so foolish as to throw herself at the unnatural fighter, but was using her blade to distract the goshe.

The goshe feinted towards Kesh then moved to finish Irato off – bursts of cracking light racing down his arm to the tip of his long-knife. Irato threw himself aside before the man's lunge could reach him and in the same moment Kesh jumped for the goshe's back. Driving down with her knife she stabbed him between the shoulder-blades and the goshe staggered forward, crying out in pain.

His knees buckled, dragging the weapon from Kesh's hand as he reached for the wall's support. Irato didn't give him time to do anything more, driving a blade up under his ribs while smashing a knee up into his face for good measure. The blistering light winked out and the goshe went limp, folding in a blood-spattered heap on the ground.

'You're getting good at that,' Enchei said admiringly. He jerked Kesh's knife from the goshe's back and wiped it on the corpse before offering it over to her. 'That's your second elite.'

Kesh nodded as she stared down at the other dead man. His eyes were open, staring straight up, bloody abrasions from the wall covering one grey cheek. 'They're all to blame for Emari,' she said in a quiet voice. 'Or others like her – they're all guilty of something similar.'

'Reckon you're right there, but let's not hang around for the rest.'

Enchei discarded his axe and waved the others forward. Kesh glanced at Irato, but if she was looking for any contribution from the man she got nothing, and with a shake of the head she fell in behind Enchei.

A doorway banged shut on their right as they ran single-file down the narrow street – Enchei caught a glimpse of small faces through a half-open shutter, frightened children hiding from the murder outside. By contrast, a teenage boy with long whitish hair sat on a dirty brick wall ahead where the street forked, dressed just in cropped trousers and an ill-fitting shirt. He seemed entirely unconcerned by the armed figures running towards him and watched them with studied indifference.

Enchei ducked low as he reached the fork, but no more goshe appeared to attack them as he'd expected. He looked left and right, trying to decide which way to go while Irato and Kesh joined him. The young woman stared up at the youth watching them. He had a spiral tattoo on his cheek that ran down his neck and underneath his shirt – not some local gang marking, Enchei guessed, but some sort of clan mark.

'The stair this way?' Kesh asked him, pointing to the wider of the two forks.

The youth shook his head and nodded in the other direction.

'Sure?' she asked, fishing out the last of her coin and holding up a fat copper piece called a merchant.

The youth nodded. 'Quickest route,' he said at last in a local drawl.

Kesh tossed the coin towards him and the youth's hand snapped it from the air like a striking snake. Enchei ran ahead, leaving the other two to follow as the fork took them to a nearly-straight stretch of brick-walled houses. A wall of white seemed to shine at the far end and he realised it was sky at the open flank of Coldcliffs.

'Come on!' he called back, 'we're nearly there.'

The only reply was the sound of Kesh's feet as she and Irato pursued him, but it was enough. In seconds they found themselves blinking at the sudden brightness of a massive open space between supporting pillars. Attached to the left-hand one was a shallow, curving slope that led up to the upper levels, but their attention was on what lay beyond the pillars. The great stairway down to the regular streets of Tale stood only twenty yards off, and Enchei felt a flicker of relief as he saw no black-clad assassins waiting among the scores of figures walking in all directions.

He led his companions at a brisk walk towards the stair, motioning for them to sheath their weapons. If they did look out of place, no one seemed to care as they went about their morning, ignorant of the small, bloody battles already fought across Coldcliffs that day. The wind was as strong as it always was at that height, a brisk buffeting sweeping up from the city beyond as they looked out over the view that was the only thing to distinguish this cold and ancient structure.

Dominating the vista was the Imperial Palace, its vastness only emphasised by the sight of the city's distinct districts surrounding it, but there were many more buildings to pick out. Lord Omtoray's squat fortress on the shore of the Crescent; three black blocks from which two slender towers rose, while half a dozen similar thorns topped the palazzos of lesser Dragons. The abrupt cliffs on the Crescent's eastern flank where House Eagle's nobles perched, the green spaces of Wolf and Raven Districts and street after street of blue-tiled walls in Leviathan – all contributed to a strange mosaic that was the Empire's heart.

Enchei looked around for pursuers one last time. 'No sign of Narin,' he said grimly.

'You think they've caught him?'

He waved them forward and they joined the mass of people heading down into the streets of workshops and houses of Tale. 'Too soon to say,' he decided. 'Getting you two off the street is all we need to worry about right now.'

Kesh glanced back at the curved lines of Coldcliffs. Neither Narin nor any goshe had followed them out. 'I think we're clear.'

'Aye – but let's take no chances,' Enchei said. He pointed to a side-street where long ribbons of brightly-coloured cloth fluttered in the morning breeze. 'There's a shrine to Lady Dancer down there. Will give me a good view of anyone following.'

'And Narin?' Kesh pressed. 'What if they've caught him?'

Enchei scowled. 'If they have, looks like I'll be getting on my knees to pray.'

'Pray?'

'Aye – our friend Lord Shield, might be time he lent a hand.'

Kesh looked startled and beside her Irato unconsciously touched his hand to his injured ribs.

'You can contact a God?'

The older man grinned wolfishly. 'Course not – we'll need a demon for that.'

Narin turned the corner and stopped. The street ended a few yards ahead at a pig sty, of all things. He looked back, breath catching as he glimpsed movement then realised it was a child darting from one house to another. He could taste blood in his mouth – somehow he'd bitten his tongue as he tripped a few streets back.

'Where now?' he muttered, cautiously retracing his steps until he could find another path.

The sounds of the slum were punctuated by cries and shouts – noises he couldn't translate into words, but he heeded their warnings none-theless. Somewhere nearby someone was crying and calling out, a plea for help lost in the babble of pain and frantic breath of the injured. He steered clear, finding another path and hating himself as he did so.

I should be running towards those in need, he thought distantly. His hand tightened around the grip of his stave as he left the voice behind. *I'm failing in my duty – Lord Shield, let it be for a good reason. Let them find a clear path to safety.*

Narin knew he couldn't have been far behind the others, but thus far he'd seen nothing of them, nor of the goshe pursuing. His path through the slum had been erratic, turned left and right by the form-less sprawl of Coldcliffs' tiny streets. The Investigator wiped a sheen of sweat from his face, his heart hammering away in his chest.

At last he turned one final corner and his field of vision seemed to blaze with welcome light. Then he faltered as he saw a dark figure standing in the middle of the open ground. Ragged coat dancing in the breeze and hood pulled forward to shade his face, the goshe looked like a demon of legend and Narin felt his heart go cold at the sight.

All around the goshe people edged past him – his head twitching left and right as he stared at each one's face. He stood ready to kill, knives drawn and blood on the blade of one. Slumped against a wall to the left was a local, with a tattooed gang member bending over him and wrapping a wound to his arm. Clearly they'd challenged him, but this goshe at least seemed disinclined to kill anyone but his target.

Narin edged back around the corner. The goshe hadn't seen him yet, but Narin couldn't see a way past him. He closed his eyes a moment and willed the fatigue from his body, taking in long deep breaths as he thought.

Find another way?

Just thinking back at the path he'd taken made the suggestion seem foolish. He'd taken his time crossing the district, he knew – they'd have each exit covered by now.

He looked down at his stave and straightened the leather vambraces Enchei had made him wear. They felt familiar on his body; similar enough to the long padded gloves he wore for dachan or stave training.

'Time to see if all that training has done any good?' he asked himself, feeling light-headed at the idea.

A memory of Rhe on the training ground appeared in his mind, the two of them trading blows and practising against the weapons of criminals. The goshe had a knife; that meant Narin had the better reach, whether or not the man was unnaturally quick.

Don't give him time to think, Narin realised, drawing the dagger from his belt and slipping the stave behind his back as Rhe so often did.

How many times had he seen it? That shaft of white appearing from behind Rhe's back with blinding speed – both on the training ground and the streets they patrolled. So long as he timed it right, he could crack the man's skull before he was in range of those knives – or at least stun him. Certainly anything more than a glancing blow would get Narin past and off down the stairs with a fighting chance of escaping.

'Maybe the city's right,' Narin added with a bitter little smile, readying himself to sprint around the corner and at the goshe. 'Maybe I am a hero – just waiting for the time to show it.'

He didn't wait to consider the answer there, just threw himself forward and ran as fast as he could towards the exit. It took him a few steps to realise the goshe hadn't moved, but in that moment the man saw him and tensed, blades out wide as Narin rushed towards him. The Investigator kept up his charge, knife held ready out in front so the goshe could see it.

He covered the ground quickly, a cry of fear and rage escaping his lips as he charged forward. The goshe barely moved, just twisting to have one knife forward, the other back and ready to strike. Narin didn't slow and in seconds he was there, knife still held out before him like a novice fighter. The goshe began to move as Narin neared, one blade ready to deflect Narin's own knife safely past, but it was nothing like far enough. Two paces away, the Investigator checked and swung his stave around with all his remaining strength.

He saw the goshe's eyes flash wide, one arm instinctively rise, but it was too late. The stave whipped around with brutal speed, years of training and fear combining. Narin felt the crash of impact shudder up his arm and the goshe's head snapped sideways. Blood sprang up in the sun-kissed air and Narin found himself staring at a single drop of red as it reached its zenith and began to fall. He realised the man's ear had burst open – most likely the goshe was dead.

All around him people started to scream and flee. Narin half turned, mouth falling open, instinctively about to try and reassure them, but the words would not come. He watched the terrified faces with a strange disconnected sense. The sounds were muted in his ears, the movements slowed and dream-like. The wide stone steps lay before him, the crowd parting like dawn fog and he started forward.

The way was clear and he found a new strength in his limbs as he made for it. Safety was within reach, he could feel it like warm sunshine on his cheek. Then his vision went black and he was thrown backwards.

Pain blossomed in his face, his knife and stave fell from his hands. His head struck the edge of a step with a crack that seemed to split it open. Through blurry eyes he stared up at the clouds and clear blue sky that hung over the city. Then a dark shape moved across his view. Narin tried to roll away, but his body refused to obey. He could only lie there, jaw moving soundlessly as though calling for help.

'There's always more of us,' he heard a woman's voice say in the distance. 'Surely you've learned that by now?'

251

Narin's scrambled thoughts were still deciphering her words when the woman reached a hand out towards him. Something glinted in the light from the tip of her finger, steel-bright and so sharp he barely felt it slide into his neck.

He saw her mouth move but the words were dulled whispers only. Narin felt himself sink back into the cold embrace of the rock below and the shadows lengthened until they enveloped him entirely. Then he felt nothing.

CHAPTER 18

Somewhere in the dark of his memory, a hundred bells chime. There is a distant echo of pain somewhere, but his mind is far from his body and other sensations eclipse it. Slashes of pink cloud hang above the city as the bells ring out and the crowd sighs as one when a woman's voice sings out over them, a single, glorious breath that builds and rises to envelop the entire amphitheatre. Just as the singer's lungs must surely burst, the note is taken up by scores of choristers and the evening sky is filled with sound.

A long garden leads into the amphitheatre and from a dark pavilion there, a woman dressed in white runs. Pale-skinned with dark hair streaming behind, she sprints between the serried ranks of choristers and musicians. Three more follow, dark-skinned women with shaved scalps – all barefoot as they race across the grass and vault the principal singer effortlessly.

Coloured banners flutter in the breeze from a hundred poles around the outer edge of the amphitheatre. Greatest among them is one fifteen feet high, white and bearing the stylised image of a dancer in mid-step. More dancers stream down the walkways, some dragging onlookers with them, and the musicians strike up a frenetic pace as the voices of the choir begin their prayers.

Narin stands and watches as the scent of cooking pork wafts over him from makeshift kitchens behind. Slabs of different meats sit on two dozen hot plates and turn on spits, the scents of chilli and garlic fill the air alongside the prayers to the Ascendant Goddess, Lady Dancer. Flames cavort within great stone bowls edged in brass and ten feet across, spread around the amphitheatre to blunt the winter chill.

He pulls his jacket tighter around his body. It is not a cold evening by winter's standards, but near to the year's end all the same. The Festival of Dancer comes close to longest night and the priesthood long ago embraced their place in the celestial calendar. While Narin is there to preserve order, most of those attending are there to eat the warming fare, drink and dance with abandon.

With long misty nights given over to the spirits and demons of darkness, the population of the Imperial City long ago chose this one to reclaim it for the mortal realm. The music and song were said to chase away the creatures of night, just as the dancing chased away the cold fingers of winter. Some would dance until dawn, the younger priests and priestesses leading them every step of the way, while the Lawbringers watched over them all.

'Have you come to dance with me, Master Narin?' he hears a honey-sweet voice say at his ear.

Narin almost jumps in surprise – so lost has he been in the hypnotic steps of the dancers. There beside him, a vision of beauty in a plain white dress, is Lady Kine, the firelight sparkling in her eyes.

'I…' He remembers himself and bows. 'My Lady, I cannot, I regret …'

Lady Kine tosses her head back and turns to the dark shape beside her. 'He refuses me as my husband abandons me,' she gently laughs to her companion, who says nothing.

'Siresse Myken,' Narin says in greeting to Kine's bodyguard.

The stern Wyvern warrior says nothing in response, she merely inclines her head to him as protocol requires. She keeps a respectful distance back from her charge, pistols holstered as ever across her belly.

'Lord Vanden is not here?' Narin asks, feeling a guilty sense of relief as he says the words.

He truly likes the man and hardly knows how to accept the patronage he has offered, but in his company greater formality is required. Away from him, Lady Kine's laughter comes more easily and Narin craves the sound like a drug.

'My husband is no devotee of Lady Dancer,' Lady Kine says, 'even before his injury. And of course, frivolity is not becoming of a warrior.' She covers her smile as she indicates her bodyguard, whose caste prohibits much and pride forbids even more.

'His health continues?'

Lady Kine inclines her head. 'He remains weak, but the worst is over – as you would know if you had visited us recently.'

Narin lowers his eyes. 'I have not wished to intrude.'

'I wish you would come more often,' Kine says in a quiet voice that makes his heart ache. 'Your visits bring us both great pleasure.'

254

He looks up to see her lips slightly pursed, as they always are when she is being earnest, rather than the studied blank expression of polite conversation. Behind her, the female knight, Myken, watches him with unblinking eyes.

Narin has never spoken more than a dozen words to Myken, but he has come to respect her all the same. He feels sure she has seen his foolishness around Lady Kine, bears witness to every fumbled word and hopeless expression, but she has said nothing when others might have forcefully put him in his place.

'My duties keep me busy,' he mumbles. 'I have little time for calling on my betters.'

He can feel Kine withdraw slightly at that. 'Is that how you think of me?'

'You are noble caste,' he says, 'I am craftsman. I would not want to take up too much of your precious time.'

She does not speak for a while, both of them watching the fervent dancers and crowd as though stones on a stream-bed.

'Siresse,' Kine calls eventually, 'I am cold. Might you fetch me some chilli squid and a cup of spiced wine? I will be safe in the company of Investigator Narin.'

Myken bows and disappears into the throng. Narin feels suddenly shy and terribly alone, both thrilled and anxious to be there with Kine amid the uninterested masses. She is known in the area of course – this is Dragon District still – but dressed to dance with no marks of caste or position visible to attract the attention. There are dozens of Wyvern women attired almost identically, Kine is marked out only by her beauty and in the fire-light most eyes are drawn to the movement of bodies only.

Narin turns to face her but the words die in his throat. He knows he does not have long before Myken returns, but he does not know what he wants to say to break the air between them.

'I'm sorry,' he blurts out, 'I did not mean to be cold towards you. Forgive me, I would never mean that.'

'There is nothing to forgive,' she says. 'You are here with me now.'

He looks into her eyes but cannot read her expression. Her lashes flutter then she looks away, returning her attention to the dance but easing her body a fraction closer to his in the same movement. He feels an ache to close that gap further, to feel her breath on his cheek as she speaks.

'In my dreams, we will have danced,' Kine says so softly he can scarcely believe he has heard her correctly. 'Danced all night, all alone here with only the Gods to witness it.'

There is a sadness in her eyes that tears at his heart. He reaches out and touches a hand to her arm. Her fingers, clasped demurely together, unfold and close around his.

'We will have danced,' he repeats in a choked voice. 'In my dreams we will always dance.'

'It is all I could wish for, to belong with you in that dream,' she says and slips her fingers from his hand. 'All I will ever wish for.'

'Kine.'

Narin woke to darkness and the jangle of pain. It took him a while to realise the faint croak had been him speaking. He tried to move and immediately regretted it, tried to blink and whimpered in pain as black stars burst before his eyes.

Against his back he felt the harsh press of metal, tight ropes binding his wrists to something solid. Bunching his fingers provoked arrows of pain, darting from from fingertips to shoulders.

There was movement ahead of him, shifting shapes in the gloom that drifted silently closer. He kicked feebly. His legs were free but his arms and shoulders were bound securely to something he couldn't move a fraction. He took the weight off his shoulders, his legs protesting.

'Awake, eh?' came a voice from the darkness.

A shape moved closer, indistinct but big – that much Narin could tell. He blinked and tried to focus, but through the fog of his mind he realised it wasn't just lack of light. The man – and it had to be a man, given the size – was dressed all in black and hooded, or so Narin thought. As he came closer the whites of his eyes became clear, then the white of his teeth as the man smiled.

A Dragon, then, Narin realised, *and big even for one of them.*

'Where am I?' he said, little more than a whisper but he saw from the man's grin that he'd heard.

'You really think you get to ask the questions here?' the Dragon asked.

Narin tried to move his head again. His neck screamed after what felt like hours of unconsciousness, but he managed some small movement left and right. The faint outline of a door was visible, the suggestion of a wall on either side. The room smelt damp and cold on top of the stink of urine Narin guessed was his own. A dungeon perhaps, but one little used and larger than a single cell.

He tried to think, to clear the mess in his mind, but everything was an effort and he soon found himself slumped down again – legs barely supporting his weight despite the increased discomfort it caused.

'Don't give up, not yet,' the Dragon whispered in mocking encouragement. 'Make a fight of it at least.'

'What do you want?' Narin slurred.

'Me? Nothing.'

Narin forced his head up again. 'Why … ?' he hadn't the strength to finish his sentence but again the Dragon understood well enough.

'Oh, you'll answer questions soon enough. But not from me, I don't care what you've got to say.'

Narin watched helplessly as the Dragon reached down and grabbed his left ankle, hauling it up and sending fresh jolts of pain through Narin's arms. He tried to kick forward at the man but found he could barely move and the dark-skinned man's grip was strong enough that Narin did nothing more than haul at his bonds and cry out in pain.

'That all you got?' the Dragon laughed, the grip of one meaty hand more than enough to hold Narin securely. 'Save your strength, you'll need it.'

The man waved his free hand in front of Narin's face. The Investigator was slow to focus on it, but as he did so he saw white sparks jump suddenly between the Dragon's fingers. In an instant the open hand was wreathed in crackling, darting threads of light that left tangled trails across his vision.

'No,' the Dragon continued. 'No questions here – just think of me as the warm-up act.'

With that he jammed his palm against the bare sole of Narin's foot. Narin screamed. It felt like a dozen blades had been jammed into his skin. He writhed and kicked as he shrieked, barely aware of anything but the pain that filled his entire body. His knee seemed about to explode as shooting fire lashed through him, but he couldn't break the man's impossibly strong grip.

In the next moment it stopped and Narin was left shuddering and trembling in the dark once more. The dark afterglow swam before his eyes as he desperately tried to breathe again, drawing in shallow, laboured breaths that hurt as much as they relieved.

'Enjoy that?' the Dragon asked conversationally.

Narin flinched at the sound of the man's voice, looking blindly around as every nerve in his body still clattered and burned. A voice from deep inside screamed for him to reply, to say anything that might stave off another burst of lightning a few moments more.

'No,' he whimpered, panting for breath after saying just that.

'No? Ah well, the next hour or so ain't going to be much fun then,' the Dragon said as he delivered a casual punch into Narin's thigh with one massive fist. That evil grin shining through the darkness of his prison didn't waver as the blow landed.

'And after ...' Narin croaked. *Keep him talking, let him talk rather than burn me – Stars of Mercy, how long can I hold on?*

'After that?' the man said, thinking it a question rather than all Narin could manage in one go. 'After that it gets worse. She's got questions for you and when she's back, you'll answer 'em. This here's only a taste, to let you know what refusing her'll be like.'

This time he didn't even see the light before pain took him in its teeth. Narin convulsed and howled through a haze of agony – unaware if he was kicking or fighting it at all. The pain was everything; even the smell of burning flesh and the fire in his lungs as he screamed were just distant things outside the pain.

Once it was over he hung limp from the bonds around his wrists and chest. If the Dragon spoke he couldn't hear it past the crashing bells that filled his head. Slowly it began to recede once more and he felt himself breathing again, grateful even for the pain that brought.

At last he found his body again and drunkenly swung his head from side to side until he worked out how to lift it and look at his torturer.

'After ...' Narin repeated, struggling to keep his eyes on those cold white teeth.

'After?' the Dragon said. 'Ah, sorry – did I break your concentration there? My mistake, you weren't finished.'

'After,' Narin said with a loll of the head that could have been a nod of confirmation, 'you won't be laughing.'

The grin widened. 'Really? Sure about that? You ain't going nowhere, friend, and you couldn't take one of us even at your best – we're blessed like that!'

'Me, no.'

'Your friends? Irato maybe? Friend, this place is so well warded the Gods themselves won't find you and there's more'n just me here.'

No Gods? Narin thought with a tremble of fear, but he fought it down again. *These goshe aren't Gods,* he reminded himself, *whatever they think. They're no match for Enchei, let alone the Gods.*

'He'll find me.'

'Who?' the Dragon asked with sudden interest. 'Who'll care enough to risk their neck for you? No God, I promise you that.'

'Old man,' Narin said after a long moment. 'Old man'll find me.'

'One old man, eh? That's all you got? No Gods? No House soldiers or Astaren strike-team? Just an old man.'

'One old man,' Narin confirmed, stars bursting before his eyes as he nodded.

'I like those odds.'

Narin forced himself to grin, feeling saliva and blood dribble from his mouth as he did so.

'You're all going to die,' he whispered.

The Dragon's smile at last went away. 'What was that? You want more of the pain? Fair enough.'

'Where is it?'

The Investigator turned, eyes widening as he recognised Lawbringer Rhe. There was blood on the Investigator's face, smeared trails running from a shallow cut at his thinning hairline and dirt on his cheek. More blood stained his sleeves, hands and jacket – more than could have come from such a wound.

'In there,' said the man, 'I think.'

Rhe's cold eyes fixed on the Investigator. 'You think? Are there other exits?'

He shook his head. 'I don't know, but I was trying to ...' He gestured helplessly behind him. Beside a water-trough lay the body of another Investigator, a woman and younger than her colleague. Her chest had been carved open by some brutal weapon, that much was obvious.

'You stopped to help her,' Rhe said levelly. The man flinched and bit down on his lip. There was no hint of praise or condemnation in Rhe's voice, but as he returned his attention to the building ahead it was clear he would have not done the same.

'What's your name?'

'Me?' The man swallowed, gaze still on his younger charge. He was a paunchy man in his forties – many Investigators were never raised

259

to Lawbringer status but were experienced enough to train others. She would have been his responsibility. 'Investigator Fenin, sir.'

'What happened here?'

'I … I don't know.' Fenin ran a hand over his face, trying to clear the sweat and dirt but only managing to make it worse. 'Demons, demons in the city.'

'There's word of sickness.'

Fenin nodded and pointed to the houses behind, cramped rooms set around a fenced yard. They were in the north of the city, in one of the poorer parts of the Imperial-controlled Arbold Warrant.

Rhe crossed over to the entrance to the nearest yard. The air was almost silent, none of the usual bustle or chatter one expected from a street like this. As he entered, a face bobbed up at the window, a local woman with tears streaking her face.

'They won't wake,' she whispered, clearly in shock. Rhe approached her and she stumbled back, away from the window. His view of inside was clear enough to confirm his fears. Three figures lay on the low bed, two shifting feebly and pawing at the blanket draped over them all.

'Fever?'

The woman shrank back from his question, but nodded eventually. 'They're burning up, that demon's brought a curse with it.'

'How quickly has it come on?'

'I saw them last night – ate with them!' He could hear the pleading in her voice, her desperation and fear.

Rhe didn't respond. He cast around the room, noting the table in the centre and the discarded clothes beside the bed. 'They were able to dress this morning,' he stated. 'One fetched water and there's smoked fish out on the table.'

'I went to their neighbours, to fetch help,' the woman moaned. 'They're sick too. That's when I saw it, the demon!'

'Stay with them,' Rhe ordered, 'bar the windows and doors – make them drink if you can.'

'Where are you going?'

He ignored her and returned to the Investigator out in the street. Fenin hadn't moved from beside his dead colleague.

'Get up,' Rhe said, as he passed the man.

Without waiting to see if Fenin followed, Rhe went to the building indicated by the Investigator earlier. It was down an alley between two stone walls – a half-open doorway that looked like a workshop from where he was. As he came closer there was a flicker of light inside and his hand went to the hilt of one pistol. Reminded of Kesh's account, he moved more cautiously as he approached the door – ready to draw and fire, but he saw nothing more as he got to the door.

A glance behind told him Fenin was following, stave in hand, but he stopped at a gesture from Rhe. The Lawbringer slipped his own stave from behind his back, holding it in his left hand to deflect any blows, and stepped around the door to look inside the workshop. All appeared in order as he adjusted to the gloom within. He could see a pair of tables with tools neatly arranged on top, the goods of a leatherworker on display. He noticed an upturned chair before the hearth, then a figure crouched at a pallet half hidden by the brick chimney and workbench.

Rhe took a step closer, trying to make the figure out, but as he did it suddenly rose and turned. The air of the workshop crackled with darting light and he glimpsed a long body and slender limbs lit up by the staccato bursts – some sort of dark, patterned hide and a hairless, misshapen head. The demon darted forward and Rhe brought his pistol up on instinct – firing with unerring accuracy at the demon's chest.

The room seemed to explode with light and Rhe reeled from the blinding flash. There was a screech from the demon, but it was impossible to tell if the sound was one of rage or pain. Rhe dropped his gun and drew the second, retreating from the doorway with his stave held straight out as he struggled to clear his vision.

Nothing attacked him. There was no sound at all from inside the workshop so Rhe advanced cautiously. Clearly this wasn't some goshe assassin, but demons did not risk the daylight – he had never heard of such a thing in all his years, quite aside from the coincidence of a demon attack just as the goshe were being investigated.

Do the goshe have their own pet demons?

Rhe put the thought from his mind and darted around the door once more, pistol levelled. The workshop was empty. He entered, gun still at the ready, and saw the room led around a corner where another door was situated. He advanced towards it but stopped in the middle of the room, noticing something on the floor where the demon had been standing just a few moments ago.

Rhe crouched and picked a piece up. The workshop had been recently swept so the debris stood out. It was dark brown in colour and unlike

261

anything he'd seen before. Certainly not clothing or armour, it felt light in his hand and looked more like an oversized reptile scale, but the broken edges showed ragged strata like a fraying fingernail. More worryingly, amid the remaining pieces he saw the crushed remnants of his bullet. Whatever the plate was, his pistol hadn't penetrated it.

Rhe stood and retrieved his first pistol. Clearly the bullet had hurt or frightened it at the very least and the creature had eyes and a mouth like any other. He would just need to find a vulnerable spot and a second shot might prove invaluable. The gun loaded, he set out in pursuit.

'It's been too long,' Kesh said, jumping up from her seat. 'They've got him.'

Enchei nodded as he looked again out of the half-closed shutter. 'You're right.'

'So we're just going to sit here?'

The tattooist scowled. 'No. It's time to find some help.'

He rose and went to the cupboard at the back of the room, then hesitated and glanced at his two guests. The three of them were in his room on the first floor of a non-descript tavern a few streets away from where they'd escaped Coldcliffs. It was a typical rented room; few furnishings or possessions on view, just a table, two chairs and a bed with a battered clothes trunk pushed up beside it. Just the sight of it had made Kesh's heart ache for her boarding-house home, and the little sister who'd never be cleaning a room like this ever again.

'Well?' Kesh demanded. 'What now?

Enchei shook his head. 'Remember, I don't know either of you and I ain't one to share my secrets easily.'

'Should we leave?'

'No – and keep away from the window. Last thing we need's one of them getting lucky and seeing you look out.'

He opened the cupboard and surveyed what was inside. Kesh went to look over his shoulder and made a puzzled sound. A few shirts and trousers hung there, a small bag and heavy pair of boots slung carelessly on the floor.

'How's any of that going to help?'

Enchei pointed to the bed where she'd been sitting. 'Sit back down; I just got something to do.'

'Something you don't want us to see?' Kesh turned to Irato, who was perched on the trunk, behind the open cupboard door.

'Something I don't want you to see,' Enchei confirmed. 'And something you don't want to investigate yourself.'

'Why not?' Kesh said as she complied and sat back down, the door obscuring her view.

'Because I've booby-trapped it. You don't want to die horribly, keep well clear of the cupboard.'

He moved forward until he was half-inside then reached out to run his hand down the right-hand wall. Kesh and Irato both instinctively leaned forward as they heard a click and something thump down inside the wall.

'A false panel?'

Enchei paused. 'You're pretty inquisitive for someone who's got caught up in a dangerous conspiracy.'

'Can you blame me? What I don't know has almost got me killed a few times this Ascendancy – I'm not exactly trusting of anyone's secrets.'

'Well, keep clear of mine,' Enchei growled. There was a grating sound and a slight grunt of effort as he pushed something back. 'Right, you two stay here. I've just got to …'

Kesh was already up and halfway to the cupboard. 'Oh no, we're going with you. It's our lives on the line too, remember?'

He didn't respond for a moment, just stared at the blank back of the cupboard until seeming to come to a decision. 'Fine, but you don't tell anyone what you see here – understand? Once this is all over, looks like I'm moving home anyway.'

'Because we've seen your cupboard?' Kesh said. 'Must be one hell of a secret compartment.'

Enchei didn't respond, he just gestured for her to go inside. Kesh peered forward at the space where the right-hand wall had been and saw a narrow corridor, barely big enough for all three of them to fit in.

'A hiding place?'

The walls were bare brick, the ceiling and floor thin boards of wood that were warped with age. To her surprise it was relatively clean and free from cobwebs; smelling faintly of dust and the oily tang of metal.

'There's a door at the end. *Do not* open it until I've shut this up behind us, okay?'

She nodded and entered the tight space, Irato following wordlessly behind. 'What would happen?'

'I told you, you'd die. We'd all die in fact, so just wait until I say.'

They did as they were told and eased themselves inside, waiting for Enchei to pull the cupboard door shut again and replace the cupboard wall panel. Once he'd done so, the hidden corridor was plunged into darkness and Kesh felt her heart quicken. She could feel Irato at her side and the big fighter's presence was suddenly oppressive in such a confined space.

He can see in the dark, she thought to herself, *they both can. He could kill me now and I'd never even see it coming.*

Kesh swallowed her apprehension. After all this, she wasn't going to let herself succumb to foolish thoughts – there was more than enough to fear outside on the city streets without her imagining more.

'Now what?' she said in a quiet voice.

'Reach out your right hand,' Enchei said from somewhere past Irato. 'There's a door latch at waist-height. Lift it and hold it up a moment, then open the door.'

She did as instructed, her heartbeat sounding loud in her chest as she held her breath. As the door opened and light once more enveloped her, she breathed out with relief and stepped out into the room beyond.

Kesh looked around. It wasn't much different to the room she'd been in, just bigger and a little more comfortably furnished. 'This is your secret?' she said sceptically, 'a few rugs and a bigger bed?'

She nudged the rug with her toe. It was of decent quality, an intricate geometric pattern woven into it, but hardly anything remarkable. Crossing the room she went to the window, remembering to keep to one side, and tried to look out. The glass was dirty and covered in dust, but only on the outside, she realised as she wiped a finger down it. Also, the mullions were not wood as one would expect, but iron.

'They're bars,' Kesh said in surprise, 'you've made yourself a safe little cage here.'

Enchei grunted as he entered and closed the door behind him. 'Something like that,' he said cryptically.

Rolling back the rug he revealed a trapdoor in the floor and hauled on the iron ring set into it. Beneath there was a set of stairs leading down into the room below – the light similarly dimmed by a caking of dust on the windows, Kesh guessed.

'These rooms are both yours? How can you afford them?'

'I own the tavern,' he said with a shrug. 'Or rather, I helped the owner buy it and he's getting rich because of it. He knows to keep well clear of my part.'

'What's behind it, then?' Kesh frowned as she tried to remember, but she'd rarely been this way and not noticed anything much when she had.

'An empty shop-front. The innkeeper uses it for storage.'

They all went down into the lower room and the first thing Kesh noticed was the lack of stairs. The floor was all wooden boards without rugs covering them, but she could see no doors or any other way to access the empty shop below.

'How do you get down?'

'You don't – I removed the stair myself. There's no way up if anyone breaks in below.'

The room looked like it was also just a storage place. Even in his secret life Enchei wasn't much for comforts, Kesh realised. A pair of large, iron-bound cupboards dominated the room, while at the back there was a strange sort of brick outcrop covered with wood that served as a worktable. On it she saw the sceptre the goshe had used to drain the light from Narin's rooms, now half-disassembled with metal pieces lined neatly up and glass fragments set to one side.

'Have you worked out what that is?' she asked, pointing at the sceptre.

'I knew already, soon as I saw it,' he replied, waving Irato over to the table and pointing at the far end. 'Help me lift this and put it on the floor.'

'So what is it?'

Enchei stopped. 'A device for blanking out all the light in the room – a pretty crude one too, but it tells us something about how skilled these goshe are.'

'Is it good news, then?' she said, watching the two men lift the tabletop off to reveal a dark well-like opening despite the fact they were on the first floor.

He brightened. 'Aye, it is actually. Tells me some about their magic, what they're likely to have up their sleeves. You could sum it up as crude, but effective. Any one of them I can handle easily enough I reckon, but if they've got the army we think they do ... well, that could be tricky for all involved.'

He waved them back and peered into the well then, to her surprise, hawked and spat down it. If there was a splash, Kesh didn't hear it, but Enchei smiled all the same.

'You're not so different from any other man,' she said with a sigh. 'Show you a height and you'll spit off it, a tree and you'll piss against it.'

The smile turned into a grin. 'If you say so,' he said, but then a serious expression took hold of his face. 'Now – you two want to stay, you keep quiet as mice and don't bloody move. In fact, sit down on the floor, there's no telling how long this'll take.'

Kesh and Irato exchanged looks. The former goshe hadn't spoken since they'd made it to the tavern door an hour or so earlier. Apart from cleaning his weapons in a methodical manner and wiping the worst of the blood and dirt from his clothes, he'd done almost nothing. Kesh herself had been too jittery to keep still for long, but Irato had been more like an automaton wound down after the running and fighting were over.

Once the pair had settled, Enchei fetched a hide bag from one of the cupboards. He pulled from it a long coil of thread like thick fishing line with a small bone securely bound to one end. Kesh caught a glimpse of symbols inscribed into the bone before Enchei dropped it down the well, wrapping the other end tightly around two fingers of his left hand. Next he retrieved a length of thin copper wire and hooked it around something inside the well.

As he ran that across the well-mouth Kesh realised there were small hooks on the inside wall, fixed to a band of copper nailed into the brickwork. Keeping the thread dangling down the centre of the well, Enchei caught the wire around each of the five hooks to create a star-shaped web across the well-mouth. That done he knelt at the side, holding the thread high and clear of the copper wire as he began to mutter under his breath.

Kesh strained forward to try to make out what he was saying, but it was no language she'd ever heard – nothing spoken on the docks even resembled it. Enchei continued in a monotonous drone and she reluctantly eased back again into a more comfortable position, realising he was repeating some mantra or invocation over and over with barely a pause for breath.

It took a long time for anything more to happen. Kesh fought the urge to squirm where she sat, uncomfortable on the floor, but risked only brief glances at Irato out of the corner of her eye before returning her attention to the aging tattooist. Irato was almost perfectly still the whole while, barely blinking, as though hypnotised by the sight.

A few days ago I would be shocked by this, Kesh realised with sour humour. *I thought demons were enemies of the Gods and of all mankind, I*

266

thought most magic was heresy and dangerous. Now ... who knows what's true? Demons saved me from Perel; Enchei shows no hatred or fear of the Gods – and I can't believe a practising shaman would be tolerated amongst the Astaren otherwise.

She paused, remembering every silly rumour she'd heard about the fabled warrior-mages. Somehow, in their exhortations and warnings, the priests had carefully separated the Astaren from the foolish and the mad who consorted with demons. The sanction of the Houses, of the rulers of the Empire, somehow made it safer, or was theirs a different form of magic? Or was it all one – power jealously guarded by those who wielded it?

Was he ever a shaman or anything like it? she wondered. *Was he born with the sight or did he learn it? If he had it as a child, why join the army as a scout when the Astaren would certainly be looking to recruit anyone with the necessary gifts?*

A rushing sound broke her train of thoughts. Kesh blinked in surprise as she realised Enchei had broken off his chanting and the air in the room was no longer still. Motes of dust swirled in the empty space between them, eddying away from the well-mouth. The air seemed charged now, the fine hairs on her arms suddenly prickling with a sensation she couldn't put a name to. Irato felt it too, she realised. The man sat imperceptibly more upright – alert and ready for action once more, and that was enough to spark apprehension in Kesh's belly.

The sound became louder and faster, the susurrus dance of wind over the well's brick surface rising up as errant strands of Enchei's hair began to flow freely. But then it changed, the whisper became not the sound of the wind but the voice of it. Kesh stiffened, biting her lip to stop herself calling out as a deep sound echoed up the well – barely fathomable in its hollow tones, but she realised there were words in there somewhere.

As the demon, or whatever it was, spoke, Enchei nodded slowly. He hadn't moved from where he knelt, twine still raised above his head.

'You do me honour, great one,' Enchei intoned. 'I beg you are not offended by my precautions, feeble as they are.'

'*The lesser kin are ever hungry,*' replied the voice from the well. '*A fool and his soul are easily parted.*'

'I beg a boon of you, great one.'

'*Speak it. Prayers unvoiced fall like ash.*'

'I seek the assistance of one in the heavens; I ask an emissary is sent.'

'*For what purpose? The Gods command, mortals obey.*'

'To save a friend, to right a wrong done to your kin.'

'*The lords and ladies of heaven bear the pride of Gods. The brave and the bold die swiftest.*'

'The friend is an Investigator of the Lawbringers; known to Lord Shield and charged with a mission by him. I believe him taken by our enemies.'

'*Prayers are for temples. The faithful know their place.*'

Enchei shook his head. 'I cannot pray, my voice is lost to me.'

'*An awestruck man loses his voice for prayers. A cautious man cuts it out.*'

'It is so.'

'*This boon I will grant. The scent of your soul I will mask.*'

'I am in your debt, great one.'

'*The wind sings a song of loss. There is a prize Lord Shield seeks.*'

'I believe Lord Shield does not know what he seeks.'

'*Stillness in heaven brings order. Your Gods remain young for this world.*'

'I understand. What belongs to your kin is not for the Gods of men.'

'*An emissary ascends to the heavens. A servant will await you in the coldest corners of the city.*'

Abruptly, the rushing wind broke off and faded away to nothing, leaving a tense stillness in the air. The room was silent. Enchei remained kneeling with head bowed a few moments longer before he stood and began to reel in the thread.

'What was that?' Kesh breathed.

'One of the Apkai,' Enchei said, back turned to her. 'The highest order of demons, beings of ages past that were unimaginably powerful before the Empire ever came about.'

'Like the Kraken God or the Shepherds of the Drowned?' Kesh shook her head in disbelief. 'Sailors would call such things the old Gods when they were in their cups. Can we trust it?'

He turned, a flush of annoyance appearing before he composed himself. 'Trust? It's an ancient being of vast power and intelligence. Our only protection here was its indifference – to it, we're as significant as insects.'

'Then why did it help us?'

Enchei sighed and began to wind up the copper wire he'd strung across the well-mouth. 'You might say that to the fox-demons, the Apkai are Gods.'

Kesh frowned. 'And that's reason enough?'

A flicker of a smile crossed Enchei's face. 'Now you're starting to think about these things properly. No, that's not reason enough. The higher orders – Gods and demons – they have their own games to play and a balance to maintain. Had I asked it to find Narin itself, likely I'd not have a soul right now. Only Shield's involvement won its interest – either it knows what the fox-demons have lost or it wants to know, given another player's already interested. Either way, it's happy to be owed a favour.'

'And now?' Irato spoke up abruptly, looking up at Enchei.

The older man scowled. 'Now? Now you get to see what toys I've got in the other cupboard. 'Cept of course you don't. You've seen enough of my secrets today, so bugger off upstairs the both of you – I need to get ready.'

Kesh looked him up and down. Enchei was still wearing the same clothes he had been in since morning, some sort of armour underneath his clothes and a variety of weapons. 'More ready than you are already?'

An evil glimmer appeared in his eye. 'When you're fighting on the streets o' the biggest city in the whole damn Empire, it's best not to attract too much attention. But my guess is, wherever they've got Narin they're far from prying eyes. So I've got a few other surprises hidden away.'

'What about us?'

'You'll only just slow me down, the pair o' you.'

'I'm coming,' Irato declared.

Enchei shook his head slowly. 'No, you ain't,' he said with finality. 'I'm playing this my way now and my secrets are my own. It's enough of a risk that I'm using those secrets to rescue him – you two are going somewhere safe and you're staying there until I come get you.'

'Where?' Irato asked, just getting in ahead of Kesh's questions.

The goshe had recognised an order, she realised, and was already onto the next matter. With an effort Kesh bit back her argument and let the tattooist reply.

'You know Tale well enough, Kesh?' Enchei asked.

She nodded.

'Good – you know the tavern towards Dragon District, the Broken Field? Round the back o' there you'll find a smokehouse. I've never been there with Narin, he don't know it, but the owner owes me a favour. She'll take you in; give you a plate o' smoked crayfish if you ask nicely too. I'll come find you once I've got Narin somewhere safe.'

'You're not bringing him?'

Enchei's face went grim. 'Man'll need a doctor first, I expect.'

'And you expect us to wait patiently with some friend of yours?'

'Pretty much. Sure she'll have some chores if you get bored.'

CHAPTER 19

Dachan proved popular for several centuries among the citizens of the House of the Sun, before a long and steady decline. Intended to maintain the sword-skills of a banned warrior caste, it was never embraced by the lower castes and eventually even those with warrior blood realised the Emperor's hegemony was never likely to return. It only took them two hundred years to notice this, remarkably swift for most military thinking.

From *A History* by Ayel Sorote

Near midday, Law Master Sheven appeared in the street and hurried towards Lawbringer Rhe. The broad old man looked harassed and lacking sleep, but his voice remained clear and loud as he outpaced his attending Investigators.

'Lawbringer Rhe, how many victims do you have?'

'Of what?' Rhe replied. 'We have two matters to worry about here. I've yet to decide which is the greater concern.'

Sheven stopped and looked past Rhe to the row of houses where they had discovered twenty or more people stricken with fever. 'They are not related?' he asked in a dubious voice.

'I don't know, but having chased the demon myself I have not fallen ill.'

'Tell me what you do know.'

Rhe nodded. 'We have eight houses in this street with people I cannot rouse. They have some fever that came on swiftly this morning from what I can tell. I have Investigators checking all surrounding streets and several have already reported similar incidents. The demon I pursued managed to escape me. It can move very quickly and must have found a hiding place, given we are nowhere near the Crescent or anything larger than a stream.'

'This fever, do you have any ideas?'

'I am no doctor,' Rhe said, 'and my first reaction would have been to send for one from a goshe free hospital, but for … recent events.'

Sheven scowled and unconsciously shifted the scimitar at his side. 'Do you have evidence they are connected?'

'None.'

'And yet you're suspicious.'

'Naturally,' Rhe said. He turned towards the nearest house and Sheven fell in beside him, motioning for his attendants to remain where they were. At the gate Rhe glanced at his companion. 'Doctors and fevers, demons and goshe, this can be no coincidence.'

'The demon you saw, what form did it take?'

'Man-shaped and long-limbed – a dark hide tough enough to withstand a bullet to the chest.'

'So nothing like the assassins Investigator Narin and his friends fought off?'

'They were human, nothing more. This … this could never pass as one.'

'Does it match the allegations you mentioned?'

Rhe was quiet a moment. 'There was no description there,' he said at last, knowing the Law Master had intentionally not asked for details earlier. 'But no, this was far from what I had been led to expect.'

'There were no other reports of demons,' Sheven said, 'but we've had a dozen instances of fever breaking out. People are already starting to panic. I have had to post guards at the free hospital in Raven District and no doubt the other one in Arbold will soon have more patients than it can cope with.'

Rhe looked around the street, where Investigators and civilians alike watched them with worried faces. The sun bathed the street in warm light and gulls called overhead, while swifts cut through the cloud-specked sky. The city seemed peaceful then, the day promising summer rather than disease and demons. He shook his head, suddenly worried how it would look at nightfall. If they had a dozen reports by midday, how many more would follow? And once darkness fell, how many more demons would he be chasing?

'Has there been word of Narin?' he asked, trying to ignore the question for the time being.

'None. I'm told they never reached Wyvern's corner of Dragon

District, they diverted to escape their pursuers and disappeared into Coldcliffs. Reports of what followed are confused, but at least three locals are dead and we have the burned remains of five people we assume were goshe elsewhere in the city.'

'Burned?'

Sheven grunted. 'Not the first of those we've had recently, eh? But a worrying increase as much as anything else.'

'We must hope Narin knows what he's doing,' Rhe said finally. 'If there are informants within the Lawbringers, we can do him little good for the time being.'

'And your investigation?'

'Cannot continue today. At least a dozen instances of fever? This disease must have taken a hundred people on the first morning; by this evening there will be chaos on the streets.'

'I will have every Lawbringer assembled and sent out to keep order. The searches of each Shure will have to wait, you're right. But if we have demons haunting the streets we will need help.'

Rhe's lips tightened as he realised what the Law Master meant. 'You would go begging to House Dragon for assistance?' the nobleman from Dragon's ancient enemy asked.

'What choice would we have?'

'Having Dragon soldiers enforcing the law, searching the streets of every district, would not prevent chaos – it could spark war overnight.'

'They would not permit any other House to do so – they're the power here. What else would you have us do? Ask your kin instead?' Sheven said coldly.

'Either the Lawbringers rule the Imperial streets, or we are an irrelevance.'

'And when our lack of powder-weapons leads to these demons cutting through our ranks?'

'The law requires us to sacrifice,' Rhe replied, prompting an astonished look from his superior that only lessened when Rhe clarified his words. 'Those of us with noble blood will be at the forefront of the hunt. We were born to sacrifice ourselves first in the name of a higher cause.'

There was a long moment of silence. Finally, Sheven made to head back the way he'd come, but he paused first. 'Any of your caste good at curing fevers?'

'I doubt it.'

'Then go and make plans for this evening. I'll try to get control of whatever's happening here. And may the Gods be looking down on us all – this is only the start.'

His mind was in darkness, threads caught on a swirling breeze. From some-where he heard her voice, heard Kine calling his name.

'Narin – come meet your son.'

He felt tears on his cheek, felt himself blind and helpless. No matter how much she asked him to, he could never see the child. His eyes were gone, plucked out and lost in the cold churning ocean. His tongue was heavy as he tried to speak, tried to explain, and Kine did not understand.

He heard her scream at him, heard her beg to understand. He tried to explain, about the goshe he'd found, about the little girl who'd been murdered, but still the guilt burned at his skin. It traced hot white lines over his body and blackened his flesh.

He begged for her forgiveness, but the guilt just burned hotter still. Soon he was drowning in her tears.

Father Jehq tilted the Investigator's head up and pushed up one eyelid. The prisoner saw nothing; his pupil was almost as large as his whole eye, but glassy and unfocused. Sweat dripped from the man's hair and cheeks, running down from the steel band clamped around his temple like a crown. The band had a network of thin metal threads across the top and engraved symbols around its edge – each one gilt-plated and faintly glittering in the weak light.

After a moment, Jehq released Narin's head again and stepped back. He pulled off the steel band and placed it on a side table, taking great care of the delicate steel threads. He wiped the greasy sweat from his fingers and turned to the man beside him.

'You gave him too much,' he said eventually. 'Put too much in the band. He was too weak to take it.'

'He's going to die?' Uttir, Synter's second, asked. The Detenii from House Iron kept the anxiety from his voice, but Jehq could see it all the same. He was afraid of screwing up so soon after being given his position.

Jehq shook his head just as the prisoner cried out again, mangled words spilling from the man's lips.

'Kine, I'm sorry. My oaths ... I can't see him.'

Jehq gestured to the man as though making a point. 'He won't die, but he's no use to us like this.'

'Isn't it supposed to make him answer our questions?'

'Oh, he'll tell the truth all right,' Jehq said scornfully, 'but first you have to get him to listen to your damn questions! He's babbling; raving like a madman, but I've no doubt it's all true. Unfortunately for you, he was too weak when you gave him the dose, and then enhanced its effect with the band. You've scrambled his brains – he's no use to anyone like this. The man's so fixated on this Kine woman he can think of nothing else.' The aging doctor shook his head.

'What can I do?'

'Nothing. It'll take a few hours for it to wear off. Then he'll be coherent again.'

'And then?'

'And then he'll be useless for tracking Irato down. He'll tell us everything he knows, I'm sure of Synter's skill in that department, so you better hope it turns out to be useful still. I'm certain Irato will have gone to ground by then, so he better have something else to give us.'

'Can we release him?' Uttir asked hopefully. 'Follow him and see if he can lead us to Irato?'

Jehq looked down at the naked Investigator – sweat-soaked and scorched by Kodeh's preliminary tortures. It had been enough to make the man pass out, then Uttir had come to pour a concoction of the late Father Polagin's devising down his throat. It was one they'd used for years now; dampening a person's will so they were more open to questioning. It was most likely that the Investigator's thoughts had latched onto his lover or wife as an escape from the torture. The drug Uttir had given him had just sent that on a loop through his mind, leaving no room for any other thought.

'We shall see,' Jehq said eventually and headed towards the barred door. 'It's Synter's decision, go report to her.'

The district of the Imperial City controlled by House Redearth was a quiet corner of the city by the standards of the rest. Their homeland was far to the south at the heart of the Empire's lesser continent, flanked by the plains-ranging hunters of House Wolf and the taciturn warriors of House Iron. The Lords of Redearth cared little for the politics of the Empire, their lands being fertile and peaceful for the main. House Iron's spears faced west, not east, to ward off the raiders of House Leviathan while the Desert of Wolves protected much of their other border.

For Synter's purposes, it also meant the district's population was evenly split between paler locals and the red-brown skin of Redearth natives, so she walked without notice through the afternoon bustle. Most of the district was made up of long, enclosed housing blocks and smaller compounds, the lords and warriors of Redearth presiding over isolated communities that echoed the feudal states that characterised their homeland.

Each one displayed flags at every corner, colourful announcements of allegiance that mostly corresponded to the Houses of Redearth, Whitemountain and Condor, with a scattering of lesser emblems she did not recognise. Her destination, once she reached it, could have belonged to the minor Houses under Redearth rule, only the lack of decoration on its surrounding fence a sign that it was not owned by a noble family.

The gate was open so she slipped inside to a courtyard of neat bare earth. The training ground was empty, but a pair of black-clad men rose from an open-fronted room on the right. Synter cast around for a moment before she spotted the altar-table standing in the shadow of a long overhanging roof. She bowed to it as any visiting goshe would, and the attendants visibly relaxed.

'I must speak to the Shure-Master,' she called to the pair, both Redearth natives.

'Your name, Mistress?' replied the nearer of the two, a tall man with long hanging hair and startling amber eyes.

He wore a gun-holster across his belly – the pistol grips bound in cloth so as not to be immediately within reach while he was wearing goshe-black. It was unthinkable for a warrior to be outside without his weapons on his person, of course, and this was the compromise most adhered to rather than invite trouble.

'My name is not important,' Synter said as she walked up to the men. She blinked and sensed the tiny flutter of light in her eyes as another of her Blessings worked its magic. Both men straightened immediately, commanded to obedience by the changes Moon's Artifice had worked on them as a baby.

'Mistress,' the warrior said, bowing. 'Follow me, Master Nyl is this way.'

They crossed the courtyard and the goshe opened a door for Synter to enter. Within was a wide hallway with racks of weapons on the walls and a stairway leading up to the second floor. Without prompting, Synter headed up the stairs and unexpectedly found herself in a comfortably-decorated hallway.

'The Shure-Master lives here?' she asked her guide.

'He does, Mistress. Our Shure is open to all, day or night, and Master Nyl has renounced his ties of family, as have several of our brothers and sisters.'

But I see he brought some of his money with him, Synter privately observed, running a finger over an ornate wooden table that faced the entrance to the stairs with a gilt mirror hanging above.

There was a study door past a long woven tapestry depicting four white mountains. She opened it to find a comfortable private room with a grand desk before a pair of tall windows that overlooked the training ground below. A large dining table took up much of the other half of the room – laid with silver cutlery as though Master Nyl had been expecting Synter and her whole team for dinner.

Standing behind the desk was an ochre-skinned warrior caste of middle years; clearly not a Redearth. Synter guessed by the tapestry on the landing he was a Whitemountain, principal of the Major Houses under Redearth's dominion.

'Mistress?' the man inquired, glancing at her guide before returning his attention to Synter.

Another tiny stutter of light in her eyes told Synter he was hers to command – not that she'd have doubted it. To reach the position of Shure-Master one had to be one of those irrevocably changed by Moon's Artifice so she didn't bother with niceties.

'Master Nyl, I have a task for you.'

The man bowed as the door closed behind Synter, her guide with-drawing without waiting for instructions.

'I live to serve the Order,' Nyl said. 'May I offer you anything?'

Synter shook her head. It was a strange sensation for her, a woman not used to this sort of goshe. Like all of the half-dozen others she'd met today, Nyl could function perfectly well without guidance, lead his small flock and maintain the Shure without any input from the leaders of the goshe. Except when presented with the Blessings of Command they were as free-thinking as Synter's Detenii, skilled leaders and teachers, yet unblinking in their obedience.

Synter was more used to her Detenii teams, fighters not bound by anything more than loyalty and unity, or the slaved goshe they used as expendable agents – ones that hadn't taken to the poison so well and were little more than mindless drones.

'Nothing, thank you,' she said awkwardly.

Nyl indicated for her to take a seat in an armchair and she did so, the nobleman settling easily on the other side while he waited for his instructions. After a moment's pause Synter caught up with herself and pulled a small leather-wrapped flask from her coat pocket. Earlier there had been seven sitting there, but this was her last stop before she went to interrogate the prisoner they'd taken that morning.

'You have a water-butt here, or something similar?'

'For drinking from?' He nodded. 'Downstairs, by the kitchen.'

'Pour this into it then assemble all of your goshe open to *command*.' She spoke carefully, ensuring the word was accompanied by another flash of light in her eyes. 'Have them take a flask each home and drink it with their families. Tell them it is blessed by the priesthood of Lady Healer. They should not be wearing goshe clothing.'

'I understand. There is talk of plague in the city; some say the wells have been poisoned by demons.'

She nodded. 'Those already open to command will be less affected, it will take longer for them to succumb if they do at all – giving them time to fetch help and ensure their plight is known.'

'And once they are ill?'

'Wait for the morning. The city will be gripped with fear of plague, a suggestion will be made that the victims are removed from the city to contain it. You will order your remaining goshe to assist in the evacuation, tell them the Order has been shamed in the eyes of the Emperor and this is the price of our penitence. They will assist the city's doctors, Lawbringers and anyone else involved in the evacuation of the sick.'

'Where are they being taken?'

'Confessor's Island,' she replied, 'our sanatorium there. It's a short boat-ride away and the only sensible place to contain such numbers.'

'How many?'

'Several thousand, we believe. The goshe must all travel to the island, but we must avoid any connection between the Order and the plague where possible – aside from our doctors being the best ones to treat it.'

Master Nyl bowed and took the flask. 'I shall do as you command.'

Out in the pale afternoon sun, Enchei checked the inn environs. He shrugged his shoulders, strangely discomforted by the feel of armour around his body again. The weight was no problem, the slight constriction on his movements negligible, but with it came memories that proved far less comfortable. The armour seemed willing to accommodate the changes almost two decades had imposed – as he knew it would – but as he'd fitted the overlapping plates onto his body Enchei had felt a profound sadness settle over him.

The armour came in two distinct parts; a flexible one-piece suit as durable as a wyvern's scaled hide with separate pieces of plate that locked into place over it. It had been made specifically for Enchei, almost forty years ago now by Astaren mage-priests, and would outlast him despite the changes they had wrought on his body at the same time.

The suit remained strong enough to resist the crossbows of the goshe, as it had proved early that morning, but the plates would survive far greater impacts and Enchei suspected he'd need all that protection if he was to rescue Narin alone. Crucially for him though, it was all far thinner than regular armour and under normal clothes would just make him look bulky – until he put the helmet on.

I'd hoped never to do this again, Enchei thought sadly as he started off down the street. *I'd hoped all this was behind me.*

The memories kept on coming. Focusing on the task at hand did nothing more than quieten them; they were too strong to deny entirely.

The coldest corners of the city – nothing a demon likes better than to be cryptic and dramatic at the same time. So now I have to trawl dead-end streets and graveyards, while Narin's time grows shorter.

In his mind he heard voices; the death-cries of comrades, the rage of ancient Gods. He saw the sky burn, a palace larger than the Emperor's own collapse in on itself, and mountains fall.

All I've seen; all I've done and still death isn't done with me. It's a wager you never win, my teachers said that often enough, but somehow it doesn't seem to matter.

He walked on, a shapeless cloth bag slung over one shoulder and his leather coat clutched tight in his hands despite the mild weather. The inn was located on a side-street connecting two larger ones. As he reached the corner, Enchei shook himself from his thoughts and checked his path ahead. The sight was enough to stop him in his tracks – knots of people standing in the middle of the street, many carrying weapons while others lay on the ground, in the street and open doorways.

Paint adorned the white lime-plaster walls of many of the buildings, hasty scrawls in red and black that conveyed their message easily enough. The circular symbols of Lady Healer and Lady Pity, below them the gibbet-like motif of Lady Magistrate – three Gods together whose devices spelled only one thing: plague.

Enchei cast his gaze up and down the street. Four houses on this one alone; two next door to each other, the other two a short distance away. Quickly he moved up to be within earshot of the nearest group and discovered those on the ground were not dead, but in the grip of some sort of fever.

'How long they been sick?' he asked the nearest of the group, a fleshy man with pox-scars on his cheeks and thinning hair.

The man jumped at the sound of Enchei's voice, half-raising the cleaver he clutched.

'Half the morning,' the man replied eventually, the fear evident in his voice. 'People been just dropping in the street 'cross half the city, they say. All these damn foreigners, bringing their diseases to the city,' he added in a quieter voice, apparently assuming Enchei was a local.

Enchei scowled and nodded, keen to make a friend in anyone willing to pass on gossip.

'Half across the city?' he said in an awed voice, 'and all today? Pity preserve us.'

'There's talk o' demons too – up in the north districts,' the man continued. 'Folk saying it's demons what brought it. There's word the Lawbringers are going to shut the city down, impose a curfew until they can hunt 'em down.'

Before Enchei could reply there was a shriek from across the street. They all turned, instinctively recoiling, only to see a woman in a white servant-caste scarf stagger as she walked. She reached out for those around her, looking for a steadying arm, but her hand was slapped away and she was driven sideways by the desperate blow. She wavered for a moment while all those around her retreated, clearing a space for her to stumble another few ungainly steps, then folded to the floor with a thump.

No one moved for a long moment, they all just stared aghast at the limp body on the ground until a woman's voice broke the quiet.

'Cowards! Fools!'

A slender young woman pushed her way forward through the fearful crowd that watched as though waiting for the woman to rise a demon.

'Help her,' the young woman called to no avail. She reached the woman's side and knelt, gently tilting her head to check for injury. Satisfied she was not badly hurt the younger woman lifted the invalid's head and eased an arm under her shoulders.

She looked up and glared around at the onlookers. Little more than twenty years old and unmarried from the way she was dressed, Enchei realised she would have been strikingly attractive if it hadn't been for the tear-streaked dirt on her cheeks and red-rimmed eyes.

'Help me, one of you!' she demanded, but no one moved.

Enchei wavered, glancing down at the bag he carried – well aware he had a mission to complete, but transfixed by the determination in her voice. She was obviously of local blood, with light brown hair and deep blue eyes, yet there was something to the set of her jaw that snagged him. In an instant his thoughts were back at the day on which he had left his home, almost two decades past; all too aware he'd never return.

Gods of the high peaks, he thought as a mournful ache appeared in his chest.

From nowhere the scents of lavender and mountain pine filled his nose and the ache intensified – the laughter and shouts of children briefly drowning out the hush of the city street.

Unable to bear it any longer, Enchei slung the long strap of his bag over his head and stepped forward, tugging his own white scarf loose from around his neck. No one spoke as he advanced towards the woman, tying the scarf across his mouth so that his face was obscured from those watching.

'You don't need to cover your mouth,' the young woman said, in a gentler voice than she'd used before. 'I've been with my family all morning without getting sick; it's nothing in the air causing this fever.'

'All the same,' Enchei said gruffly. He knelt beside the ill woman and slipped his arms underneath her, lifting her easily and following the young woman to the nearest open doorway.

'Bring her in here,' she instructed, pointing to a blanket lying on the floor on the far side of the small room. Through another doorway

Enchei glimpsed three figures lying side by side on a mattress, faces slicked with sweat but as still as the dead.

'You've been with them all day?' he asked.

She nodded. 'I don't know what's causing the illness, but I feel fine. I've been tending the neighbours too, since I'm the only one not scared to go near them.'

'How long have they been ill?'

'Since early morning. I was last up, at work until past midnight.'

Enchei looked down at the woman on the cracked tile floor. He didn't want to investigate her body too carefully for signs of plague or other disease, but from what he could see it seemed more like a severe fever than anything else. That in itself was easily enough to kill, but the speed at which people were being taken ill made it unlike any fever he'd seen before.

'I have to go.'

'Go?' the statement seemed to take her by surprise. 'Well, of course. Thank you for helping me,' she added gruffly.

'Keep them drinking,' he advised, looking her straight in the eye for the first time. 'Good luck.'

He turned his back before she could say anything, not trusting himself not to linger if she asked.

Foolish old man, he chided himself. *Narin needs you, nothing else matters – certainly not your misplaced guilt.*

Careful to avoid the looks he received outside, Enchei left and headed towards the public thoroughfare. Out on that bustling avenue he tugged the scarf down and uncovered his mouth, needing to avoid attention more than he needed to hide his face now he was among the crowds of day.

Enchei walked with his head low, ignoring as much of the confusion and fear he saw as possible. Clearly the rumours were correct; this fever was widespread and indiscriminate. At one point a curtained litter hurried past, its bearers almost running in their haste. The herald clearing the path for them was barely about to keep ahead of his charges.

He didn't see who was within it, but the markings declared it a House Wolf nobleman. If the nobility was getting sick too, the problem was a greater one than anyone could have expected, but more likely they were just keen to be off the streets – away from the unwashed masses most susceptible to disease.

The coldest corners.

The former Astaren focused on those words, let his thoughts circle them as a point of reference. The effort dampened his memories of years past, quietened the voices enough to let him decide where he was going. There was an underground market just across the canal in the Cas Tere Warrant, some sort of ancient cellar network that had survived long after the great building above it had fallen. It was the best and nearest option he could think of aside from Coldcliffs, and Enchei had no desire to try there unless he'd run out of options.

I could head west instead, Enchei thought as he walked briskly east along the thoroughfare, towards the Fett Canal. *The House Dragon vault cemeteries? They're cold and lonely, a good place to be unobserved.*

He shook his head, dismissing the idea. Demons were certainly not afraid of sanctified ground, but the cemeteries were of the Gods; demons would not use them by choice. *The cliffs of Eagle? The wind gets channelled down those rocks; there are streets that spend half the year frost-rimed in those parts.*

Enchei paused as the thoroughfare opened up ahead and he was afforded a sight of the Fett Canal. Traffic on the canal itself was as busy as ever, but there were fewer pedestrians on the towpaths than he'd have expected. It was the experience of that morning's flight that stopped him. Somehow the fugitive group had picked up additional pursuers as they travelled along this canal. Enchei wasn't sure how it had happened, but had to assume the goshe had kept a lookout stationed somewhere nearby for whatever reason.

Just to be safe he cut into the alleys on his left, winding his way through narrow, rubbish-strewn streets until he came out on the canal again. This time he faced not the wide, stone-built Spinner's Bridge that spanned it for the public thoroughfare, but the Poor Man's Bridge. It was an aging, wooden affair, the Poor Man, with slimy boards and space only for two men to pass, but as such any lookout was unlikely to be stationed so close to it.

He crossed just as a barge reached the bridge, the bargeman following tradition and whacking the apex of the Poor Man as the boat reached it. It was the lowest of the four bridges spanning the Fett Canal and the local folklore varied on the reasons for the dangerous tradition. Some claimed the bargemen disliked having to duck their heads and were hoping their combined efforts would one day make it fall. Others thought that striking it brought luck, but Enchei was fairly sure the men just found it entertaining to cause those on the bridge to jump.

Either way, the bridge didn't fall and no assassins pursued Enchei into the alleys of Cas Tere, so he soon found himself back on the public thoroughfare, heading towards the cellar market that was his best bet. Most likely the demon had various emissaries out in the city waiting for him – a tendency towards the cryptic was one thing, but losing a day because your contact was too stupid to understand a subtle reference wasted everyone's time.

The cellar market had the advantage of an underground stream running along its north wall from a tunnel as old as the massive, ancient cellar. Given it really was an old, albeit disused and fouled, well that Enchei had found in his inn, the forgotten waterways under the city would make the market an easy place for any demon to reach.

Before long he was standing across the street from the open steps that led down into the market. The ground above was clear of buildings, unusually for this part of the city, and only a quartet of fat chimney stacks rose up from the ground there to ventilate the chambers below. Business seemed to be continuing as usual, a regular stream of people heading in and out with goods in hand. Enchei spent a while watching those in the streets around the entrance, habit forcing him to be circumspect before heading down into somewhere with only one exit.

After twenty minutes and two full circuits of the area, Enchei was satisfied and walked down into the market. His eyes wavered momentarily between his natural and unnatural vision before settling on a strange, dimmed version of normal sight – the colours washed out, the detail picked out in faint threads of white. The temperature dropped immediately, the wide stone rooms seeming to feed off the heat of his skin and going from chilly to cold as he headed further into the warren of chambers.

He passed stalls of fresh produce, then rows of crusted baths where fresh seafood lurked, tentacles and eyestalks wavering uncertainly in the permanent gloom. Furtive figures lurked on the fringes of pools of light from oil lamps that lined the walkway, some appearing as misshapen and bizarre as the creatures on sale there. A burst of chatter came from a side room and Enchei paused at the doorway to glimpse wide-eyed monkeys in cages, darting polecats and the sharp click-click of bats further back. He walked through it all, bag slung across his front to dissuade the thieves who haunted the underground chambers.

He reached a fork and paused, glancing left before remembering the drug dens lay that way. He turned right down a narrow path towards two vaulted chambers of butchers – the two trades occasionally intersecting, if local gossip was to be believed. Whatever the truth, it was the butchers who made most use of the underground river that passed briefly through the cellars, and there he headed.

The stink was palpable, despite the cold that prickled his skin and the pails of water used to sluice down the floor. Children scrubbed at the pitted stone slabs and Enchei realised the day was done for the butchers, but no one challenged him as he passed through the tangle of bloodstained tables of wood and stone. It didn't pay to be overly curious in a place such as this, where figures keen to avoid the light went about their work. The butchers themselves were clustered about an oval archway, laughing and drinking while peering down at something Enchei couldn't see. From the sounds, he guessed something was being made to fight for them to bet their wages on.

The river itself was little more than a stream, but swift as it made its way to the Crescent and the bloodied remnants of the underground trade was carried off to the sea. It emerged from an opening a few feet high and Enchei couldn't help glancing down into the blackness of that oval tunnel. Even he could see little there, just a faint curve of stone above the water too regular to be natural. It appeared to be empty so Enchei returned his attention to the rest of the room. As he did so, an unnaturally slim figure seemed to fold itself around one of the counterforts that projected into the room and curved up to the peak of the roof.

Enchei's senses seemed to blossom into life. Discordant sounds danced out across the room like the clicking calls of a bat – a dozen different sounds that no one else there could hear. At the same time he saw darting, flickering movement within the figure's cloak and it drifted towards him as though supported merely by air.

He couldn't make out the figure's face, but he didn't expect to see anything there as he approached it. His own body reacted to the figure's presence – arms and hands tightening inside his armour, ready to fight, knees bending slightly as he readied to attack or flee.

A pattern of light traced through the air before the figure's cowled face, illuminating nothing of the blackness within. Shapes and movements evolved so quickly no normal man would have been able to make any sense of the images, but Enchei had been expecting it. He blinked once as the pattern seemed to etch itself onto his eyes and twisted into the semblance of sense to his mind.

And all without truly understanding how it is done, he reflected, as he had so many times before. *The explanations were always perfunctory – they wanted me as a tool, a weapon to be wielded, not a scholar. For the enlightened masters of the nation, they always were jealous in guarding their knowledge.*

– You are the one, came the demon's silent words. *– You are the mortal blessed by our lord's favour.*

'Don't know about that,' Enchei muttered as he formed a reply. He raised his hand and skeins of light danced briefly across the surface of his palm.

– I am the one.

– We are the emissary. Kneel before us.

'Like buggery I will.'

– No. Give me the message your master sends.

– You will show us greater respect, mortal.

– The message, now.

The demon's reply was jagged edged and intensely bright.

– We will tear out your soul!

Tendrils of light unfolded from within the drifting dark cloak that hid the demon. Enchei just snorted and slapped his light-traced hand towards the nearest. As it passed through, the tendril seemed to burst. The demon recoiled hurriedly, tendrils writhing around its slim form until they were withdrawn again.

– Try that again and I'll cut your balls off, he signalled.

The demon kept very still, uncomprehending his threat, but now aware of the danger he could pose it.

– Your master gets to speak to me like that, Enchei continued after a pause. *– You just get to leave without being killed if you give me the message now.*

There was a long moment where only blackness was visible within the cowl, but at last tiny threads of light appeared again.

– The being of the night sky you call Shield accedes to your request. It has traced the steps of your friend, but he is now beyond Shield's sight.

'I expected as much,' Enchei said. *– Where does the path end?*

– Here.

The light traced an image suddenly, a plan of the city as seen by a being of the night sky. Enchei watched as the image rushed towards him; the scale dropping as quick as a striking falcon as the districts, then streets, became visible. Lastly the shape of a building came into view, the outline of a door-lintel and the smoky trail of Narin that led inside.

Enchei nodded. The image had imprinted itself on his memory; he could see exactly where in the city they had disappeared from Shield's sight – most likely the building was warded against demons and avatars of the Gods alike.

– *Thank your master for me.*

The cloak merely collapsed in front of him and fluttered untidily to the floor. Enchei found himself standing alone, staring at a wall a few yards behind. He coughed and turned, realising one of the boys cleaning the room had stopped to watch him and wonder what was going on.

'You can fuck off an' all,' he said, half-drawing a knife at his waist as a threat – choosing to look like just some local thug rather than anything more gossip-worthy.

The boy glanced over at the gaggle of butchers, still intent on their sport then returned Enchei a level look. With a shrug he went back to his mopping.

CHAPTER 20

Narin stands and watches her from a darkened corner, cocooned from the songs and laughter that ring out across the great hall. Tapestries of snarling wyverns adorn every wall. Birds sing from gilt cages on each of the two dozen round tables. Most of the hall's occupants are at the tables; warriors kneeling while the nobles and religious caste sit on fat velvet cushions of purple and blue.

The hall is in fact five rooms; arranged in the shape of a primrose, Narin remembers her telling him. Curved stone archways separate the rooms, normally blocked off by painted wooden screens, but for the feast it is all one room.

For the first hour the feast proceeded across strictly formal lines – host lord and his honoured guests in the central room below a great glass dome through which the night sky is visible. The noble, religious and warrior castes each in a room of their own, with the honoured merchants in the last and furthest. It is there Narin has remained, even after the formalities are done and the segregation relaxed, offered only the cheapest wine they have. He takes a sip from his cup and is reminded that its quality remains better than he can afford himself. Only a merchant's wife has bothered to speak to him all evening – as with all formal events, the arms of every person present are bare. There is no hiding his caste-mark from his betters.

He glances to his right and sees the merchant's wife immersed in conversation with an aging warrior – the Wyvern's long braided hair now white against his dark skin. He realises he was terse in his replies, his discomfort at being the lowest-born person in the room a burr against his skin. His resentment at her assumed condescension turns to embarrassment at his rudeness. He wants to go and apologise, but does not know how and in the next moment Kine rises from across the room.

He feels his breath catch as for a moment she looks him straight in the eye. The babble of the feast fades to nothing and he is lost in the white flash of her eyes, the brief glimpse of teeth before she covers her smile. She wheels away from the tall priest she had been talking to, a butterfly darting from his raven's clutches. Her arms are in constant movement, each gesture precise and intended as she navigates the press of revellers, greets friends and deflects well-wishers, all without a word spoken.

Narin follows her through the hall, circling in the opposite direction. The palazzo hall is packed with people, but one end is opened up to the enclosed gardens. Lord Vanden is from the inland reaches of Wyvern's domain – not for him the arid, desert-like gardens that echo the home of real wyverns; he prefers the towering, humid jungle.

It is a garden to get lost in and as soon as Kine slips through the hanging fronds of an unknown tree, she has disappeared from sight. The garden is small by noble standards – vast by Narin's reckoning. Yellow-tinted jars placed amongst the undergrowth shine a soft light, but to Narin it is a confusing thicket he blunders blindly through.

Wyverns are a hot-blooded breed – he knows that much at least, and keeps close to the candlelight. Soft moans come from the darker corners, followed by an abrupt cry of pleasure that breaks like a startled bird. Narin turns to follow the sound on instinct then looks away again with his cheeks warm.

From nowhere Kine stands before him, a gentle smile half-hidden by her slender fingers.

'My Lady,' Narin blurts out, ducking his head in some semblance of formality.

'Investigator,' she acknowledges, performing a playful, almost girlish curtsey. She holds out her hand. 'This way, there are benches away from the darkened corners.'

She leads him along a tangle of tiny paths, winding past canopied seats and cloth-decked pergolas until they are in the furthest corner where a curved stone bench sits – exposed to the light but hidden by expansive trees.

'I am glad you came,' Kine says, releasing his hand briefly as they sit. 'Are you enjoying the feast?'

Narin's words falter. 'I … not much,' he admits, hanging his head. 'I have no polite conversation, no refined interests to offer for discussion.'

She acknowledges his words with a squeeze of his hand. 'I thank you for coming then. My heart is lighter just for seeing you across the room.'

'Any discomfort is worthwhile,' he declares with as much gallantry as he can muster, 'just to sit here with you. To be alone with you.'

He sees her eyelids flutter up, instinctively checking for anyone who might be watching them, but at the same time she cannot help but smile. Even turned slightly away from him and lips instinctively covered by her fingers, the sight warms Narin's heart.

She turns towards him just as he leans forward. There is surprise in her eyes, but she reaches to him all the same and they brush lips delicately. The taste of her lips and scent of her skin are intoxicating.

The smile on her face afterwards awakens a hunger for that taste again; a desire more powerful than he has ever imagined he could feel. He kisses her again and this time it lasts much longer; his hand pressed gently against her back, hers bunched into fists around his tunic as she pulls him close.

Reluctantly, she breaks away and again checks for witnesses. 'Not here,' she whispers breathlessly. Even in the faint light he can see a flush in her dark cheeks. 'If we are seen, we would be killed.'

'Where then?'

'There is a teahouse, near the Harbour Warrant,' she says after a moment, straightening her dress, composing herself. 'The Feathered Serpent, do you know it?' He nods. 'I go there with friends to play cards the first day of every ascendancy. Wyvern and Longtooth noblemen gamble on Firstdays; my husband never misses that, be it cards or bloodsport.'

Narin nods and she stands, checking once more before cupping his head in her hands and kissing him hard on the mouth.

'The others will leave at nightfall. Come find me after dark, I will have a few hours.'

Cold water slapped across his flesh, sluicing the warmth of his dreams away. Narin gasped and shuddered under its impact, then howled as the movement drove iron rods of pain down through his arms and shoulders. Hung from manacled hands, toes scraping feebly across the stone floor, his body was alive with pain and his head fogged and dizzy.

He tried to look up, to focus on the face ahead of him, but he could make out nothing. The scene swam in front of his eyes and the pain from his arms and back nearly overwhelmed him again. There came an abrupt jerk on the chain holding him up. Narin moaned, but after the initial movement he found himself being eased down to the floor. It was cold and hard but Narin could not tell if the tears spilling down his face were caused by pain or relief, however short-lived they might be.

'Better?' came a voice above him.

Narin squinted up. Still unable to see properly, he was at least able to work out it wasn't the Dragon who'd tortured him. This one wasn't nearly so dark-skinned or broad, with long slate-grey hair.

'Water,' Narin croaked and was rewarded by a cup being brought to his lips, his head supported as he drank. A voice at the back of his head – Enchei's, he thought distantly – told him that this was the time to try to escape, but he could barely move. Lifting his head was beyond him, let along overpowering some magic-enhanced goshe assassin and fighting his way free. Instead he just found himself pathetically grateful for the trickle of water that made it down his throat.

'Got some questions for you now,' the new gaoler stated once Narin was finished with the cup.

'Fine,' Narin gasped as he sank back on the floor. 'Doesn't matter now.'

'Because Irato's already bolted from wherever you were going to meet him,' the man stated. 'Aye, thought as much, but there's still a lot you can tell us.'

'And you'll just believe me?' Narin said, confused.

'You want Kodeh to come back here and start cutting bits off you?'

Just the memory of the Dragon's lightning-wrapped hand pressed against his bare skin was enough to make Narin whimper and try to curl protectively up.

The man laughed. 'Didn't think so.'

'Still don't see why,' Narin coughed after a while, desperate again to be talking rather than anything else. The room was lit just by a lamp; nothing to indicate the time of day or how long he'd been passed out.

'Should still be some of the drug in your body,' the man replied conversationally, 'that'll keep you chatty.'

Narin blinked up at his captor. Through the fog in his mind he realised the man's voice was young; he hardly sounded older than a novice, despite his grey hair. *House Iron*, he realised slowly, the room briefly spinning as he tried to shift position on the floor.

'Drug?' he said slowly. Narin blinked and saw bright bursts of light behind his eyelids as he did so, the room coming only reluctantly back into focus. 'I can't lie?'

His captor laughed again. 'Try one.'

'I ...' It took Narin a long time to think of anything at all, but at last something did come to mind. 'I'm Lawbringer Rhe.'

'There you go then, you can lie.'

'How would you believe anything I said, then?'

The man crouched at his side, close enough that Narin could smell the leather of his boots and strange, pungent sweat.

'Did they tell you at Lawbringer school that you can't beat a true confession out of a man? Well, that ain't exactly right. You can make an innocent man confess to anything, damn right – but some bastard you know's guilty? Someone you know has something to tell you? He's got to be tough before he's gonna lie convincingly when you're burning the skin off his body. Tougher'n you, I reckon.'

Despite himself, Narin shuddered, imagining the pain all too easily.

'Yup, there you go – and I ain't even touched you yet.'

The goshe bent lower, his face so close to Narin's he only had to whisper, as soft as a lover. 'But the other reason you're gonna tell me everything? You want to know that?'

Narin stared up at the suddenly-malevolent smirk on the young man's face and felt a cold shard in his belly. He didn't say anything, terrified of what might come next, but the man continued anyway.

'Aye, I reckon you do. See – the drug I gave you, I gave you too much. No bloody use to me o' course, what with you babbling like a madman and not hearing any questions I had for you, but that didn't stop you talking.

'So answer me this, brave lawman – who's Kine? Fancy gambling that with all the power of the goshe at our disposal, we wouldn't be able to find *her*?'

The map in his mind took Enchei to a corner of the city he'd rarely visited, far enough from Coldcliffs that he had to wonder how they'd managed to get a subdued Narin so far across the city without attracting attention. The Kayme Warrant was a small, mostly residential district on the northern edge of the larger Eagle District. Many of the servants and labourers working in Eagle lived in Kayme and its buildings were some of the oldest in the city; cramped, narrow streets with little logic to their layout. As a result it was the poorest of the northern districts and rife with crime.

A good place to get lost in, Enchei realised as he entered the district, *and the locals are unlikely to be helpful to anyone pursuing Narin's kidnappers.*

He stopped before a small well at a crossroads of five streets and watched the locals go about their day. The fever had taken hold here too, he saw, with hastily-daubed symbols on walls and fear in the eyes of those fetching water. They all eyed him with suspicion, but were almost as wary of their neighbours as they went about their afternoon chores. Very little talking took place between any of them and Enchei was careful to move on quickly, resisting the urge to stop and question the locals.

He passed a long passage between houses that had an aging lead roof covering it, but at the far end he could see daylight and a street beyond. *A good place to get lost in,* he repeated to himself. *Hidden from the Gods, even.*

It was only mid-afternoon, but it seemed like evening was drawing in early. Grey clouds massed overhead, the sun banished behind a gloomy, unseasonal curtain.

Hoping the rain would intensify and keep locals off the streets, Enchei pulled on his long leather coat and headed into the heart of Kayme. Before long, he found himself surrounded by half-derelict tenement blocks and warehouses. A broad, forbidding building rose from the heart of them and instinctively he knew that was where he was headed, despite the map telling him his destination was an abandoned shop-front nearby. That backed onto a crumbling tenement full of noise, children and babies creating a clamour that hung over the building like a cloud. Any cellar would be small and cramped, any strangers or screams quickly noticed.

In a part of the city this old, Enchei knew there would be disused sewers and tunnels dating back to the Greater Empire. Criminals and vagrants inhabited most of those, but he had no doubt the secret soldiers of the goshe would have cleared out a patch for themselves and sealed it off. The large, four-storey building hidden within the tenements was significantly older than its neighbours and had once been grander. That meant thicker walls and proper foundations, perhaps even several levels of cellars – perfect for keeping prisoners.

He walked a long lap around the building. There were no signs of life. The upper floors showed signs of fire damage, while the lower windows were barred where there weren't shutters blocking any view of within. There were two exits beyond the principal one, which was half-hidden by a blockish portico that looked dangerously unstable should anyone try the door. He lingered near each of them for as long as he dared – one a tall street door, the other a smaller alley exit.

293

Realising he couldn't waste as much time watching as he'd like, Enchei chose the alley door as the more likely to give him safe access. He stepped into the recess of the doorway and surveyed the obstacle. It was sturdy and fitted comfortably into the frame, with little yield when he gently pushed on it.

Most likely a recent replacement that's been aged to blend in.

He placed a black metal disc the size and thickness of a child's palm on each thick hinge bracket. On the back of the discs was inscribed an incantation in the language of a forgotten race, ornate words that spiralled inward to a tiny crystal shard at the centre. Enchei pressed his thumbs against each shard before walking away, leaving them attached to the door.

Enchei counted silently as he took a lap of a neighbouring tenement block to allow the discs time to work. It was one of many skills the mage-priests of his homeland had planted into his mind, bypassing the learning process to burn it directly into his memory. The seconds slipped past, entirely absent from his attention, which was occupied with watching for threats but keeping perfect time.

Worried for years about that, I did, he thought as he completed his circuit. *Whether they'd taken out some of me to make space for it all. Was years before I learned how much useless space was in my head, how much they could put in there without me even noticing. Doubt Irato would appreciate that little nugget of wisdom, though.*

As he returned to within view of the alley door, the desultory rain turned into a sudden, intense burst that scattered what few residents were in sight. Enchei scowled up at the sky as heavy drips worked their way down his neck. He found himself a darkened corner that would be mostly hidden from the building Lord Shield's ghost-map had shown him and began to run through his plan of action in his mind. The seconds slipped past at the back of his mind, unnoticed as he waited for his charms on the door to have their effect.

He had no idea what state Narin was in now, but had to assume he was talking and giving them everything he knew. That meant the inn was likely compromised, his identity too, perhaps.

And once more, I'm left with just the clothes on my back.

Enchei sighed and reached into the bag he'd brought with him, slipping his hands into the mesh gauntlets that were part of his armour. Once they were in place he felt the metal grow faintly warmer and the mesh tighten briefly against his skin before settling on a comfortable fit around his hands. It had been years since he'd worn these, his hands already sufficiently deadly for almost any circumstance.

No time for careful reconnaissance. I'm just going to have to march in that back door and hope there are no surprises I can't deal with.

The countdown in his head came to an end and Enchei stepped out of his temporary hiding place, heading back towards the alley door he was planning on using. It was the most likely exit, given he doubted anyone going into that abandoned shop-front would leave the same way. Other tunnels were also a possibility, but he didn't have the time to search for them and once he was away from potential witnesses he had other tricks he could employ.

He slung his bag over one shoulder and quickly moved to the alley door, walking lightly with his senses open to anything that might indicate he'd been seen. The city was quiet enough; no unnatural calls or warnings overlaying the muted voices of children, no scuffle of feet or steel on stone.

At the door he surveyed his handiwork and gave a nod of satisfaction. There was no outward sign of damage to the thick, rusting hinges as Enchei pocketed each disc, but with a metal-clad finger he scraped a furrow of brittle metal shards from the topmost hinge.

From the bag he withdrew what looked like a baton of the same black metal, with a handle that took up half its length and a blunt, rounded tip. One last check behind him and he slammed the butt of the baton into the lower hinge. Under the impact the metal crumbled, falling like soil at his feet.

Enchei tensed, but he heard no alarm – mundane or arcane – as the door lurched a shade. It was a solid construction, thick wood bound in studded bands of iron, but like any other door, without hinges its strength meant little. Stepping back from the recessed doorway, Enchei moved almost halfway around the corner before he smashed the baton into the second hinge. He pulled his arm back after him as quickly as he could, but no flash of fire erupted from behind the lurching door, nor any other form of trap that he could detect.

Almost disappointed in his opponents, Enchei moved back around to grab the creaking door as it sagged back. Held up only by the lock and frame around it, he punched forward into the wood with the stubby points of his gauntlets. Once he had a firm grip he levered the

295

door open enough to slip around it, the grind and groan of the iron lock the only sound.

Inside it was dark, only the outline of an empty double-height room visible in his white mage-sight. He pulled the door behind him and secured it as best he could with a length of wire. That done he dropped his bag on the ground and pulled the last item from it, an all-enclosing helmet with a curved, featureless face-plate. He slipped it on and felt it mould tight around his skull, setting his senses tingling. He looked around again and this time saw more than an empty room. There were ghostly trails stretched at random across it, an invisible residue of magic hanging in the air – a web spread throughout most of the room to warn of anyone breaking in.

Enchei nodded appreciatively. He'd chosen correctly after all; unless by some terrible coincidence he'd stumbled upon an Astaren stronghold.

And not even I'm that unlucky, he thought as he stepped forward, baton ready in his hand. He paused. *Probably. Almost certainly.*

There was a path through the webs, oblique but clear. No doubt that was how the goshe left the building. Whether or not they could actually see the webs, they knew the path through so the warding would always remain active.

Someone's not sharing, he guessed as he walked silently forward, then stepped to the side and moved in an arc towards the far side of the room. *Now ain't that a familiar story? Unless their elite are too damn stupid to be trusted to lock up behind them, whoever set this is making a point that they've kept some knowledge from their servants. Paranoia and jealousy; they'll be the death of the strongest man.*

Once he was through the web of wardings, Enchei found himself at a narrow corridor leading to a smaller ante-chamber. Halfway down it he stopped, some sixth sense bringing him up short. The floor was paved with square tiles, many broken and tilted after years of use. The pattern they traced in his dark sight was chaotic and scuffed by a hundred boots – all except for the one section at his feet. He peered closer and discerned the edges of a single slab separate from the rest.

Carefully he picked his way over the slab, feeling a small prickle of pleasure as he got past the deadfall trap. But for his unnaturally sharp vision, he'd never have noticed the difference in dirt on the slab. He couldn't see what lay underneath, but even with his Astaren armour he didn't want to be falling onto steel spikes or the like.

One arcane defence, one simple one. Doesn't mean there aren't others, but all but the most paranoid mind would consider that sufficient for anywhere people have to walk on a regular basis.

At the end of the corridor he tightened his grip on his baton and edged around the corner, watching for guards and further traps. The room was also double-height, a rickety-looking iron balustrade running around the top, but otherwise empty. Bare of any furnishings, it also lacked a door and for a moment Enchei was puzzled as he walked cautiously into the centre of the room. Then the scuff-marks again came to his assistance as, on the right hand side of the door, he saw boot-prints on the wall at chest height. Looking closer he realised the rail was different there – newer and securely bolted down. With a few steps run-up he pushed himself up the wall and caught the rail with his right hand, quietly pulling himself onto the walkway.

There was an open doorway near that and at last he heard some signs of life. There were voices just a few yards ahead, lines of light around a door. Enchei crept forwards, readying his baton as he reached the door. He listened for a moment. Two voices; too muted for him to hear properly, but he guessed they were Dragons from the depth and rhythm of their accents.

Crouching, he put his fingers to the gap at the bottom of the door, rubbing his thumb and forefinger together while running an arcane script through his mind. The friction of metal on metal produced a faint sound too high-pitched for any normal human to hear but, as Enchei silently chanted, a shape of the room beyond the door appeared in his mind. The image was crude, a shadowy sense rather than any clear picture, but enough to tell him the rough size and the location of the goshe within.

He rose and waited a moment longer. The voices had faltered while he was sounding out the room, but then they continued – clearly unsure if they had heard anything at all. Enchei didn't wait for them to compare notes. He burst through the door and charged for the nearer of the two goshe. With the image of the room in his mind he didn't stop to take in his surroundings, just let his body drive forward with the baton leading the way. The nearer man was facing his way so Enchei levelled the baton and squeezed the handle.

A stream of distorted air seemed to erupt from the end and struck the man full in the face. His head snapped back as though he'd been

297

punched and Enchei turned the baton towards the other man, who was rising from his seat and reaching for a knife. The weapon knocked him backwards into the wall, knife forgotten as his hands went instinctively up to cover his face. Neither collapsed insensate though.

Damn, they've got defences in their minds.

Enchei whipped the baton back across the face of the first goshe. The solid rod connected with his throat and Enchei felt bones snap under the impact. A second blow took the goshe on the side of the head and he was falling like a dead weight even as the second finally staggered forward a few steps.

Enchei levelled his left hand at the other goshe and the whisper of a half-dozen darts burst from the hump of armour on his arm. They caught the man full in the face, tearing through his dark skin in a spray of blood. In the next moment he was falling too, limp as only a dead man could be, and Enchei was alone in the room.

He looked down at the baton and shrugged. *So much for not killing everyone I meet.*

The room was seven yards across, two racks of three beds occupying the far wall with a stove, table and chairs in the centre of the room. An open cupboard on his right housed the goshe's equipment and weapons – all mundane in construction, Enchei saw with relief as he cast his eye over the bags and sheaths there. Irato's possessions had been exactly the same – clearly, if the goshe possessed anything more powerful it wasn't part of their usual kit. Which gave him an advantage.

The only object of interest in the room was a faintly glowing crystal ball. Wisps of light floated listlessly inside it. It wasn't clear what it was for, but Enchei had to assume it was a way to alert the guards to any tripping of the wardings. He left it alone and headed for the only other door, again crouching to sound out what was behind before opening it.

There was a steep flight of stone-walled stairs, a solid and secure path down into the belly of the building. It was pitch black, but he could tell it led not far underground so, shutting the door behind him, he crept down and found himself in a basement room with two open exits. The left-hand was a tunnel of some sort. He could see an uneven curved roof that appeared to be some sort of ancient sewer leading towards the entrance Lord Shield had shown him. The other was steps down to a deeper level, far below ground and more recently dug than the sewer.

The air smelled of cold mud and water, a cloying scent of recent excavations as well as old, crumbling brick. Above that was the acrid stink of urine, and blood too, perhaps. Enchei had seen enough dungeons to recognise the aroma and headed for the steps, but before he reached them a white figure loomed like a vengeful spectre.

The man was quick and big, covering the ground fast enough that Enchei didn't react in time and felt a boot slam into his chest with the force of a hammer. The aging fighter was thrown against the wall behind him, while the pale giant whipped a pair of long-knives from their sheaths and jumped forward.

'Uttir!' he barked as he stabbed down.

Enchei darted to one side and smashed his baton down on the nearest blade. The impact jerked it from its owner's grip but, as it fell, bursts of lightning leapt from the giant's mailed fists. Sparks exploded over the baton and Enchei felt his arm jolt and go rigid for a moment. Both men flinched from the burst of light, but Enchei reacted fastest. He punched at the giant's arm and felt the armour burst under the impact, following it up with a swipe of his protesting arm across the man's face.

Somehow the giant jerked back out of the way and slashed with his remaining knife, but Enchei turned into the blow. He met the giant's arm with his own and grabbed the man's wrist. Bending the elbow back on itself, bones snapped horribly under the pressure. In the next moment Enchei slammed the handle of the baton down onto the giant's nose with all the strength he could muster. The blow shattered his face, blood bursting down pale skin as he dropped.

A second goshe appeared up the stairs, moving fast but this time not quick enough to prevent Enchei levelling his left hand. A spray of tiny steel darts studded the goshe's cheek and throat, some punching right through into the brick behind. The man gave a startled gasp and ponderously began to tip backwards, beads of blood appearing at his wounds before he crashed down.

Nearby, the giant's legs were twitching feebly, telling Enchei he was dying too. He stepped over the body and headed down the steps to the dungeon below. He kept his arm outstretched as he went now, ready to fill the narrow corridor with a storm of darts. Three doors led off to the left, spaced evenly down the brick-lined corridor. The first contained a naked, blood-streaked man he guessed to be Narin, but didn't stop to check until he'd confirmed the next two rooms were empty.

299

Once that was done he returned to Narin. The Investigator hung limp from a chain fixed to a ring in the ceiling. A jug of water and an unlit lamp sat on a small table, well out of Narin's reach, but other than that the room was empty. The Investigator's legs trailed feebly over the stone floor, legs and stone streaked with bodily waste. Enchei took no time in lifting him to relieve the pressure on his arms, wincing at the shudder and recoil from Narin despite his relief that the man was still alive. Through split, swollen lips, he heard a feeble sound, though whether it was pain or something else Enchei couldn't tell.

'You're safe now,' Enchei said to him, easing Narin back down to a relatively clean patch of floor. 'Stay calm, Narin.'

Narin's hands were roughly bound with chain; the links looped through the ring above but were not actually locked in any way. Instead the weight hanging on it kept the chain too tight to slip, making it impossible for someone as weakened as Narin to free himself.

Enchei fetched the jug and gently sluiced Narin down, washing the worst of the filth and blood off and letting a little fall over the Investigator's face. He saw Narin's tongue twitch out a little to catch some of the drops and smiled in the darkness.

'Aye, you'll live,' Enchei whispered to his friend. He cradled Narin's head, supporting it so he could see into the younger man's eyes. 'Time to find you some clothes. I ain't carrying you naked on my shoulder, that's for damn sure. Nothing I want to grip there.'

CHAPTER 21

The number of high-born Lawbringers is a de facto secret within the Empire. In this one situation the Great Houses are wilfully blind to the number of gun-trained soldiers serving the Emperor so long as it is not flaunted. Lawbringer Rhe's utter lack of political sense has hardly helped the matter, but when considering an Empire-wide balance of power, what are a few armed incursions between friends?

From *A History* by Ayel Sorote

The last light of evening was a gilt arc over the western horizon. Thick trails of cloud striated the sky; bands of white graduating through shades of grey. Behind them hung the dark shapes of Knight's divine constellations – appearing as distinct grey pinpricks while the sun was near the horizon. The Order of Empress hung almost directly above them in the sky – just waiting for the sunset to cast its own light on the world.

Lawbringer Rhe stood on the eastern shore of the Imperial Island and looked out across the Crescent, beyond the high towers of Eagle District, and at the Gods who had passed during the day. Unnoticed by all but the priests who would scan the daytime sky for the faint sight of their lord or lady, what remained of the Order of Emperor above the horizon was hard to make out in the cloud-streaked evening. The Lord General was the only daytime constellation he could discern; the rest he could only guess at.

'Sir,' called one of his companions, a diminutive woman who fell short of his shoulder. She pointed north, towards the Arbold Warrant. 'A signal – there!'

He turned to look. More than a mile away a white flag streamed in the fading light, swept from side to side by the one of the novices

Rhe had sent out. The novice stood near the mouth of the river that defined the border between Arbold and Kayme.

Both Imperial warrants of the city. Is that a good thing or not? He knew there would be more guns in House-controlled districts to deal with the demons, but once the warrior caste got a taste for hunting demons how carefully would they discriminate in the dusk?

'In,' he said, stepping down into the boat where a team of oarsmen sat ready.

Behind him the small woman, Investigator Soral, boarded with four others and the oarsmen set off. Rhe crouched at the bow of the boat as they headed across the Crescent, adjusting the sword on his back as he did so. It had been years since he'd carried such a weapon, not since he'd left his homeland in the north to come here and pledge his service.

He glanced back at the others. All noble-born, each had been taught to fight with sword and gun, then put aside their blade during their time as Investigators.

And I am told those noble-born Investigators will refuse to wear a sword, if they are raised to Lawbringer rank. My choice was my own yet they follow me like sheep. Law Master Sheven finds it instructive, being of the religious caste, but I am just unsurprised.

His gaze was noticed by Soral who raised her chin a little, awaiting instruction, but he looked away and the small woman did not question him. From a Major House under Eagle, rival to Rhe's own House Brightlance, Soral was a typical House Fox warrior – compact and narrow-faced, with startling yellow eyes.

While she was very young to participate in such a dangerous assignment, Rhe had chosen all of the Investigators on marksmanship alone; trusting the training of their caste to ensure they would stand with him when they found their prey. After his encounter earlier, he had pulled together every gun-permitted Lawbringer and Investigator. Divided into units, they had been assigned sections of the city to patrol, ready to respond to more demon sightings.

'Demons walk the city streets,' he said abruptly. 'An affront to our Gods and their blood descendant, the Emperor. An affront to the honour of the Lawbringers. I will die before I allow this in our city.'

The stern men and woman in the boat each nodded briefly or grunted agreement.

'They are stronger than men and command magics we cannot understand. Take them down and make certain of any kill. Questions?'

No one spoke and the rest of the short journey passed in silence. Even on the other side, the white-faced novice who greeted them did so without words. He bowed briefly to Rhe and waved them forward, heading at a trot down a nearby street. Rhe followed, running tall and stiff with one hand on a pistol grip. The shadows were long in the narrow street, the air close and sickly from the refuse underfoot. It didn't take them long before they had passed a dozen plague symbols across the doors of houses.

The street itself was deserted. He saw a few fearful faces at windows, but every door was shut and he guessed barred as well. As dusk deepened, Rhe found himself heading down gloomy, unlit alleys that ran parallel to the river. A rat scampered across their path, making for the river and the novice turned left there, heading for wherever the rat was fleeing.

Rhe followed him and drew his pistol instinctively as the novice faltered. Ahead was a market square where a dozen or so stone pillars supported a broad roof at the centre, all pitted with age. On the ground was a body, what remained of an Investigator, while through the pillars Rhe saw a large figure moving. He pointed and his companions also drew their guns, fanning out behind him.

Rhe advanced ahead of the rest, skirting the square with one eye on the various alleys and streets leading off it. The demon was quite unlike the one he'd pursued. It had pale skin that shone in the waning light, but something like shadows slipped across its naked, angular body. As he got closer Rhe saw it had caught a dog and was bent over its struggling form – twice-jointed arms picking at the creature's body with deliberate, careful movements.

All of a sudden the elusive shadows on its body sharpened and quickened, becoming dark circles that raced for a moment then snapped still. Rhe felt his breath catch as he saw the circles surge towards him, clustering in the nearest part of the demon's back while the rest of its skin became as white as snow.

Gods above, they're eyes!

The demon jerkily turned, the shadow-eyes staying focused on Rhe as the body moved around. Its face was blank, just scars where its eyes and mouth had once been – the nose a mere impression on its hairless, earless face. He took a slow pace forward, determined to buy a few moments and let the others line up a good shot. The demon ducked its head, eyes swirling off around its body to form new clusters as it caught sight of the other Lawbringers.

Rhe blinked and realised its long fingers had begun to twitch, white light starting to emanate from the thin digits. He wasted no time in wondering what was about to happen and levelled his pistol. The demon recoiled from the movement, eyes spinning around its body as the others did the same, but the light continued to grow so Rhe pulled the trigger.

The crack of his gun echoed around the square, his bullet snapping the demon's head back. More shots followed his; one caught it in the shoulder and the force twisted it around, another lower down and it faltered but remained standing.

As Rhe went for his other gun a second shot caught it in the head. This time there was a spray of something against the sky behind – grey, not red, but the demon reeled and he knew they'd hurt it.

More shots rang out, two in quick succession as the last two Investigators fired their pistols. Rhe advanced while the demon was distracted, closing the ground with his second gun ready. Less than ten yards from the demon, he stopped and aimed. The demon's hands were now painfully bright to look at, haloed in the gloom by pure white light. Rhe lowered his gun a shade, aiming at the raised palm of the demon, and put a bullet right through its spindly hand. From somewhere there was a high sound of pain, near-inaudible to human ears, and the wound in its hand turned black. The light faltered, shadows seeming to fill the skin of its limbs as more bullets rocked its body backward.

Rhe charged, longsword drawn and ready to strike. The demon failed to notice him, so intent was it on the injury he'd done, but then his first blow sheared through the blackening limb. The demon screamed again, this time a sound so loud and high it felt like daggers in their ears. Rhe staggered sideways, clutching his head as the sound seemed to explode off the surrounding walls and strike him on all sides. His vision blurred and shuddered, his muscles suddenly turned to liquid inside him.

Rhe tumbled backwards as a white shape cut through the confusion and crashed down just in front of him. Finding his sword still in his hand Rhe slashed blindly, catching nothing. The movement seemed to return him to his senses, however; the feel of swinging a sword was

304

so ingrained in his body that from somewhere he found his composure return. Unable to see properly, guided by the light of its remaining hand, Rhe stepped away from a second swing and struck up at where its arm should be.

He caught it a glancing blow, but life-long training drove him on and he chopped down at the hand in the next instant. Something burst under the force of his blow and he twisted sideways as the light dimmed. The demon was ahead of him, bowed over the blackened ruins of its hands and he hacked down at the back of its neck. The blow sent it crashing to the floor – not severing the neck but enough to cripple the demon. Rhe stepped back, blinking away stars from his eyes as he heard the running footsteps of his colleagues close by.

He opened his mouth to shout an order but the words died unneeded in his throat – drowned out by the double-crack of pistol shots that burst the demon's head apart.

Night had fallen by the time Law Master Sheven came to find Rhe at his station on the bank of the Crescent. Behind his grey beard, Sheven's face was a mass of anxiety. Bows from the Investigators went unnoticed as he hurried up to Rhe, scimitar flapping on his hip.

'Lawbringer – you've had a successful night?'

Rhe did not respond for a moment, at last inclining his head. 'We killed two; reports from the other teams give us a total of five.'

'But we have taken losses?' Sheven finished, seeing the grave expression on Rhe's face.

'At least six of ours dead – perhaps thirty civilians at the hands of the demons. I have no way of knowing how many have been killed accidentally, but I myself witnessed one instance.'

'What did you do?'

Rhe turned briefly towards where the flag-wielding novices would now be ready with torches in the darkness. 'Nothing. It was unintentional and he was a House Wolf nobleman, they were a servant.'

Sheven ducked his head in acknowledgement. Putting anyone of the noble caste on charges was fraught with difficulties at the best of times, especially when the victim was low-born.

'How fares the rest of the city?'

Sheven's shoulders sagged lower. 'Chaos. The fever has been reported in every district of the city bar the Imperial Island itself.'

'Deaths?'

'A handful only, but that will change.'

'You are sure?'

Sheven nodded. 'The Emperor sent us his personal doctors to assess matters. Those who died today were the weakest, but the fevers are running hot. More will die in the night and it will continue that way.'

'The cause?'

'They are still arguing that. It is not plague, no matter what the common folk say, but nor is it some simple fever. It is too swift for that; too widespread over the course of a day. From what I've gathered they are leaning towards some sort of ill vapour rising up from the water in the night. The fear is that the breath of those stricken could infect everyone nearby. The doctors are frightened, truly fearful for what tomorrow may bring.'

'They want us to quarantine the entire city?' Rhe asked. 'Or perhaps close the bridges to the Imperial Island and pretend the Crescent isn't easily crossed by boat?'

'They are frightened for the population; there has been a suggestion of moving those who are ill into quarantine to protect the rest.'

Rhe frowned. 'Moving them? Where could possibly suit such a large number of ill people? We would need an army of doctors.'

'A suggestion has been made,' Sheven said, distaste dripping from his words.

It didn't take Rhe long to realise why. 'The goshe,' he said flatly. 'They comprise the greater part of doctors in this city. They are the ones willing to care for the sick – and they are the ones with a leper colony and sanatorium five miles off-shore.'

Sheven growled some form of agreement. 'One Imperial lady raised the idea with the Emperor at court – Princess Kerata. You've seen her before.'

'The An-Goshe, she was part of their delegation. Meanwhile, our numbers are wholly occupied by this fever and the demons that accompany it. We are unable to pursue our investigation of the goshe, leaving this Father Jehq and his conspirators free.'

'Don't forget the favour they might win with the Emperor,' Sheven added sourly.

'The timing cannot be a coincidence, but leaving aside how they managed such a thing – to what purpose is this all?'

'Investigator Narin had not been able to discover that from the turncoat?'

'Narin!' Rhe gasped. 'You've not spoken to him yourself today? Has there not been any word from him, from any of them?'

Sheven shook his bald head. 'None, nothing since they disappeared into Coldcliffs.'

Rhe nodded. 'I suspect running to Lord Vanden Wyvern was always a feint for the sake of informers in our ranks.' *And given the girl's story, the last thing we need is a fight on the streets of Dragon – magic-enhanced goshe being seen by an Astaren agent. This is a test of the Emperor's law; it does not need a bloodbath to match the Ebalee Trading Company.*

'I had still hoped to hear from Narin by now. This turncoat goshe might yet be able to provide us with something to unravel this mystery.'

'I trust Narin,' Rhe said plainly, 'he will find us when he can.' *I may not trust the tattooist, but like us not he'll see the other three safely through this.*

'And until then?' Sheven sounded like a tired old man for the first time Rhe could remember. 'What is our plan?'

'The Emperor approves of this goshe suggestion?'

'He does. Lord ald Har could provide no sufficient reason to refuse it.'

'Then we cannot waste our strength fighting it. Order on the streets of the city is our priority, whether or not the goshe have caused this to distract us. In the meantime, we must have faith in Narin that he can uncover what lies at the heart of all this.'

'Faith?' spluttered the Law Master, as though he were warrior caste rather than religious.

Lawbringer Rhe inclined his head. 'Narin will resurface, or they are all dead and our leads died with them. I have faith in the man,' he said, adding in his mind, *and faith in his secret Astaren helper.* 'He will not fail us, but until then, faith must serve.'

CHAPTER 22

He saw her in the cell, naked. Her rich, brown skin glistened with sweat and blood. She hung just as he had; arms bound and stretched up, head sagging. Her hair fell limply across her face. Her breasts were marred by cuts, the small swell of her belly battered and bruised. A trail of blood led down the inside of her thighs and Narin tried to scream, but no sound would come. He looked down at himself and saw he was clothed and free. A goshe mask covered his face and his gloves were stained with blood. Still the screams stayed in his head, unable to break out to the dream-world beyond.

Narin blinked, wincing at the light above him. Through bleary eyes he looked up at an unfamiliar ceiling and gingerly lifted his head. He was in a narrow room, barely large enough for the bed he lay on and a chair currently occupied by Enchei. On a single shelf was the candle that provided the room's only light. Through the half-shuttered window he could see it was dark outside. The occasional spatter of rain made it through the gap and onto the bare wooden floor.

'How's the pain?' Enchei grunted, looking up.

Narin tried to roll on his side, his bruised and burned body protesting mightily. 'Hurts,' he croaked.

'Aye well, that's what happens. Should be starting to fade now, though.'

'Why?'

Enchei's expression was something between a grimace and a grin, but Narin couldn't tell which. 'Worked my arts on you. It ain't going to stop the pain, but it'll fool your mind into mostly ignoring it a while.'

'How long?'

'Couple of days. There's a payoff waiting at the end, I promise you that, but that's all I can offer.'

'It'll do. That's long enough.'

Enchei leaned forward. 'You sound angry. That's good, hold on to that.'

With a hiss and a gasp Narin eased himself a little more upright. 'Angry?' he echoed with what little force he could muster. 'They tortured me. I shit myself with the pain, screamed myself hoarse and they didn't stop. And you think I'm angry? Piss on you.'

'Trust me boy, angry's as good as it gets. Something like that can break a man, leave him a wreck, so be glad at what you've still got.'

'Glad?' Narin coughed, gingerly tugging aside the blanket that covered him to look down at his torso and legs. His stomach lurched at the memory but in the end there was nothing much for him to see; thin bands of white bandage covering each of the five worst areas of hurt. 'Is it bad?'

'Not so bad – the pain'll have been worse than the damage. They didn't focus on one part, just burned fresh patches o' skin for each question they had, it seemed. A doctor'd tell you to stay off your feet for a while to come, but I don't think you got the option there.'

Narin glanced over at the window. 'How long until dawn?'

'A few hours yet. Time enough to talk then catch another few hours before the streets get busy and we can move you.'

'Talk?' Narin eased back against the head of the bed. His muscles felt weak and shaky, the sour feeling of fear in his stomach making him want to retch.

Enchei sat back again, looking down as he fumbled with his pipe. 'Aye. Before anything else we need to talk.'

Narin didn't say anything but the older man didn't seem to expect him to, and busied himself a while until the pipe was lit. Eyes still lowered, Enchei's voice dropped when at last he did continue.

'Torture makes every man talk,' he said at last, almost reluctantly.

'I don't need this speech,' Narin growled.

'You ain't getting it, boy,' Enchei snapped. 'They did some shit to you and that's for another day. I'm just saying – you told 'em something and we need to know what before we go further. No matter what it was, we need to know. I'm in this fight to the end, that's how I'm made, but if they know my secrets I need to hear it just as I need to know what you told 'em about Irato and Kesh.'

There was a long silence. Narin stared at the wall, completely still despite the crash and howls echoing through his bones. The sickening crackle of the goshe's lightning, the pain that blinded him and the heavy blows that had rocked his body.

'Hey! Stay with me now,' Enchei commanded. 'There's no time for remembering, not yet. Talk.'

A surge of revulsion and hatred for his aging friend washed through Narin. He found himself drawing his arms and legs protectively up to his body, the urge to retch building, but Enchei did nothing in response and eventually Narin relaxed – gaze fixed on Enchei's weather-worn face.

'Talk,' Narin said, almost choking on the word. 'I've had enough of that for a lifetime.'

Enchei nodded. 'Fair enough. You tell me where I go wrong, then. You told 'em how you found Irato and how his memory got wiped away. You told 'em about Lord Shield taking an interest. You told 'em about Kesh, how she got involved, about the foxes that saved her.' He took a deep breath. 'You told 'em about me—'

At that Narin shook his head. The Investigator was watching Enchei intently, his fists curled tight around the blanket as though fighting the urge to flee.

'You didn't tell them about me?' Enchei said slowly. 'That's the bit you kept back.'

'I ….' Narin coughed. 'I called out Kine's name – they'd given me something and I dreamed of her. When I woke they asked who she was, threatened her.'

'And they made you hate 'em – made you want to beat 'em. So you held out as long as you could and made damn sure you kept one thing back.' Enchei nodded with understanding. 'You told 'em we didn't know what their plan was, that we only had a few guesses and half-baked ideas; enough to make sure they didn't run and hide. Enough to think they could still win at this game. And you held back something that could really hurt them.'

'I'm going to kill them,' Narin croaked, hands shaking with both rage and terror. 'All of them.'

Enchei scowled. 'You're sounding like a man with nothing to lose there and that ain't healthy. Being determined to die for the cause ain't the best way to win – it's the best way to die.'

'I've got nothing,' Narin said in response. He gestured to his feet, the bruises and cuts on his body. 'Only Kine and the baby matter. I'll never be a father to it, I realise that now. Even if we get Kine out,

310

Lord Vanden will never let an heir go if it's a boy, never let a girl live. It'll never be mine, but if these goshe win it might be dead before it's ever born.'

'You know,' Enchei said eventually, 'I never thought of you as some cold-hand gambler. You're an honest lad at heart, brought up well and not a cruel bone in your body.' His expression was a twisted smile. 'But you've just thrown the stars there, haven't you? Told them what you needed to ensure it's all or nothing now. They make their play and we'll be trying to screw it all up – that's why you told 'em everything but what I am.'

'I want to kill them all.' The passion in his voice surprised Narin, but Enchei only nodded sagely.

'Maybe they did break you a bit,' the tattooist said, 'just enough to make some sharp edges.'

Narin looked away, eyes blurring as exhaustion crept up on him.

'Get some rest,' Enchei suggested, seeing the change in Narin. 'There's a pair o' blades under your bed, case you want 'em. I'll be back with some food after sun-up. Need to go see what the new day brings us.'

Narin managed a nod and Enchei left, carefully shutting the door behind him. The Investigator stared after him then, with some difficulty, dragged the chair towards the door and wedged it as best he could under the latch. That done he sank back down onto the bed and wrapped himself around the blanket, curled up at the end of the bed. Unable to close his eyes, Narin just stared at the wall until the tears crept out and tiny shudders went through his body.

'Whatever it takes,' he whispered to the empty room. 'I'll kill them.'

Lawbringer Rhe jerked awake, hand reaching for a pistol before he had registered where he was. He lay in a warehouse between two stacks of crates on a clear patch of flagstones. With only a blanket underneath him, his back protested as he moved but insistent voices cut through the confusion of sleep. Grainy light filtered through the air and told him it was daytime, but nothing more.

'He's asleep – you'll wait.'

'Bugger that, my message's important. He'll want it now.'

Rhe frowned, trying to fit faces to the indistinct voices he could hear. He sat up and leaned back against a crate, casting around for a moment for his pistols only to find them where he'd left them. The double-sheath hung from a nail that protruded from one of the crates, just beside his head.

'You will step back,' the first voice said angrily. Investigator Soral, Rhe realised.

The yellow-eyed woman had been utterly fearless the previous night, had revelled in their hunt – much to Rhe's surprise. A natural thief-taker she was not. Clearly, Soral had joined the Lawbringers for some other reason, because she was far more of a warrior than Rhe. It was the victory she lived for, the crash of battle echoing in her head.

'Gonna shoot an unarmed man?' the messenger asked scornfully. 'Wouldn't want my blood to stain your honour now, the stuff's difficult to get out at the best of times.'

Rhe grunted and rose. That was Enchei, the tattooist friend of Narin's. Even if he'd not recognised the voice, Rhe could think of no other low-born so happily disrespectful of a warrior caste. He shook out the jacket he'd been sleeping under and pulled it on.

'Tell you what, Siresse, how's about we wake Rhe and ask him? If he doesn't want to hear my news as soon as possible, you can give me the kicking I so richly deserve.'

'Soral!' Rhe called, realising he needed to interject before she drew a weapon. Whichever way that went, it wouldn't end well.

He rounded the crates and advanced toward the warehouse door. On either side of him were Lawbringers and Investigators, most scowling up at the intruder whose raised voice had interrupted their sleep. 'Investigator, I am awake now, so I will see him.' He pointed at Enchei. 'You – outside.'

They went out into the light, leaving Soral to shut the door behind them and the rest to get back to sleep. They had all worked hard that night and the day would bring work enough that an hour more sleep would be precious. The morning was dull and grey, drizzle falling on the pair as they walked to the water's edge. The warehouse had been commandeered for the night as useful space near the Palace of Law, serving as the hub for Rhe's demon-hunting bands.

'Adopt a more respectful tone towards your superiors,' Rhe ordered Enchei once they were out of earshot of anyone. 'Your background does not give you licence to insult – unless you are operating openly here, you will play the role of your allotted caste.'

312

'I've only got one tone, if she don't like it that's tough for her. We got more important things to talk about right now.'

The Lawbringer shook his head. 'No. We stand for the Emperor's law; we protect the society of his Empire. You will conform to it or you will have me to deal with.'

Enchei coughed in surprise. 'That's a threat, is it?'

'A statement of fact. I have no interest in what you are or what you once were; the law remains the same. This goshe business, demons, plague – you and your friend Narin. You are all subject to the law of the Imperial City and anyone who defies that must know I will come for them. This is the certainty the Lawbringers offer.'

'And that's why you've not called in the troops?' Enchei asked. 'Gods – it's pride, isn't it, you want to deal with this yourself. You want the Lawbringers to have a victory of their own. No matter that the goshe have forbidden magics at their disposal, you're determined to keep House Dragon out of it.'

'We are either the authority in this city, or an irrelevance.' Rhe stared straight into Enchei's eyes. 'I will die before I give up any such authority and the law applies to you as it does anyone else. Know that I will treat you no differently, should you defy that authority.'

Enchei didn't speak for a moment, the two men staring each other down, before he snorted and shook his head sadly.

'Pity the fools who follow a fanatic,' he growled. 'Aye, I believe you – and I believe you'll not flinch at the cost. Can we get back to the damn point now?'

'Narin sends word? Our information is incomplete, but there is talk of an Investigator being kidnapped in Coldcliffs.'

'He's safe now, resting up. They gave him a fair beating trying to find out what we know – what Irato told us.'

'So now they are aware of how little that is and can pursue their goals without fear that we'll be there ahead of them?'

'If you want to be a little ray of sunshine about it, sure,' Enchei sniffed. 'One thing I've found over the years though; careful plans tend to be delicate. Some ignorant bastard wading blindly into the middle of it tends to screw everything up as completely as informed opposition.'

'That is your plan? To wade in blindly and hope you get in the way?'

Enchei cocked his head. 'Had someone else in mind for the ignorant bastard, but close enough.'

'So you want our assistance?'

The older man looked away, east towards the sun as it fought to break through the clouds. 'Now there's a question,' he said.

'What do you mean?'

'Narin says there are goshe informants within your ranks.'

Rhe stiffened. 'Are you saying you cannot trust us with you plans?'

'Worth considering, don't you reckon? Now, they might realise they're giving themselves away by passing on any more information, but you've seen yourself that some are willing to sacrifice themselves for the cause.' Enchei hawked and spat a ball of phlegm into the water. 'But they don't even have to do that; they could just muddy the waters and hamper any response when the critical time comes.'

The Lawbringer was quiet a long time, realising the truth in Enchei's words. 'We are not an army,' he said finally. 'There is no clear chain of command. A few traitor Lawbringers could indeed sow confusion with only modest effort.'

'There anyone on the Vanguard council you can trust completely?'

'Yes, Law Master Sheven certainly – and of course the Lord Martial.'

'Will they take you at your word? Evidence is in short supply at the moment.'

'I believe so.'

'Good. It might be Narin can get some help at court too, find out if there's anyone trying to put pressure on you there.'

'You cannot trust the court – the goshe have already been making moves there.'

'How?' Enchei demanded.

'This sickness sweeping the city, I don't know whether the goshe started it, but they're keen to get involved. They're making every effort to be the ones tasked with caring for the sick.'

'What's happened?'

'A suggestion has been made to the Emperor, one supported by his doctors. The sick are to be transported to Confessor's Island to reduce the risk of infection to the rest of the city.'

'Their leper colony? But what do they gain from that?'

Rhe shook his head. 'I do not know, but it cannot be a coincidence. With what you say, I will ask the Law Master to ensure we're involved as much as possible. If he is supervising, perhaps he can discern their intentions and frustrate them a little – enough to buy you time to find out their goal.'

'Sound enough,' Enchei nodded. 'What about these demons I've been hearing about? They the source of the sickness?'

'I cannot tell, but they do not seem anything more than monsters. I fail to see how they could carry out instructions and those of us hunting them are not yet sick. The monsters are moving through affected and unaffected areas alike, but the sickness has been kept to clear pockets for the time being.'

'So they're a distraction, something to keep you busy – you personally, perhaps. They know Narin's your protégé, just as the whole city knows you'd be the one leading any sort of demon-hunt on these streets.'

The suggestion startled Rhe. It made sense, yet he hadn't even considered it as he went about his duty.

'Perhaps I am easier to confound than I had realised.'

Enchei grinned and nudged him with an elbow. 'Don't worry, happens to the best of us! Right I'm away. Kesh and Irato will be waiting for news.'

Rhe watched the man set off towards a boat-station, where a handful of watermen lounged by their craft, waiting for the first fare of the day. For a moment the whole world seemed to recede from view; Enchei and the buildings behind him blurring into nothingness. All that remained was the flow of the Crescent at his feet and the rush of blood in his ears.

He felt adrift and unsteady, suddenly frozen with indecision – a rare sensation in his structured, unequivocal life. Then it faded and he found himself staring across the glittering waters of the Crescent. The scent of saltwater and wood smoke drifted over him, prompting Rhe to turn into the wind and look to the eyrie palazzos of Eagle District atop the jutting cliffs on the far shore.

'A distraction?' he muttered. 'Perhaps so. But if I ignore it, how many deaths might be on my head?'

Rhe sat down, the lonely cries of seabirds in his ears and the water of the Crescent lapping against his boots. There was a broken piece of stone nearby and he picked it up, turned it over in his fingers for a while. It was nothing remarkable, just a fissured chunk of rock, smooth on one side. Once part of something larger, some constituent piece of the city, now useless.

He tossed the fragment into the water, watched it be swallowed up by the Crescent and headed back inland towards the Palace of Law.

*

Kesh stood at the door as Enchei headed off down the street, his coat flapping in the breeze that rushed off the sea. Once he was out of sight she bolted the door shut and returned to the back room where Irato waited with the owner of the smokehouse.

Enchei's friend was a tiny woman of local extraction called Pirish who had apparently run the smokehouse single-handedly for decades. Her face was a mass of wrinkles and her hair perfectly white, but she'd carried long heavy racks of smoked fish with as much ease as Irato.

'So you're safe then,' Pirish commented. 'That's good news.'

Kesh frowned and flopped back into the seat she'd been occupying for half of the morning. 'Not quite safe,' she said at last, 'but not hunted at least.'

'So don't go knockin' on the nearest Shure gate, easy enough.' Pirish shrugged. 'Don't expect you'll be spendin' much time on the streets today anyways. Sounds like it's gettin' worse out there.'

Kesh glanced back at the door she'd just closed and nodded. Caught up in their own troubles, they'd still seen the fear taking hold in the city. Even unaffected districts were tense, with strangers being treated to hostile looks from nobles and peasants alike.

'And this city's so bloody divided, the goshe are the ones the Emperor turns to for help.'

'This ain't the Emperor's fault,' Pirish said sharply, 'and now ain't the time for blame.'

'I know,' Kesh said, raising a hand to acknowledge the old woman's point. 'I'm just trying to work out what to do about it all.'

Pirish turned to Irato. 'How 'bout you? Ideas?'

The former goshe was sat in the corner, still and silent as usual. He seemed to jerk awake from a trance as Pirish directed the question at him, but when he opened his mouth he had nothing to say.

'Come on, boy,' she urged. 'They emptied your memories, not your wits, right?'

'I …' He nodded. 'Sorry. Still finding it hard to think, my head's filled with fog all the time. I can hear what you're saying, understand it too, but it doesn't go further in till you catch me out like that.'

'Well, time to think,' Pirish concluded, sitting back in her ancient, battered armchair.

The back room was a tiny space clustered around a tiny black stove; little more than an alcove from which a narrow stair rose to Pirish's private rooms above. A packing crate served as a table, around which a handful of mismatched chairs were clustered.

'It, ah – we're still not safe,' Irato said slowly. The blunt lines of his head were accentuated as he struggled to form his thoughts, reminding Kesh that he was a fighter still – that she could direct him to act more easily than she could expect decisions from the man. 'Kesh maybe, I doubt any of them got a good look at her face, but Narin and I need to keep out of sight.'

'None of us are safe if we don't stop them,' Kesh asserted angrily. 'Enchei reckons this sickness is part of the goshe plan and it sounds like they're keen to transport people to their leper colony – a long way from prying eyes. How about rather than hiding here we go back to the docks, see what gossip's going round the taverns?'

'You think you can do it without being seen? What about me?'

Kesh looked Irato up and down. Her feelings towards the man were a strange conflict of hatred and sympathy, but beyond either of those she felt there was a debt between them. Irato had said he wanted to atone for his role in Emari's death and a burning part of Kesh's heart wanted to make sure he did exactly that.

'You're coming with me. You need someone to do your thinking for you, fine. You're doing what I say and when I say it, understood?'

She felt a moment of contempt when he nodded his head immediately, unthinkingly obeying like a trained dog. But then she steeled her heart against it – Irato was a killer, most likely, had been a killer until the night Narin had found him. If he ran risks doing as she ordered, it was no different to the way he'd been living before and that was the penance her grief demanded.

'Goin' ta disguise him as a woman?' Pirish said with a cackle. 'You're easy enough to hide among the crowd, this one … not so much.'

Kesh hesitated. 'Good point. Got any suggestions?'

Pirish stood and looked down at Irato, cocking her head to one side as she thought. 'Shave his head, trim that excuse for a beard – mebbe we could stain his skin too. I know some leatherworkers and tanners; they might have something that'll stain him darker than he is now. Won't smell good, but like as not folk'll think it's some plague-preventative.'

Kesh also rose and went to where she'd left her few belongings. As soon as they'd reached the smokehouse she'd removed the gauntlets and shirt Enchei had given her, pulling off everything that felt constraining on her body. She reluctantly pulled on the shirt of thin, steel plates, belted the knife sheaths to her waist and covered it all with her jacket. That done she turned to Pirish.

'Do you have a shawl I could borrow? A scarf for my hair, maybe?'

The old woman nodded and headed for the stairs. 'Aye, easy enough. All gettin' added to the favour Enchei now owes me anyways.'

'You're still leaving right now?' Irato asked.

'Yes – I can't go straight to the dockworkers I know, they spend half the day on the wharves in plain view of everyone. So if I'm to find out anything useful, I need to be leaving messages with folk I can trust and that'll take longer.'

'How will I find you?'

'There's a thieves' den in the Harbour Warrant, tavern called the Black Bat. It's north off the main road, out towards the furthest tip. You won't get any trouble there, none you can't handle so long as you don't start it. The Lawbringers don't bother with the place, though, so keep an eye out. I'll find you there.'

Once Pirish had fetched a shawl and scarf for her, Kesh headed out through the smokehouse's workroom and back to the street. As she opened the door the sun broke through the clouds and bathed the street in golden light. Kesh squinted up at the sky as she finished tying the scarf. There was a string of bulky clouds massing in the sky and the wind was bringing forbidding grey bulges in across the mainland.

This sunshine won't last long, she thought as she set off, head low and aiming for the familiar streets of home. *Might be the dockers'll beat me to their favourite pubs. I could do with a bit of luck for a change.*

'There you are,' Narin said, dropping his knife on the bed. 'I was starting to wonder.'

Enchei stood in the doorway and looked Narin up and down, a bundle of fresh clothes in his hands. 'Feeling better, then?'

Narin looked down at his body. He was half-undressed, wearing nothing more than underclothes and half a dozen bandages. His skin was pale and blotchy with bruising and he hadn't yet brought himself to investigate what his wounds looked like.

'Better,' Narin said hesitantly, as though fearing to tempt fate. 'Better than I should be, that's for sure.'

'Aye, well, you can thank me later.' Enchei closed the door behind him before depositing the clothes on a spare chair. He stood in the middle of the room and removed a pair of weapons from his coat pockets before sitting – a short, brass-banded baton and his short-sword. 'Just remember there's a price. You'll crash like an addict in a few days and think your head's gonna burst.'

'But until then, I won't feel the pain?'

'Most o' the pain,' Enchei corrected. 'But you'll still be tired and weak, still do your body damage if you work the injured parts too much.'

'Is this shaman work or the magic you learned, ah, after?'

The tattooist shrugged off his coat and went to sit. 'There's a difference?'

'I don't know, that's why I'm asking.'

'Just be glad it works.'

Narin didn't speak for a while and merely stared at Enchei. The older man weathered the look blankly until Narin gave up. 'Fine, keep your secrets; we've got better things to do.'

'Aye, so we do.'

Enchei launched into a quick description of Rhe's activities and the news of the sickness flowering in various corners of the city. When he got to the suggestion of the woman from the An-Goshe council, Narin's face darkened as he guessed the rest.

'What's the betting,' he started slowly, 'that if Lawbringer Rhe organised a search party of that island, he'd be recalled before he could hunt down Father Jehq? Assuming the man's even there.'

'Pretty damn good, I'd guess – and the only way we could find out is by forcing the matter. At which point we could be hamstrung at the vital moment.'

Narin stood up suddenly, wincing as he stretched burned patches of skin. 'There's a way!' he gasped, reaching out to steady himself on the back of a chair.

'What? How? Hey, careful there, you're still weak, remember?'

'That bastard Imperial!' Narin continued once he'd caught his breath a little. 'Remember Prince Sorote of the Office of the Catacombs? He's a power-broker and collector of secrets. Before a few days back, membership of the goshe wasn't something we had a problem with – it probably wasn't such a closely-guarded secret then and even if it was, he might be able to give us an idea of what we're dealing with. He must have heard the discussion at the Emperor's court, witnessed what sort of support they might have.'

Enchei urged Narin back down onto the bed. 'Aye, you could be onto something there. Puts you even deeper into his pocket, mind.'

'What – more so than knowing a secret that could get me murdered within a few hours? That's a risk I'm happy to take.'

'So I see.' Enchei stood for a moment, frowning down at Narin as he thought. 'It might give us an idea of what we're contending with, but let's hope Kesh can find out some of what's going on at that island.'

'What do you mean?'

'Said she'd be working her contacts in the harbour, hunting for clues about what the goshe are up to if this island is the focus of their plans. Anything they're planning there, they'll have to ferry all they need over from the city and they'll need seagoing ships to do it, I expect. That means the Harbour Warrant, unless they've got some deal with House Leviathan to use their docks and that's unlikely.'

'You've sent her out to spy?' Narin demanded. 'Since when does she have contacts rather than friends?'

Enchei snorted. 'Sorry, habit there. Aye, she's got friends in the warrant, folk who're likely to trust someone they've known their whole lives. And no I didn't send her out to spy. I'm amazed the girl's patience for hiding out lasted this long, in all honesty. In any case, we need to know more before we can do anything to stop these bastards and she's as much a part of it as we are. You need to lose some of that chivalry o' yours or you'll trip over it before this is through.'

'She's a civilian,' Narin protested. 'She's not ready to be part of this fight!'

'So're you in my eyes, remember that. She's got a good head on her shoulders, does Kesh, and there's plenty o' risk to go around. She can take her fair share if she wants, I ain't askin' her to kick down the door of the nearest Shure.'

'You think she can find out what the goshe are up to just by asking sailors?'

Enchei shook his head. 'No, but she might be able to provide another piece of the puzzle. We know some, might be we can guess enough o' the rest.'

'What do you mean?'

'Well, we know they stole something from the fox-spirits somehow, whether it was a secret or an object. We know Irato's memories got scrubbed away by this Moon's Artifice, we know he and others like him were probably dosing babies with the same stuff – so they were doing something similar to their memories. It doesn't affect basic things like how to walk, stuff anyone needs to be useful, but it does clear out space in their heads. Could mean they're ready to be controlled by magic, could be they're ready to have some demon hide inside their heads, or most likely a dozen other things too. Point is – we don't know yet, and we can't guess with what we have.'

'So we need to know why people are being taken to this island,' Narin continued. 'Whether it's a ruse for something else, whether they need the people – whether the sick will wake up with no memories either. Oh Gods!'

Enchei looked grim. 'Aye, could be a thousand or more folk as good as dead to their families already. I ain't happy about letting Irato near his former comrades in case they can exert some power over him, some magic I've never seen before. If this came from demons it might be different to anything any Astaren has seen before!'

Narin shook his head and reached for his clothes. It was a struggle, but after a moment Enchei went to help him dress in the clean clothes and ease on his boots. The more Narin moved the more he felt the bruises deep in his flesh – some of the fainter patches of discoloration overlaying an echo of pain that seemed to radiate out from the bone. By contrast, his largest and darkest bruise, the one over his ribs that surrounded a burn, was no more than tender. Narin didn't want to know what it would be like after Enchei's efforts wore off, however.

'You ever been to the goshe island?' Enchei asked as he pulled Narin's jacket on over his shoulders.

Narin shook his head. 'I doubt any Lawbringer has in years, why bother? It's a misshapen lump a mile or two across. I've seen it from a boat – the leper colony at one end, in the shadow of the hill, and the goshe sanatorium at the other. Maybe a few hundred people live there in total and that's including the patients of both.'

'So a nice, private space for them to get up to anything they fancy? And probably cliffs around most of the edges making it easy to defend.'

'Close enough.'

'That'll be fun, then.'

CHAPTER 23

The Imperial City is comprised of eleven self-governing districts – one for each of the Great Houses plus the Imperial Island – and another nine are administrated warrants. When dividing up what was left after the Ten Day War, the Great Houses ignored the ruined sections within the old city boundary and disputes prevented any correction of the oversight. As a result, some conquered territory fell back under Imperial control. It seems lawyers can succeed where the Imperial Army failed.

From A *History* by Ayel Sorote

A sunset of outrageous glory crowned the western horizon as Kesh left the tavern. Huge layers of cloud were stacked across the sky, bands of red, orange and pink overlaying a golden haze where the sea boiled into the sky. The whole street was bathed in an orange twilight and for a moment Kesh was dazzled by the low light, unable to make out the shapes of the shadows behind it. Her fingers closed around the hilt of her dagger, but then she saw the street was almost empty and relaxed again.

The sickness had taken a firm grip on the eastern flank of the warrant, she now knew. Whole streets were near-silent as most of their inhabitants lay abed, wracked with the fever. Some had died, according to tavern gossip. Rumour said the Lawbringers were poised to close down sections of the city, or order every eatery and tavern shut to limit infections, but Kesh had her doubts. The clusters of infected streets were spread across the city with no pattern she could see, but clearly it was too wide-ranging for any efforts at containment to work.

Stars in Heaven – even this goshe quarantine idea is better, Kesh realised glumly as she set off into the sunset, head bowed against the glare of evening.

She was on a wide avenue set behind the warehouses that overlooked the harbour wharves. On her left were gated yards and workrooms while down the right-hand side was as varied a display of eateries, shops and taverns as could be seen across the city. She was not far from her home but resisted the urge to turn and crane her neck around these squat buildings for the outcrop it sat on.

Just a glimpse earlier had been enough. Without lamps to illuminate it, the boarding house had been a dead silhouette against the deep blue sky. Kesh had dragged her gaze away before she had a chance to see what state it was in – whether it was shuttered-up or ransacked, whole or a burnt-out husk.

'Eyes on the water ahead,' she muttered as she walked down the centre of the near-deserted street, 'nothing pretty in the wake.'

She couldn't remember where she'd first heard those words, but now they echoed in her father's voice at the back of Kesh's mind. Before she could get lost in her memories of the lost, however, a flash of movement in the shadows caught her eye.

Kesh stopped, half-drawing her knife before she remembered she was in the middle of an open street and trying not to attract attention. Unusually empty it might be, the avenue was a much-used one and it was unlikely she'd be alone there for long. She checked behind her, back down the street, but aside from a handful of figures loitering outside a card-house, there was no one there.

Again she caught a flicker of something pale in the dark and this time she followed the movement to a stack of barrels outside a high-fenced yard. Kesh took a step closer, ready to draw her knife. As though in response to the threat, a scuffle of movement came from behind the barrel and a bone-white tail swept briefly through the air.

Kesh relaxed a touch and took another step forward. A dart-shaped head peered around the barrel at her, eyes completely black. A russet streak ran from between the fox's eyes and back over its pale head. Quite different to the rusty-red foxes she'd seen before, Kesh was momentarily transfixed by the sight. In the twilight the pale fox seemed to shine with an ominous light. Though she could see no ghost-spirit around it, Kesh was certain this was no chance sighting.

'Hello demon,' Kesh whispered as the creature stared at her, unblinking. 'Have you been watching over me all this time?'

The fox-demon tensed fractionally, lowering its head but never breaking eye contact. Whether it was a response to her words or something else, Kesh did not know, but she found herself holding her breath as she waited. The fox took a delicate step out from behind the barrel, affording Kesh sight of a greyish ruff of fur around its throat, but then it turned and vanished from view. When she went to follow it, Kesh saw only a blank space in the shadows and felt a slight shiver run down her neck. As before, when she'd seen one in the street in Moon District, the fox had simply disappeared from sight with an ease that seemed far from natural.

Remember, Kesh warned herself, *they're demons. Whether or not they saved you once, they're not of our world.*

She looked around, trying to see any possible paths of escape, before realising a pair of men were advancing up the street towards her. Keen to be moving before they came close, Kesh gave the barrels a final look and continued on her way.

The street began to taper as she left the more prosperous parts behind and neared the furthest point of the Harbour Warrant. All remained quiet – fear of the sickness had ensured that – but Kesh realised she hadn't seen plague-symbols in a while. She hesitated and checked around, casting her mind back to the last time she'd seen them. Enchei had pointed out it was the poorer districts taking the brunt of the illness, as was the usual form, but here she saw nothing of the sort.

Most of the houses in this part were single-storey buildings, huddled close in the lee of the rocky outcrop that deflected the waves of the Inner Sea. A few taller, much older structures punctuated the view and it was below the great sweeping roof of one of those that Kesh spied the tavern that was her final destination. The steep slate roof bowed with age in the centre, the tired walls held up only by a ramshackle collection of buildings that had been tacked onto the sides over the years. Named the Black Bat, it didn't keep the same regular hours as its namesake, but welcomed the daylight as little.

She'd visited it twice in her life; just enough to know you didn't do so lightly and that the interior was a confusing warren where privacy was the order of the day. It was only a childhood friend that had taken her anywhere near the place, but now she found herself hoping he'd been successful in his less-than-legal life.

The windows at the front were shuttered, dim light spilling around the edges and illuminating a crudely-cut bat shape at the centre of the shutter. She pushed open the door and found herself in a cramped hallway a few paces long. A man sat at a counter, shadowed from the candles above her head by a wooden partition she knew contained an improvised portcullis.

'Need something?' the man said with a local drawl, looking her up and down.

'A drink'd be a start,' Kesh replied, determined not to show any fear now.

'You sure, love?' The man was not quite what she'd expected from this place, being clean-shaved and dressed more like a travelling merchant than local thug. He was large, there was no doubt about it, but hardly the sort who'd run to fat after years of hanging around a bar. 'Sure you ain't lost?'

'I'm sure – just after a drink with a friend of mine.'

'And who's that?'

Kesh nodded toward the door facing her. 'Well, two actually. One's waiting here to meet me, a stranger to you, but I'm hoping to find Hirl Jastar.'

That seemed to surprise the man. 'You a friend of Hirl's? How come I've not seen you around here then? Bugger spends more time here than me.'

'I'm not in his line of work.'

The guard chuckled to himself. 'Shame,' he said at last, 'most o' his girls are on the skinny side for my tastes.'

At that Kesh gave a cough of surprise. The last time she'd seen Hirl the man had been a thief, among many other things, but running girls? *Maybe it has been too long. Maybe this was a mistake.*

'He's a pimp now?'

'Must've been a few years since you've seen the boy,' the guard laughed. 'Aye, he's been running girls a year or two now, couple o' boys too I think. Must do well out of it, given he's still allowed to drink here.'

'Well?'

The guard nodded. 'Boss fucking hates pimps,' he explained. 'Most weaselly bunch o' cowards you ever met, I promise, but Hirl pays his money and don't mess up his girls, which sets him apart and keeps him a place at the card tables. Most pimps got a bad fucking temper on 'em – like their discipline a bit too much – but Hirl I never heard gave out anything more than he really needed to.'

Kesh nodded, suppressing the slightly sickened feeling in her gut. Hirl had always been a cocky young man, ready enough with his fists should a challenge present itself, but she hadn't expected this of him.

'Am I getting in then?' she asked quietly.

'Sure, just you be careful in there. Most ain't so friendly as me.'

'I know.'

The guard tilted his body to one side and pressed a pedal hidden behind the counter. Kesh heard a scrape from the other side of the door and nodded her thanks, pushing it open to reveal the dim, smoke-laden main room of the tavern. It occupied much of the original building; an oval bar jutting into the centre of the room with four enclosed booths flanking the door and a spiral stair leading up to a gallery where tables lined the outer wall.

A few faces turned her way, but Kesh knew enough to not show any interest in the patrons. Instead she approached the bar and asked for Hirl as she ordered a drink.

'Never heard of him,' the greasy-haired barman said automatically.

'He's a friend of mine,' Kesh persisted, 'and I know he spends most of his time here.'

The man scowled at her as he pulled a clay bottle from under the counter and poured Kesh a cup of wine.

'You don't look like a friend o' Hirl's.' As he pushed the cup towards her, the man leaned forward. 'This ain't a good place for a scene, girly, you hear me?'

'I hear you,' Kesh replied, determinedly not reacting in any way, despite conflicting urges to flee and punch the man right in his gap-toothed mouth.

A low whistle broke her train of thought and the two of them turned towards one of the booths. In the shadows sat a large man dressed in black – it took Kesh a moment to recognise Irato with a shaved head and brown skin, but when she did she gave him a companionable nod.

'I'm not here for a scene,' she repeated, 'but either way I'm guessing no one wants a stranger wandering through your rooms looking for Hirl, am I right?'

The barman grunted. It wasn't his job to pass messages, but she was right all the same.

'Your name?'

'Kesh.'

'Chane,' he called behind him towards a young woman barely out of childhood. 'Find Hirl – tell him there's a woman called Kesh here to see him.'

The girl, a Wyvern with coffee skin and long flowing hair, bobbed her head and slipped away. Kesh paid for her wine and went to join Irato in his wooden-walled booth.

'Any trouble?' she asked.

He shook his head. 'Just a job offer. They all reckon I'm some hired knife, new to the city and looking for work.'

'Better than thinking you're an easy mark.' Kesh paused for a while and watched Irato stare down at his beer. If she didn't know better she'd have thought he'd been drinking for hours and was planning on finishing the night in the same pose.

'We really need to work on your head, don't we?' Kesh commented.

'What? Why?'

'We're having a conversation, but you just forgot that.'

'You asked me if I'd had any trouble. I didn't.'

Kesh sighed. 'You've been waiting for me here for an hour or more, waiting while I looked up dockers and sailors in four different pubs.'

'Yes.'

'Pity's sake,' Kesh breathed. 'Don't you want to know what I've learned?'

That seemed to wake Irato up a bit, a tangle of confusion and realisation crossing his face before he nodded. 'Anything useful?'

'Not as much as I'd hoped,' Kesh admitted, taking a long swallow of wine. 'The Lawbringers have chartered every ship they can, drafting them all into service to carry the sick out to Confessor's Island. It's hard to tell whether the goshe've been up to anything else round here, but supplies to the island haven't increased. There's a ship that does the run most ascendancies – a local fisherman. They took supplies yesterday, same amount as before, so if they're planning anything it's to be lost in the chaos of tomorrow.'

'Nothing more?'

'I'm hoping Hirl will know if there's anything more.'

'You're friends with a local criminal? Doesn't seem like you.'

'We grew up neighbours; I've known him my whole life. Can't say we're really friends these days, been living different lives, but it might be he'll do us a favour for old times' sake. This bar's owned by a major player in the warrant, this is where the important people drink and talk. Anything Hirl doesn't hear during the day on the wharves, he'll hear at the card tables.'

From across the main room a voice broke the furtive hush. 'Well bugger me sideways with a Stone Dragon's lance!'

Kesh jumped, reaching for her knife on instinct. Irato was standing by the time she regathered her wits and put a hand on his arm. She turned to see a familiar face bearing down upon her, smiling broadly even as he kept a weather eye on Kesh's companion.

'Hirl,' she said, slipping from her seat to greet the newcomer. 'Good to see you again.'

He was bigger than she'd remembered – not much taller than she but significantly broader. Though he was local stock with pale skin and brown hair, Hirl had the build of a House Dragon warrior. He was dressed well, wearing a dark, patterned doublet that had been cut to suit his large frame. In one ear was a trio of diamond studs, the significance of which was lost on Kesh, while on his belt was an ornate dagger. It all added up to a man doing well out of life.

Hirl's massive arms reached out to embrace her, but Irato edged forward and there was a tense moment as the two men faced each other down.

'Easy there, chief,' Hirl murmured, far from intimidated by the taller man. 'This ain't the place to settle whatever business we got, hear me?'

'Hey,' Kesh said, doing her best to push the big goshe back. 'What are you doing?'

'I …' Irato turned to look at her and retreated from her expression. 'I don't know.'

'Well let's sit and be a bit more friendly, eh?'

Hirl waved to the barman. 'Aye, put on your friendly face round here,' he added, sliding onto the bench alongside Kesh. 'Owner tends to do somethin' about faces that don't look so nice.'

A drink was brought over for him and Hirl took a moment to look between Kesh and Irato as he drank.

'So,' he began at last, 'it's been a while, Kesh. How you been keepin'?'

She scowled. 'Not good of late.'

'That why you brought a bodyguard to see an old friend? Some exiled Wyvern warrior to watch your back?'

Kesh gave a start. 'No, that's not it. Hirl – I need your help, but, ah, but I can't tell you too much. I don't mean any disrespect –'

'Disrespect?' Hirl echoed. 'Who do you think I am, Kesh? Some crime-lord you bow and scrape in front of? You're still the girl who kicked me off the harbour wall an' had ta drag me out the water again after.'

She shook her head. 'Sorry, I just didn't … I've not seen you in a year or two. Didn't want to presume too much, and the man on the door said … well. I just wanted to be careful not to treat you like the boy you once were, the one I knew. I don't know much about what you're about these days, but I didn't come here to cause trouble.'

Hirl nodded. 'Fair enough. But you're here now, so tell me what you're into.'

'I can't. It's not even a story I'd know how to tell, but I don't want to spread the danger round any further than I have to.'

'And the bodyguard?'

'Isn't a bodyguard,' she said. 'Hirl this is, ah …'

'Perel,' said Irato slowly as Kesh faltered.

The name sent a shock through Kesh as effectively as if Irato had placed his hand on her chest and unleashed his lightning weapon. She felt herself cringe as she looked into the goshe's eyes. He was focused again, frighteningly so – like he had been when they were fighting his former comrades.

The loss of his memory and uncertainty was eclipsed by some in-built sense. Kesh couldn't tell whether it was natural or something the Moon's Artifice had done, but she recognised the readiness to kill easily enough.

'Sure. Perel it is then,' Hirl drawled. 'So, you're in something together, whatever it is, and you want my help.' He took another long drink and leaned back against the wooden partition of the booth. 'And how can a humble businessman help an old friend?'

'I'm hoping you hear most of what goes on around the docks,' Kesh said. 'I've not been around much these past few days and we run in different circles anyway.'

'Got myself a colourful set o' friends these days, it's true.' Hirl grinned. 'So you want gossip rather than anything that's gonna get in the way of my drinkin'? Sounds easy enough.'

'Thank you.' Kesh hesitated. 'It's, ah, gossip about the goshe I guess. You heard anything around the harbour itself? What they've been up to round here?'

'Goshe?' Hirl's smile faltered slightly. 'We've all been hearing about them. Cut the throat o' some Lawbringer didn't they?'

'They tried,' Irato growled. 'Might be trying again.'

'That's what you got caught up in?' Hirl gasped, briefly the young man she'd known again. 'Bugger me, you really are in some shit then.' He paused and glanced nervously around. 'Hang on, just what damn company you been hangin' around? This ain't a place you just bloody walk into if you're workin' for some o' the names I heard mentioned recently. Shit – bodyguard-man, Perel, whatever your name is. You better not be one of 'em or we're all fuckin' dead, get me?'

'He isn't,' Kesh said hurriedly. 'You want the truth? He's as bad a criminal as anyone here. We've just been dumped into some strange company and we've not got much choice about who keeps us alive at the moment.'

Hirl frowned and took a while to settle again, the cocky grin gone from his face now. 'So you want any gossip about the goshe, or just what they've been up to round here?'

'Round here, but I'll take anything you've got. They're going to be transporting all those who're sick with this fever to their quarantine island. We're thinking they might be using that as a cover for something else – something major. Have you heard about anything strange round these parts at all?'

'Always some crap goin' down round here,' Hirl replied. 'The goshe ain't usually part of it though. Let me think. There was a body in the harbour this mornin', some sailor drowned I heard. Not so unusual that, given the shit they drink, but somethin' I guess. If they're takin' the sick out ta Confessor's Island though, they'll need boats. I've heard nothin' about them hirin' any themselves, not the fishin' fleet or nothin' – just the Lawbringers.'

'That's all?'

'So far's I've heard.' Hirl raised a hand. 'Hold up here a moment. Let me go ask one or two faces out the back. They don't keep social hours, if you see what I mean, charitably keepin' an eye out for sailors at risk o' drownin'. If anythin' strange goes on, cover o' night's the best time for it, no?'

Kesh nodded and Hirl slipped away into the murky gloom again. They had finished their drinks by the time he returned – long enough that Kesh was thankful of Irato's presence. From the looks a few of the patrons had cast in her direction, they knew they had outsiders in their midst.

330

While Enchei might be happy for men to underestimate him in a fight, Kesh was glad Irato looked every bit as tough as he was. Few people would idly pick a fight with him, outsider or not, and it afforded them the space to sit quietly as they waited.

'Miss me?' Hirl asked as he took his seat beside Kesh again.

His swagger had returned a touch now, which she took as a good thing, but Kesh had the sense not to rush her old friend as he called for another drink. As it came, she took out a silver coin to pay for it, thinking it was the least she could do, but Hirl waved it away.

'Don't you worry about that, it didn't cost me anythin' more'n a favour I'm glad to owe anyways.'

'Glad?'

He nodded. 'Got some serious men in this place, some o' the biggest sharks in this part o' the Inner Sea and those who work for 'em. I owe a man somethin' small, he'll come collect one day. You do business with the big fish right, they come around again. I'm workin' my way up, not fightin', and they likes a man happy ta put in an honest day's work. So ta speak, obviously.'

'Any news, then?'

Hirl gestured expansively. 'Wouldn't let down an old friend now, would I? Last night – reckon this is what you were lookin' for.'

'What happened?'

'Well – man I know was takin' a late stroll, keepin' the sailors safe, when he thought he saw a likely candidate. Kept an eye on him from a respectful distance then saw the man had friends. All dressed similar, could easily have been goshe now he comes to reflect on it. Anyways, they had a crate they brought through the streets – big enough to fit a man inside probably, but two of 'em carried it easily.

'They looked jumpy so he gave 'em their space, but reckons he saw them load it on a fishin' boat. Two stayed with it, keepin' watch, but the rest left. Didn't go straight off though, was still there after the dawn tide when all the rest were gone. Which is a bit odd to my mind; it's only goods comin' in that get inspected and taxed. You want to get rid quick, no one'd stop you.'

'Draws attention though,' Kesh said. 'All the fishermen would know it'd headed out early. It's a few miles to the island and the tide's against you, I doubt they'd be back before the rest were around and getting ready to go.'

'If you say so.' Hirl leaned towards her. 'So what was in the crate?'

'No idea,' Kesh said. 'Wish I did, but that's a whole other mystery. Hirl – fancy doing me another favour, one that pays this time?'

The burly man brightened. 'Pays? Depends what we're talkin' here. Reckon I'm out of your price range.'

Kesh smiled and thought of Enchei, sure he had a variety of means beyond his Imperial wages. 'I won't be the one paying,' she assured him, 'but the job's small anyway. I could probably do it myself, but I'd prefer paying over the odds to a man of your connections.'

'Now you're playin' my tune. What's the job?'

'I need a boat, as small as can still make the trip out into the bay. One just a couple of people can manage, waiting somewhere it's not going to get commandeered by people ferrying the sick out to the goshe island.'

Hirl nodded. 'Of the sort that don't get seen so easily after dark too?'

'If you can manage it, yes. Ir— Perel, how much money do you have on you?'

An inspection of their coin-pouches bore a handful of silver pieces and she pushed them towards Hirl. 'To start with,' Kesh explained. 'I can get more brought here for you, just let me know how much you need.'

'How long do you want the boat for?'

'Two nights?' she guessed. 'Maybe three. Tied up and ready to take out whenever we need.'

'It'll cost four times what's on the table, I'd guess. Any lawmen goin' in this boat?' Hirl scowled. 'Might be it's tied up somewhere they don't want Lawbringers ta see.'

'No one looking like the law,' Irato broke in, 'and no one who'll come back to investigate the boathouse after or care about what they see in the meantime. Any comeback will be down on Kesh so we won't be risking it.'

Hirl fixed Kesh with a sharp look. 'You better be good for that, it's my arse too if it doesn't hold. Old friend or no, you get me on the wrong side o' these men and I'll kill you.'

The cold certainty in his voice made Kesh hesitate, but she accepted anyway. Narin would be glad to agree if it helped them all survive the next few days.

'Done then,' Hirl declared, sweeping the coins off the table. 'Give me till midday tomorrow to track someone down. I'll be here lunch tomorrow, come by with the money and I'll tell you where ta go.' He glanced down at their drinks and winked at Kesh. 'Looks like you're both empty. Since I got all the rest o' your money, best you hop it, eh?'

With that the man knocked back the last of his own drink and headed back into the depths of the Black Bat. Kesh and Irato stared at each other across the table a moment longer, then Kesh realised the man was waiting for her again. She sighed and pointed toward the door.

'Come on then, let's go. Don't want anyone on the streets to mistake you for a demon in the darkness, now do we?'

Kesh led the way out, taking care to thank the guard before she left. The street beyond was starlit, a silver sheen from the Gods spread out over the dark ground ahead. She looked up to where Lord Shield's constellation led the Order of Knight across the night sky. Past the zenith was the Order of Empress, half-obscured by narrow phalanxes of cloud. Only three of the circling Ascendants had all their stars clearly visible, the number preferred by diviners.

'Archer,' Kesh whispered to the cold night sky, 'Thief, Assassin. Not a cheering set.'

She took a few steps forward, but faltered as she saw a brief flash of white out the corner of her eye. Kesh turned, but there was nothing to see. She opened her mouth to speak to Irato, emerging from the Black Bat behind her, but he waved her forward down the street.

'Not a good place to linger,' Irato said, pushing gently on her shoulder to urge her on. 'Let's move.'

Kesh stumbled on, her mind fogged by the wine she'd drunk that evening. In her memory a flash of white darted behind a barrel, a narrow face observed her from under a food cart, a rusty pelt darted toward the goshe attacking her.

Kesh gave a gasp, reaching to grab Irato's arm. For a moment her mouth failed her and she just croaked a warning to him. The goshe turned to frown at her just as a ghostly form burst from the shadows.

Irato flinched away from the movement but the demon-spirit drove straight on and swept right through his body. The goshe reeled as though struck, but in the next moment he had his knives drawn.

'Wait!' Kesh cried, but her shout went unheeded.

A rusty-white blur darted forward and Irato turned and slashed in one movement. His blade opened a shallow furrow on the fox's shoulder as it dodged away from his reach, but another was already closing behind him. Kesh saw a white mist appear around it, quickly coalescing into a misshapen wolf-ghost looming large over the fox. Another came forward and she recognised the pale fox she'd seen earlier. Tethered to its body by threads of faint light was another ghost-form – a massive, sleek shape with long, curved teeth she didn't recognise.

'Stop!' Kesh called, stepping between Irato and the demon. 'He's with me.'

Her actions caused both sides to hesitate and Kesh was careful to turn her back on Irato, hands outstretched towards the demon. Its ghostly true form seemed to fold in on itself and became a stream of mist that surged towards Kesh so fast she barely had time to move.

The smoke slipped around her body as though using her as a screen. Kesh heard Irato cry out in alarm – then pain. As she turned Kesh saw the stream coiled around his body like a snake enveloping its prey. The head locked about Irato's face while he frantically tried to tear it away.

The big man wrenched around, flailing at his insubstantial attacker. Kesh took a step forwards to help when suddenly her ears were filled with an unnatural shriek. She gasped and clapped her hands to her ears, realising it was the demon-cry of another fox. Kesh staggered as the fox screamed again and others joined it; a cacophony of noise that seemed to drive sparks down her spine and briefly locked up every muscle in her body.

Irato looked similarly afflicted, shuddering at the demon-cries and still desperately fighting at the spirit wrapped around him. Kesh watched him seem to lose the fight with his attacker as his body went rigid. The twisting cable of mist surged up and forced its way into his mouth. As the last of the mist disappeared down Irato's throat the big goshe crashed to his knees, his expression twisted into some strange mixture of wonder and terror. He knelt there, eyes wide but seeing nothing, before toppling forward to hit the ground face-first.

Abruptly the demon-cries broke off and Kesh found herself staring at Irato lying prone at her feet. He was perfectly still and felt like a dead thing as she rolled him over. The man's eyes were open, staring blankly up at the Gods above, while his stained skin was discoloured and scraped from the fall.

'Irato – can you hear me?' Kesh got no response and, checking around at the foxes, shook his limp body. 'Oh Gods, Irato – wake up! What have you done to him?'

Abruptly, Irato took a long shuddering breath, back arching before he fell down again. Eyes still looking at nothing, face empty of emotion, his lips began to move.

'Empty,' he rasped in a hollow, emotionless voice. 'Gone. A hole in its mind.'

'Irato?' Kesh gasped, edging back.

'No.'

'What? What have you done with him?'

'The thief is here, inside this host,' came the dead reply.

'What are you?' she found herself almost wailing with fear. 'A demon?'

'To your world, we are demons,' the possessed goshe said, still lying flat on its back. 'Spirits of another age, of the time before your kind.'

'Ah – but you can speak my language?'

'The host can. It is not dead but under my control.' Without warning Irato sat upright – the movement stiff and mechanical rather than anything alive. 'This one is not your enemy.'

'No – he ... he was, but he's trying to keep me alive now.'

'We believed you in danger. We were wrong.'

Kesh hesitated. 'That was you, before? When Perel attacked me? The other goshe?'

'We had your scent. We had tracked this one to your home.'

'Thank you,' Kesh said in a quiet voice, fighting back tears. 'Thank you for saving me.'

'You are their enemy. We are their enemy,' Irato said blandly.

'What have you done to him?' Kesh stepped closer and moved around Irato to look the man in the eyes. 'Can you possess anyone?'

Irato got to his feet jerkily and finally focused on Kesh. 'No. This one has been opened to us.'

'Opened?'

'There is a hole in his mind,' the demon replied. 'His memories are gone, removed to make space in his mind. This is what was stolen from us.'

'Space? Space for what?'

'We ride the minds of many creatures, we can move from one to another if they carry certain bloodlines. We have no form of our own, they are our vessels.'

'He's a vessel? For what?'

'For anything with power. His mind is open, he has been prepared.'

335

'For demons?' Kesh shook her head. 'For your kind?'

'We are a voice on the wind; this one has been prepared for thunder.'

'Something bigger than you?' Kesh asked. 'A higher order of demon?'

'Something greater,' Irato confirmed. 'Many of us could inhabit this vessel. Come.'

He spoke louder then and three foxes trotted forward, unwary now. Kesh took a step back and watched the demon-spirits leak out of the foxes like morning mist; three separate trails coiling around Irato's body before slipping silently down his throat.

'Why? Why would the goshe do that?' Kesh asked.

'No human can make use of this,' Irato said by way of answer.

Kesh kept silent, thinking furiously for what it might mean. *This is what was stolen? The ability to empty a mind, to make space for a demon-spirit inside it?*

'What was stolen? A secret or an object?'

'They are the same.'

'With this object they made the poison? Made Moon's Artifice?'

'The poison opened a path in the host's mind. The object can link one path to another, can send spirits down those paths and bind them together.'

'Can …' Kesh started hesitantly, 'can Irato hear me? Can he speak with you in his mind?'

The possessed man closed his eyes and went very still. Kesh felt a flicker of fear run down her spine before Irato seemed to jerk awake again – eyes wide with alarm and panting for breath.

'Blood-lit stars!' the big goshe gasped, 'what happened?'

'Irato, is that you?'

He nodded and roughly rubbed his hands over his face, hissing slightly as he found the scraped skin from when he'd fallen. 'They're quiet for the moment. Gods, I can feel them in my head!' Irato winced and tilted his head one way then the next, as though trying to dislodge water from his ears. He gave up and shuddered.

'Did you hear what it said?'

'Some,' he said with a scowl. 'Was screaming for a while there. Not paying attention to a whole lot to begin with.'

'It told me what the poison had done to you,' Kesh said. She grabbed his arm as though to emphasise her point. 'I think I know what the goshe are up to!'

336

Irato blinked at her, still dazed by the possession. 'You do?'

'I think so,' Kesh said. 'We need to find Enchei and Narin, tell them all this. Ah – demon, can you hear me? Will you come with us to find our friends?'

Irato's face smoothed out, the animation and emotion draining to nothing in seconds. 'We will come.'

'You don't need your fox-vessels?'

'They will follow, but this mind is better suited to us than any animal.'

Kesh nodded and waved Irato forward, starting off down the street as fast as she could. 'Come on then, we don't have much time.'

CHAPTER 24

How the Gods ascended to the heavens remains a closely-guarded secret –
perhaps the greatest secret in the entire Empire. It is said the God-Emperor
and God-Empress studied the millennia-old texts of a long-dead race, excavated
horrors and journeyed far into the uninhabitable Shadowrain forest. Accounts
of the demon-war they fought mere months before their ascension suggest not
all beings were as surprised by this glorious event as their subjects.

From A *History* by Ayel Sorote

Night had fallen by the time Enchei and Narin reached the Imperial
Palace. While it was late, neither thought Prince Sorote of the Office
of the Catacombs was one to keep regular hours. As they asked for
directions it became clear the Emperor had not retired for the evening
either; which meant the entire court and the many hundreds who
served it remained awake as well.

Occupying the north-east corner of the Imperial Island, the Palace
had water on three sides and one grand entrance on its western
flank. A small bridge crossed the canal on its southern flank, but
passage was reserved solely for those of the Imperial caste and senior
Lawbringers. All others entered via an enormous form of portico
thirty yards square that stood like a tower without sides. One hundred
pillars, one for each of the noble houses of the Empire, supported a
convex roof that gathered rainwater in a chamber hidden by ancient
and fantastical decoration.

Narin and Enchei, the former hampered by his injuries, walked under
this remarkable structure and like all other visitors they stopped to
stare at the great complex. The Imperial Palace was divided into four
distinct areas and paths to each of these led off from where they stood.
Ahead was the Great Court, the vast seven-storey building centred

around the Emperor's public throne room; a hundred-yard vaulted hall where all matters of state were presented to young Emperor Sotorian.

Dozens of offices and lesser audience chambers flanked this; rising high around three sides of the throne room's peaked roof like a crown, four slender towers for tines. It was commonly-held that a U-shaped garden had taken root up there in the space between, sheltered by the outer walls, and a small army of gardeners was required to tend it lest the beautiful high windows to the throne room be covered.

The blunt wedge tip of the Great Court was dominated by huge grey doors, embossed with golden suns twice the height of a man, that led into the throne room. Behind that the central block widened to five hundred yards on the far side, with stone tendrils reaching out to the huge wing south of it and great square towers to the north. The tips of the curved rear swept down to become covered bridges that connected it to the Emperor's crescent-shaped residence and the enclosed ground served as a formal garden of renowned magnificence.

Narin had been inside the Great Court only twice in his life, but he knew that each room was no less than twenty feet high and in many cases thirty or forty. Built by a long-dead race, the Palace had never been designed for human proportions and it dwarfed its current inhabitants. It was said that the upper levels of the Great Court, the largest single structure in the entire Empire, were only fitfully used; the proportions and layout of each chamber proving increasingly eccentric as one ascended.

Of the other two remaining paths, the right led to the palazzos of the extended Imperial family. There, a central s-shape extended for a mile down the flank of the entire Palace complex, smaller wings branching organically off and graduations of long sweeping roofs resembling the petals of some twisted flower. The left-hand path was where Enchei and Narin headed – walking into a chaotic tangle of interlinked, overlapping buildings where the Palace administration was housed. Great blocks of ancient stone buildings loomed in rows of four above the mess, a dozen in all and each one large enough to be a lord's keep.

While the Great Houses controlled the greater part of the Empire, there remained trade corridors and disputed territories under the Emperor's authority. The merchant princes and consortiums that had risen to power in these places occasionally possessed the wealth of noble houses, but were careful to preserve the caste structures of the Empire. Ever mindful of their position – and the fate of the massacred

Ebalee Trading Company – they employed brokers from the Imperial caste in their official dealings and maintained permanent trade missions at the Imperial City.

They entered the web of streets and were abruptly presented with a dizzying array of flags unknown to anyone outside the world of trade, well-lit by gas lamps and lanterns hung above every doorway. Almost immediately a handful of lounging children approached them, each one in a knee-length coat of varying styles, but all with the blue collar of the merchant caste.

'Message, sir?' asked the tallest of them. 'Directions maybe?'

'You know the Office of the Catacombs?' Narin said.

'Aye, sir,' the boy of twelve or so replied.

There was a flicker of disappointment on his face as he spoke; clearly Prince Sorote was not a profitable source for the local runners. The boy nudged a younger child beside him, a button-nosed girl with tangled hair.

'She'll take you, sir. It's not far.'

The girl scowled, but didn't argue. With a wave of the hand she trotted off down a darkened side-alley, not looking back to see if they were following. Narin and Enchei exchanged looks and fell in behind, having to hurry to match her pace. The girl didn't wait for them and disappeared through an archway while Narin negotiated a path around two portly merchants dressed as finely as any nobleman. The archway led to a wide, dog-legged boulevard of taverns and eateries that spilled out into the street, but once past those they found themselves walking twisting streets of shuttered buildings, all closed for the day, and soon Narin had lost all track of the path they were taking.

It took them ten minutes on an unnecessarily oblique route through the warren, but at last the girl stopped before a curious square building with a dark slate roof, a dozen yards across and only two storeys high. Lamplight shone around the edges of a shuttered window, but it hardly looked like somewhere an Imperial interested in Lawbringer Rhe would base himself.

'There, sir,' she said, pointing with a grubby finger.

Narin looked sceptically at the small house even as Enchei tossed her a coin and headed to the door. As the girl scampered off, Narin managed a grunt of thanks and joined his friend as the tattooist banged his fist on the closed door.

From inside there was a scrape of furniture then footsteps approaching the door. Without asking who they were, the door was jerked open and a servant stood there, looking them up and down.

'You are not who I expected,' the lean, balding man stated.

'Rarely are,' Enchei said before Narin could speak. 'We're looking for Prince Sorote.'

The servant glanced behind him at something in the room Narin couldn't see. 'For what reason?'

'Is he here?' Enchei continued, ignoring the question. 'If he is, he'll want to see us.'

'Let them in,' called a voice behind the servant. 'Finding out what they want will probably waste less of my time.'

The man stepped back and Narin entered, looking around with surprise as he found himself in a single room with a mezzanine level occupying the farther half. Three heavy oak desks separated by bookcases stood on the left, with the stair to the upper level on the right and a wide cellar entrance at an angle beneath the mezzanine. The doors to the cellar were open, but what Narin found strangest about it was the size of them – each one six inches of wood bound with a dozen fat iron rods.

'Investigator Narin,' called Prince Sorote from the mezzanine, his voice tinged with surprise. 'I must confess, I had not expected you to come visit me so soon.'

'Needs must,' Narin said, one look at the man's face enough to blacken his mood considerably. 'I've got a favour I need to ask of you.'

'Indeed?' Sorote descended to meet them, putting aside a pistol belt as he came and gesturing for the door to be shut behind them. Much to Narin's surprise the servant then retired down into the cellar. 'And who is your friend?'

'Enchei Jen, yer Lordship,' the tattooist gabbled in an obsequious tone.

He advanced on the Imperial in a curiously hunched manner, some comical effort at bowing while he walked. Hands outstretched, Enchei dropped to one knee, head still bowed low, and took the astonished prince by the hand – reverentially kissing the large seal-ring that Sorote sported on his middle finger.

'An honour to be in yer presence, yer Lordship.'

Sorote withdrew his hand and examined the seal-ring with a fastidious sniff. 'Yes, I'm sure it is. And why are you here?'

341

'My Lord Sun,' Narin began, 'you know already the Lawbringers are in conflict with the goshe. This relates to that ongoing situation.'

'I had thought,' Sorote broke in, 'when the law was broken it was simply described as a crime. Or does the size of the goshe order elevate this to a conflict?'

Narin tried not to glower. 'Indeed, my Lord. The exact nature of the crime is, well, difficult to frame in legal terms. The extent, however, makes this not simply a case of hunting down a culprit.'

'This fever gripping the city,' Sorote said, 'and the goshe plan to evacuate the infectious to Confessor's Island. Are they behind the fever? Do you have proof?'

Narin tried not to look surprised as he shook his head. 'We have evidence of very little, and given the situation I hardly know how to gather it without starting a war.'

'Now you have my interest,' Sorote said with a smile. 'Come upstairs and we will discuss it further. Hentern!' he called down to his servant. 'Refreshments for my guests!'

He led them up the stairway to where his own desk was situated, a slender mother-of-pearl- and jet-inlaid antique of the most beautiful craftsmanship – currently piled with papers. Beside it was a second desk unlike any Narin had ever seen. The top was not flat but undulating, eight or nine rows of channels running across it, each a hand-span wide. Nestled in several grooves were stone cylinders about a foot long and covered in tiny symbols.

'What are those?' Enchei breathed in wonder, taking a step towards the cylinders until Prince Sorote pointedly stepped into his way.

'Nothing that concerns you,' he said firmly. 'Ancient research, nothing more. The Office of the Catacombs is dedicated to the study of history.'

'Whose history?' Enchei asked, backing reluctantly off.

Sorote frowned at him and pointed to a pair of chairs, well away from the desk, where the pair could sit. 'Hardly the matter at hand. You have come to speak to me about the goshe?'

Narin glanced at Enchei as they settled into their seats and the tattooist gave an imperceptible nod of the head. The fawning servant routine could easily result in a battering around the head, but it was worth the risk if it afforded Enchei enough time to see whether Sorote was under any sort of influence.

'I have,' Narin said at last, feeling a flush of relief. 'You're a power-broker, you deal in secrets.'

'I hear things,' Sorote corrected, 'due to my rank and connections. But I am a historian by trade, in as much as one of my caste can be said to have a trade.'

'You found out my secrets easily enough.'

Sorote raised an eyebrow in Enchei's direction. 'I take it I can speak openly?'

Narin grunted and the Imperial nodded.

'Very well – influence is currency within the House of the Sun, only a fool would deny it, and Lawbringer Rhe is an influential man. You are in a unique position to influence that man, but as much as anything I seek knowledge – his opinions are closely guarded and I would know whether I have a potential ally in him, for all Rhe disdains politics. I am not the schemer you believe me to be, I merely look at the structure of this Empire with a historian's eye and I would do what I can to strengthen its foundations. We are at a disadvantage to the Great Houses in almost every way; the least we can do is ensure those of the same mind work together.'

Narin shrugged. 'Sounds almost convincing, that,' he said, 'but I think I've lost my faith.'

Prince Sorote narrowed his eyes at the Investigator, taking note of the harder edge to Narin's voice. 'Faith takes many forms, Master Narin. A man can choose to believe – or at least, to choose that something is worth believing in.'

'Right now I'm finding it hard enough to believe I'm going to survive the next few days – but I guess that's not going to stop me trying to, so that's faith of a sort.'

'And you, Master Enchei?' Sorote said. 'What is your part in this? You're no Lawbringer.'

'We're friends,' Enchei said simply. 'No great mystery in it, but I've served an army term or two and ain't scared to fight. Might not be so young now, but I can still give Narin the run-around on the dachan court. Until I feel properly old I'll not stand by while some two-bit gang murders little girls and tries to kill my friends.'

'Little girls?'

'The woman you saw me with at my home, Kesh,' Narin explained. 'Her sister had been poisoned by something a goshe carried, but instead

343

of helping the girl at the free hospital they killed her and sent an assassin after Kesh.'

'And that's why they came after you at your home? To tie up that loose end?'

Sorote broke off as his servant, Hentern, appeared with a tray of glasses and a decanter of wine. Narin waved it away when offered, the distant ache of his injuries enough to dull his wits more than he'd like, but Enchei eagerly accepted and gulped down half a glass in one go. His thirst quenched, or at least the show of low-caste unease performed, the tattooist relaxed. He sat back in his chair, glass dangling idly from his fingers, while he watched Sorote and Narin continue the conversation.

'That is why they came after us – and we suspect they were given our location by someone within the Lawbringers. You've seen the influential members they boast from across the Empire.'

'You are looking to root out the spies? Is that the mission you've been given?'

'I'm not honestly sure what my mission is,' Narin admitted. 'I'm just trying to stay alive and even Rhe agrees that's only going to happen if we stop the goshe from completing whatever they're up to.'

'And what they are up to involves transporting the city's sick to Confessor's Island, judging from the day's discussions at court. Have you been able to work out why? Are they clearing districts of the city? Targeting their enemies with the fever? Casting the blame in a certain direction? Or are these fever victims to be used for something else entirely?'

'We don't know,' Narin said, raising a hand to ward off Sorote's questions. 'But their island stronghold could easily hold the answers we need – the question is, how do we find them?'

'Without spies reporting it or hampering your efforts? So you came to me; a man who is interested in the allegiances and circumstances of the House of the Sun's influential figures.'

'If we can free ourselves to move on the goshe, we might yet prevent whatever it is they're planning. It involves magic and demons, that much I am certain of – if the Astaren were to hear of this it would spark a bloodbath,' Narin said with urgency. 'The goshe have some hold over their members – they obey orders without question, they are being controlled by a small number within their order. The Astaren would kill every goshe they could, but most were infected as children, very likely, and can hardly be blamed for the actions of the few.'

'A bloodbath?' Sorote echoed with astonishment. 'You underestimate them, my friend.'

'What do you mean?'

Sorote gave a weary shake of the head. 'It would spark a bloodbath yes, but only on the first day,' he said gravely. 'Most likely, House Dragon stepping in to massacre anyone who faces them. But that's not the biggest problem – it's the following day we have to worry.'

'Why?'

'Because then, reports of this forbidden magic reach the ears of other Astaren, probably several Great Houses at once. These all bring forces into the city to try and mop up what remaining goshe there are. If there is magic and demons involved, none of them can risk their enemies discovering an advantage that could tip the balance between them. They'll fight over the bodies of goshe and any hospital or building owned by them. Open warfare on the streets of the Imperial City for the first time since the Ten Day War.'

Sorote stood and tossed back the remains of his wine. 'I will help you, Master Narin,' he said, 'if for nothing else than to try and keep this city from catastrophe. I have records of Lawbringers I believe to be members of the goshe, yes, and furthermore I can provide you with a map of Confessor's Island. It will be outdated I am sure, but should give you the lie of the land for any action the Lawbringers might intend.'

Narin stood and bowed to the man, the flicker of bitterness in his stomach lessening slightly. 'Thank you, Prince Sorote,' he said with more formality than his greeting.

'Prince Sorote,' Enchei echoed as he knelt.

'It will take me time to assemble the information,' Sorote said. 'Shall I have it sent to you at the Palace of Law? I have messengers I can trust.'

'Law Master Sheven,' Narin suggested, 'or Lawbringer Rhe – either of those will know what to do with the information.'

'It is not evidence enough to make arrests,' Sorote warned him. 'Whether or not some have committed treasonous acts, proving so will be difficult in the extreme.'

'We'll find a way to make use of it,' Narin promised him, turning towards the exit. 'Stopping them is our first priority – there are hundreds who've been taken by this fever already. Whatever the goshe have planned, we're going to disrupt it.' His face went stony. 'Once that's over, we can worry about arresting whoever's left.'

Between drifting drapes that hung floor to ceiling, Synter stared out across the city. Her Blessed eyes could make out the lines of the districts in the darkness, but from the upper room of her canalside eatery, Kayme Warrant was too far to make out. Still she stared, unblinking, as the cold sun of rage continued to burn inside.

'Orders?' said a soft voice behind her.

Synter didn't move. She had known before he even spoke that it was Kodeh.

'I don't know,' she admitted at last. With an effort she pulled her gaze away and turned to face the dark-skinned goshe. 'I expected us to all be dead by evening.'

'What're they waiting for?' Kodeh asked, his enormous arms tensing and flexing in anticipation.

Synter laughed bitterly. 'Seems I'm wrong again,' she said eventually. 'Been a lot of that recently.'

'Now ain't the time to blame yourself. Was no way you could've known that damn Investigator had a team of Astaren following him.'

Synter glowered. 'Blaming myself? No. Doesn't stop me feeling their deaths on my account, though – nor wondering why they gave us time to interrogate him first.'

'Disinformation?'

'If he'd been lying about Irato's memory,' she argued, 'they'd have taken the artefact by now. Our wards were to keep the foxes out, not resist an assault. What sort of long game would possibly match taking possession of it?'

'What else is there?'

'Could he be caught up in something else? They were hunting him, not watching his back? Might explain the delay.'

Kodeh's great shoulders rose as he shrugged. 'Could be they're bluffing – Astaren got Irato, but his memory really is wiped. So they let the Investigator tell us all he knows and make it look like they allowed it to happen. We assume they know everything and shit ourselves.'

Synter ran her fingers through her hair, scratching at her scalp in an irritated gesture. 'We could go mad trying to work it out, but that won't help us. They're in play somehow – that's all we can be sure of.'

'So what now?'

She patted a pouch on her hip, the contents tightly packed. 'We get ready for them. I want all the Detenii on the island as fast as we can manage, armed with our special crossbow bolts. We've been holding on to them for years now, time to break out the stock.'

'You sure the firepowder heads will work against Astaren armour?' Despite his concern, Kodeh's whole demeanour brightened as he imagined using the weapons at long last.

'I'm sure of nothing, but if they come I mean to be ready for them. Tell the Elders nothing, they'll just panic and we need them ready for the ritual.'

'They have enough to do,' Kodeh agreed. 'Near as much every ship in the city's going to be pressed into service tomorrow – each one filled with fever-struck citizens to bind to the artefact. By this time tomorrow, the moon rises.'

'I got to admit it,' Enchei said, puffing out his cheeks and looking from Irato to Kesh. 'You surprised me with this one!'

The tattooist didn't look entirely happy at the revelation that Irato's head contained a handful of demons, but made no actual complaint. Other than briefly tightening his fingers around his baton, he did nothing as he absorbed the information.

'Am I, ah, talking to a demon now?' Narin hazarded.

The four of them sat in the smokehouse, the lamps turned low in deference to the late hour. Pirish had retired once Narin and Enchei had arrived, taking a pewter mug of rum up to her bed. She'd left a thick stew bubbling on the stove, but in their determination to get their news out, no one had yet touched the food.

Irato shook his head. 'They can hear you, but it's me in here.'

'And you think this is what the goshe're about?' Enchei added.

'Don't you?' said Kesh. 'It has to be, doesn't it?'

'Depends what you think it is – this means nothing by itself.'

Kesh waved a hand at Irato in frustration. 'There's a bloody demon in his mind – a few of them!'

'Aye, but that's not a plan. From what you said the demons are riding him, rather than being passengers under Irato's control.'

'But the fox-spirits aren't the only sort of demon out there. What did you call those demon princes? Apkai? What if one of them was behind the goshe, controlling them all? What if it's building itself an army it can command, every soldier in the army working to one single purpose, each one knowing their place and knowing no fear?'

Enchei looked far from convinced. 'The demons told you this?'

'No,' Kesh said with a shake of the head, 'but they told me the object stolen from them could link up the paths between their minds and there are thousands of goshe out there. What human could control so many people? Perhaps one could give orders to a few linked to it, but an entire army?'

'But why mess up Irato's head to make so much space? Space for three demons in each goshe mind at least?'

'You said the Apkai were like Gods to the fox-spirits – could be one's using them as weapons,' Kesh persisted. 'One of them could be strong enough to keep them under control.'

'There are Shure in two dozen cities across the central isles,' Enchei argued, 'let alone those further afield in the merchant domains and in House-ruled lands, that's tens of thousands of goshe outside of the Imperial City. Ask Irato's new demon friend how many of its kind there are – I doubt there's nearly enough for each goshe, quite aside from how they would catch half the demons in the world. You can't exactly breed them like sheep.'

'So what's your explanation, then?' Kesh demanded, not intending to sound petulant but the exertions of the day were catching up with her at last.

As Narin winced and shifted in his seat, Enchei stood. The former Astaren went over to look Irato closely in the eye. 'Come out to play, little demon,' he said, 'I've got some questions for you.'

A flicker went across Irato's eyes, the dart of mist on the wind that was gone in the blink of an eye.

'We hear you,' Irato intoned.

'Good. Now – Kesh says you can use Irato's body, how about his brain?'

'The host is open to us, nothing is hidden.'

Enchei nodded grimly. 'These paths – once they're opened you could reach out to control another goshe?'

'No. We could communicate with our kin, no more.'

'But if you were stronger, you could?'

'Only from within, the paths do not extend to our animal hosts.'

'Has any of your kind been hunted? Imprisoned?'

'No, the packs tell of no such losses.'

'What if it was the Apkai doing it?'

'Their presence is like the noonday sun to mortals. We have sensed no such being in our pursuit of the goshe else we would have abandoned it.'

'And the goshe weapons ain't exactly God-like,' Enchei added. Abruptly he turned to face Narin. 'Remember that question you were asked by Lord Shield? "Who is the Moon?"'

Narin nodded. 'You know who it is?'

'Most likely this Father Jehq,' Enchei said carelessly, as though the answer didn't matter at all. 'My point is, he must've asked you the question for a reason, must have got the name from somewhere. So how about Irato's mind? Moon's Artifice takes effect while people sleep and you knocking Irato out was what inconvenienced him, no?'

Narin was hesitant now. His entire body ached in a distant way, like a fire blazing on the far side of the room. He was aware of it, but not yet close enough to properly feel its prickle on his skin. Even so the constant presence was exhausting, and following Enchei's train of thought was beyond him so he just grunted to acknowledge the man's words.

'Asleep or unconscious, that's when Moon's Artifice gets to work. Lord Shield grabbed a fragment from Irato's mind, the name of what he'd just poisoned himself with or something else about the moon, but not enough to make sense of. I'm thinking the *who* doesn't matter so much as the *what*.'

'What?' Kesh echoed. 'That makes even less sense! How does that help us?'

'Be more literal,' Enchei commanded both of them. 'What is the moon?'

'A rock in the sky, isn't it?' Narin said.

Enchei pointed straight at him with the wooden baton in his hand. 'Exactly.'

'Eh?'

'Be literal?' Kesh asked hesitantly.

'Aye – look at the whole sky and tell me what the moon is.'

'It's ...' She glanced up at the ceiling out of habit, then looked down in momentary embarrassment. 'It's what lights the night, alongside the Constellations of the Gods.' She gasped and turned wide-eyed to Enchei. 'Oh, Hammer of Smith!'

'There she blows.'

'What?' Narin demanded.

'It's a light in the sky – it's what the Gods share the night sky with. By comparison the lesser stars are just tiny pinpricks of light. The moon is the only equal of the Gods at night!'

Narin still looked blank.

'It's a rival to the Gods!' Kesh said, almost shouting before she caught herself and lowered her voice. 'They're going to raise themselves a God of their own! Whoever this moon is, the important bit is that they're planning on becoming a God.'

'On the moon?' Narin asked, feeling increasingly dazed.

Kesh clouted him around the head before she could even stop to think. 'No you fool, it's just a symbol! All this linked space in the minds of others – that's where the God will live, actually in the heads of its followers!'

'But how do you create a God?' Narin asked, scowling and rubbing the top of his head.

It was Kesh's turn to hesitate now. She opened her mouth, ready to continue her tirade at Narin, then realised she didn't have the answer and had to turn to Enchei. The tattooist shrugged at them, again unconcerned.

'Whatever was stolen from the fox-demons can open paths up between minds. Father Jehq and his cronies have most likely got a way to send their minds inside from the same source. Their combined intellects, magnified by the brain-power of a few thousand minds, living for ever as pure energy inside the minds of their minions – sounds like a God to me.'

'Combined?'

'Why not? Without bodies or any mortal concerns, why not link your mind to others? For safety, if nothing else – the more of you there are, the stronger you all are. Probably they'll end up fighting for supremacy at some point, but until then they'll link their minds and use their mortal vessels to elevate their intellects to a level closer to the Gods than the mortals they once were.'

'And their bodies will die?'

'The ones they've left, most likely not. The others have been stripped of memories, but not the unconscious parts that remember to breathe and keep the heart beating. Stars in heaven – even if the Astaren did then step in, there are Shure across the entire Empire, a thousand miles away and all open to be touched by the new God. The Astaren would never catch them all, never kill enough to murder this new God even if the Ascendants would permit such a thing!'

Narin tried to shake the muzzy confusion from his mind and sat up a little straighter. 'What do they need for all this?'

'How should I know?' Enchei asked. 'This is all just informed guess-work right now.'

'Enchei, you're as close to an expert as we've got here. Is this what you think they're up to?'

Narin struggled to his feet, wincing as he stretched the bruised muscles and scorched patches of flesh. Right now he didn't mind it. A sense of renewed purpose flooded through him, washing away the faint helplessness that had been seeping in over the past few days.

'Aye,' the tattooist confirmed. 'I reckon so, and if I'm wrong I'm not far off. The crux of any plan like this has to be how to get away with it once the Astaren find out. The goshe's answer is simple: to have so many host bodies the ringleaders can't ever be caught. I might not have the details quite right but not so much as will matter. If you're just looking to mess their plans up because whatever it is, it's a threat to the Empire, I'm right enough.'

'Good enough for me.' Narin looked around the faces of his three companions just as Irato gave a shudder and a gasp of shock, the demon receding from control of his body once more. 'I don't know about the rest of you, but I'm not going to wait for these bastards to be rewarded for stealing the minds of a few thousand innocents. I don't know what Lord Shield will do, but I don't intend to wait around for the Gods to decide.'

'You think they'd allow it?' Kesh said, startled.

'I don't know, but Shield's not exactly been keen to get involved yet. All of a sudden I don't think their interests are the same as mine. I hope I'm wrong, but you fancy telling Lawbringer Rhe we're just going to stop and sit back? There's a crime and I want to find those who deserve to be punished.'

'Got a plan?' Enchei asked quietly.

Narin shook his head. 'Not yet, but they'll start transporting the sick to Confessor's Island at first light. Some of the fever victims have already died; they won't want to wait for the rest. You said there were

351

hundreds afflicted already, more by the morning I'm guessing. If they've got goshe from all across the city helping to move the sick they'll have at least a thousand minds to play with when they are ready, maybe two thousand. Would that be enough?'

Enchei gave a snort. 'How'm I supposed to know?' he protested. 'I've only just come up with the idea!'

'Well, think about it.'

'I, ah … I don't know. Maybe – they've got more members than that spread across the Empire, but might be they need enough together in one place to start the whole thing off – souls to sacrifice for their new God while still keeping enough goshe abroad to hide the God once the Stone Dragons turn up to slaughter every still-breathing body on Confessor's Island.

'O' course, if you've got a variant that removes everything but what's needed to breathe, eat and sleep, could be you've halved the number right there. Moon's Artifice allows you to build sleeper agents over the decades, quiet enough that no one notices, but you keep this nastier one in hand for your endgame.'

'More importantly,' Kesh broke in quietly, 'they're not running and hiding.'

They all turned to look at her, realisation setting in for each of them at the same time as she continued.

'They've risked exposure and are still going. They wouldn't do that if they weren't ready – or at least close enough to be willing to risk it. We either stop them tomorrow or we're too late.'

Her mouth was an angry, bloodless line as they all contemplated the goshe succeeding in their scheme.

'So how are we going to do it?'

CHAPTER 25

*The powers that be are more than capable of defending the system they rule
– one epitomised for many by the caste structure. Direct attempts to overturn
this have ended catastrophically – from the Ebalee Trading Company to the
Famine War that crossed the Wolf-Redearth border and Leviathan's shadow
war. One cannot help but wonder if change will only come as a consequence
of something else entirely.*

From A *History* by Ayel Sorote

'I don't want you to come back.'

The words continued to echo through Kesh's head. As she walked
through the thinning mist of dawn she barely noticed the furtive
ghosts of other travellers passing. The jangle of emotion inside her
was so insistent she only distantly realised many were fleeing the fever,
heading east on foot to the city wall. Enchei's parting words had felt
like a punch, unexpected and frightening, and before she'd recovered
herself to reply the man had shut the door on her.

Do I want to go back?

She felt a traitor for even asking herself the question, but Enchei
had forced it on her. He'd sowed the seed earlier, but this time had
been almost cruel in his words. The suggestion wasn't her own, but
the decision would be – whether or not he'd sparked it.

You're not a soldier, came a treacherous voice at the back of her mind. *Your
place is at your mother's side, not trying to stop the birth of some murderous God.*

She kept to the main streets, crossing the Tier Bridge without
noticing the wind whip through its twisting, bone-white struts or the
choppy waters below. Once on the Imperial Island she hurried through
its orderly streets, just one grey-coated figure among many, and at last
found herself on the paved expanse of Lawbringer's Square.

As she approached the Palace of Law, Kesh stopped before the statue of Lord Lawbringer, one that stood a little out from the entrance as though forever on guard. Head bowed, stave-tip touched to the ground at his feet, the God looked both humble and threatening to Kesh – his intentions hidden by a stone hood pulled low.

She stood almost directly underneath the statue, staring up at the looming stone figure to look at its cold, expressionless features. It had been carved with great skill. The wide face and small features more than hinted towards the Ascendant God's heritage, for all that the white marble could hardly be more different to the near-black skin that had been Toro Dragon's in life.

The statue's presence was oppressive when viewed from there. Leaning forward, the statue looked as if it was about to topple onto her, but Kesh stayed in its lee as she let the questions run through her mind, unable to go inside yet.

Do I leave them? Enchei didn't give me time to argue – but why? To absolve me of guilt? Because he doesn't want me on his conscience? Does he truly not want me there? Would I be a liability? The boat must be easy enough to pilot, they don't actually need me. Do I risk breaking mother's heart out of rage – out of grief?

'You're no use, are you?' Kesh whispered to the statue above. 'Lord Lawbringer; as cold and unfeeling as the statues raised in your honour. Nothing mattered to you except your duty, not after the Ten Day War when you became a traitor to your own House. But I have something to lose; I have someone to hurt by my selfishness still.'

The statue did not answer, but just that empty stare was enough to cause tears to run down her cheek.

Damn you, Enchei. A bastard buried deep – that's what Father would have said about you. How can I abandon you? How can I leave Mother all alone?

She wiped her face on her sleeve and glanced up, checking for witnesses to her tears but there were none. The cry of seagulls echoed around the square as she ascended the steps, her voice quiet and wavering as she spoke to the sleepy-eyed Lawbringer waiting in the hall beyond. She felt as weak as a child as she walked through the empty corridors, sick with anticipation.

Her escort was very young, a novice few would consider old enough to be a man, but he had the sense not to speak as she shuffled feebly after him. Up one great stairway in silence, down a long vaulted room and into a narrow passage with doors set into each wall. At last the novice found the correct one and knocked gently. Just that small sound made Kesh shrink back, her hand shaking as she reached out to open the latch and go inside. But one look at her mother's face, at the delight and relief blossoming from sleepy confusion, was enough to give her strength.

They embraced a long time, Kesh's mother keening as she hugged her girl tight. Only when Teike at last released her daughter, taking hold of her hands instead and bringing her to the small bed for them to sit, did Kesh speak, the words driving a knife into her own heart.

'I'm sorry, I can't stay long.'

Law Master Sheven stood at the entrance to an alley overlooking the docks, his white robe flapping in the brisk morning wind. The mass of fishing boats ahead, most painted green with Imperial suns in a variety of forms at the prow, swarmed with activity. Beyond them waited schooners – white or blue according to the trading league they belonged to – alongside tall ships from three different Houses and a pair of massive merchant house barques at the deep-water wharf.

In the distance, the House Eagle warship, upper gun ports open in lazy threat and sky-blue sails furled, kept clear – watching and waiting as it had been since it arrived within sight of the city. Sheven had a clear view of it through the small forest of masts.

'Lawbringer,' he said softly, 'your Investigator's message expressed concerns about any Dragon involvement, did it not?'

Rhe nodded, eyes never leaving the crowd of men and women on the main dock. There was barely space to move there; a narrow path ran down the centre of the road between lines of makeshift stretchers. The sun had been up only an hour, but already half the city seemed to have descended on the Vesis and Darch Harbour Warrant.

Faces masked against infectious vapours, it was a forest of bandits that tended to the sick they had brought on makeshift stretchers in their hundreds. It was impossible to tell the goshe from the anxious relations of the fever-struck – a detail that made both Rhe and Sheven wary. All looked poor, which tallied to the half-finished map of outbreaks Sheven's aides were compiling, but the lower castes were also the main recruiting ground for the goshe.

'Perhaps we can ask those two Dragon ships to hold back from the effort,' Sheven continued, pointing to a pair of red-hulled schooners. 'We don't want to provoke that Eagle warship, after all.'

Both men wore scarves around their necks, ready to pull up when they came closer to the sick; noble purple for Rhe, religious black for Sheven.

'The schooners only have small deck-guns,' Rhe pointed out. 'What threat would they offer?'

'None,' Sheven said, 'but when both sides are looking for an excuse, are their House colours not enough?'

'You might make them even more determined to assist.'

Sheven smiled grimly. 'Certainly *you* would if the request came from you.' He looked around for one of the novices he'd suborned to carry messages for him and pointed at one. 'You; find me a Lawbringer from Dragon or one of their Major Houses – I have a mission for them.'

'And the Dragons among us?' Rhe asked softly once the novice had raced off. 'Can we even be sure about them?'

'I trust you right now, and that's about it. You have teams ready in case there are more demons sighted?'

'I do, though only one was reported last night and it was quickly hunted down. I doubt we will need any tonight.'

'But not unreasonable to assign any Dragons of ours to the teams before evening comes?'

Rhe nodded. 'It will be done.'

'Law Master Sheven?'

Both men turned to find a richly-dressed young man behind them. Of local stock, with pale skin and dark hair, he wore a beautifully brocaded jacket of blue and grey, but more notable was the fat gold collar to that jacket – the sign of the Imperial caste – and the low-slung pistol holster.

Sheven didn't move for a moment, so surprised was he, but then Rhe bowed and the Law Master followed suit.

'My Lord Sun,' Sheven murmured, 'how may I serve you?'

From the Imperial's collar hung a white silk scarf threaded with more gold, draped in a carefully rakish manner to Sheven's eyes. He was in his early twenties and his eyes glittered dangerously as he nodded an acknowledgment to their bows. Sheven could never remember having before met an Imperial who wore a weapon so casually.

While they were of the highest caste and of course permitted such a thing, custom frowned upon it when the entire warrior caste of the House of the Sun had been banned after the Ten Day War. The youth's careless arrogance was a gross provocation to any ranked House nobleman – had Rhe's life followed a different path the Imperial might have soon been dying in a duel.

'I come to assist you,' the young man declared magnanimously. 'My name is Prince Enser Kashte.'

'Assist?' Rhe asked. 'I believe loading the sick onto boats might be beneath my Lord's high station.'

'Oh indeed,' Prince Kashte said, wrinkling his nose at the idea, 'but I had something else in mind.' With a flourish he took something from inside the thick sash around his waist and Sheven caught sight of intricate tattoos on the back of the Imperial's hands before a folded sheaf of paper was offered forward.

'I share a mutual acquaintance with your Investigator Narin – this acquaintance sends you this list at the Investigator's request.'

'What is it?' Sheven asked as he opened the paper to see a column of names in elegant script. 'Lawbringers?'

'If any man was of a mind to wonder who among his colleagues might hold allegiances to other parties, a start must be made somewhere.' Kashte nodded towards the paper. 'Furthermore, if the Lawbringers find themselves in a police action of a larger scale than they are used to, certain distant relations of mine and I will be nearby and glad to assist in any service to our cousin, the Emperor, that might be requested of us by his noble representatives.'

Sheven coughed in surprise. 'You and other members of the Imperial family?' He exchanged a look with Rhe. More men with guns being added to the mix – would that be a good thing or disastrous? 'Just how many are we talking about here?'

'A handful of idle youths such as myself,' Kashte said with a cold smile. 'Feckless and of little status among the wider Imperial family as we are, I can bring you thirty whose upbringing has been mostly occupied by swordplay and marksmanship. In the unlikely event you find a use for us, we will be yours to petition for assistance.'

The Law Master blinked at him. 'And, ah, this acquaintance of yours?'

'Prefers to remain nameless, lest he gain a reputation for involving himself in petty matters of civic order.'

'Where might we find you, if we did indeed have such a request?' Rhe asked while Sheven was still lost in the list of names – many of them Lawbringers he respected and trusted.

'There is a gaming house on the public thoroughfare – the Black Tiles. I have persuaded them to open their doors early to us.'

'The Black Tiles,' Rhe confirmed. 'I know it.'

Kashte smiled and bowed with a flourish. 'In which case I depart and leave you to your ministrations.'

The Imperial didn't wait to hear Rhe's polite reply and the words died unfinished, wasted breath that faded to nothing on the breeze.

'Didn't see that coming,' Sheven admitted once he'd watched the minor prince turn the corner. 'You?'

Rhe shook his head. 'All the more surprising given how careful the Imperial family usually are,' he said. 'Does it mean we have a new ally or another player in a game we do not yet understand?'

'Narin clearly knows more if he's arranged this. Does he want us to have an edge or a fighting chance? Could the goshe have guns to use? Even with some warriors and nobles in their ranks, it's a dangerous choice to use guns on us. House Dragon would certainly hear of it and might simply react.'

'He fears worse than a handful of noble goshe ready to turn their guns on us,' Rhe replied carefully. 'As we agreed I've kept back details from you and this is one. Narin rightly fears the Dragons will send in their Astaren and that it will all spiral out of control. The goshe possess magic they can use in battle – magic no Astaren would stand to see in the hands of others.'

'Such as your demons?'

'Their elite agents possess unnatural powers, according to the reports I have from Narin and others. I doubt the goshe have a cache of guns – mass-production of weapons is difficult to hide when Astaren across the Empire are watching out for it. But I am certain their elite are more dangerous than any armed warrior caste.'

'Fortunately we're planning on making it a surprise,' Sheven said after a moment of quiet. 'Whatever their motivation or the provocation it causes, I don't believe we can turn these Imperials down.'

His attention returned to the sight of masked figures gently loading the stricken onto boats. Not all were unconscious, it turned out; many were simply weak and delirious with fever, suffering through the early stages perhaps, but the majority were carried on every form of stretcher imaginable.

The steady stream of figures walking out onto the wide stone-packed ground put him in mind of a trail of ants – each bound to the will of others and mindlessly carrying their burden back to the nest. Through the press and disorder he caught occasional glimpses of white-coated goshe doctors moving through the mass, and a few black-garbed goshe too – all carefully modest in their numbers.

As Sheven watched, the first shouts went up from several of the fishing fleet; their captains unhappy at being called into service by the Emperor's personal order, but wasting no time to be away once their decks and holds were full of the sick.

'And so we send them off,' Sheven muttered, a sick feeling building in his stomach. His hand tightened around the grip of his scimitar until he forced himself to release it. 'Cast them into the hands of our enemy – to do what with, we do not know.'

Rhe nodded. 'It is time I went to find Narin and asked him that very question. The message said he had a plan – let us hope it is worth us helping the goshe do exactly as they want.'

Cautious as ever, Father Jehq stood in the concealing shade of a copse of trees until the boat was tied up at the jetty and the sailors jumped down. Goshe attendants from the hospital, all dressed in black, trotted forward to begin the process of unloading – the first of many such efforts, if Synter's plans were falling into place. Jehq watched carefully as sacks of grain were passed over and shouldered, then stepped into the open.

A grey-cloaked man disembarked with the supplies and stood on the jetty surveying the island with such intent he did not notice Jehq at first. Hood raised to conceal his identity, the figure had clambered off the boat as soon as they arrived, not waiting for the lines to be secured in his eagerness to be on solid ground.

Jehq smiled inwardly. For all that he couldn't see the man's face, he knew it was Father Olos. Few of the goshe's inner circle of Elders were as tall as the man from House Jaguar, a native of the great island ruled by House Salamander. Fewer still were so obviously unnerved by travel across water.

'Olos!' Jehq hailed as he reached the pebble beach. 'You had no trouble at the docks?'

A lined, tanned face squinted up at Jehq from the shade of his concealing hood. At last Olos scowled and swept the hood back, inclining his head to Jehq by way of response. His eyebrows and hair were all grey now, his cheeks sagging as age sapped the vitality Olos had been known for.

'Getting busy there,' Olos grunted, his thick southern accent still barely penetrable after all these years in the Imperial City. 'You'll be overrun soon.'

'With the sick, I hope,' Jehq nodded. 'Our time is at hand, my friend. You have the artefact?' He looked around Olos at the other passenger on the boat – Caric, one of Synter's Detenii, who was serving as guard for what would be unloaded last.

'We got it,' Caric replied, stepping up onto the gunwale and glancing at the men pulling supplies from the laden fishing boat. 'Kinda wish you'd not mentioned it in front of this lot though.'

Jehq raised a hand. 'Look at me, all of you!' he commanded.

The sailors and goshe alike turned to face him and he felt a flash of light in his eyes. Every one of them gave a slight flinch as the *Command* Blessing took hold of them all.

'Good – as I thought. Stop worrying, Caric. They all belong to the faithful.'

The Detenii grunted and removed his hands from the grips of the long-knives. 'As you say,' he said briefly, still looking wary. 'Where do you want the crate?'

'The lazaret,' Jehq said, pointing to the far end of the beach.

The goshe elder looked down on the small dock from a hump of ground at the edge of the beach; a crescent perimeter of scrappy lumps of grass that separated it from the rest of Confessor's Island. At each end there were larger slabs of rock seemingly broken off from the tilting cliffs that rose up behind them. Beyond the grass there were trees to Jehq's side, small spike-leafed specimens huddled from the wind in the cliff's lee.

The open ground was penned up by an old clay-brick wall, its yellow-tinted flanks stained by rain and grey lichen. There were two gates in the wall; the nearer one being the larger while the smaller, near the far end of the beach, led into the leper colony. The lazaret occupied a sizeable tract of land; space for three palazzo-sized buildings to house the lower-caste patients and another three quads of cottages for the higher castes. In addition there were barns for the animals that grazed on the rest of the island so they could be accessed from within the wall, and a sheltered community garden.

'Into the lazaret?' Olos commented, surprised. 'You intend ...' He trailed off, but Caric gave a snort as he hoisted a crate onto his shoulder and stepped onto the jetty.

'Aye, we do. No time to be squeamish now, Father.'

Olos' expression twisted into distaste. 'Is that quite necessary? There must be hundreds at the harbour by now, if not a thousand of the fever-stricken.'

'Your compassion for our wards does you credit, my friend,' Jehq said dryly, 'but the sooner we're ready, the less time there is for us to all be slaughtered.'

Caric chuckled as he passed Olos. 'Heh – a saying the Detrult have always lived by, Father.'

An average-sized man, Caric looked strange with the large crate propped on one shoulder, but he ascended the pebble beach and stone steps cut into the turf with ease. He headed past the wide gate that led to the rest of the island, pausing only to salute a face watching him from above, and went on to the lazaret gate.

'Come, Olos,' Jehq said patiently, ushering his long-time colleague forward. 'This must be done, and they will be cared for still – you know that. Even more so than before – it will be in our interests to tend to them.'

Olos shook his head sadly. He had been vital to their plans over the decades of work leading to this day, Jehq knew that all too well, but Olos had left the hard decisions to his peers – preferring life in a laboratory to the more active role Jehq had played.

It took a moment, but Olos eventually came along and the pair trailed behind Caric; a strange mismatch, with the smaller of the two almost supporting his colleague for the first dozen paces.

'Do we have a number?' Olos asked, walking taller as they arrived at the door. From behind it they heard the heavy clack of bolts being opened.

'Of souls?' Jehq shook his head. 'Nothing so definite I'm afraid.'

'You're the one who's worked with the artefact most, are you not?'

Jehq inclined his head. 'Each mind is different – and we had never expected to factor in so many fever-born. I have a broad idea; certainly by the end of the day we will be able to touch every goshe in the Empire, even those in the eastern Shures of Raven. Synter's left us exposed, but at the same time her boldness has brought us all we need.'

'Fever-born?'

'The name we've given them to differentiate them from the moon-born – those goshe who were dosed with Moon's Artifice as children. We'd only ever thought to use those mental deficients in our care to be fever-born, a few score perhaps. Just enough souls to give the artefact power to reach the nearest moon-born and spread from there.'

Olos looked around. 'The lazar colony will need to be expanded then, the hospital too. The variant you've used will make them helpless – entirely dependent on the goshe for care.'

'And care they will receive,' Jehq reminded him, 'care commensurate with the divine spirit they will then carry.' He smiled. 'You will, of course, be in a position to ensure that!'

Olos was silent a moment, watching Caric manoeuvre the crate into a position where it could fit through the small gate. Gauntlet-clad hands reached out from within to help and together they turned it to scrape through.

'You are right, Jehq,' Olos said with a nod, 'and I am not ignorant of how we reached this point. How long do you think this will take?'

'Shoolen?' Jehq called through the gate, prompting a thin, black-skinned man to dart out. 'Have you finished here?'

'All done, Father,' the Dragon said with a subservient bob of the head. 'They're all down; had their medicine more'n an hour past.'

'Then we're ready to proceed,' Jehq confirmed. 'Go up to the hospital and finish off there.' He turned to Olos. 'We need physical contact for each one, but it should only be a matter of moments to complete the process. Our pet demon is quick about its tasks and it was born just for this.'

'And so the moon rises,' Father Olos intoned. The act of speaking the words seemed to give him strength and he went inside with renewed purpose. Jehq watched the man with a small smile.

'Indeed it does,' he muttered. 'Let's just hope the stars don't get there first.'

It was chilly in the Lord Martial's chamber – a round room on the top floor of the Palace of Law, exposed to the vagrant sea breezes through three tall windows. Rhe stood perfectly still in the middle of the room, hands behind his back and staring straight ahead at the painting of the Emperor facing him.

On the Lord Martial's polished oak desk was an oil lamp from which shone warm golden light. It resembled an orrery, the head of the lamp a great brass sun with the constellations of the Gods cut into it, while through the windows shone a colder light from the grey sky.

'You and Law Master Sheven are agreed?' Lord Martial ald Har said at last. 'This is the correct course?' He looked up from his desk, his startling red-tinted eyes looking infernal and incongruous with his lined, aged face.

'We are, my Lord. If we are wrong, if the girl has lied and circumstances have worked out to deceive me, the result will simply be wasted effort and my personal humiliation. That is a price worth paying, but I am not wrong. This much I know.'

'Men will die. This is unprecedented.'

'I understand. We do not suggest it lightly, but the reckoning has come.'

Ald Har let out a heavy sigh and stood. Walking around the desk he headed to the nearest of the double-height windows and opened it. The window faced south-east, towards Confessor's Island. On a clear day the awkward lump of Confessor's Hill was visible seven or eight miles in the distance, over the headland outside the city. He was quiet a long while – long enough that Rhe was forced to wonder what was going through his mind.

'Answer me this, Lawbringer,' Lord ald Har said after a long while. 'Do you aspire to this office?'

Rhe blinked. 'I ... I do not know,' he admitted at last.

'No? You are the presumptive heir in the eyes of the city – not to me, unless I live well into my dotage, but to someone, surely?'

'I realise others consider me so,' Rhe said stiffly. 'It is not the only thing expected of me by some.'

'Ah yes, Godhood. Well then, do you aspire to that? To be an Ascendant God and live among the stars?'

'I aspire to be worthy ...' Rhe stopped. 'No, that sounds rehearsed and I would not have you think of me that way. I have thought about it, it is hard not to when the city's gossips suggest such a thing. But Godhood? How does a man even consider such a thing? The later

Ascendants were all raised – or rather noticed by the Gods – through near-perfection in some discipline. They were considered supreme by mortal standards, but what does that mean to me? There is a Lord Lawbringer already; what would perfection in my chosen discipline bring me? How could that even be measured?'

Rhe shook his head. 'And most importantly – when I see I am not suited to a mortal supremacy, the position you hold, how could I aspire to higher?'

'You feel yourself unworthy?'

'Worthiness cannot be so easily judged – suitability is another thing entirely. You are the Emperor's servant, but you are also the face who must defend this corner of authority against the Great Houses; against the priests of every temple and likely factions of Imperial castes too.'

Ald Har nodded at that. 'We are servants of the Emperor, not noblemen. You of all castes are aware of that.'

'One look at my assigned rooms is reminder enough,' Rhe said. The Lord Martial turned with a questioning look, but an awkward smile told him it had been a poorly-executed attempt at levity rather than a complaint.

'Administration can be learned,' ald Har continued. 'There are clerks able to manage the load and the Law Masters are yours to command.'

'I know, but it would not be enough. You are an inspiration, a leader – I ... I am an ideal at best. The others choose to believe what they will about me and so my legend is furthered, but that does not equip me to manage politicians, to negotiate or be a leader of men.'

'Yet that is exactly what you intend to do.'

It was Rhe's turn to be silent for a while. 'I suppose so – but while it was ideals that brought me to the Lawbringers, I was always out of place in my House. Unwilling to live a life of idleness, I could see no place for me within the military. I am not a man to follow; I am not a man to lead. I heard one playwright called me an army of one, but they don't know how right they are.

'I despise soldiers as deeply as courtiers. The single consuming purpose of combat – that I understand, but the unthinking, thuggish aggression men mistake for prowess? They could be an army of dogs, trained to heel and worked up into frenzy when required. But the strictures of an army, the regulations and structure? The forced shelter of comradeship? The purpose I aspire to – I crave – is not to be found within an army. I do not know if it is even to be found within the Lawbringers, but here at least I know that my efforts can be turned to a greater good.'

'Have you read the writings of Lord Duellist?'

'I have.'

'And?'

'And he and I are of the same mind,' Rhe hesitated, 'except in one respect.'

'Which is?'

'The man who was to become a God thought to teach others what he had learned, to tell the whole world the shape of his thoughts.'

The Lord Martial gave him a long appraising look. 'When you read his treatises, you couldn't understand why he'd bothered to write such a thing down?'

Rhe nodded. 'I was young and it had never occurred to me that others would not think that way. He described the shape of the world, nothing more. What need do I have of reading the sky is blue, that the Gods orbit above us? For Duellist it was the end of a journey of enlightenment. In my heart I feel no awakening, no understanding or revelatory insight. There is just the prism through which I view the world – I cannot truly conceive how others might believe the sky is green. And that is, perhaps, the reason I will never be suited for Godhood.'

'Nor for this room,' ald Har said, gesturing around them. There was a flush to his cheeks, Rhe saw. Anger? Disappointment? 'Not that you cannot think as others might, but that you don't struggle. There is no conflict within you, no doubt or interest in the path not taken. That is why I fear to approve your scheme – you don't fear death. You don't fear anything, not truly, and what happens to those who follow a fearless man?'

'I can offer no assurances there,' Rhe said quietly, feeling stripped to the bone by the aging Lawbringer's words. 'Only that I will be at the fore of them when they meet danger.'

'That is precisely my fear. However, I can see no other course of action, so you have my approval – and may the Gods be with you.'

CHAPTER 26

Many see the Empire as a great tapestry, an intricate design of beauty and skill. Unfortunately, the analogy can be extended – our rigid society is a tight weave indeed. Unpick one part and more than you ever intended could unravel, so the Astaren are careful to cut off any idle fingers poised to pull a stray thread.

From A History by Ayel Sorote

Narin watched the rain fall through half-closed curtains. It lasted only a few minutes, a brief shower to wash the harbour clean as the second wave of boats set out for Confessor's Island. He stared at every face below him, careful to keep back in the shadows of the darkened room, but driven to try and pick out individuals among the crowd.

Most were masked, supposedly against the fever, and were impossible to identify. He began to fit builds to those men and women he knew; a fearful imagination that folk he trusted might yet turn out to be one of the goshe. There, a heavyset man with tightly-rolled shirtsleeves, black hair cropped close to the scalp, could have been Irato at that distance. Three or four who could have been Enchei, greying hair and average builds – one, Lord Vanden with coffee-coloured skin and a slight paunch. There was even a substitute for Kine, slender and dark with her hair tied back in a bun – but the gait gave her away as a stranger.

Her, at least, I'd know. Even in such a crowd, I'd recognise her.

Cartloads of the sick arrived from every alley, the fever-struck propped limp against each other or lying flat on stretchers. Some were carried or dragged on improvised travois, brought by others in the clothes of their trade; surely too many to all be goshe. The people of the city – fuelled by fear of leaving their sick neighbours close to family or driven by concern for the stricken – had mustered of their own volition to help the goshe.

The white-clad doctors and their helpers – a few in goshe black but many more not so conspicuously dressed – moved among them, identifying some who'd succumbed, guiding others towards the boats. Not all were insensate, Narin noticed during his vigil as one hour dragged on into a second. A fair number were enfeebled, able to walk with assistance, and he saw those given preference on the boats.

Law Master Sheven had Lawbringers out on the harbour walk too – only a small number, but they were engaged in an opposite effort wherever possible. The enfeebled were mostly the stronger adults, fit and healthy men and women most likely to be trained at a Shure. In the name of mercy, Sheven's small cadre of supervisors were trying to get the old and youngest preference, without sparking a confrontation. They had no way of telling whether the sick were genuine or not, but they could at least hamper the rate at which goshe soldiers were transported to their island.

'How're you feeling?' Kesh asked behind him.

Narin gave a start. He'd not heard her come in. 'Me? Well enough.' He shifted his feet and unconsciously put one hand to his stomach.

'There's no place for heroics here,' she warned him. 'You sure?'

'So speaks the woman who shouldn't even be here,' Narin said in reply.

'That's different – I'm staying to do what I can, but I'm not pretending to be strong when I'm not.'

'Good for you.' He gestured to the long rows of sick out on the harbour walk. 'It's almost midday and they're still loading most of this second journey. Doubt they'll get more than four trips.'

'Have you been able to keep count? Any idea how many are out there?'

'Hundreds,' was all Narin could say.

He flexed the scraped, scabbed fingers of his right hand, watching the skin move as he tested his strength. His stave stood to one side and Narin picked it up, rolling his shoulders in a few slow strikes to test how easily he could use the weapon.

'Get some rest,' Kesh advised, watching him carefully. 'What they put you through, you need some sleep. We're not moving until close to dusk anyway.'

'I can't sleep.' Narin turned back to the window, careful to keep his expression hidden from Kesh. 'I've tried.'

He heard a tiny sound from her, abruptly cut-off as Kesh thought better of arguing. For a moment his eyes did close and his head bowed, but it was not sleep that gripped him and his hand was shaking by the time he looked up again.

'Is Enchei here?'

'Went back to the inn, said he had to fetch a few things.'

'Is that safe?'

Kesh gave a snort. 'Seems the old man can handle himself. If they've bothered leaving anyone to watch the place, they'll get a nasty surprise.'

'Irato?'

'Downstairs, seeing to our weapons. It was either that or he was just going to stare at the wall for the next few hours, so I gave him a job to do.'

Narin looked around for his own daggers, then remembered he'd left them with the rest of their weapons. The house belonged to a family Kesh knew, or what was left of it anyway. The father and two youngest children had been taken by the fever and sent to the island on one of the first boats. There was a mother and son left, but along with hundreds of others they had packed a few belongings and left early in the morning – keen to be out of the fever-struck city until the worst was over.

How many had made that decision Narin couldn't tell, but Kesh reported a steady stream of people heading towards the outskirts of the city. On her return journey from the Palace of Law the numbers had been marked – there were easily more fleeing than there were helping the sick to the docks. By the end of the day, he knew, things would start to get desperate. Panic would set in, violence would break out and shops would be looted, most likely. Where the limited numbers of the Lawbringers would be placed amid all that, Narin didn't quite know.

'What did your mother say?'

'What?' Kesh asked, startled. 'My mother? What do you think? She was angry. She's still grieving for Emari, for Pity's sake – what did you think she'd say?'

Narin shook his head. 'I'm sorry, I was just thinking about Kine. I'm not going to have the chance to say goodbye.'

'It's not going to be goodbye,' Kesh insisted fiercely. 'We're getting through this, okay?'

'You don't know that.' Before Kesh could reply Narin held up a hand. 'Wait, I don't mean to be sounding so sorry for myself. I just meant I …'

His expression turned to one of frustration and his shoulders sank as he struggled to find the words for what he now felt.

'You've unfinished business?' Kesh asked quietly. 'The baby you and Enchei were talking about earlier?'

'Pretty much,' he admitted. 'I don't know what's going to happen, got no damn clue, but I've not seen her since this all started. I don't know how she is, what danger she's in — I've not even been able to try and do something about it. Can't say I know what I should be doing, but ah, stars in heaven! I wish there was time to at least try. We're risking our necks and you know it – that part I don't mind, a Lawbringer's got to accept that. But … Ah …'

'But doing so while Kine's in danger goes against your oaths,' Kesh finished.

'Gods, it's more than the oaths! What sort of a *man* does that? Puts a woman and child in danger without even trying to do something about it?'

Kesh was quiet a while, then she came closer and took hold of Narin's arm. 'Look at yourself, Narin,' she said. 'You've been attacked and chased halfway across the city, then kidnapped and tortured; you're only upright because of some damn magery of Enchei's. Now's not the time for blaming yourself or asking what more you could have done. That you're still going is better than could be expected of anyone.

'Now come downstairs, sit and eat something. You want to do something for Kine? Make sure you've got enough strength to survive the night, that's all she'd ask for. That's all she'd pray for.'

'Not sure what use I'm going to be in a fight,' he said, wincing as they headed for the door. 'Certainly not against any goshe elite.'

'Neither of us will, but when were we ever going to try to win a fair fight? Enchei's got something far better in mind. It needs a few brave men to pull it off, but I think we can find a couple of those.'

Narin smiled weakly. 'A brave woman too.'

'Pah. I'm not brave, I'm clever – and I intend to be alive at the end of this.' Kesh patted his hand. 'I'll leave bravery to you idiots.'

Fragments of orange cut across the sky as the sun reached the horizon. White-robed doctors on the speckled pebble beach seemed to shine like beacons in the fading light. Above them, against the darkening sky, were the cloud-smeared constellations of Knight, but all eyes watched as the last wave of boats came in from the city. The crests of waves out in the bay beyond glowed brief and elusive in the evening light, faint echoes of the great beacons on the headland beyond.

From above the main gate, Synter watched the boats drive for the beach, each captain eager to unload his fever-stricken cargo and turn around before night truly took hold.

'Atash,' she called softly to the man below.

The Wolf turned to look up at her, the last of the light imbuing a strange fire to his yellow eyes. 'Aye, sir.'

'Father Jehq says we're close. We won't need all of these.'

'I should kill 'em?'

'Don't be stupid,' she snapped. 'Point is, get the first couple dozen up to the hospital quick as you can. Might be we don't need them at all, but they can't hurt. The others we'll still use, but most importantly we need that starting jolt.'

She looked back towards the hospital; a torch-lit lump a mile off. 'Here come your helpers. Get the first lot unloaded and send 'em on, then lock down the beach. No one goes anywhere until you hear from me or you feel the moon rise, okay?'

Atash grinned nervously. 'Aye – the moon rising with a thousand voices in my head. Reckon I'll notice that!'

'Damn right you will – until then, keep sharp. If any God or demon's paying attention, I reckon they'll notice too.'

The man gave her a sloppy salute and headed back down the beach to meet the first boat. Synter checked around at the forces they'd left there. Only thirty-odd goshe stood on the beach, weapons hidden or lying flat on the ground so it wouldn't look like they were quite so obviously on guard. Ten Detenii occupied the wall, crossbows with firepowder heads to hand in case the worst happened.

On the road behind her came another two hundred goshe in a disordered column. These ones were all moon-born; loyal and trained soldiers of the goshe, but still cattle compared to Synter's Detenii. Most had pulled on their black goshe jackets once they'd deposited the last load of patients at the hospital, the building's grounds now almost entirely filled with silent, insensate fever-born. Their weapons were stashed in a temporary armoury inside the gate, but more than a few had used their polearms to make stretchers anyway.

Jehq would be finishing off the last of the fever-born now while the other Elders completed preparations for the ritual. The fever had taken people in a range of ways, but once the artefact had been touched to their heads they were as still as the dead. Indeed, Jehq had told her most would be dead by morning if a critical mass wasn't reached.

Synter had watched it happen with a faint chill of dread – in part because this was at her instigation, but mostly at the simple sight of a thousand living corpses whose minds would soon be linked. She was glad she wasn't the one doing the work there. Jehq had looked drawn as he'd carried the bluish-grey block from one fever-born to the next. The shards of gold-flecked quartz set into the artefact pulsed with inner light as it touched each one – a flush of hungry delight from their enslaved demon, Synter imagined, as it consumed soul after soul and slowly grew in strength.

The first boat reached the dock and Atash grabbed the rope thrown at him. He tied it off and trotted up the short ramp one of the goshe dropped against the side. Synter watched him hop onto the deck as the ship's sailors, all still masked against the fever, started moving the first of the enfeebled patients forward. It was a practised routine now and even before the reinforcements made their way through the gate and down the beach, Atash's men and women had half the first boat unloaded.

Synter looked up at the remaining ships drawing up to the shore. Even with the second jetty they'd constructed and the deeper-drafted ships winching down their shore boats laden with the sick, much of the daylight had been lost unloading at the island end.

'Least it won't matter this time around,' she muttered. 'That first boat's got enough for Father Jehq's needs. The rest can wait.'

A second ship pulled up to the jetty, buffeting it as it came in a shade too fast. The jetty shuddered and men stumbled, Atash jumping up to bellow remonstrations at the captain even as its lines were secured.

Synter couldn't hear what was said, but whatever was called back Atash didn't seem to like it. Her hand tightened as she watched the Wolf drop onto the jetty and race up the lowered gangplank.

Seven hells – now's not the time, you damn fool!

She glanced towards the steps that ran down to the ground, momentarily undecided whether she should go and sort it out herself, but Atash was a Detenii. She knew perfectly well he'd have won any fight by the time she got there, by which point she'd just look stupid in front of one of her less-respectful soldiers.

Synter hissed with irritation and reached down to grab her crossbow instead. 'If that's not sorted quick,' she commented to the nearest man on the wall – Frayl, a Redearth from her team whose skin looked rustier than usual in the waning light – 'someone's getting shot. I don't care who.'

Frayl grinned and nodded, hefting his own bow. From a small table beside him he tapped one of the firepowder quarrels they had on hand. 'One o' these'd shake 'em up!'

'Spark a bloody panic more likely,' Synter said, a trace of regret in her voice. She looked up at the boats and frowned. There was a staccato light shining on board the fisher Atash had boarded. 'What the fuck's he doing?' she breathed. 'Showing his Lightning Blessing for the whole damn Empire to see?'

'Ah, Synter?' Frayl said, doubt showing in his voice, 'I don't know much about boats but ain't those coming kinda quick?'

She looked around. He was right; many of the fishing fleet hadn't furled their sails or checked their speed – they were driving straight for the beach.

'Shit and damn,' she said – just before a gunshot echoed out across the beach.

Rhe watched the goshe stagger, driven to a halt by the force of his bullet. The Wolf's mouth hung open, his expression more one of astonishment than pain. Movement on the deck stopped as the Lawbringers and Imperials stared at the goshe – thin curls of lightning still flicking lazily around his hands. Rhe had shot him almost point blank, just as the goshe darted forward to strike, and a faint cloud of smoke from the pistol was all that stood between them. The goshe tried to say something, but as he did so his heart seemed to give one final beat and blood poured from his chest.

The goshe wavered and fell to one knee, lightning vanished and hands now clawed in pain, not rage. His yellow eyes were wide and staring at the Lawbringer who'd killed him, then his strength failed and he toppled forward.

Before the body was still, Prince Kashte was moving past and bringing his rifle up to aim. With brass chasing and intricate scroll-work the Imperial's weapon was a work of art, but he levelled it with practised movement.

'Lawbringer?' he muttered as he took aim.

The word stirred Rhe into action. He'd barely had a chance to announce his purpose to the Wolf before the goshe had attacked, but one guard's action wasn't enough. As Law Master Sheven led a group of Lawbringers off the boat Rhe stood high on the gunwale and raised his voice.

'I am Lawbringer Rhe – drop your weapons! I am here to search for the fugitive goshe doctor called Jehq.'

Behind him, the remaining minor princes levelled their guns, covering the Lawbringers as they filled the jetty and ran down the beach. Before any response came, a great creak and scrape filled the air as the first of the boats beached themselves hard on the pebbles and more Lawbringers dropped into the shallow water.

Rhe looked around at the panic-stricken goshe on the beach. Most stared back at him unmoving or looked to their fellows, waiting in vain for someone to take charge. A handful drew what weapons they had on them and waited for the Lawbringers to come, several of those glancing back up at the defensive wall behind them. The Lawbringer followed their gaze and saw more figures in black up on the wall, barely visible in the dark. One carried a blazing torch, however, and the light it cast showed crossbows in the hands of those beside him.

'My Lord Sun,' Rhe called to Kashte, 'the wall.'

'I see them,' Kashte replied. 'Do you want me to fire?'

'Hold until they fire,' Rhe commanded.

'Doesn't seem sound advice, Lawbringer.'

Rhe glanced down. Prince Kashte had a small smile on his face but he continued to line up a shot. 'You are a man of the Lawbringers for tonight,' he said coldly, 'and that is our lot.'

Just as he turned back a fizzing spark corkscrewed down from the wall. Rhe followed its erratic path to the far end of the jetty where—

A thunderous detonation broke the night as a man-sized sun erupted there. Rhe reeled away, arms up to cover his eyes from the blinding light. Behind him he heard Kashte and his fellows return fire, a stutter of whip-cracks ringing out around him. Screams filled the night, blurred streaks of light searing through the dark as Rhe tried to recover himself.

From elsewhere there came more gunshots, a second party of Imperials and high-caste Lawbringers on boats landing either side of the jetty. Rhe dropped to one knee as he heard quarrels thud into the wood of the boat. He tried to blink away the pain in his eyes but the blur remained and he could do nothing but hope not too many were similarly affected.

'Lawbringer?' Kashte called from somewhere nearby, 'are you hurt?'

Rhe shook his head. 'Can't see properly,' he said, wincing at the sting in his eyes. He looked towards the sound of Kashte's voice and at last found things resolving themselves. 'Go!'

The Imperials didn't wait to be told twice. Rhe sensed as much as saw them leap the gunwale, his eyesight only just improving enough to blearily make out the goshe from the beach charge to meet the Lawbringers. The goshe carried long-knives for the main part and were already outnumbered. Only fervour drove them forward and it wasn't enough, as they were cut down in moments by the longswords and halberds of the Lawbringers.

Rhe touched a hand to the sword on his back, reminding himself of its presence. He stood and returned his spent pistol to its sheath, not trusting himself to reload the weapon properly yet. Heading down the gangplank Rhe glanced at the shattered and burning wreckage at the other end, then trotted towards the beach, pulling his sword as he went.

Ahead of him he saw Kashte, rifle in his hands, dodge back from a wild slash. Likely trained as a duellist just as Rhe had been, the Imperial showed a street-fighter's instinct as he kicked at his attacker's knee then swung the butt of his rifle at the man's head. The goshe staggered under the glancing blow and only then did Kashte draw his gold-hilted sword and calmly hack into the goshe's neck with it.

Rhe blinked. The style wasn't a duellist's, now he saw it, nor was the man's weapon a delicate rapier. Its blade was twice the width of a rapier, with a basket hilt – more suited to the battlefields of centuries past than high-born disputes. At the sight, Rhe couldn't help but wonder who this mutual friend was, and what part he played in the Imperial House that his underlings wielded such weapons.

By the time he reached the beach, the last of the goshe had been cut down; even the two doctors in white had picked up weapons and died rather than flee.

None surrendered, Rhe noticed distantly. *Narin was right – they've been made fearless fanatics.*

The goshe on the wall had stopped firing momentarily, outnumbered by the guns on the beach, and for a moment Rhe wondered if they had fled. He looked around at the scores of white- and grey-clad Lawbringers and Investigators as they disembarked from a dozen beached boats, forming disordered knots on the open beach. Realisation struck him. *They're just waiting for us!*

'Prince Kashte!' he yelled.'The wall!'

Even as he spoke, a burning object arced high up in the air, barely starting its descent again before exploding in another eye-watering burst of light. Two more swiftly followed and tore through the crowd of Lawbringers.

'Clear the wall!' Kashte responded, dropping to one knee. Several of his fellow Imperials did the same and in seconds the first rifle shots echoed across the twilit beach. Rhe saw a dark shape tumble from the wall, but at the same time more quarrels thumped down and struck the first group of Lawbringers to mount the beach. Then another burning quarrel darted drunkenly down and exploded at the feet of the nearest of them. Rhe caught only a glimpse as he turned away, but the white light illuminated a snapshot of spraying blood and torn limbs.

Kashte's troops were quickly joined by the noble Lawbringers and the sound of gunfire came more quickly, forcing the handful on the wall back down again. Those few goshe who did chance further shots discovered how accurate the Imperials were with their beautiful rifles. Rhe left them to it, running along the beach and shouting to impose some sort of order on the invading force. The Lawbringers were not an army, of that he was painfully aware, and even the basic instructions he'd given regarding keeping to designated units proved difficult.

There were several hundred Lawbringers on the beach, many soaked from the waist down. A few dozen more were wading, completely sodden, out of the water even now, dragging their weapons along behind having swum in from the rearmost boats.

'Get in line!' Rhe yelled again and again, dragging the halberd-wielding Investigators into rows. 'There's more of them!'

His reminder that they were expecting several hundred goshe to be on the island seemed to drag their thoughts into order. The assigned squad leaders added their voices to his until they had their men together and facing the same direction.

Rhe returned to the jetty where his gun-wielding troops had spread out, wary of the goshe's bombs. The cries of wounded men intruded on his attention at long last and Rhe realised several terribly-injured

375

men had been dragged back to the boats. Among those bloodied but still standing was Law Master Sheven, his robe torn and blackened.

'I'll survive,' the man said, noticing Rhe's look. 'Just you get this done – they're not going to wait around for us.'

Rhe nodded and raised his sword. He opened his mouth to shout for them to advance when the main gate opened. Out of it raced a disordered mass of goshe. The high-castes reacted first – their ragged volley cutting down the first dozen defenders – but then Rhe's order was lost as the Lawbringers roared their defiance and charged for the enemy.

Rhe found himself frozen for a moment, astonished at the reaction of his colleagues, but instinct drove him forward. In one smooth movement he drew his second gun and shot down the nearest goshe. Then the two makeshift armies crashed together and screams once more filled the air.

Synter risked a look over the wall just as the moon-born goshe reached the Lawbringers. Chips of stone flew up as a rifle-shot glanced off the wall and she was forced back down again. Below her, goshe were still pouring through the gate so Synter scuttled over to the nearest steps and shouted at one of the men she recognised below.

'Caric!' she shouted over the noise, having to repeat herself before the Raven turned towards her. 'Shut that fucking gate! We need to hold the Lawbringers here, not kill every last one. Let's not lose more minds than we need to before the Elders are finished.'

Caric nodded and used his Blessings of strength to shove aside the knot of goshe between him and the gate. The moon-born yielded to him and soon he'd driven the gate shut and dropped the bar to hold it in place. Synter reached the ground and cast around for faces of the Detenii, but it was difficult to spot them with many of the goshe slipping on the black hoods of their order.

'Detenii,' she called, seeing a few heads rise at that, 'on the wall – Caric, get twenty crossbowmen up there too. You,' she pointed at the nearest man who looked old enough to be a Shure master, 'what Shure are you?'

'Arbold Crescent-side, Mistress.'

'Take forty men and head into the lazaret. Set ambushes there for anyone trying to push through – Caric, you're in charge here until I get back. Contain them as best you can, hear me?'

'Done!' the man replied and started to pick out those with crossbows to herd them up onto the wall.

She left Caric to it, the chance that this was a distraction of some sort occupying her mind. The noise of violence was continuing on the other side of the gate, but Synter was well aware she didn't need a victory here and now. The Lawbringers had brought in extra guns from somewhere and right now all she needed was to keep them from the hospital, a mile away at the far end of the island. She had a good four hundred more goshe in reserve around the island and three further teams of Detenii who'd taken no losses in the skirmishes of recent days.

We're too close now, Synter thought angrily as she started back down the road towards the hospital. *I won't let them stop us now.*

As though the Gods had answered her, the sun slipped below the horizon and the sky darkened further. Up above, rain clouds were massing on a stiffening breeze coming in off the Inner Sea. Synter broke into a sprint.

The smuggler's boat cut the water with barely a sound. Kesh looked over the lowered mast and saw the sun had disappeared below the horizon. Soon the sleek black boat would be near invisible to the island's lookouts. She'd lowered the sail and mast almost half an hour before, letting the tide drag them closer to the island. Hirl's price had been steep, but the man had at least delivered the goods, she was glad to see.

The small boat was simple to handle and fast, its small sail doing the bulk of the work as they slipped out of the city and began a wide circle around the island. The beach where the Lawbringers were landing was on the western end of Confessor's Island, a lumpy protrusion little more than a mile long. Most of its coastline was made up of high, jagged cliffs. That beach was the only safe place to put in on the whole island.

'Time to row,' Kesh announced, seeing a scowl cross Narin's face as she did so. 'Not you, Narin – you'll need to save your strength. The three of us will be enough.'

He shook his head. 'I'll pull my weight.'

Kesh didn't bother arguing. There was a spark of anger in Narin's eyes since Enchei had rescued him. It cut through the fatigue and whatever pain he was feeling, Kesh realised now.

Tomorrow perhaps, we need to do something about that, she thought. *Until then, it's what might just keep him alive.* She paused and almost smiled inwardly. *Tomorrow it's my problem? Strange – I'm thinking of them as brothers yet I hardly know them. Wonder what it'll be like when this is all over?*

With the four of them rowing hard and the tide assisting, they quickly reached the island. Once they were close, Kesh withdrew her oar and tapped Narin on the shoulder, indicating he should do so too. The Investigator didn't argue and just stowed the oars while Kesh took the rudder and guided them in to a sheltered section of cliff to tie up at.

'And now?' she asked sceptically, looking up at the almost sheer cliff above.

Tilted slabs of slate cut sharp lines in the remaining light. It looked an impossible climb, the handholds few and treacherous for sixty feet before the scrappy clumps of earth and grass at the top.

'Now I climb,' Enchei said, a broad smile on his face. 'Not done this in a few years, more's the pity.'

'You can make that?'

He looked up to the top. 'This? With one hand tied behind my back. Trust me, girl, I've scaled worse.'

'And then?' Narin joined in.

'Then I'll lower a rope for you and Irato.'

'What? What about me?' Kesh asked. 'Don't tell me you're getting chivalrous, old man.'

He shook his head. 'Someone's got to stay with the boat, keep it from breaking on these rocks or attracting attention.'

'Good enough job for a girl then?' she snapped.

'Hard enough,' he replied. 'It's a sailor's job and you're the only one o' those we got.'

'Oh, spare me platitudes.'

Enchei shrugged. 'Fair enough,' he said before abruptly grabbing Kesh by the arm and dragging her close. 'Someone's got to stay with the fucking boat, understand? And you're it – 'cos you're the best sailor and the worst fighter, and I'm in charge. Being quick with a knife's little use when everyone else has something longer and you're not in some cramped little alley. Narin's not in the best shape, but he's been training for years and he's bigger'n you so that's the difference. You don't like that, complain to the Gods above and see if they give two shits.'

Kesh stared back at him, struck dumb by the muted outburst. Eventually, she nodded and Enchei released her again. From inside the covered section towards the prow he retrieved a bag he'd slung there and began to pull items from it. To Kesh's surprise, the first thing he retrieved was a strange sort of silk cloak. Once the bag was mostly empty he slipped its cord strap over his head and pulled the cloak over that. Dark grey and so thin it wouldn't keep out any sort of breeze, the cloak hung limp from his shoulders down to his knees – blending almost perfectly into the evening gloom.

'A cloak?' Narin asked.

They were all dressed in clothes retrieved from the goshe killed at Narin's rooms. The bloodstains had been roughly scrubbed out and the tears sewn shut – perhaps not good enough to pass formal inspection but easily overlooked in the dark. Enchei had ripped at the sleeves of his before they left to fetch the smuggler's boat – Kesh hadn't got a good view, but there was something bulky strapped around his arm like an oversized vambrace.

'Relic of my former life,' Enchei muttered, settling the loose hood back on his shoulders before he slid his short-sword into a baldric and a stubby baton into a sheath. 'My armour's proof against most things the goshe have, but I'd prefer not to be seen in the first place.'

Lastly, he pulled a shapeless piece of thick black cloth, rolled it tight and tossed it to Narin. 'For later. Hides things even from a God's sight.'

The Investigator nodded and tied it to his own weapon belt as Enchei slipped on a pair of gauntlets with dull points on the fingertips, then hung a coiled rope from his baldric. At the end of the rope was an iron spike to be hammered into the ground so the others could follow him up the slope. Lastly he retrieved a helmet and, with an instinctive frown at the three people watching him, fitted it around his head.

Kesh exchanged a look with Narin. It wasn't clear how Enchei could see anything at all; the face-plate of the bizarre helmet was perfectly blank, but he seemed to be untroubled as he climbed out of the boat and took a grip on the rock.

'Are you sure about this?'

'Shut up and wait,' came his reply, Enchei's voice apparently unencumbered by the helmet covering his mouth. 'Irato, you follow up the rope when I give the signal – Narin, tie yourself to the end and we'll pull you up, just remember to walk up the cliff to keep the rope as clear as you can.'

He gave the cliff one more speculative look then began to climb with remarkable speed, barely pausing to look before finding the next hold. The silk cloak drifted fitfully in the breeze as he went, blending so unnaturally well into the dark rock that if he had stopped, no idle observer would have noticed him.

Kesh looked over at the other two. Narin was watching with equal astonishment, while Irato's face was tense and inscrutable.

'You going to be okay?' she whispered to the goshe. 'Not going to find yourself under their control?'

'The demons say not,' he replied, looking far from reassured. 'Not as long as they're in there, anyway.'

'Are the other goshe vulnerable to them?'

He nodded and began to check his various long-knives, hatchets and crossbow. 'Long as they get close enough and have time to break their defences. Probably the ones with the fever they can take at will.'

Kesh fell silent again, feeling a faint sense of horror at the idea of demons lurking in Irato's mind. They had been mostly quiet over the course of the day, but Enchei had spent half an hour engaged in some sort of clipped, one-sided conversation with them. Kesh still wasn't entirely sure of what had gone on there, but they'd emerged with a plan of sorts for the island.

On the cliff, Enchei paused at the top and crept up over the edge – holding on without any apparent difficulty until he chose to advance out of view. After that there was silence for several minutes, long enough for Kesh's anxiety to blossom into panic, before the rope slapped sharply against the cliff-face and made her almost cry out in surprise.

Irato gave the rope an experimental tug. Satisfied, the former goshe took it in both hands and began to walk up the cliff-face.

'Just remember,' Kesh said to Narin, 'don't get reckless up there. Kine's going to need you alive, so keep your head and leave the fighting to those two.'

'I remember.' His eyes lowered. 'Don't worry about me.'

Seeing how quickly Irato was moving up the cliff, Narin made a last check of his weapons before it was his turn too. One of the daggers Enchei had given him was sheathed in his belt, the other replaced by a sword, a simple slashing blade to suit Narin's stave training. Confirming they were both secured tightly, Narin slipped on the black goshe hood he'd brought with him and stood to tie the rope around his waist.

Once it was secure he gave a tug on the rope and felt one return as the slack was quickly taken up.

'Keep safe,' he said to Kesh as he stepped up onto the edge of the boat and rested one foot against the cliff.

'You too,' she said in a quiet voice. 'Good hunting.'

His response was lost as Irato and Enchei began to haul on the rope and jerked him up through the air. Narin turned back towards the top of the cliff and took the first few stuttering steps up. Against the darkened sky he quickly faded to just a blur of movement and Kesh found herself looking away.

She pulled on her own hood to hide her pale skin from what starlight there was and checked for her crossbow inside the covered prow. Finding it, she hunkered down, feeling a little better with the loaded weapon in her hand.

At the top of the cliff, Narin scrambled over and found himself face to face with a dead man. He gasped in surprise and almost let go of the cliff entirely as Enchei chuckled softly nearby.

'Didn't expect them to have guards?' the older man said softly. Both he and Irato were kneeling just to one side, puffing slightly after their exertion.

Narin glanced to his left and saw a second body not far away, stashed in a slight hollow so it wouldn't be visible from the rest of the island.

He struggled up and untied the rope from his waist. In the distance, he could vaguely make out the shape of the goshe's sanatorium complex, about two hundred yards away. There was little cover, just sporadic clumps of gorse no higher than his knees on this more-exposed end of the island. Away to the left, the ground sloped down towards the pebble beach the Lawbringers would be landing on. In the distance, Narin fancied he could see the faint flash of gunshots, but he couldn't be certain and the wind was behind him so any sound was drowned out. The misshapen, bare-topped lump of Confessor's Hill was a looming presence in the distance, its rocky peak edged in dull starlight while, lower down, a black tangle of trees nestled in its lee.

'Now what?'

'Now I go scout things out,' said Enchei. 'You two stay here like you're on guard until I fetch you.'

Before the man could leave, Irato suddenly gave a shuddering groan and doubled over. They watched him in alarm as, without warning, sparks briefly burst from his fingertips and a ghostly white mist leaked from his eyes and mouth. It lasted only moments, thin tendrils of mist questing out before coiling back on themselves and returning into his head.

'No,' the man croaked, fist bunching with pain around the stem of a gorse bush and snapping it with ease. The crack of wood seemed to bring him back and with one final gasp Irato looked up, a pained expression on his face. 'They've done it.'

'Done what?' Narin demanded with mounting panic.

'Something has awakened,' he intoned – all expression falling away from his face as the demon took over. 'The path is laid.'

'Path?'

'The paths between minds,' the demon confirmed. 'They are linked. This one we have protected, have cut the links before his soul was touched by their servant.'

'Servant?' Enchei asked sharply. 'What servant?'

'An abomination – mindless slave to their will, formed from the clay of our kin.'

'That's what's linked the goshe minds? Can it control them?'

'If instructed – but it possesses no will of its own. It is not truly alive, merely a tool.'

'So we don't have long,' Enchei concluded. 'No time to scout, just follow behind me and try not to get killed, okay?'

'Law Master!' Rhe shouted, over the chaos of the goshe on the beach fighting to the last man. 'We need to break down that gate!'

Law Master Sheven hurried over to him, pushing through the throng of Lawbringers and Investigators on the beach. 'We'll need a ram,' he called back before he reached Rhe. 'One of the boats? A mast?'

Rhe looked back at the debris of beached fishing boats up on the shore. 'The shore boats,' he replied, pointing. 'That small one there, we can lift that.'

'Not with those firebomb crossbows,' Sheven warned. 'You keep those goshe on the wall down or we'll be burned before we get it near.'

Rhe nodded and Sheven set off back to the waterline where a cluster of rowboats from the larger transport ships lay. A few were making the journey back to their ships, looking to carry the remaining Lawbringers ashore, but the smallest had been left abandoned on the pebble beach.

Sheven physically grabbed half a dozen men and shoved them towards it, shouting instructions as he went. It took him a few moments to get them in order but Rhe left him to it, knowing the belligerent Law Master would bawl them into line soon enough. Almost unbidden, his hands went about the routine of reloading one of his pistols, but then he stopped halfway as he saw a figure rise up from the first boat to have arrived.

Not dressed as a Lawbringer, the woman stood jerkily and looked around. Then another hauled itself up beside her, this one a dark-skinned man dressed like a shopkeeper.

Are they recovered from the fever? Rhe wondered distantly before a more alarming thought struck him. *Stars in heaven, are they under some goshe compulsion?*

Before he could move or speak, a thin band of mist swirled around the man's throat, shining bright in the gloom of an overcast night. Then he guessed the truth – not goshe, but the other player Narin had mentioned in this. Demons.

His mouth fell open just as a cry of alarm came from the men nearest, but the fever-stricken citizens moved as though in a dream – unaware of everything around them, and only a shout from Rhe stopped his men from turning to attack this new threat.

More figures rose from the deck of the fishing boat – three, then five, then ten. They swarmed forward with one purpose, tumbling over the gunwale of the boat and down into the waist-deep water below.

Rhe took an instinctive step forward then recovered himself and finished loading his remaining pistol in case he was wrong. The men and women continued to come forward over the edge of the boat as the first few waded through the water and up onto the beach. The white mist now surged and swarmed about then, three or four ribbons around the head of each – moving with purposeful, sinuous grace.

From the water at their feet came more nightmares; misshapen creatures like spider-limbed monkeys that swarmed up between the demon-possessed people. Blade-shaped claws dragged their dark, glistening hides over the pebbles, crawling alongside the possessed like hounds of the lower hells hunting the living.

In the face of this, the Lawbringers frantically parted, scrambling to get out of the way as the stumbling possessed advanced. The demons seemed not to notice and they continued up the beach towards the wall. Cries of alarm and panic rang out all down the half-formed ranks of Lawbringers, all thoughts of the goshe forgotten until the crossbow bolts started to hammer down into the possessed – rocking them back and tearing mortal wounds in their flesh, but not stopping any of those they struck.

Rhe shouted for Kashte to resume the shooting that had tailed off in the shock, but before he could do so the leading possessed was struck by one of the corkscrewing fire-bolts. She exploded into flames, the trails of mist being thrown outward by the force as their vessel was torn apart by the force. Several trails dissipated entirely under the impact while one other was thrown up into the air. The faint impression of a ghostly wolf glowed against black sky as Rhe shielded his eyes from the conflagration, then the trail dropped back down to join the dance of spirits around the head of another possessed.

Gunshots rang out once more, bullets cracking against the stone parapet of the wall. The goshe were given no more opportunities to fire as the possessed surged forward. Once they were near, Rhe saw their mouths fall open, jaws hanging loose for a moment – but then the demon-cries began. The air seemed to split apart as scream after scream burst from their mouths – a garbled, high-pitched sound no human could ever make.

On the beach, many Lawbringers dropped their weapons and clapped their hands to their ears, assailed by the intensity of the demon-cries while, on the wall, several goshe were even more affected by it. Rhe watched one man howl in pain, crossbow abandoned as he threw himself around, trying to escape the noise, before tumbling backwards off the wall.

Those less assailed continued to fire down at the demons. One pulled a pouch from their waist and jammed a burning torch inside it – a bag of fire-bolts, Rhe guessed. They wasted no time in dropping that over the edge and ducking back out of sight again before the riflemen could line up a shot.

The explosion ripped open the ground at their feet, throwing even the demons to the ground and ripping half a dozen apart in the process. The swirling spirits recoiled and drew back, but their monstrous hounds were undaunted. Even those injured in the explosion hauled themselves forward again and began to climb the wall with terrifying ease, long claws digging into the mortar as they scrambled up towards the goshe.

Rhe didn't see them reach the enemy. Before he could think to call the advance and urge his comrades on in the wake of the demons, a deep and thunderous roar rolled across the sky. Icy dread slithered down his spine as the ground trembled underfoot. It was unlike any sound he'd ever heard – the rage-filled bellow of some monstrous creature, but somehow he recognised it still.

Even as he turned, he knew what he was looking for – from the tales of his own House's centuries-old wars, from the fate of the Ebalee Trading Company and a dozen other fragmentary accounts. A roar that heralded the death of armies.

From the water at the far end of the beach rose a new terror – faceless and stone-skinned, pale ghosts emerging from the gloom. Larger than all but the tallest men, the thick-limbed figures stood in the shallow water and surveyed the fighting ahead. Their booming war-cry crashed against Rhe's ears once more, shaking his bones as the first of the figures began to advance. They looked like living statues, skin as cold and seamless as carved stone, with long cylinders of the same material slung under their right arms like the stub of a lance.

The nearest statue lowered its lance and pointed its concave tip past Rhe, towards the wall. The Lawbringer dropped to the ground in anticipation and others nearby did likewise. There was a rushing sound and Rhe saw the air ripped apart as intense heat washed against his skin. He didn't move in time to see the gate be struck by the Dragon's Breath, but he heard the conflagration as it erupted into flames and the stones around it shattered.

A rare spark of fear fluttered in Rhe's heart. Few who witnessed this ever lived to tell the tale, but famous it was all the same. The Stone Dragons had announced their presence in death and flame.

CHAPTER 27

Of the Astaren there are many tales, but few are recognised as truth. Only those of the Stone Dragons are given credence because House Dragon is happy to demonstrate their power to the entire Empire. One must wonder what other weapons they keep secret when the Lords of Dragon are willing for their enemies to know the terrible strength of these battlefield destroyers.

From A *History* by Ayel Sorote

Synter took a step towards Father Jehq, axe half-raised before she even realised what she was doing. Without lowering the weapon, she composed herself and asked coldly, 'What do you mean, leave them?'

'There is no time,' Jehq replied. 'You heard the call of the Stone Dragons. Either they hold out or they're already dead.'

'I can't leave my men to die! I don't care about the moon-born goshe, but there are Detenii out there too.'

'And we will mourn them,' he said calmly, 'but there is nothing we can do. Caric is no fool, he'll disengage and leave the rest to die. We must complete the ceremony or we are all dead.'

'How long?'

Jehq looked back down an open stairway at the lavish hall below. Six large pillars supported a central dome painted black and studded with silver constellations, while a square cloister of alcoves and door-ways surrounded it. The pair stood at the edge of a balcony with a view over the front courtyard. Beyond it, the leper colony was visible in the distance, columns of flame rising up from several parts as the Stone Dragons did their work.

'Assuming those flames don't reach the houses where the lepers have been left? It is hard to gauge. Mother Yliss is gone, Pallasane is being drawn now,' Jehq noted.

A woman's body lay discarded on the ground beside the crystal-studded artefact while the tiny form of Father Pallasane knelt before it, forehead pressed against the largest shard. 'It does not take long, but only when we are twelve at least will we be strong enough to control what we have created.'

'So you're number twelve?'

'I am.'

'Shit, we're running out of time. I'll take the teams we've got here and set up some sort of delaying action – at least the Stone Dragons followed the Lawbringers in. I don't know what made them decide to act, but we caught a break there. Gives us space to ...' She tailed off and there was a moment of complete silence.

'What? What is it?' Jehq snapped, turning. He followed her gaze and faltered too. 'Is that ...?'

'Yes,' Synter breathed. 'The Gods come to claim us.'

A light blossomed beyond the courtyard wall, then a second and third. Synter looked left and right to see more bursts of light – encircling them. Directly ahead was an enormous man, bearded as she remembered from the temple worship of her childhood and dressed all in white. On his left arm was a silver vambrace around which the air glittered, describing a large disc shape in the air – Lord Shield.

Thirty yards to Shield's right was a tall man with long dark hair and faintly glowing red eyes; Lord Huntsman, a great spear of starlight in his hand. Away to the left was the cold porcelain face of Lady Archer, a burning arrow nocked, while beyond her was the more-familiar figure of Lord Duellist, hand resting on his fabled blade.

'Well, there you go,' Synter croaked, recovering from the shock first. She pointed towards Duellist. 'Didn't you want to have a word with him?'

Jehq coughed in astonishment. 'You make jokes, now of all times?'

'I ain't dead yet,' the woman declared, standing taller as she faced the Gods down. 'And they're not rushing in to stop us.'

'But why?'

'They can smell what we've just done,' she realised. 'They heard the call go out and touch all the moon-born goshe – and they want it. Gods love power as much as any man, just they can take it more easily.'

'But they've got competition from their own? They're facing each other down?'

'Aye – more important than anything, they can't let another take it. They're waiting for one to blink and take the first step. That one's likely to be cut down by all the rest, but it could spark a war in heaven and none of 'em fancy that much.'

Jehq blinked and squinted forward at the darkness surrounding the shining Gods. 'What's that?'

'What?'

'I … I can't see so well – the air's …'

'Oh seven hells!' Synter exclaimed, blinking furiously. 'That's not natural – what is it?'

The air had changed around them and a haze of tiny glittering motes began to overlay the island. Judging by the reactions of the avatars of the Gods, the same was happening everywhere – each one searched for the source of the disturbance but none seemed to find it. To Synter's Starsight-blessed eyes it was as though the very air had frozen and each fragment of water vapour was now a sparkling ice crystal drifting on the breeze. Thousands upon thousands of tiny dots of light, filling the air around her and catching what faint light existed – eliminating any advantage of sight the Blessing gave her.

'Someone's levelling the field,' she said, squinting out over the courtyard at the indistinct shape of Lord Shield. 'Some sort of magic, blinding even those with sight better'n our Blessings. One of them, or the fox-spirits maybe – the Ascendants can barely see in this, same as us.'

She closed her eyes and concentrated, suppressing her Starsight for a while as she tried again with normal eyes. Now it seemed a thick fog covered the island – one heavy enough to obscure the light of the Gods above and all but a faint glow of the flames in the distance. Normally, her Starsight would penetrate even the worst mist, but if anything it was easier to see through the fog than the supernaturally glittering haze. The air shone like a sandstorm of silver, but barely moving rather than blowing on past.

'They're going,' Jehq said, peering forward as far as he could. 'Look! Lady Archer – she just vanished.'

'Whichever one's created this, they've got a plan,' Synter said, thinking fast. 'Do they want us to succeed? No, that makes no sense. The Lawbringers!' she gasped. 'That's where they've been getting their help – some damn God's sitting in the background. Shield or Lawbringer no doubt, they want this to play out and have that bastard Rhe deliver them the artefact without starting a war in the heavens.'

'Then we've still got time,' Jehq declared. 'Get the Detenii out there – once the moon is risen, I'll be able to gather your teams to the fold without you touching the artefact.'

Synter gave a start, unaware of that, but as soon as she'd opened her mouth she realised it wasn't the time to argue. 'Fine, we're gone.'

The woman slipped her black mask over her face and she headed down the stairs, yelling for the Detenii. He watched her go as activity in the hall below continued, oblivious to the strange detente that had apparently been reached outside. In the centre of the pillared hall the last scraps of Father Pallasane's tattered soul fled his body and the still-warm corpse flopped sideways to the floor. One of the goshe attendants hauled the tiny body away as the stout figure of Mother Eyote kneeled in his place. She looked out of place wearing goshe black, but Jehq remembered her in her younger days.

Athletic and strong, she'd shared his adventurer's spirit and been one of the first to jump at the chance of an expedition. Warrior caste, Jehq recalled, his thoughts lingering on the nights they'd spent together – back in another age so it seemed – when he'd explored the scars and tattoos of her muscular body. Never a flicker of fear from her as they travelled the demon-haunted depths of Shadowrain forest, but now she was just as broad-hipped and careworn as any mother of grown children.

In Synter's wake, half of the moon-born guards also left – minds linked and obeying her commands as one perfect unit. A dozen remained as sentries, walking the dark walkways overlooking the hall, and two dozen more were on the perimeter. The hall was lit by lamps set in high alcoves on every wall, oval archways leading to the wards that occupied most of the sanatorium's bulk and justified the high walls around it.

Jehq spared one last glance in the direction of Lord Duellist before he too headed down. The darkness of the island was overlaid by a shifting insubstantial curtain that obscured almost everything. The God he had once met had vanished back to his lonely constellation in the heavens.

'We will speak soon, my Lord,' Jehq whispered to the night. 'Soon we will meet as equals.'

*

Dazed and horrified, Rhe and Sheven followed in the wake of the Stone Dragons as the leper colony burned behind them. It was unclear whether there was anyone inside – only the nearer buildings were burning, but if the wind turned the flames could take the rest with ease. There were no cries for help however, no shouts or screams to alert them. Reluctantly, they had moved on, leaving a handful on the beach in case any innocents were caught up in the chaos.

'This can't be natural,' Sheven declared, gesturing with his scimitar at the sudden fog that had enveloped the island. 'You think it's those demons?'

Rhe nodded. 'You saw the spirits moving round them like mist. They're not so different from this. But it might be the goshe too. The Stone Dragons aren't moving so fast, look. They're not far ahead – might be they can't see well either and are wary of an ambush.'

He had barely finished speaking when yells broke the air. Rhe heard the clatter of quarrels on armour and the ring of steel, then the Stone Dragons roared. Again, that great heave of breath split the air apart. The mist was torn open and Rhe saw figures smashed from the path of the Dragon's Breath. Limbs were ripped away and clothes ignited. The sense of dread in Rhe's gut grew as the stink of burned flesh filled the air.

The Stone Dragons marched inexorably on. Groups of goshe threw themselves at them – Rhe guessed they were just as disorientated by the mist, for though they attacked fearlessly it was as an armed mob charging, not a trained army. The Astaren of House Dragon slaughtered those in each assault with brutal ease – drawing short wedge-like blades to wield with their free hands or using their lances as clubs.

Rhe's sword was sheathed on his back now, his pistols holstered. The Lawbringers were a hushed and humbled column trailing along behind Rhe and Sheven. Prince Kashte and his Imperial cohorts kept close to Rhe, pride keeping them at the fore of the battle despite the blood and charred entrails scattered across their path.

Rhe walked with a stiff determination, fighting the urge to shrink down and be bowed by the oppression of death and entombing fog. The light of the Gods was hidden; the scorched and torn ground as much their guide as the stone-bordered path that cut through the gorse-studded heather. The Stone Dragons were indistinct pale shapes behind a curtain of fog and Rhe found it easy to imagine they were the hungry ghosts spoken of in his people's folklore.

He knew the demon-spirits now lurking elsewhere in the miasma overlaying the island were a more likely source of such stories, but he was an Eagle-hegemony by birth. At war with the neighbouring House Dragon more than a dozen times since the fall of the Greater Empire, it was more than possible that these killers of men had been glimpsed as they went about their brutal business.

Rhe found his hand tightening and forced himself to put such thoughts from his mind. *I am a Lawbringer – a warrior of my House no longer.*

He found his head bowing under the weight of it all.

Punish the guilty. That armour they wear is evidence enough to one of my birth, but there are boundaries to even the Emperor's law.

He struggled on; fighting back the hate with every step, reminding himself there was another purpose to leading his brethren there. They had at least several dozen dead already and the risks of this mission were great enough without foolishness on his own part.

But, one day, we will see even the Astaren answer for their crimes. One day I will see no man or woman above the law. Even the Astaren will be subject to it.

The resolve was a cold, sour knot in his belly, but it gave him strength and Rhe marched on.

One day. Until then, let Narin steal this prize out from under them. Let the great Astaren know failure.

Synter hunkered down in the fog, fighting to control her confusion. She couldn't remember the last time she'd been out in the pitch black with only her normal vision to rely on. The air was close and chilly around her, shockingly dark, while every tiny sound she made was amplified to her ears. With her Starsight the fog had seemed to envelop her, glittering and swirling, but even now she could discern little through the gloom.

Ten yards away she could just make out the dark shape of another Detenii similarly crouched in the gorse. By the size, she could tell it was Kodeh. Only the pale Leviathan giant, Ushernai, had matched him for bulk – the pair a strange balance of light and dark.

But Ushernai's dead, she reminded herself. *Most likely it was these damn Stone Dragons who killed him.*

She looked at the crossbow in her hands. The fat clay head of the quarrel gave it an awkward balance – they flew like a drunken firework, impossible to aim at any distance, but it was the only weapon they had against the Astaren. Nothing else would crack that armour or do anything but attract their attention.

Just as well I can't see far in this crap anyway, Synter thought with a smile. *With luck they're as lost as me. If not, this is going to be the worst ambush in history.*

She glanced up in the direction she hoped the leper colony was. It was impossible to tell exactly, but they'd used the path that ran to the beach as a guide. Ahead of her there was nothing, a ghostly curtain through which she could hear only fragments of noise. Voices and shouts, demon-cries and the roar of the Dragon's Breath as it obliterated men and foliage with equal ease. Just coming out this way to lay in wait for the Astaren in staggered groups, Synter had been playing games with her fears. Shapes in the fog, drifting illuminations and whispering voices on the edge of hearing – she had no idea what was real now. Something had created this infernal, yet blessed, unnatural curtain of fog – hiding them all from each other, levelling the ground for the goshe whether or not that was the intent. Somewhere at the back of her mind was the whisper of the moon-born minds – not linked to her but a growing presence in the air around her and all the Detenii.

Some sixth sense prickled on her neck and Synter readied her crossbow. From somewhere off to her right there was a fizz and thunk as one of her team fired their bow. She was following the weapon's sputtering path without thinking; left hand touching crackling sparks to the clay head's fuse.

She saw a faint light twist through the fog before the sharp crack as it erupted into light. An indistinct outline blossomed not far away, a massive silhouette in the process of turning just as she sighted her sputtering weapon.

Synter felt her guts lurch as the Dragon's Breath coughed and a long lance of air distorted away towards the bolt's source. While she pulled the trigger on her own weapon the luckless Detenii exploded into flames.

Leaning into the kick of the crossbow, Synter watched breathlessly as her quarrel darted forward, twisting through the air as Kodeh's appeared an instant behind it. Then it struck and the air turned white as a double explosion split the air.

She flinched away from the blinding burst of light, intent on running in case a Stone Dragon was taking aim, but was dazzled and stumbled after a step or two. Synter let it turn into a roll, tucking her shoulder down and regaining her feet in a long-ingrained movement. The world returned with fitful trails of light and hazy details, but she kept moving – crouched low but going as fast as she could to get clear of the inevitable retaliation.

Inside, she crowed, wanted to howl Kodeh's name and see the satisfaction on the brutal Dragon's face. His countryman was dead, she was sure of that – the Stone Dragon had been hit by both weapons.

Somewhere behind there was a roar of rage and the whump of Dragon's Breath tearing through the undergrowth, but Synter was well away.

Got you, fucker. Time for you to feel fear – you're in my shadows now.

Enchei ghosted forward through the fog. The air was cool on his face, now exposed to the night. With his helm on he had been able to see almost nothing as a million tiny motes glittered all around him. The breeze had been stilled and the cold scent of fog overlaid a distant flavour of something else. Something that would have been all but imperceptible had it not stirred faint recognition in Enchei.

The Apkai, he realised with a chill. *Should've known that demon would be keeping a close eye on me.*

What allegiance the fox-demons might hold to the greater kin he'd invoked, Enchei couldn't imagine. The realm of the supernatural was separate to all but a few Astaren, so remote and alien were the minds involved. A few were altered and trained to deal with demons and the avatars of Gods, but for the main they used the tools this unnatural side of the world provided and kept a healthy distance from its denizens.

There must be some threat out here, Enchei realised as he continued in a rough skirting of the sanatorium, leaving the more direct path for Narin and Irato. *The Apkai must be slowing something or someone up – buying us time to stop the goshe. Not surprised; if I was a Stone Dragon on standing duty in the Imperial City, I'd investigate all this just to stave off the boredom.*

Almost from nowhere two shapes loomed suddenly in the fog. They were walking from right to left – a patrol, Enchei guessed. He levelled his baton and the air shuddered. First one, then the other, folded up and collapsed as limp as a corpse. The aging warrior grinned to himself as he stepped over their unconscious bodies. A man and a woman in goshe clothing, their spears abandoned on the ground.

Before he'd gone much further he heard a voice cut through the pale night. On instinct Enchei crouched and slipped the hood of his silk-like cape over his head. Quite still, he peered forward, trying not to move as he identified where the speaker was. The voice was muted by the fog; somewhere up ahead was all he could tell. He edged closer.

'I tell you I heard something,' insisted one.

'What was it?'

Enchei froze again, keeping as low as he could and trusting his cloak to hide him from searching eyes.

'In my head – like a burst of noise, but far away.'

'From where?'

The first man grunted. 'Don't know, but I heard it.'

Enchei looked down at the baton in his hands. It was a simple tool, one that filled its victim's head with sound and light normal senses couldn't perceive – but enough to overwhelm the mind and cause them to black out far more effectively than a blow to the head.

So this link between them ain't complete, he realised. *He heard something, an echo of it, but has no clue what it was and there's no God in his mind to figure it out.*

'Hey, who goes there?' one of the men snapped abruptly. 'Stop where you are.'

'Where's Father Jehq?' replied a gruff voice – Irato. 'Take me to him.'

'Who are you?' the man repeated, a little uncertain now. 'What Shure are you two from?'

'Do what I say,' Irato commanded.

Enchei felt a slight frisson as Irato spoke; a faint spark of something unfamiliar running down his neck. Whatever it was, the goshe's attitudes changed in a heartbeat.

'Yes, sir – he's in the main hall. They're in the middle of the ceremony.'

Learning all sorts now, aren't I? Enchei thought as footsteps began to lead away. *Those demons have been rooting around in Irato's mind – looks like they've found some toys to play with there.*

Silently, he followed at as great a distance as he could. Narin had been quiet the whole time, acting subservient as he'd been ordered.

394

Before long, the outline of the sanatorium's high walls appeared in the distance and Enchei circled away from the men he'd been following. He didn't want to go anywhere near the door they were heading for — his plan was a little more oblique.

So far, so good. Now we just have to hope Jehq doesn't kill Irato as soon as he recognises him.

Enchei touched his fingers to the contents of the bag on his back. Inside was the mace-like object the goshe had used to blank out the light in Narin's rooms, hastily repaired.

Got a little surprise for you, Father, Enchei said inwardly, *trust me — you won't like it, but by then it'll be too bloody late.*

CHAPTER 28

To be a hero in the Lesser Empire is an unenviable thing. Many aspire to such a status, but few truly attain it and fewer still survive it. First into the breach in battle and targeted by younger warriors in duels, glorious retirement is rarely an option. A sensible man would not wish for such a thing, but bravery and sense are rare companions.

From *A History* by Ayel Sorote

A levelled crossbow met Irato at the door. With an effort, the renegade goshe did nothing, merely looked forward and waited for the other man to make his decision. In those few heartbeats he felt a sudden liberation, a clarity of mind as the fog of uncertainty and loss parted. Here there was only the moment, the pivot around which his death or salvation would turn.

'Unfuckingbelievable,' the tall man at the door growled. 'I should kill you where you stand.'

'Probably,' Irato agreed. 'Not your call though, is it?'

He had no idea who the man was even once he'd slipped off his black mask. Long curls of brown hair framed a pale, fleshy face. Irato couldn't guess the man's heritage, maybe somewhere in the remote east, Houses Raven or Ghost, but his accent was local.

'You search him?' the man snapped at Irato's trailing attendants. He peered forward at them and scowled. 'Of course not, you just did what he told you. Do it, now!'

Irato didn't resist as he was grabbed and pushed against the jamb, three pairs of hands swiftly removing what weapons he carried.

'Bind his hands,' the man continued, tossing forward a knotted cord while keeping his crossbow pointed at Irato's face.

This was done quickly and only then was he admitted to a dark hallway, lit solely with what illumination crept through an archway at the far end.

'Move. Try anything and I'll not bother showing you to the Elders first.'

Irato complied and walked as directed, keen to be inside and face to face with his former comrades. Through open doorways he saw bodies, dozens upon dozens on every spare piece of ground available. The hundreds of fever-struck citizens, minds sacrificed to the God these goshe were trying to bring into being.

'Just leaving them there like dead meat?' he asked, catching a glancing blow around the head for his troubles. Irato staggered a few steps before recovering himself, his unnatural resilience stretched by a steel pommel or cosh.

'They'll survive the night, long enough for us to reach all the goshe across the Empire. You, on the other hand, won't be so lucky.'

'You reckon?'

Another blow dropped him to one knee. Irato blinked away the stars that danced at the corners of his eyes and slowly forced himself upright again. From what Kesh had said, his old self was an arrogant man who'd not keep quiet even with a blade at his throat. To Irato's surprise, the role wasn't so hard to play as he'd expected.

'Shut up and move.'

'I'm going,' Irato said, lurching forward before he found his balance again. 'It's Jehq I'm here to see anyway, not his pets.'

There was an intake of breath, but the elite behind him was no fool and could tell when he was being needled. The man didn't reply, but nor did he strike Irato again. Irato knew he was strong enough to stave in a man's skull if he got careless out of anger. Killing a traitor while he tried something was easily explained to the man in charge, they'd be naturally suspicious of his presence. Cracking that same traitor's skull out of irritation while taking him to be interrogated however … Well, that wasn't the thinking of a man likely to share much of his master's successes.

At last they came to a candle-lit hall. Great brass stands flanked an inner ring of pillars, gleaming in the light, while candles shone from every alcove around the outer wall. He glimpsed more bodies through one open doorway – clearly they were not standing on ceremony, despite what they were doing in the centre of the room. With their souls and minds lost, or given over to the God that would inhabit them, he guessed they'd be invalids at best – living corpses at worst – but the goshe would need them alive for certain.

A stuttering flurry of oaths and curses heralded Irato's arrival in the hall. Despite himself and the prospect of death, he felt a quickening in his stomach at the alarm his presence had sparked. Unknown faces advanced towards him, some with weapons half-raised until older faces shouted for them to stop. It took a few moments for the senior goshe to restore order within the ranks, but Irato wasn't complaining as it gave Narin time to put some distance between the two of them.

The hall was finer than he'd expected of a sanatorium; intricate detailing on every cornice and pillar, a geometric mosaic on the floor and the black central dome painted with constellations of both the Gods and the lesser stars. The greater stars were silver studs, connected by stylised lines, while the lesser constellations were also faintly described, but dominating it all was the great silver moon at the very peak, detailed with concentric bands of script he couldn't make out.

To his left was a wide stairway that led up to the open air, while he guessed the three largest iron-banded doors led to the sanatorium wards. Narin had said this was where the city's lunatics ended up – or at least the poor majority of them, given that high-caste patients were mostly treated at a smaller version in the city. Irato only knew that any such knowledge was lost in the black hole of his mind, which he guessed meant he'd visited this place often.

Somehow, the poison, Moon's Artifice, had separated out parts of his mind – stripping out his memories but leaving the more remote details. He knew the history of the Empire, the Ten Day War and how the smugglers of the Horn Coast plied their trade, but the existence of anything on this small island escaped him entirely.

There were guards lining the walls, half in cloth masks, he was glad to note. Narin would be able to blend in easily enough; the faces on view showed half a dozen descents so it was unlikely they all knew each other. There was a clear differentiation between the elite around the inner pillars and the goshe standing guard beyond that. The regulars hadn't reacted at all to Irato's presence, just a docile noting of the reaction he inspired in the various elites and elders presiding over the ritual in the centre.

There, a bluish-grey object a little smaller than a man's leg stood in a wrought-iron stand – irregular crystal shards set into its body which glowed with fitful light. A balding man with grey, lined cheeks and liverspots on his hands knelt before it, forehead pressed against the largest shard.

'So our errant son returns,' declared a slim, white-haired man, advancing ahead of a gaggle of goshe elders. 'A little late for redemption, don't you think, Irato?'

'Never too late – isn't that what the priests say?'

Jehq, or so Irato presumed, cocked his head to one side. 'Not many, no. I don't remember you being an attendant at Pilgrim's or Pity's temple anyway.'

Irato shrugged, happy to keep the man talking. He could see the curiosity in the man's greyish cheeks and guessed he could play this out a little longer. 'I'll take your word for it, just sounds like something a priest would say.'

'Jehq!' snapped one of the elders behind, a woman with a ruddy face and thick arms whose sleeves had been rolled up to reveal five or six long scars. Defensive wounds, Irato assumed.

'You're wasting time. He's obviously here as a ruse.'

'You didn't capture him, Sho?'

The elite with the crossbow shook his head. 'Man just walked in with a few guards acting attendants. Guess you didn't think about traitors when you made that Command Blessing,' he added with a hint of black humour in his voice.

'I suppose not,' Jehq mused.

'Sho, kill him,' the woman barked.

Irato felt a prickle on the back of his neck, but couldn't tell whether it was his imagination or the cold tip of a quarrel.

'You let your bitch talk for you?' he said to Jehq hastily, trying to delay matters long enough.

Jehq smiled thinly as the bitch advanced past him and wasted no time in planting a firm knee into Irato's groin. Her strength was remarkable and Irato's effort to twist sideways did little good, the impact almost lifting him from his feet.

He dropped, gasping at the blow and feeling the tremble of sickening pain rumble swiftly along behind it. In moments Irato's stomach was cramped with bands of hot iron tightening around him. His involuntary cry was a strangled and muted thing; it was only the shooting pain that garbled the woman's words as she bent low over him.

'Just for that, I won't kill you. Tonight of all nights, we shouldn't be wasting bodies so you get to go the same way as the fever-born. Hear me, Irato? I'm going to strip out that mind of yours, take all the words away from your big mouth. You'll live out the rest of your days in a cell here, shitting the bed while I use your mind in your place.'

She stood again. 'Bring him.'

The elite, Sho, gave an amused grunt and handed his crossbow to one of the goshe guards. Drawing a dagger, he touched it to Irato's throat and dragged the renegade, one-handed, by the collar into the centre of the room. Just as they reached the limp bodies of several old men and woman, Irato convulsed and spewed his guts up over the floor as the sickening pain in his guts was exacerbated by the movement.

He lay face down for a moment, panting to catch his breath with his head propped against the cooling body of a plump, middle-aged woman. Only then did the demons in his mind dull the pain in his balls to a level he could tolerate.

Out of the corner of his eye he watched the woman stalk around him just as the man kneeling before the artefact fell back, lifeless. She shoved the body carelessly out of her way and tugged the crystal-studded artefact from its holder, brandishing it like a mace as she advanced on Irato.

'You go first,' Irato suggested in a hoarse voice, angling his body around in an attempt to get to his knees. 'Think I'll pass on it entirely. Lost the taste for grand delusions.'

'Delusions?' That seemed to throw her for a moment, but she was not a woman to be surprised for long. 'I'd ask what happened to you to change your mind, but I'd be wasting time and I really don't care that much.'

Without ceremony, she raised the artefact as though it was a javelin to be hurled and carelessly drove it against Irato's forehead. The impact rocked him back, but instead of being knocked over backwards Irato felt his head clamped against the artefact by some invisible force. Almost instantly, the end of the artefact became hot against his skin. He felt a moment of pure blank terror inside just before his ears began to echo with the high, savage cries of the demons inside his mind.

In the next moment everything went perfectly black.

*

Weapons were out before anyone knew what was happening. The stuttered moment of complete darkness made most of the goshe freeze, but not all. Sho's dagger slashed toward where Irato had been while he drew a second knife, but the edge caught nothing. In the next heartbeat his Starsight blossomed into life and the hall reappeared in his mind – a shade etching both detailed and beautiful. Before he could move, the white etched lines seemed to shudder and wrench before his eyes. Sho staggered, hands to his eyes as he fought the urge to puke or drop to his knees. His Starsight stuttered, dimmed then reasserted itself and finally he found his bearings again.

The artefact was a blazing light ahead of him. Irato had somehow got his hands free and was wrestling with Mother Terail over it. Before Sho could close the ground between them Irato wrenched Terail off-balance and slammed an elbow down into her eye. Terail shrieked and fell, whereupon Irato darted out of the way of Sho's slash and yanked a long-knife from the belt of a blinded guard.

Sho took a step towards the man, about to attack, when pain exploded in his side. He was thrown off balance and stumbled over the howling figure of Mother Terail, barely stopping himself from falling. Dazed, Sho looked down at his side and saw the black mess of blood leaking out of a neat tear in the cloth – all neatly detailed in white and grey by his Starsight.

Behind him, sword in hand, was a masked goshe, while to Sho's complete astonishment a Darkness Sceptre swung crazily above the man's head from an upper window. The sceptre was a black tear in the tapestry of his Starsight, but clearly damaged – the darkness sputtering fitfully as it blurred the neat white outlines around it.

Irato has allies? How many traitors are there?

The goshe who'd stabbed him took advantage of Sho's astonishment to kick him in the ribs and drive him into the nearby pillar. The pain worsened and Sho's legs buckled underneath him.

Sho tried to stand, legs treacherous beneath him, as Irato tossed the artefact to his conspirator. The tall figure of Father Olos hurled himself at the man, a corona of spitting light surrounding his reaching hands. Somehow the goshe managed to avoid him, twisted improbably around and out of Olos' hands as the Father overbalanced and stumbled. The goshe whipped his sword across the man's head in an artless swipe, but hard enough to crack the Father's skull and drop him.

The goshe sheathed his sword and wrapped a piece of cloth around the artefact, blanking out its light before he slipped it into some sort of quiver. Sho watched this happen with an increasing sense of detachment. His side was numb now, his fingers cold. Irato put his long-knife to work as another of the Elders made for the masked goshe. Dangerous though they were, each seemed to move as though drunk, flailing for the burly Detenii while he ducked and sliced with impunity.

Sho sank back, defeated by the seeping chill. Eyelids drooping, sight dimming, he watched the masked goshe sprint for the door. Those in his path swung wildly for him, some blows seeming to connect but having as little effect as the efforts of the Elders. Behind him went Irato, dragging the blinded guards into the path of the Elders and making for the stair to the balcony. Causing chaos while his conspirator fled, Irato selflessly brought the wrath of the goshe onto himself as he made for the upper floor.

The darkness was almost complete around Sho now. His thoughts moved as slowly as the reeling Elders and goshe, but even as he sank into unconsciousness a question lingered in some small part of his mind.

Why?

Irato wasn't a man to sacrifice himself. Irato wasn't the sort to cover some stranger's escape, and the masked goshe was no Detenii – that much Sho could see. They were a tight-knit group built over years and betraying that wouldn't be for selfless reasons.

Why then? What did I miss?

The darkness took him before any answers came.

Narin ran without thought. The quiver slapped and rattled on his back, the only thing that was real in the grey murk of outside. In the vague distance there came dulled sounds and diffuse lights – nothing he could make sense of and he had no time to try. A clatter at the open sanatorium gate behind him turned into the heavy tramp of boots in pursuit – not slowing to check on the guards Narin had surprised there. Angry shouts echoed off the high outer wall as they fanned out, his small head-start enough to let the fog swallow him up.

Clumps of grass seemed to leap up at his knees out of the dark. He careened around them as best as he could without slowing, but skidded off the side of one and his foot went from underneath him. As he thumped down onto his side, the bruising from his torture seemed to burst into life again. The impact drove the air from his lungs and for a moment his vision went white with pain.

It was the chill and damp touch of mud against his skin that brought his senses back. He used his sword to push himself up, leaning on it like an old man before fear overrode the hot flowers of pain in his muscles. He pushed forward, lurching wildly until he caught his balance, but then he stopped.

Narin looked left and right. In the tumble he wasn't sure if he was facing in the right direction any more. There were no stars or features of the land to guide him, nothing but that damned fog hiding everything from sight.

He took a hesitant step forward, deciding to go straight and hope he'd not got turned too far around. In the next moment a dark shape loomed out of the fog, a goshe with a long black scarf wound around his face. The goshe stopped in surprise as he saw Narin and the two looked each other up and down. The other was taller than he, broader too and for a moment Narin felt Irato's name form on his lips. Then he realised the man carried a curve-bladed spear and just as the goshe began to say something Narin lunged forward with his sword.

It was an awkward thrust, but the sword slid easily enough into the goshe's chest. The goshe gave a wheeze, something between disbelief and agony. Narin hesitated, arm extended, as the spear dropped from the man's grip. The goshe looked down at the steel in his chest and staggered back, drawing himself off Narin's blade, knees buckling as he began to wail piteously and clasped his hands to the blood flowing from the wound.

Narin watched the man's pain in horrified fascination. It had happened so quietly, so smoothly, that he froze at the sight of a man dying before him. Then the goshe flopped sideways, one hand out to break his fall and somehow keeping upright as the fear and panic in his voice increased. That spurred Narin into action again and he chopped down at the goshe's neck with all the force he could muster.

He felt the blade snap bone and plough on through. The dying man spasmed and went still, the blade caught deep in his body. Narin wrenched it back out again and stood looking down at the ruined mess of meat that had so recently been a man. His breathing was ragged and pained for a long moment of silence as revulsion welled up inside him.

Narin wanted to vomit, but managed to force himself to turn away and take a few steps. Suddenly he was filled with a need to escape the deed and he broke into a run again, racing blindly through the fog with the hot stink of terror in his nose.

The crack of wood rang out from somewhere on his right and Narin veered left, almost falling when he saw a huge shape loom up ahead. Unable to stop he stumbled away from it and thumped into the bare stone of a jutting lump of rock. The rough edge snagged his sleeve and he heard the cloth tear as he was jerked to a halt. Narin groaned as the impact sent a shooting pain down his sword arm, the weight of the weapon suddenly dragging his arm down.

He cast around for anything that might tell him where he was, but aside from the broken-topped rock he could see nothing. He stood and gasped for breath, working his shoulder in a circle to try and get some feeling back. As his panic increased, he yanked the goshe mask from his head and gulped down the cold night air, trying to make sense of where he was going. Skirting the rock, he turned in a full circle, but all he saw was the air tear apart some twenty-odd yards away and a path of yellow flames leap up from the ground. In its wake a man shrieked, clothes alight and flailing fruitlessly against the terrible fire, before collapsing to the ground and falling silent.

He started off in the other direction, trying to move stealthily to avoid the attention of whatever terrible weapon had done that. After a few yards he stopped, seeing pale shapes in the fog – waist height and still. He edged closer and realised it was a woman crouching, wearing just a thin white shirt and skirt. She was crowned with a halo of bright mist and as he neared her it began to move and swirl through the air.

Narin raised his sword but the woman did not rise, only turned her head towards him. Her eyes shone in the darkness, lambent orbs inside her head, and with a lurch Narin realised she was not goshe, but some native of the Imperial City. The shining mist, he guessed, was a fox-spirit possessing her and, as though to confirm that, her hand awkwardly rose from the ground and beckoned him forward.

He found himself obeying, almost relieved at the sight of a fox-demon out in the darkness. Irato had said there would be others on the island, secreting themselves on the boats of fever-struck, but Narin hadn't realised until then they had also taken over the minds of people. He headed towards her, sword brushing the low twists of gorse that covered

404

the ground, but before he could reach her there was a sudden rush of bright mist away from him.

The woman barely had time to turn her head before the fox-spirits had abandoned her and a searing path of fire tore through the fog. It struck her with the force of a God's punch, smashing her backwards as her hair and clothes ignited. Unlike the previous victim, though, the woman fell without a sound and didn't move again as the flames hungrily consumed her.

'Hello precious,' whispered a voice in Narin's ear.

He tried to turn and bring his sword to bear, but was struck a terrific blow on his shoulder. It jerked the weapon from his hand and a kick sent him sprawling on his back. Dazed, he looked up at a black-masked goshe who held a crossbow in hands that crackled with trails of lightning.

'Miss me?' the woman said.

Narin's stomach lurched as he recognised her; Synter, the woman who'd captured him at Coldcliffs. Rage and terror clashed in his mind as Narin scrambled for a weapon, but Synter just laughed and darted forward with unnatural speed. She grabbed his wrist and twisted his knife from its grip, tossing the weapon off into the darkness. Shoving him back down again, Synter retrieved his sword and threw that after it.

'Now keep quiet or the bad man will get you,' she hissed, raising her crossbow.

Narin looked past her and blearily made out a faint shape in the fog – visible only because it was huge and as pale as bone. Slung under one arm was a long, fat weapon of some kind – not a spear, he realised after a moment, but shorter and with a blunt snub tip. The figure turned towards them as the air around Synter's crossbow cracked for one fierce moment and some sort of fuse ignited on the quarrel.

She fired and dove for the cover of the rocks Narin had just left. He glimpsed a corkscrewing trail of light race towards the giant before the air above where she'd been standing was ripped apart.

A great wash of heat slashed down onto his skin, causing Narin to cry out and wrench his protesting body away. Mere yards away the undergrowth blossomed yellow and orange, then a crack split the sky and a fiercer light exploded around the giant – a Stone Dragon, Narin realised as he rolled through the blessedly cool, damp grass.

When he looked back up, Synter was nowhere to be seen but the Stone Dragon was still standing. It stormed towards him with weapon levelled, casting around for the goshe. Its armour was flame-scarred and cracked, Narin saw – blackened down one side of its torso with a fissure running down the all-enclosing armour that looked more like porcelain than steel. A broad-bladed short-sword was in its other hand; almost as long as Narin's but stubby in the fist of the Stone Dragon.

It closed on him rapidly, but Narin realised one leg was moving more stiffly than the other. Synter had hurt it, but it was far from dead. Closer still and Narin could see the faint contours of nose and jaw in the shape of the helm, while large almond-shaped indentations indicated its eyes. The Stone Dragon's gaze paused only briefly on him, just long enough to confirm he was no threat and return to the rocks where Synter was hiding. It moved obliquely, searching for others while it hunted her. Narin could see no more of the Astaren, but he knew there would be others. House Dragon was not in the habit of using anything but excessive force.

From behind it, Narin heard the clatter of running feet through the gorse bushes. The Dragon was already turning, its weapon casting a blast of infernal heat across the ground. Three figures of flame appeared in the dark, while a fourth reached the Dragon only to have its spear-thrust turned with contemptuous ease. Narin blinked in shock as he watched the fat blade drive into the attacker and rip out their side with a casual flick. The goshe fell dead, but in the next moment a second spitting quarrel flew through the night and exploded into blinding light a few yards shy of the Stone Dragon.

The terrible weapon carved a path across the ground as he turned after Synter, but then a bigger goshe burst up from the ground with an enormous flanged mace. Moving with the unnatural speed of the elite, the goshe swung the mace down against the Dragon's arm and managed to force it off balance before lunging forward with the spiked head. That smashed into the Stone Dragon's damaged side and something erupted in the breach with another great flash and crack of thunder. This time the wound was greater and the Dragon was thrown backwards, staggering while the goshe batted away the heat lance. Then Synter was there, the air filling with crackling light as she darted in to drive a knife into the wound and up into its body.

The Astaren dropped, groggily trying to break its fall with its sword, but its arm folded under the weight and it crashed face down, dead. Synter's companion – broad enough to be of Dragon descent himself

– made sure with one overhead blow. That done, the goshe dragged at the heat lance attached to the Astaren's arm trying to tug it free.

At first it was stuck fast but he persisted – driving the top spike of his mace into what appeared to fix it in place while bursts of lightning raced from his hands. Under such assault the clasp popped open and the goshe gave a triumphant shout as he hauled it clear and held it up.

'Careful,' Synter warned him, 'who knows what it'll do if you try to use it.'

The big man nodded and lowered the weapon. 'Time to play later,' he agreed.

The two of them approached Narin, still lying dazed on the ground. His cheek prickled hot from the near miss by that heat lance and his legs were incapable of supporting him, so Narin could only watch them come.

'Think you've got something of ours,' Synter said. 'I felt the ritual be interrupted and from the shape on your back, you've got something that belongs to me.' She cocked her head. 'Time to kill you I think. You've been enough of a pain right now and your Astaren friend here ain't going to help you now.'

With one practised movement Synter sheathed her knife in favour of a pair of hatchets and resumed advancing on Narin. The Investigator scrabbled backward through the scrub, gorse bushes dragging at his clothes and scratching his back. He tried to stand and run but his legs failed him and before he could try again the other goshe had circled around him. The man gave him a hefty kick in the side; enough to knock him back down and leave him wheezing at Synter's feet.

'Now'd be a good time for any last words,' she commented idly. 'Anything?'

'Yes!'

That seemed to surprise her and Synter lowered her axe a touch. 'Oh. Yes?'

'I, ah, yes,' Narin gasped. 'He, ah, he wasn't my friend.'

'No?' She glanced back at the Astaren. 'Well he's dead now, so either way you're fucked.'

The other goshe gave a grunt that Narin took to be agreement, but then the man unexpectedly lurched forward and almost toppled on top of Narin. The man staggered a few steps before straightening, one hand clasped to his forehead as though dazed by a blow.

'What was that?' Synter demanded, turning.

'His friend,' called a voice from the gloom of fog.

A dark, ghostly shape drifted forward – then seemed to tear apart as Enchei raised an arm and his cloak opened. Narin only heard a deadly zip through the air and the repeated thwacks of something striking. He saw nothing part the fog, but the goshe Dragon shuddered under the impact and gasped in shock and pain. He stood a moment longer, frozen to the spot, until a second flurry of Enchei's darts cut through the night and felled him.

Synter had already dived away from the path of the shots and rolled back to her feet, kicking onto the attack in the next instant. Enchei let her come until the last possible moment, jerking to one side to avoid a blow and stepping in to batter his shoulder against the goshe's. It deflected her momentum and he turned gracefully away, content to let her come again. She obliged him, slim axe-heads slicing through the air with remarkable speed as she wove a path towards him. Enchei carried his short-sword and baton, but seemed unconcerned about the goshe's lightning-swift slashes. He backed steadily away, weapons low and merely flicking at the strokes that came sufficiently close.

'Fight, you fucking coward,' she yelled, only to have Enchei step abruptly forward and drive a boot into her midriff.

It didn't knock her over, but she reeled under the impact and afforded Enchei space to level his baton at her. Synter was rocked back by some invisible impact, one hatchet falling from her hand as she sank to her knees, too weak to stand.

'You want to kill her?' Enchei asked. 'Reckon those Dragons are getting close so we don't have much time.'

'You're not a Dragon agent?' Synter croaked before Narin could make up his mind. 'Then you're just as dead. You'll never get off the island, not with the artefact. You know once you're out of this fog the Gods or Dragons will find you in a heartbeat. Give it to me and you can still get out of this alive. When the moon rises, we'll be strong enough to see you right.'

Enchei gave a snort. 'Reckon I know what brought this mist down; that gives us a fighting chance.'

Synter straightened. 'Kill me then, just, first – tell me why? You're not working for any of them, you're not loyal to the Gods – what's in this for you?'

Enchei turned to Narin as the Investigator struggled to his feet. Before either could speak Synter exploded into movement, chopping forward at Enchei and catching his arm a glancing blow. The next missed, the third tore through his cloak. Though she kept coming close, Enchei remained a step ahead of each movement of that savage flurry. At last an opening came and he hooked her axe, hauling Synter off balance. He brought his baton up at her chin in the next moment.

She tried to twist out of the way but it cracked against her black face-mask and rocked her back. A downward stroke from his sword severed her wrist but the killing stroke came from Narin. He'd taken a long-knife from the dead goshe and drove it into her kidneys as Enchei's cut fell. The goshe arched, a howl of pain breaking her lips before shuddering to a halt.

'Why?' Narin snarled in her ear. 'Because of a little girl called Emari – for the thousands you've poisoned and robbed of their minds. You don't get to just do that.'

A huff of pained breath was Synter's only reply. Narin realised he felt nothing now. The horror of killing he'd felt previously had gone, and now he was just cold and numb inside. He held her, pinned for a drawn-out moment, then jerked the blade from her back and let her fall.

'They're coming,' Enchei said, glancing over his shoulder.

He levelled his left arm and Narin caught a flash of movement. Tiny darts thudded into Synter's mask, one bursting her eye apart. With one final jerk she stilled.

Enchei went over to the other goshe and hefted the heat lance that he'd pried free. 'We've got our prizes, time to move.'

Narin let himself be shoved away and the chill night folded in behind them.

CHAPTER 29

More successful than heroes of folklore are the brazen rogues. In a world of Gods and demons, monsters and superhuman warriors, cunning is the normal man's last defence. To insult such beings is to invite a swift death – to outrageously demand to their faces that the entire world submit to one's will might yet see a man through when all options are exhausted. History is silent on how many attempt this and fail, however.

From *A History* by Ayel Sorote

Lawbringer Rhe followed the screams and stepped over the corpses. Dozens of goshe had thrown themselves at the Stone Dragons, but few had even got close enough to be cut apart by their brutal blades. In the wake of the Astaren's advance, his ragged corps of Lawbringers, Investigators and Imperials had trailed without resistance. The fires of the leper colony raged unabated behind, an orange glow through the unholy curtain of fog.

Explosions echoed across the island, accompanied by dull flashes of light. How many goshe elite with those terrible crossbows there were, he couldn't tell, but the reports of their fire-bolts came from all directions. The Stone Dragons had proceeded up towards the sanatorium strung in a line, but all order had been lost as teams of elites launched attacks from all directions. Each Astaren was an island now, a fortress of destruction amid the sea of fog that confounded them all.

He judged they were close to the sanatorium now. As Rhe began to imagine the horrific final slaughter to come, a faint outline of its walls appeared ahead. He looked to his right where Law Master Sheven walked and realised he could make out more figures beyond the man than earlier.

'Is the fog easing?'

'This is no fog,' Sheven growled in response. 'It's some demon's spell to hide them from the Stone Dragons.'

'But is it waning?' Rhe persisted.

The white-bearded Law Master stopped and looked around, grunting in acknowledgement. 'It is,' he said. 'Are the demons driven off?'

'Something has happened.'

Rhe looked up and at last saw the distant pinpricks of the Gods above. Lord Shield's constellation was almost directly overhead, the whole Order of Knight gradually reasserting their divine light once more. A gust of breeze swept down to wash over his face and continued the steady erosion of fog. When he returned his attention to the sanatorium walls he saw figures there, but they vanished from view almost immediately – retreating from the sight of a pair of shadow-scorched Stone Dragons.

'It's over,' he realised dully, 'they're not defending it.'

'And now?'

Sheven got his answer from up ahead. As the fog melted away around them, one of the Stone Dragons levelled its heat lance at the walls. A great roar cut though the night, the air ripped apart and flames exploded over the surface of the stone wall. A few moments later its comrade joined it and the crack of stones bursting apart rang out over the island.

The wall blackened and groaned fearfully. Ear-splitting crashes echoed from deep inside and the wall visibly shuddered under the assault. Satisfied, the Stone Dragons broke off their assault and one marched up to the wall, punching its blade straight into the weakened stone. Once it'd hauled that out again it stepped back and kicked forward with one massive armoured boot – stamping forward into the stone to knock out a whole section of wall.

Off to the right, Rhe saw another Astaren emerge from the darkness like a vengeful avatar of the Gods – spitting flame at the gate, which caught in moments. Red blades of fire leapt up into the sky and Rhe felt a sudden chill. This was too arbitrary to be merely dealing with the fighters. They were going to kill every last one of the occupants – goshe and fever-stricken citizens alike.

'No!' he yelled and broke into a sprint. Before he really knew what was happening he had run up to the wall and stood between it and one of the enormous Stone Dragons. 'Stop – withdraw!'

The carved face stared impassively down at him, but Rhe could sense the hatred in the Dragon's stance. Though he was a Lawbringer and part of the House of the Sun now, his face marked him clearly as from a house within the House Eagle hegemony – House Dragon's long-standing rival and enemy.

'Step aside, Eagle,' the Astaren rumbled – his deep voice unmuffled by the all-enclosing armour he wore.

'I will not,' Rhe declared, staring defiantly up. 'There are innocents within and criminals I intend to arrest. I will not let you slaughter them.'

'Criminals?' roared the other Stone Dragon, turning to face Rhe and pen him in against the wall. That close, Rhe could feel the heat from the stones as clear on the air as the mounting anger of the Empire's most volatile warriors. 'Your law does not apply – these goshe will answer to us for the forbidden arts they have used.'

'No.'

The Stone Dragon took a step forward and levelled its heat lance at Rhe's face. 'You cannot stop us, you cannot compel us or order us, Eagle. Get out of my way or you will die.'

'No,' Rhe repeated, speaking clearly and slowly. 'You will walk away – you have asserted your power already. The elite are yours as you choose – they are changed by magic and as such are your prize, but the rest of the goshe are mine along with the fever victims. Their minds have been changed, their will stolen from them. They are victims above anything else.'

He was careful to keep his hands away from the pistols sheathed on his stomach, but equally determined to show no fear.

'The compassion of Eagles,' one commented scornfully. 'These people are changed or sickened by magic – they are beyond your help *and* your compassion.'

'I am a Lawbringer of the House of the Sun,' Rhe replied. 'I have my oaths and my duty – this crime will be unravelled and the guilty punished, but the innocent shall be protected, whether that is from the goshe or from you. Whether this was a crime against the Gods or the Emperor's law, my duty remains.'

The Stone Dragons exchanged a look as the third made its way over and a fourth appeared behind them.

'Kill him,' one stated flatly, 'and any who stand in our way. All those changed are forfeit; this sickness must be cured in fire.'

412

'Look behind you,' Rhe said.

The Stone Dragons did not, but Rhe got the impression their arriving comrade had communicated the sight anyway. The Lawbringers Rhe had led onto the island were formed up in their units once more, arranged in a long arc around the Stone Dragons no more than twenty yards behind.

He could see their resolve now. The fear and confusion of battle, the terror of demons and Astaren – all this had melted away from their hearts. What was left was only their duty and the man who epitomised it. They were with him and would serve the Emperor's law with their dying breaths if need be.

But the symbol is enough. My duty is to ensure that does not happen, not seek battle.

'Give the order,' the first Stone Dragon said. 'You think we cannot kill them all? You think we would even lose one of our own?'

Rhe felt his own contempt rise now, an emotion he had rarely felt in all his years. But now, in the face of such arrogance and callousness, he was filled with it.

'I think you would kill us,' he confirmed. 'If that is your wish, you will do so. But it is what comes after that matters. How you reached this island I do not know, but anyone using these waters knows there is a House Eagle warship patrolling them.'

'Now you claim your heritage again?'

Rhe inclined his head. 'I acknowledge the House of my birth, as will they. Do you think that warship will contain no Astaren of House Eagle? In this time of tensions, you think such a lack would be permitted by the Lords of Eagle? Do you imagine they are not aware of what is happening right now with whatever arcane methods they have at their disposal? With the Gods looking down on this place and that warship bearing witness, do you think you could slaughter us with impunity?'

He looked from one faceless Astaren to the other. 'To murder the servants of the Emperor and men and women of every Great House serving under his banner – to murder the sick and the enfeebled. To murder a nobleman of House Brightlance and men of the royal family itself with impunity? If it is war with the rest of the Empire you seek, go ahead.'

To make his point, Rhe pointed to Prince Kashte who stood slightly ahead of the rest alongside Law Master Sheven. The Imperial stood easily, leaning on his rifle with such casual disregard for the threat to his life, as only a distant cousin of the Emperor could manage.

'Royal blood, noble blood and innocent blood. So what is your prize to be? The elite and the secrets their altered bodies contain, or a war even your armies cannot hope to win?'

The Stone Dragons were silent a long while, but eventually one jerked in a stiff attempt at a nod.

'Very well, you have your innocents, Brightlance. Bring us the elites – alive or dead, we do not care.'

'Of course you don't,' Rhe replied, turning his back on them to skirt the wall and rejoin his men. 'Your kind never do.'

It didn't take Enchei long to find the boat again, though how he managed it Narin had no idea. The fog hid everything and they couldn't even see Kesh below, only the vague outline of the smuggler's boat as it moved below. Enchei jerked the rope twice to be sure it was her, receiving three tugs on it in response. Satisfied, he checked around one final time then began to pull up the rope to tie it around Narin's waist but the Investigator stayed his friend's hand.

'I'll climb, just give me a moment.'

Enchei's reaction was impossible to make out, but the man's hesitation told enough. Narin's hand trembled on his friend's arm – because of the exertion or his encounter with his captor, Narin wasn't sure himself, but it remained noticeable.

'Best we don't hang about here.'

Narin gritted his teeth. 'Just … half a minute, okay? Let me get my breath back.'

'As you wish,' Enchei said with a curt nod.

He looked down at the plundered heat lance he carried, careful to keep his hands off the grips though Narin could see nothing that looked like a trigger.

'What are you going to do with that? Sell it?'

The question brought a snort of laughter from Enchei. 'Sell it? Oh sure, just what I need is to spread a little chaos – let some madman get his hands on it to start settling feuds.'

'What then?'

'Don't know, if I'm honest, habit mostly. To an Astaren the weapons of the enemy are more precious than their weight in gems. Since it was just lying there I thought I'd help myself, you never know when you might have need of something like this. That cloth I gave you'll shield it from curious spirits or irate owners until I can hide it somewhere safe.'

Enchei pulled the rope up with quick controlled movements and tied the weapon onto it, lowering it down for Kesh to retrieve. Before long, a tug on the rope told them it was clear and Enchei offered the rope to Narin.

'Ready now, or want me to go first?'

Narin peered over the cliff. 'I'll go.'

Ignoring the ache of fatigue in his arms, Narin began to lower himself down, walking backwards down the cliff with the rope cradling the small of his back. He took it slowly, playing the rope out through his gloves in small controlled bursts and before long he found himself at the rocky outcrop where they'd tied up. Kesh straddled the edge of the boat with one foot on the rock and the other inside, using the strength of her legs to keep it close since it was only secured at one end. She gave him a relieved smile as she helped him over and into the belly of the boat.

'All safe?'

Narin didn't answer at first as he slumped down and panted for breath. The quiver on his back jutted over his shoulder at an uncomfortable angle, but it was a while before he could find the strength to shift himself to a more comfortable position.

'Don't know,' he said at last. 'Enchei's coming down now, but I got separated from Irato.'

'What? When?'

Narin shook his head and started to paw at the quiver on his back, eventually pulling it off and stashing it under cover by the base of the mast. The contents were still securely wrapped in the cloth Enchei had given him that, by the feel of it, had chains of metal links stitched inside it.

'In the sanatorium – we split up to sow some confusion, but this damn fog made it impossible to do anything but run.'

The scuff of boots on rock made them both turn. With what Narin now thought of as typical speed and recklessness, Enchei descended the cliff and dropped lightly onto the rock beside Kesh. In quick succession he removed his helm, cloak and sword, bundling them away beside Narin's quiver.

'Any sign?'

'Of Irato? No, but he'll be here. Probably skirting whatever's going on between the Stone Dragons and the remaining goshe. Give him some time, he'll be here.'

'And then what?' Kesh asked. 'That artefact – if this all went as you planned, that artefact is actually connected to the minds of all the goshe?'

'Aye, looks that way.'

'So half the Empire's going to want it. Even if there's no God residing in their minds, there are thousands of goshe across the ten Great House hegemonies – all just waiting for commands from whoever's got that artefact.'

Enchei grinned. 'Didn't figure you for a power-player in the making.'

'I'm not!' she hissed. 'I'm the one who doesn't want every bloody Astaren in the Empire tracking us down.'

'Don't you worry about that – look, the fog's easing.'

'What's that got to do with anything?' Narin asked.

'Means I've been right more than once tonight. It's unnatural, any fool could see that, but Irato's demons ain't powerful enough to manage that – not in a way that confounds Astaren.'

'Lord Shield?' Narin asked grimly.

Enchei raised a finger to correct him. 'Is just one of the beings we've had contact with in the last few days, so don't assume too much. Shield's kept a weather eye on you, sure enough. I'd never have found you otherwise and as soon as we leave the island, the fog starts to lift. Can't be a coincidence, that.'

'And do you have a plan when our benefactor comes calling?'

Enchei patted her on the shoulder. 'Not really something you can plan for, hey? Best we just roll with the punches if that's what happens – do what seems sensible under the circumstances.'

They fell into silence at that idea, Kesh staring anxiously out over the black water as she thought. The light of the stars cut slender slivers on the crests of the bay's waves, a blank landscape that extended featureless for miles into the distance.

When it came, the double-twitch on the rope made both Narin and Kesh jump with fright. Enchei chuckled and gave the return signal and soon the bulky shape of Irato was smoothly descending the rope. At the bottom, he crouched and regarded the other three with a suspicious set to his shoulders – face hidden by his black goshe mask.

'All good?' Enchei asked.

'All has gone to plan,' Irato replied in a hollow voice that made Narin realise it was the demons speaking for him.

The big goshe then shook himself like a dog and his voice returned to a mortal timbre. 'Your trick worked perfectly, all the minds connected and all of 'em relying on altered eyesight they stole off the demons in the first place.'

Kesh scrambled forward to help him out of his cloak and the harness of straps that held his weapons in place, bundling the lot at her feet.

'Even the ones who realised something was up,' he continued, 'couldn't figure it out and still trusted what the demons made them see. Was like some shadow-painting held over the real world, one that moved and changed with every second. I think a couple would have sworn they cut Narin's head off only to watch him walk away.'

'Aye, was quite a show,' Enchei said, keen to be out over open water as fast as possible. 'Let's shift before anyone starts wondering exactly what happened.'

He cast off and Kesh slipped back fully inside the boat, letting Enchei and Irato push them away with the oars while she manned the tiller.

Once they were away from the rocks, the two men pulled hard on the oars to put some distance between them and the island. Narin just sat in front of them, too tired to care that he was doing nothing to help now, until Kesh went forward to hoist the small mast back up. Together they raised it and Kesh secured the main support rope before gathering up the wrapped artefact and heat lance.

'I'll stow these in the prow lockers and tie the other supports,' she said, 'you start freeing the sail.'

Narin nodded and left her to it as he fumbled with the ties that kept the sail furled. Once it was all done they headed out towards open sea rather than retrace their route with the tide against them. It was a longer route, but with a number of divine constellations now visible and beacons on the city cliffs, Kesh was certain she could navigate the sand flats easily enough.

Narin slumped beside Kesh at the tiller and watched the receding island with an apprehension that didn't fade when he could no longer be sure where the land and sky were divided. Even the light of the Gods was lessened to his city-born eyes, the darkness of the open sea something he'd always found to be intimidating and humbling. Before long he lifted his gaze to the heavens, seeking out the diamond constellation of Shield.

Only Shield and Pity, the Ascendants who led the way across the heavens at the end of the month, were properly visible past the streaks of cloud that overlaid the sky. Appropriately, in the Order of Empress that preceded Knight across the night sky, it was the constellation of Lord Thief that was most visible. Narin smiled at that, hoping one Ascendant would be looking favourably on them this night, but even as he thought that he sensed a change in the water around them.

'What's happening?' he asked as Enchei and Irato began to grunt with the effort of hauling their oars back. Similarly, Kesh yanked hard on the tiller and hissed as it refused to move under the pressure.

'We're dead in the water,' she said, looking around. 'Snagged on something maybe?'

'Worse,' Enchei replied, giving up his efforts and indicating that Irato should too. 'We're over deep water now; this isn't a sandbar or weeds.'

'So what?'

'Don't think we're alone out here.'

Narin felt his hand reach for his sword on instinct, then felt foolish as he realised what Enchei meant. 'Where?'

His question wasn't answered as they all stared out at the water around them. Starlight still caressed the low peaks of waves in the distances, but the water for a good ten yards all around them had calmed. It wasn't that the surface was freezing, Narin realised, but simply that the wind and current wasn't affecting it – the sea surrounding them falling still and flat in seconds.

Once all was motionless, he realised there was a faint glow on the surface just a few dozen yards from where he sat. He kicked Enchei's boot and pointed, all four of them staring over the starboard side of the boat towards where Narin guessed the island was, somewhere in the inky distance.

'What's that?'

'The demon,' Enchei guessed, his voice a whisper now.

As he spoke, Narin realised the glow was moving slowly towards them, picking up speed as it snaked its way forward before it was at the edge of the stilled water. There it diffused into the glassy section of sea until a faint glow filled the water all around them. Narin exchanged a glance with Kesh and saw his own apprehension reflected in her face.

'What now?'

'Now we wait,' Enchei replied, motioning for them all to stay where they were. 'Sit and wait for our betters.' Ignoring his own advice, Enchei went and fetched the quiver from the prow and put it under the rower's bench with one foot resting gently on top as though worried it would escape.

'Guess the cloth might hide the artefact, but not the rest of us,' he said with a wry smile at Narin and Kesh.

Nothing happened immediately, but after half a minute a shape broke the surface of the water on Enchei's side of the boat and rose ten or twelve feet in the air. It was hard to make out exactly. Comprised entirely of curves that folded in on themselves, it was not a solid shape but the outline of one – tiny streaks of white describing the shape of something that had no physical form.

Narin squinted forward, trying to impose some sort of order on what he saw. He heard Kesh give a tiny gasp just as it finally resolved into a smooth, spiralled column that tapered then abruptly flowered into an oval overlaid by layers of horn-like curves. In the heart of that was a trio of almond shapes he imagined to be eyes, set above a circle of a mouth behind which a tapering funnel ran down like a gullet before spreading again to join the edges of the column.

'A dangerous game you play. Gods and demons as pieces on a board.'

Narin flinched at the sound of the demon's voice, deep and echoing as though also folded back in on itself, like its light-traced body. It sent a tremble down his limbs, resonating through him as though the voice had a physical presence in a way the body failed to.

'The game was not ours,' Enchei declared in a loud voice – apparently familiar enough with the demon that he refused to be cowed. 'We could only play to the rules of others.'

'A game spoiled is a game won. Spoils lost can prove a prize yet.'

If Enchei had a response for that, he didn't get the chance to voice it. A clap of thunder broke the air and all four flinched away from a blinding flash of light that emanated from the other side of the boat. Blinking and biting back a curse, Narin turned to see a more familiar figure standing on the water opposite the strange, insubstantial demon.

Tall and bearded with rusty-brown skin and white clothes that shone in the darkness, a skein of starlight glinted like the ghost of a shield to announce the Ascendant God's identity to all present.

'A messenger receives no spoils of war, Apkai,' Lord Shield declared in a booming voice – without antagonism or belligerence, Narin noted, but in the assured expectation the demon would not challenge him.

'*No war was fought here, Ascendant,*' the demon replied. '*Thieves were hunted, thieves were robbed.*'

'Mortal souls are bound here,' the Ascendant God replied, 'the theft is two-fold.'

'*Death comes to all mortals. The fleeting may not overshadow the eternal.*'

'You would fight me for this relic of your kin – here under the stars?'

'*Only a fool starts an uncertain war. Only mortals age and diminish.*'

'Investigator Narin,' Lord Shield said, shifting his focus. 'I charged you with a holy mission. An answer I required of you and you have done your job well.'

I have? Narin wondered. *I never got that answer … but I suppose it was the investigation Shield wanted, the rooting out of this prize rather than the names of the men and women who wanted to become a God.*

'I, ah, I thank you, Lord Shield.'

'And what do you suggest now? Both demon and God have a claim on that artefact you have hidden away beneath you.'

Narin blinked at the Ascendant God in confusion. He knew Shield wasn't really asking his opinion, but surely the Gods had the advantage of any fight? With the whole Order of Knight looking down on them? Or was Shield actually trying to work out his next move – how to win the artefact without calling on his brethren, at least one of whom had to be stronger than he.

'I don't know, my Lord,' Narin admitted, trying to give himself time to think. 'Does it really come down to claims?'

'You sit between us, our prize hidden beneath you – would you prefer us to fight?'

'No, Lord,' he said hurriedly, all too easily imagining how long he'd survive stuck in the middle of such a battle. Narin couldn't help but check the object at his feet and felt a touch of relief as he saw it safely nestled there.

'But there is no law here,' he continued hesitantly. 'No right or wrong that can be enforced. One of you will take it or the other will – my choice doesn't figure. Either you strike a bargain or you fight, what else is there?'

He glanced over at Enchei and noticed the former Astaren was keeping well out of the conversation. *Trying to keep away from Shield's notice, or does he just have more to lose?*

Without warning, the light from Lord Shield's starlit arm intensified, prompting a ripple of infolding movement from the demon. There was a groan from the stilled circle of water as darts of light rushed down from the stars above and impacted deep into the water around them, while a dozen spinning funnels of mist sprang up.

Narin fought the urge to cringe, realising they were preparing to fight, but found himself shoved to one side as Kesh grabbed at the quiver beneath Enchei's seat.

'Enough of this!' the woman growled over a building rush of water and wind all around. 'There you go, there's your prize!'

She grabbed the contents of the quiver and hurled it up into the sky with all her strength. The air seemed to shudder then freeze above them as both entities reached out towards it. The wrapped object reached its zenith and stopped – turning slowly, as though time had slowed for it.

'Look at what you're willing to fight for,' Kesh yelled, standing up and turning from one immortal to the other.

The object continued its gradual spin and at last a corner of the cloth fell away, slipping down and pulling the rest of it away from the pair of wooden clubs bound together with twine.

'Still want your war in heaven?' Kesh roared defiantly. 'Which of you wants it most? Ready to kill for it?'

The light around them dimmed, the air quietened.

'The artefact is still on the island?' Lord Shield demanded. 'It is not on your boat, that I can sense. There is … there is a second cloth.' The Ascendant God stepped closer, anger brimming from his every word. 'What have you done with it?'

'Put it out of your reach,' Kesh replied, her own anger matching the awful majesty of an enraged God.

In his mind, Narin pictured a small, limp body – barely breathing on the stairs of her home. He saw the aching ball of loss Kesh had been carrying for all these days, the fear and pain she had shared with her mother only this morning, intensified by her need to walk away again and see this through.

Now she seemed to unveil it like starlight and wore her loss as armour against the majesty and terror of their presence. In the face of that, Narin's own confusion and alarm seemed to fade. Kesh faced both the God and the demon down, unafraid of their wrath and uncaring of their claims.

'The artefact has linked thousands of minds – human minds that no demon has a right to. Enough minds for the goshe to almost create a God of their own. Power like that I think no God needs, so I deny you both.'

'*Where does it lie?*' the demon intoned – less obviously enraged, but the threads of light composing it continued to surge and twist. '*What can be hidden from land and sky?*'

Kesh took a composing breath. 'Enough, I reckon. I've been on boats my whole life, but suddenly all those stupid superstitions and tales you hear sailors tell don't seem so fanciful. You want to know where it is? It's in the deep – sunk without a trace and far from your grasping hands.'

'You serve *them*?' Lord Shield roared.

'No, my life's my own,' Kesh said with a shake of the head. 'Each of you had a pawn here; someone you'd got your hooks into and hoped would do your dirty work. But neither of you has a claim on me and no bloody demon of the deep sea does either.'

The young woman sounded weary to Narin now, disappointed at a world more imperfect than she'd expected. Still there was no fear in her face, not even as she paused and took a long breath. It was time enough for Narin to reflect on what they were doing, but unlike him Kesh remained fearless.

The moments stretched out to the thump of his heartbeat, loud in Narin's ears, and only when the tense hush was almost unbearable to him did Kesh speak again.

'Until a few days past I'd never have believed there was such a thing as a Kraken God – or any of the other dozen daft stories that get whispered by your watch-mate or a drunk old-timer. If the priests ignored whatever sailors whispered it had to be a lie, right? But now I see each of you here and I'm wondering if there's not something to the stories.'

'You trust in the dwellers in the deep?' Shield growled. 'Child, you cannot know how foolish you are. Powerful they may be, they are no Gods and they bear no love for mortal life.'

'Trust 'em? Oh I don't trust 'em – but the stories are few and far between. If I can't trust a demon or a God with the souls of all these goshe, mebbe best the artefact ends up somewhere neither will dare fetch it.

'Your dwellers might be monsters, but all that matters to me is that they don't give a damn about us either. It's not that they just don't care, they're not interested either – not in Gods or demons, mortals or anything in between. They've got their realm in the blackest deeps and rarely leave them; that's something the stories all agree on.'

She paused and took a long breath, taking a moment to look one then the other in the face before she spoke again.

'You know what I realise now? I've been to temple all my life, prayed for health and a better world – for the soul of my da and all the other sailors who don't come back. But what's that done for me? What's prayer done for anyone? Do you really care? Do you even know our names and ever intercede? I doubt it.'

'Your frustrated prayers are at the heart of this?' Shield asked with contempt.

'No. I don't mind that you don't answer prayers – just that you pretend to care for those who worship you, for those who might devote their whole lives to your name.'

There was a tear on her cheek now, her voice wavering for just a moment. 'What's at the heart of this? A little girl who deserved better. Her name was Emari and she was my sister. She was caught up in all this and was killed as an afterthought, disposed of quietly and none of you Gods or demons cared.'

She shook her head, bowed under the weight of grief. 'None of you even knew her name and so I'm done with the lot of you.'

The silence and stillness around them became a palpable cold on Narin's skin. He fought the urge to look up, to see more arrows of light fall from Shield's constellation. The wrath of Gods fell from the heavens, that much he remembered from temple scripture. It was all too easy to imagine the darts that had crashed down become searing flashes of fury, but nothing came.

The demon Apkai did not speak further, but the threads of light that composed it slowed, its form gently unravelling and fading into the dark. In moments it was a mere impression in the air then nothing and the water around them began to move once more. Narin found himself letting out a breath he hadn't even realised he'd been holding in, and all eyes turned to Lord Shield.

'You play a dangerous game, mortal.'

423

'It's no game,' Kesh said with sadness in her voice. 'I wouldn't expect a God to understand that.'

'I have not entirely forgotten mortal life. I remember grief still, I remember loss.'

Lord Shield looked up at his stars above for a moment before returning his attention to Kesh.

'You are right that we cannot know the names of all those lost, but we are Gods still. Perhaps it is easy to forget that. For all those who died at the hands of the goshe, for all those who had their souls and minds stolen – your sister's name shall be written in the lesser stars on the last night of my ascendancy for ever more. That I offer, to honour their memories – a memorial in the night sky to the innocent.'

With that the God turned and walked away across the quickening sea, the light receding with every step until he vanished entirely and they were all alone. The boat rocked gently with the movement of the tide, the slap of water against its side the only sound above the thump of Narin's heart.

Kesh lowered her head for a long moment, the pain still raw in her heart. And then it was conquered and she looked up with a familiar glare at the men staring aghast at her.

'Well? What are you all waiting for? Get rowing.'

'Aye, captain,' Enchei laughed, pulling hard on his oar. 'When even Gods submit to honest words, man can only obey.'